DAMN NEAR DEAD

AN ANTHOLOGY OF GEEZER NOIR

Edited by Duane Swierczynski

Busted Flush Press
Houston 2006

Damn Near Dead

Published by Busted Flush Press

Compilation copyright © 2006 by Duane Swierczynski
Guest Introduction copyright © 2006 by James Crumley
Editor's Introduction copyright © 2006 by Duane Swierczynski

First Printing June 2006

ISBN: 0-9767157-5-9

Design & Illustrations: Greg Fleming
Layout & Production Services: Jeff Smith

BUSTED FLUSH
PRESS
P.O. Box 540594
Houston, TX 77254-0594
www.bustedflushpress.com

CONTENTS

For Lou. Bernice. Walter. Eleanor. Hilda. Jim.
The toughest people I know, dead or alive.

GUEST INTRODUCTION
Geezer Wisdom

By James Crumley

People often suggest that life should be a learning experience. Perhaps something like a nice, small Southern liberal arts, with a final exam, which if you pass, lets you drift softly into a pleasant eternity. If life is like college, I've screwed up again: I missed the assignment. I was deep into the anthology, wondering where these mean old people came from. My wife showed me the title page. As usual, knowledge changed nothing.

Another college failure: I never understood what a short story was supposed to be. Although over the years I leaned on the bar among the best: Dubus, Carver, Yates . . . For me the short story was always a way to practice writing, to try out a novel idea, or gather chump change for beer. I'm not sure if I've ever written one for fun. But that doesn't matter. I had fun with these stories. Some of them had pot holes—stories told in dialogue, funny names that were supposed to reveal character, and mistakes—but all in all, the stories were professional. And the array of angry geezer villains limping through them, speaks to a deep, abiding, and fearfully explicit imaginations among these writers.

(As a senior citizen myself, I can verify that the humiliations of aging are nothing to the horror of getting short. Be careful around old, short folks.)

My teacher and friend at Iowa, Verlin Cassill, always maintained the story should be a pinprick in the arc of a character's life, a tiny shot of the action that reveals the beginning and the end. When it works, it's terrifically effective. As it does in Megan Abbott's "Policy". The pinprick is like a diamond solitaire in your eye, your last sight vague sparkles among blood. But it ain't the stars of heaven.

Many of the stories are about business or economic failure, middle class stories, touching for sure, but hard for a working class kid to sympathize. Too soft. But Ray Banks's "The Ballad of Davey Robson", a hard bite of the real world, the place where nobody plays golf and everybody is one paycheck from being homeless. And speaking of golf . . . Victor Gischler's "Duffers of the Apocalypse" garners a bit of new and detailed version of middle-class hell into a vision of a cleansing, fiery tornado, full of laughter.

Since it's an anthology of mostly American writers, a lot of stories take place in the U.S. Aside from Mr. Banks, they are a number of fine stories that don't depend on local knowledge. Zoë Sharp's "Last Right" draws us sharply into the Mexican world of murder and revenge for a visit. Charles Ardai brings us into the world of Irish gangsters, a pleasant visit to an unpleasant society where honor and loyalty count for more than life. Then Mark Billingham in "Stepping Up" makes us step down to the underground where old boxers go to aerobics class as punishment for their sins of omission.

Two other out-of-area-code stories will knock your socks off, assuming that you have them on. Colin Cotterill in "Has Anyone Seen Mrs. Lightswitch?", set in Laos, creates the perfect voice for the novel of intellectual detection. Sherlock Holmes, eat your heart out. Dr. Siri is twice as smart, doesn't have a drug problem, and is more charming than Holmes could ever hope to be.

Ken Bruen's "The Old Gun". Someone who only knew the name asked me about the story. "It's as if," I said, "you're a fifteen-year-old Irish boy leaning on a roadside rock, sucking on a pint and considering self-abuse, when an old country priest, as knotty as last winter's potatoes, catches you in mid flog. When he lectures you, stone chips fly off the rock. Then he pulls out a pistol. And you pay attention for the rest of your life. Carefully."

It's no secret that I've been around this business for forty years, so I guess that makes me a geezer. A geezer with an attitude and a gun. I know I've slighted my old friends with this introduction. Robert Ward, Jenny Siler, and Laura Lippman. Solid writers. But I thought I should give new people some space, and I'm sure I missed some fine stories.

When you get into your sixties, try to pick up a four-hundred-page manuscript. And don't misplace any pages.

I want to thank Duane Swierczynski for talking me into this, plus all the writers who made a chore into a pleasure.

Missoula, Montana

EDITOR'S INTRODUCTION
Respect Your Elders. Or They'll Kick Your Ass

By Duane Swierczynski

I was just sitting downstairs in my living room, idly watching CNN with my wife, wondering how the hell I was going to introduce the collection you hold in your hands.

Then Paula Zahn introduced her big story:

Two elderly women in Los Angeles. In their 70s. Grandmother types, if a little glammed up. (This was L.A.) Charged with mail fraud.

But they were also, according to an LAPD spokesman, prime suspects in two hit-and-run murders.

Seems these little old ladies had cooked up a murder-and-insurance-scam plot—taking out meaty policies on a pair of homeless guys, then (allegedly... maybe...) running them down in the back alleys of L.A.

Those ladies are the kind of geezers you'll find in this collection.

My kind of geezers.

When people think "senior citizens" and "mystery fiction," certain images come to mind: the kindly old amateur sleuth with a ball of yarn in her lap, cat on the sofa and a dead body in the foyer. A cup of tea, a plate of finger sandwiches, a severed head in a pink gift box. Jessica Fletcher, Miss Marple. Fixodent and forget it. Genteel stuff like that.

That's—pardon my language—a bunch of horse puckey.

Truth is, getting old is the most hardboiled thing you can do. Make it past 65 and your hair starts to go. Your body fails you at inopportune times. You begin to suspect you're surrounded by idiots. You have values and morals the rest of the world seems to have forgotten. Kids won't stay off your lawn. You're the ultimate outsider. Cast aside. Ignored. Expected to die peacefully, in your sleep.

Not the seniors in this collection. You're about to enter a twilight world where turning 65 can mean you're the last woman standing. Or the guy too stubborn to die. It's the boulevard of broken hips. The land of the old, the bold, the uncontrolled.

I'm talking about old people... who kick ass.

The idea for this anthology came right from the twisted mind of Busted Flush Press owner David Thompson, who clearly has grandparent issues. I thought it was brilliant, but at first, was a little puzzled at why he thought I was the guy to edit this anthology. Sure, I'm getting up there in years (as of this writing, I'm 34). And yes, I do have kids, which means I've passed along my DNA, which means I'm biologically useless to the world and have begun my slow, desperate march to the grave. (Happy Father's Day!) But it's not like I'm ready for the glue factory. Maybe David assumed I was an old soul.

Anyway, I was a little worried about approaching writers for this anthology. I felt compelled to issue a disclaimed in my e-mail pitch to each one: "I assure you, this is no comment whatsoever on your age, but..."

Then I had the bright idea of running the stories in age order, from Whippersnapper to Grand Master. Most writers took it in stride, and happily coughed up their birth years. Laura Lippman should have slapped me, but didn't. Dave White was in a panic for weeks about being the youngest contributor in the anthology, and I tortured him with tales of a wildly talented pre-teen noir author I'd discovered. Al Guthrie was vaugely surprised that, when he looked up the year on his birth certificate, he was younger than he'd thought.

But otherwise, as the young kids say, it was all good.

Huge thanks to David for giving me the chance to work with some of my favorite writers, and in many cases, beg them for a story. Thanks to every single contributor, who not only nailed the concept, but surprised me with the depth and range of their stories. The big worry about "high concept" anthologies is that the stories run the risk of following predictable patterns. That is not the case here. There's not a single story like another. (If you find two that are alike, I blame the Alzheimer's.)

Most of all, thanks to you, dear reader, whether you're over 65 and angry at the world, or under 65 and wish you had an excuse to wave your cane in the air and curse a lot.

I hope you enjoy the stories. I sure as hell did.

Philadelphia, Pennsylvania

PART ONE:

TWILIGHTS AND GOODNIGHTS

MY FATHER'S GUN

DAVE WHITE

Dave White (born 1979) is a middle school teacher from New Jersey. His story, "God's Dice," appeared in The Adventure of the Missing Detective and 19 of the Year's Finest Crime and Mystery Stories, *and he's currently at work completing his first P.I. novel,* When One Man Dies. *Despite his weird affinity for lime-green sweaters, the name "Dave White" is one you're going to be seeing a lot in the years to come.*

MY FATHER'S GUN
by Dave White

It was a Thursday. Jeanne was off to teach and run some errands, while I put the finishing touches on my office—a coffee maker and a throw rug. The desk, the chairs, a few pictures and the "Jackson Donne Investigations" sign on the door were all in place. It was going to be an early night for me: Rutgers basketball, TV dinner, and a Coke. Clean and sober three weeks, the Coke part still made me cringe.

Tomorrow, the phone company would show up and set up a line, and I'd officially be in business. Until then it was just going to have to be my cell phone, which rang while I was watching a Rutgers campus bus rumble down George Street from my second story window.

It was Jeanne's mother. I didn't even know she had the number.

"Jackson, I have a problem."

"What's up, Mrs. Baker?" I asked, figuring that something in the house broke and her husband was playing cards at the church.

"Leonard has run off."

Leonard was Mrs. Baker's—I still couldn't bring myself to call her Sarah—husband.

"What do you mean run off?"

"He's not here. He was upset all day. It's the anniversary and he's been acting mopey all day."

"The anniversary?"

"Yes," she said, and paused. I could hear the *beep* of the microwave in the background. "He could have gone to John Roland's place."

"I'm sure he's fine, Mrs. Baker. He's always been in control. He's the boss. Smoking jacket and pipe kind of guy." I laughed.

She didn't. It was like she didn't even hear me.

On the street two women browsed shoes in a Payless window. The sun had set, and a sharp, cold wind pulled at their scarves.

"Who's John Roland?"

"A friend of Leonard's. Leonard always goes to see John on this date."

Sarah Baker didn't sound worried to me. She spoke clearly, calmly, and the microwave meant she was eating. But there was just a tinge of tension in her voice, like she was trying to hold it together. Like her brain told her there wasn't any reason to worry, but her heart said otherwise.

Leonard and Sarah were married apparently since the beginning of time. They had Jeanne when the biological clock was ticking so loudly they couldn't hear either end of the conversation. Mrs. Baker probably thought she should know her husband better than this. She should know where he was.

"What's special about today, Mrs. Baker?"

"I wish he owned a cell phone. We should really look into that. Listen, Jackson, are you busy?"

I reached over to the table and plugged in the coffee maker.

"No," I said. "Not really."

"Can you check in on John and see if Leonard stopped by?"

"Did you call there, Mrs. Baker?"

There was silence on the other line. This time the microwave didn't even beep.

"No."

"Why not?"

"Please go look, Jackson," Mrs. Baker said. "Leonard took his gun from Korea with him."

♪♪

"Hey, guess what? I've got a case," I said.

My car cruised along River Road in Piscataway heading towards Route 287. John Roland lived in an apartment not far from the on ramp. Mrs. Baker gave me his address.

The road, dark and winding, ran next to the Raritan River which was littered with chunks of ice.

"Congrats!" Jeanne said, her voice traveling through the shit reception of my cell phone. "What kind of case is it?"

"Your mother wants me to pick up your father."

"What are you talking about?"

I gave her the gist of the earlier phone call. I left out the part about Leonard Baker taking his old revolver with him. When I finished, I asked, "What's this anniversary your mom kept mentioning?"

Jeanne clicked her tongue like she always did when she thought. "Oh, is that today?" she asked. "Man, I remember when I was a kid dad would always act a little weird around this time of year. But I haven't been around too much lately. You know, a dinner here or there, that's it. I thought maybe he got over it finally."

"What?" Everyone was dancing around the subject and it was starting to piss me off.

"Dad's sister died when they were kids. I think she was shot. I don't

5

know the whole story. He never talked about it in front of me, and it's only what I can remember picking up over the years. Little tidbits here and there, you know?"

I wanted to get off the phone so I could play with my defroster. The cold was fogging my window and in the dark I couldn't see the lines in the road very well.

"Anyway, Dad used to go drink at some bar with Uncle John around this time of year. Come in really wasted and pass out on the couch. Do you remember the first time you came over for a family dinner?"

Jeanne was smiling, the crooked smile she always had when she rehashed our early dates. I could hear it in her voice. She probably sat at her desk, pushing her strawberry blonde hair back over her ear. Papers were strewn out in front of her, unmarked.

"Yeah. When I thought your dad hated me?"

"Right. That was the last time I remember him getting all weird. Well, that was the day after this anniversary. He was hungover."

"I remember he didn't say a word to me that whole night. Barely a hello."

"Jackson, he didn't say a word to anyone. He was too busy letting things roll over in his mind again. My mom always says he gets trapped up there this time of year. She can't even talk him out of it."

"Happens to the best of us."

"Yeah," she said. The smile was gone from her voice now. Maybe she was remembering other anniversaries. I could hear a tinge of sadness lace her words. "But every year like clockwork? I mean, when I was a kid, it was like they weren't even married. They didn't talk at all because my dad would just shut down. It was weird." She took a deep breath. "Let me know when you find him. But call my mom first. She doesn't show it, but she gets worried."

"Okay," I said. "Thanks."

"Call me when you pick him up. I'll be in class, but leave a message."

"What time are you going to be home tonight?"

"I don't know. I'm going to stop at Pathmark after class, get us some groceries. I'll talk to you later. I love you."

"You too."

I snapped the phone shut and clicked up the defroster. As the frost on my windshield faded, I saw the apartment complex on my left.

❦

John Roland buzzed me in. When I got there, his door was open a crack. No chain. Settled into a recliner with footrest extended, he sucked on an unfiltered cigarette. I could have shot him before he lifted a hand.

Barely looking at me as I introduced myself, he took smoke in deep, held it, let it out slowly through his mouth, and inhaled it again through his nostrils. Then he'd let it out in one long puff. I think he was showing off.

"I ain't drinking no more," he said eventually.

I folded my hands, resting them on my knees as I sat on a faded yellow couch. "Okay," I said.

I couldn't guess the last time Roland opened the windows. But I could guess that he had just finished a cigarette about five minutes earlier. And another ten minutes before that. The smoke hung in the air like thick, smelly fog. My nose itched from it.

Most of the tobacco he'd smoked over the years had settled in Roland's hair. What should have been a shocking white color was closer to the faded yellow of the couch. His teeth matched his hair. He wore a blue jogging suit and brown slippers open at the heel. When I entered he was watching a hockey game. The television was muted now, but the players skated back and forth.

I waited for Roland to tell me why his lack of drinking was important to me. Ten minutes passed since my entrance. I explained that I was looking for Leonard Baker. John Roland explained he wasn't drinking anymore. And a lot of smoke hung in the air.

Finally, I said, "So, you not drinking, does that have anything to do with Leonard Baker?"

He went through the process of inhaling smoke again, and then said, "Of course. You think I'd tell you otherwise?"

I shrugged.

"See," he said, "the thing is, every year around this time, Lenny shows up here and we go to the pub down the street and get drunk. But I ain't drinking no more. Not since Harriet died. From liver problems. And she just loved a glass of wine once in a while. They way I drink . . ." He trailed off.

"If I can jump to a conclusion, Leonard wasn't here tonight?"

"Jesus Christ, man. Did I say that?"

"You haven't said all that much."

"Well, if you would give me a chance—"

"I'm all ears."

He rocked back in the recliner, as if adjusting his ass into the grooves he'd made over time. "Good. Now listen." He sucked the last bit off the cigarette. "Lenny, he was here—oh—about an hour ago. We don't talk so much anymore. But he stopped by, the way he does every year. And I told him about my drinking. So we talked for a bit, maybe five or ten minutes more and he left."

"Did he say where he was going? To the pub anyway?"

Roland let the recliner down and fumbled for the pack of cigarettes. He popped one, lit it.

"You believe in fate, son?" he asked.

"Not especially. Why?" I wanted to press him for Leonard's whereabouts, but I was afraid if I pushed too hard, he'd just sit there and smoke.

"I do. Too much has happened in my life that was beyond my control. That was beyond free will. My wife, I met her because I missed my train one summer morning. We both did actually. If either of us had left our house three minutes earlier, we'd have missed each other. And, God rest her soul, my wife made my life worth living.

"Fifty years ago, too. I mean, if I hadn't opened the door to Lenny's dad's closet instead—if his sister didn't have her friend make fun of her and come running home in tears—there wouldn't be any anniversary. Would there?"

"What happened that day?"

"Not my place to say." Roland waved the cigarette in front of his face. "But it looks like fate's jumping in again tonight. Way I see it, if Lenny was going to take care of things tonight with that gun, then who was I to step in the way? But you showed up."

I leaned forward, a shock of adrenaline running through my system. "Take care of things?"

"Yeah," Roland said without emotion. "He said he was going to take care of things tonight. No more anniversaries. Especially now that I ain't drinking." He laughed more to himself. "I guess if I hadn't decided to stop drinking, things would be different too. We'd be at the pub. You see?"

"What are you talking about? Where did Leonard go?"

The moments before his answer were agonizing. He took two longs drags on the cigarette and eyed the hockey game on TV. It felt like he was turning things over in his mind, whether or not to tell me. Whether or not to trust me. Whether or not he had a part in whatever the events of the night were going to be, if that's what he believed.

"He went to see his sister," Roland said finally. "The cemetery in Highland Park. He has the gun with him."

❦

The air was brutally cold. Late February and winter was dug in like it wouldn't be gone until August. The wind whipped through my coat and clung to my arms and chest. My breath condensed before it crossed my teeth. I was trudging through snowflakes in a darkened cemetery.

As I drove along River Road, after nearly sprinting from Roland's house, I thought I could have argued that it was his fate to call the police. That people who do nothing but wait are those who believe in fate, that we control our destiny by our actions. But that would have wasted time. It wasn't my place to argue philosophy while another man wanders a cemetery with a gun. In my own experience, the man with the gun is always more important.

When I got to the cemetery, a hilly, grassy area adjacent to a church, I had to scale a locked gate. I felt the rust and chipped black paint against my palms as I climbed. Absently, I wondered if Leonard Baker had done the same.

Moving along from headstone to headstone, the wish that graves were listed alphabetically overcame me. The remains of an earlier snowfall soaked my shoes and my body involuntarily shivered. I pushed on, trying to fight off the physical and mental effects of the cold.

My stomach flipped when I found him. We were so deep into the cemetery, I could only see other graves, not the street, nor the church. The sound of cars along River Road was more a vague sensation than anything else.

Leonard Baker knelt in the snow in front of a small headstone. His arms were at his side, and in his left I could make out the shadow of a revolver. His shoulders shook. The wind picked up the sobs and carried them to my ears.

"Mr. Baker?" I said, forcing myself to speak in a level voice. Not yell, not whisper. Just get his attention.

The shoulders ceased shaking and Leonard Baker slowly turned my way. The revolver remained at his side.

"Who's there?" he asked.

"It's Jackson. Your future son-in-law."

He got to his feet and took a step toward me. For a brief moment, some moonlight shone on his face. A face that was normally wrinkled now looked tired, eyes moist. The Leonard Baker I knew was stately, a gentleman with class. The lines on his face marked experience. Now he just looked old.

"You shouldn't be here, Jackson. Did Jeanne send you?"

"No, sir," I said. "Your wife did."

He smiled faintly. At the same time a small tear rolled from his eye. "Go home. You don't need to see this," he said.

"See what? Why are you here?"

He raised the gun to his temple, but only for a second. When he lowered it, it was like he was testing its weight. "I think you already know why I'm here."

I shrugged. "It doesn't make too much sense to me."

"Have you ever lost someone close to you?"

I shook my head.

"You can't imagine the pain. The day-in, day-out pain. And to lose someone to violence, it's something you never get over."

"Tell me."

"Tell you what?" Leonard hefted the gun again. "Go home Jackson. Hug my daughter for me."

I let his words hang in the air for a moment. Their weight seemed to hang heavier on me than on Leonard. He put the gun to his temple. The image of me hugging Jeanne, telling her about her father's suicide played in my mind. The touch of sadness I heard earlier would become blatant. She'd have her own anniversary to think about year to year.

"Stop," I said.

Leonard hesitated. Maybe the force of my voice pressed the same image into his head as well.

"What are you going to do? End your life because your sister died fifty years ago?"

"You don't understand," Leonard said.

"Then make me. And then you know what? If it's so bad—if you have to kill yourself—then I'll walk away." I put my hand to my chest. It probably sounded stupid to both of us. We both had to know I wasn't going anywhere.

"My sister died fifty years ago today," he said. "It was my fault."

"How?"

"It was before Korea. The reason I joined the army. My friend John and I were looking for my father's liquor closet. John was opening and closing drawers and closets and he opened one and found a gun."

I knew where this was going, I could already sense it, but sometimes it's better to let people talk. The wind seemed to grow colder the longer we stood. My ears burned.

Leonard hefted the gun again. "It seemed like a good idea. John was always talking about fate. He said it was our fate to find the gun and to go out and try target practice. No one was around in the neighborhood anyway, so we could just shoot in the backyard.

"We went outside and John was setting up a target, when Emily came home crying. She wasn't more than ten—God I can't remember exactly how old she was. How sad is that?"

"Mr. Baker, Leonard, please. Put the gun down."

"No. Let me tell the story and then you'll see, it's time to go." His body shuddered in a sob. "It's time for me to go."

Again, I chose to remain silent.

"She was crying and she wouldn't be quiet. We just wanted her to go inside and deal with her problems on her own. Finally, she got so loud, she kept saying my name and I turned and I just wanted to scare her. I turn and lifted the gun and told her to be quiet. The gun went off in my hand. Put a hole in her chest."

He let the gun drop to his side. He was speaking through hard tears now. Trying to catch his breath.

"John ran. I hid the gun in the woods and blamed it all on some niggers that people kept seeing around the neighborhood that winter. People believed it. Or at least they wanted to. I enlisted and went away to Korea. I thought I'd die there and God would get even with me. I went to Korea because I wanted to die. But I didn't. I survived. I married. I had a child. I watched her grow. Just like Emily should have."

"And now what? Now years later, you're just going to kill yourself?" My blood boiled. Because of a mistake years ago, he felt he could ruin his wife and daughter's lives? "Seems like the coward's way out."

"I kept the gun, Jackson. It's this gun. I always told people this was my gun from Korea. But it wasn't. I kept my father's gun. The one that ended my sister's life. And now it'll end mine."

"Why now, Leonard?"

He stared at me. A few faint snow flurries fluttered to the ground. The dead remained silent among the two of us.

"Because Jeanne is going to have someone to take care of her. You're going to marry her and take care of her. And Sarah will be okay without me. We've grown apart anyway. We don't talk much after all these years of marriage. She'll be okay without me."

"That's bullshit."

"No," Leonard said sharply. "It's not. It's the truth. I couldn't ever talk about this with her. No one would talk about it with me, except John. And only when he had a lot to drink. That's why we always went out on this day. So I could talk it out it one more time with him, get it off my chest for one more year. But John stopped drinking, and he told me tonight he wasn't going to talk about it anymore. And I can't have this weighing on my heart anymore. I can't live with it beneath my skin."

"John's crazy. If he was your friend, he'd help no matter what."

"You don't know him."

"I've met him. Tonight. He was going to let you do this. He didn't want to help you."

John Roland was a lazy bastard who didn't care about anyone. He was just going to sit and watch a hockey game while his friend killed himself. Then, to clear his conscience, he'd blame it on fate.

"It's just as well. I didn't want him to help me," Leonard Baker said. "I want to die."

"Well, I'm your friend too, Leonard. And I want to be your son-in-law. I want to help. I don't want you to die. Your daughter doesn't either."

Leonard Baker lifted the revolver, not at the temple this time, but instead pressing it to his chin.

"Your daughter," I said. "You couldn't watch Emily grow up, but you watched your daughter."

"Yes, I did. And you don't know how painful it was for me. To see my own daughter go through things and only have it remind me of my dead sister. And now that I've seen her grow up, I can let go."

I expected to hear the echo of the gun going off. My body was tense and tight. But nothing happened. Leonard didn't pull the trigger. I still had time.

"You haven't seen your daughter do everything yet. Don't you want to see her laugh at her wedding? Or hold her own child in her arms? Your grandchild?"

"I—I just want to die."

"It's not time yet, Mr. Baker. Give me the gun."

His entire body shook. Tears flowed along his face. Some of the corpses probably looked healthier than he did at the moment.

"Your wife loves you. She called me, worried about you. Jeanne needs you. We need you Mr. Baker. We're young. We can't lose you yet." I extended my hand. "Give me the gun."

Leonard Baker hesitated and I saw it in his eyes. He couldn't pull the trigger. The gun lowered in his arms and the next thing I knew it was in my hand. My future father-in-law collapsed in the snow and dirt, breathing heavily.

It was my turn to heft the gun. "Even if you had tried it, Mr. Baker, I think this thing is so old it would have jammed."

It was a lie, the gun had been cleaned and polished regularly. The thing would have fired no problem. But I wanted to give his conscience an out.

He looked up at me, eyes still brimming with tears. "Damn it, I wouldn't have even been able to do that right."

We both laughed. It was an uncomfortable laugh, the kind that only relieves tension, but it felt good nonetheless.

"Come on," I said. "Let me take you home."

"Okay," he said. "Don't tell my wife."

"I won't." My phone buzzed and the caller ID indicated Sarah Baker was calling me. She was probably a nervous wreck. "Speak of the devil."

It was all a haze, nerves screaming under my skin, the loss of the use of my limbs, going into shock. When I answered Mrs. Baker was crying only able to say the words "Jeanne," "accident," and "drunk driver." The words didn't register at first, it was white noise. But as my brain put the pieces of the puzzle together, a horrible image floated behind my eyes.

I was on my knees after that, the world spinning away from me.

Somewhere I heard Leonard's voice. "What happened?" over and over again. His hand slipped under my armpit and he tried to get me back to my feet. He couldn't lift me, my vision clouded, the cemetery faded black.

ff

The wake, the funeral, the repast, they were all an alcoholic blur. I know the Bakers were there. I think I made it to one of those events, but I'm not sure which one. I fell off the wagon hard. Jeanne was dead. My world was gone because someone weaved across the yellow lines and smashed into her Geo.

It took me two weeks to be able to function anywhere outside of a bar. And that was only because the Bakers continually tracked me down and tried to sober me up. Leonard Baker was always there for me, always dragging me out at closing time. Always trying to find me before I left my apartment to go to the bar. He rarely succeeded. He tried to take me to lunch. Mrs. Baker cooked me dinner. I didn't eat, ever.

It was the end of March before the world came back into a bit of focus. I sat with Leonard Baker on a park bench along the Raritan. It was late afternoon, the sun shining on the back of our necks. In his lap was his father's gun.

In front of us a few ducks flapped their wings and quacked at each other. I had a beard and bags under my eyes. I couldn't remember the last time I'd gotten a haircut. Or, for that matter, taken a shower.

"Do you remember that night?" Leonard said as we sat. His voice was a whisper.

I didn't respond.

"I never told Sarah what happened. I just said you found me in the bar. I didn't tell her how you saved me. If you hadn't shown up. . ."

One of the ducks took off into the air. It circled a tree once or twice and landed again, its squawks even louder.

"My wife would be a mess, and the way you handled this, you wouldn't have been there for her." He let those words sit for a moment. "No one would have."

I kicked at some grass, feeling more tears well behind my eyes. There was no way a man could cry as much as I had.

"Maybe John was right," Leonard said. "Maybe you were supposed to save me that night. Because God knows if you hadn't there would have been three people dead after that night. Me. Jeanne. And you."

I turned toward him.

"I know you've put the gun in your mouth at least once since this has happened," he said. "Maybe you don't have the guts to pull the trigger either, but I know you. You've thought about ending it. And if I had died that night, you probably would have seen how easy it was to just pull the trigger."

His words rang false to me. But at this point everything rang false. The ducks kept squawking like nothing had changed in the world. People walked behind us on the streets as they did every day. Cars passed and honked and life kept going. But I couldn't understand how. How could life go on when my fiancée was dead?

"I've made a decision, Jackson. You may not like it, but it's my decision and I'm going to stick with it." He picked the gun up. "I'm not going to need this anymore. I'd been saving it for when I thought it was time to end my life. It's not time."

I watched as the gun flew from Leonard Baker's hand and splashed into the Raritan River. The ducks scattered at the sound.

My father-in-law put his hand on my shoulder. "You need someone to be there for you, like you were there for me. And I'm going to be that man. You're going to get through this. I'm not going to let you turn into me. It's not the way to lead your life."

"Fuck you," I said. "Fuck it all."

He squeezed my shoulder tight. "We're going to get through this."

The ducks settled back on the water. They seemed to be looking for something. Food, maybe, I don't know. Leonard and I sat for another hour watching them. We were silent.

Behind us the world kept moving.

Afterword

Jackson Donne is my series character and has appeared in a number of short stories. I always wanted to tell the story of Jeanne's death, a central moment in Donne's life. Figuring out where Donne was when the car accident happened was the hard part. But the idea of Donne trying to save another of Jeanne's relatives came to me and I went from there. —D.W.

TWILIGHT ON SECOND AVENUE

SARAH WEINMAN

Sarah Weinman (born 1979) is the crime fiction columnist for the Baltimore Sun *and co-editor of the publishing industry news blog Galleycat, but most people seem to know her for the wildly popular crime and mystery fiction blog Confessions of an Idiosyncratic Mind (www.sarahweinman.com). Her short fiction has appeared this year in* Dublin Noir, Baltimore Noir *and* Alfred Hitchock's Mystery Magazine. *She lives in New York, where Sarah says "it's awfully easy to be an old soul."*

†

TWILIGHT ON SECOND AVENUE
by Sarah Weinman

It was two in the morning on Saturday night and Morton Poliner was finally alone. The last customer left three hours ago, slightly annoyed at being shooed out after only his fourth cup of coffee. The wait staff hung around another hour, counting their tips to make sure they hit their weekly quotas. And somehow, Morton managed to keep his focus, hiding any inkling that something had gone terribly wrong.

Only Tomas, who'd worked the kitchen for two decades, sensed something amiss.

"You okay, boss?"

Morton nodded. "Of course. Why wouldn't I be?"

"You've been twitchy the entire night. You don't look anyone direct in the eye, like you're keeping some big secret."

A chill coursed through Morton, but he refused to give anything away. "Everything's fine, Tomas. Have a good night."

Tomas persisted and stayed another half hour, but even he too decided there was no sense in sticking around anymore. Another fifteen minutes and Morton might have broken down and told him the real reason why there would be no restaurant as of tomorrow morning.

Now he wouldn't have to.

Poliner's had been his for almost three-quarters of his life; a tiny, ramshackle restaurant at the corner of Second Avenue and Fourth Street that eventually grew upwards and across, drawing a throng of customers night after night for the pastrami sandwiches and potato knishes. Some called it a family-style restaurant, but Morton had always aimed for something more. It was a meeting place, a wellspring for the community, and an elegy for a lost generation. It wasn't modern and never wanted to be. Just like its owner.

So the décor was at least thirty years out of date. So the paint peeled off the tops of the walls and the color had faded from its original vibrant green. So what if tastes had changed and moods had altered? Poliner's had earned its reputation for a reason: good food and friendly service, with Morton Poliner at the epicenter. He was there every evening, greeting the customers like he was one of the wait staff, demurring whenever someone dared to offer him a tip. Give it to my boys, he said time after time. They're the ones who do all the work.

But after tonight, there wouldn't be any work. Poliner's would belong to someone else, given a new name, new look, a new function. And even though Morton wanted desperately to hang on, to board the place up with him still inside, that couldn't happen.

It was his own damn fault, and now he had no choice but to let go.

Morton stood in the center of the restaurant and slowly turned in a circle, taking in everything one last time. There were so many mementos: the snapshot of him and his next-door neighbor Gershon Edelman taken the day they broke ground on the restaurant's foundation; the 30th anniversary plaque given by the previous mayor; the black-and-white photo of him standing in between DA Morgenthau and Chief Medical Examiner Helpern, Cuban cigars dangling from each of their mouths; the 8x10 of his grandniece Kelsey in her high school graduation finery, her arm securely wrapped around the waist of her childhood friend Daniel; and his favorite, the crayon extravaganza Kelsey gave him a decade ago. Every week for a year afterwards, she made a point of visiting the restaurant to see if the picture was still up there. And every week, it was, to the ten-year-old's delight.

But tomorrow, it wouldn't be.

He wondered if Kelsey would ever forgive him.

Morton reached over and removed the drawing from the wall. He'd have to put it in a safe place where no one could find it, make sure it didn't suffer the same fate as everything else here.

He knew he'd brought this on himself. It had been so easy to retreat into denial, into thinking that old wounds wouldn't reopen, that he could keep the restaurant forever. It had taken very little effort to shove his transgressions into increasingly smaller compartments until he thought he'd forgotten them completely.

Being here, all alone, was a stark reminder of how wrong he was.

Morton checked his watch. Ten minutes had passed, or maybe hours. Time was an elastic thing for him lately; sometimes he would close his eyes for a moment and find he'd lost an entire morning, while other days seemed to crawl by, every detail to be preserved in his memory.

Like the day Poliner's opened for business, all the way back in— what was the year?—1952. Running a restaurant had been his grandfather's dream, then his father's. Neither of them had enough money to open one so each had to settle for whatever they could get – tailor, blacksmith, garment worker, diamond trader, all the typical things a Lower East Side man was supposed to do. But the Poliner men loved their food; Morton couldn't remember a time when his father wasn't criticizing his mother's cooking, annoyed that she had overcooked the chicken or made the *cholent* too bland.

"I can do better!" his father said every time.

19

"So if you can do better, why don't you make some money at it?" his mother would yell back.

He didn't, but Morton would. It took hard work, determination and astonishingly good timing – as well as tacit approval from the rival gangs run by the McGradys of Avenue B and the Castellinis of Houston and Ludlow – but when the day came and customers lined up around the block to eat at the tiny restaurant with his name on it, he didn't ask if it was a dream, if he would wake up and everything would disappear the next day.

It was his right, and his duty. And he never thought he'd be forced to relinquish it.

But even though Morton preserved some days in his life with a level of detail reserved for the best photographs, he knew how to shut other ones out completely. Someone dared to criticize the food? Out they went. If a health inspector showed up and started making noises that maybe, just maybe, the restaurant wouldn't pass the health code this year? Out they went, with an extra wad of cash in their hands for good measure. And if someone wanted to buy Poliner's, do something different or move it somewhere else? They weren't even worth paying attention to.

Morton's heartbeat quickened as another memory came back. He put his left hand against the wall, where Kelsey's painting had once hung. He did not like this memory. He did not like how it kept him awake some nights, the all-too-familiar voice mocking him with the same sentence over and over:

"I know what you did, Morton."

Because of that voice, Morton wouldn't have his restaurant anymore. Because of that voice, Morton would no longer be able to do what he loved most: making sure his customers had a wonderful time, excellent food and became, at least for an evening, a part of his community.

Because of that voice, Morton's place in the neighborhood he loved best was at risk.

There was nothing left to do but wait.

⚜

It was only a few weeks ago, but Morton had been so much younger then, still capable of going days without sleep. He was in the middle of one such sleeping jag when, well after closing time, a well-dressed man in a seersucker suit and a brown fedora he didn't recognize knocked on his apartment door.

"Who is it?"

The other man said his name. Morton shouldn't have let him in, but as soon as he heard who it was, his mind went on autopilot and his body was too numb to protest.

Morton opened the door. The other man sauntered in like he didn't have a care in the world. Of course not, considering the reason he was here.

"Remember me, Morton?"

"Should I?" he was stalling, he knew it, but the words had to be said.

Rory McGrady laughed them off. "That's not going to work. Everyone knows who I am, even if they don't care to. And without me, your entire life as it stands wouldn't exist."

Morton's palms sweated, and he felt his shirt dampen. He had to calm down. There was no other option.

"That's not true."

"You're playing the denial game now?" said McGrady, in a genial tone that worsened Morton's uneasiness. "That's awfully strange. I mean, you're the man who never shied away from your roots, that you grew up poor and fulfilled your father's dream. And you're so good at acknowledging who helped you in the past. What about me?"

"What you offered wasn't 'help,'" Morton spat.

"But you took it. Again and again, and – oh yes, what was it? – again. You could have turned me down. You could have refused."

"No I couldn't! And risk losing Poliner's?"

McGrady's face contorted into a horrible approximation of a smile. "It was your choice, Morton. You thought the restaurant was more important, so you did whatever you could to preserve the place and keep it running. And that was fine, because it suited me not to be publicly associated with it. It didn't exactly fit the image I've taken great lengths to cultivate."

It dawned on Morton that so many others welcomed this man into their home, their lives. They gladly took his money – blood money disguised as philanthropic donations – because they were eager to be associated, even in the tiniest way, with his wealth and reputation. And for the longest time, Morton had been one of those others.

Until the day when Rory McGrady casually let slip that he knew something other people didn't, nor shouldn't. And that if Morton didn't make him a silent partner in the restaurant, he might let everyone in on that secret.

So Morton took his money. He expanded Poliner's upwards and across and more customers ate there and came back. And for a while, he could forget, because McGrady believed a silent partner should stay silent.

"You never wanted attention before. Why should I pay you any now?"

McGrady motioned to the couch. "May I sit here? My back aches." He sat down before Morton could say no. "Ah, good. So much easier to speak when you're sitting, do you know what I mean? Neither of us is getting any younger."

"Cut out the bullshit or I'll throw you off the couch."

"Oh please, Morton. Enough bluster. But since you wanted a point, here it is: I'm selling my share."

Morton was elated. Finally, he'd be free! But his rejoicing lasted all of ten seconds.

"Oh, not so fast," said McGrady. "I've already found a buyer."

"Who?"

"Cervico."

Morton's face paled. Selling to them meant demolition would happen immediately. It wasn't enough that someone else would own Poliner's: they'd destroy it.

"You've seen the neighborhood. Poliner's just doesn't fit anymore. It reminds people too much of the old ways. They're going to fusion places, new cuisines. No one wants *borscht belt* when they can get Szechuan."

"And this is your way of consulting me before the fact?"

"I thought it better than you waking up one morning and finding the place imploded."

Some consolation. Morton tried to think, but nothing came. Why hadn't he slept? Because he'd been too busy working with the volunteer shelter. Too busy helping Kelsey with her college homework.

Too busy to forget his own homework.

The other man must have seen Morton's expression flicker. "It didn't have to be this way, Morton. But you should have realized that over time, my share would finally hit 51%. And then I could do what I pleased."

He had to sleep on this. Or simply sleep. "At least don't do this tomorrow. Give me some time."

"I wouldn't do that to Morton Poliner," McGrady said, oozing insincerity.

"Shut up. How long do I have?"

"Six weeks."

"Good. Then I'll find a way."

Rory McGrady laughed. "Like hell you will. You'll see the contract tomorrow. You can't get out of it."

Before Morton could respond, the man in the seersucker suit took his leave of the apartment. Morton sat on his couch, the one he'd bought with the first profit from the restaurant.

He knew he'd find a way.

It might take every bit of time he had left, but he would.

✦

Morton didn't know how much longer he could wait. An odd admission, but he allowed himself such things. He didn't want to deviate from the plan he'd finally devised only a couple of days ago.

It wasn't foolproof, but he believed it came close. In an ideal world, a secret would only be kept by one person, but that was inherently impossible. Otherwise he wouldn't have been in this predicament in the first place.

Morton fiddled with the ring on his finger. He'd told everyone that it belonged to his great-grandfather, a wedding trinket that had been passed on from generation to generation. But with everyone who could possibly refute the story dead for years, it was an easy fiction to maintain. As soon as he'd taken the ring he had filed down the surface, making sure the shiny newness transformed into a duller, more worn look.

Wearing it was a constant reminder of how far he'd come, and how things could have changed so easily.

Morton Poliner wanted to run a restaurant, but there weren't too many people who believed that someone like him had the *kishkes* to make it. Morton was twenty-five, but in many ways he was appallingly naïve. Thinking about his innocence made him wince.

He thought he simply had to go to city hall and get a permit. As soon as he explained himself, they laughed at him.

"You think it's that easy, young man?" said the woman at the desk.

"I have the money, I have the paperwork. Why shouldn't it?"

She leaned over and whispered in a conspiratorial manner. "You don't know much about the Lower East Side, do you?"

"What do you mean?"

And then, dropping her voice even lower, she explained. Two families, the McGradys and the Castellinis, had been fighting each other for over twenty years. The two factions could get bloody if necessary, but most of the time they engaged in dueling protection rackets. Right now, there was a truce: one family controlled one half of the neighborhood, while the other had the second half.

"Where do I fit in?" asked Morton.

"You're on Second Avenue?"

He nodded. "And Fourth."

She smiled, showing off a slew of missing and cracked teeth. "The

Castellinis, then. Lucky you."

And so it was, but just as he was preparing to pay them the requisite protection money – a bargain at 10% of his projected earnings per month – Declan McGrady had other ideas.

The week before they were due to break ground, McGrady paid a visit.

"I'm taking over," he said matter-of-factly.

"You can't. Silvano Castellini's already getting his cut," protested Morton.

"You're not paying much attention, Poliner. Castellini's dead. Heart attack. So everything's up for grabs."

Morton spent the next four days in a panic-induced sweat. He wasn't the only one, as the entire street suddenly became swarmed with McGrady's goons, all demanding more money and making more threats. Some decided to close down lest they pay extra; others stayed in, angry but determined not to get rookered by the new arrangement.

Gershon Edelman, his soon-to-be neighbor, was especially livid. "We have to do something," he said when Morton came to visit.

"I know, but what? We don't have enough power."

"But we don't have enough money," the older man retorted. "I know I don't have enough cash to keep my dry goods shop open. In the old country these things would take care of themselves."

The ominous tone made Morton wary. But when McGrady called him up to arrange a meeting later that night, he didn't refuse, and asked Gershon to come along.

"I'm not sure that's a good idea," said the older man.

"Why?"

Gershon's mouth hardened into a straight line. "Because you don't know what I'm capable of."

Morton put the comment out of his mind until much later, when McGrady appeared at the construction site. At first, Morton wasn't impressed with the slumlord's appearance, his wide-brimmed hat dipping slightly to the left over a face deeply lined by sun and abuse. But then he caught a glimpse of McGrady's eyes, and understood: this man ruled by fear, and always would.

McGrady surveyed the site, not bothering with formal greetings. "You have some knack, Poliner. I should have taken over this property years ago."

"You still won't," Morton insisted. "I'm not paying out to two different people."

McGrady laughed. "Semantics. Besides, Castellini's gone, and the rules are brand new. I can rewrite them as I please and I'd like to expand what I have." He suddenly whipped his head to the left. "Two of you? This is even better."

"Don't count on it," said Gershon.

"You think you can threaten me? All I have to do is put in one phone call and you'll be shipped back to where you came from. How would you like that?"

McGrady went down before Morton could register what happened. He heard the sound, he saw the bullets fly but he didn't realize anything until Gershon put down the gun and calmly walked over to where the Irishman had fallen.

Morton stared at Gershon, horrified. "Why did you do that?"

"Because you weren't going to."

"That's not a reason! I would have come up with another plan. I *did* come up –"

"Bullshit. You were going to talk your way out of it and you can't do that with Declan McGrady. You think others haven't tried? How do you think he spread himself through the neighborhood?"

"But –"

Even in the dark, Gershon's look was withering. "Enough, Morton. There's work to do."

Morton tried to find more words but they weren't there. It was awful, but nonetheless the truth: Gershon's answer was the only good one, and it wasn't his own.

The rest was easy: dropping McGrady down a well-placed hole and covering it up with the shovels left behind by the construction crew. Calling them the next morning to say that the foundation would have to be seven feet shallower, would they mind? And learning how to wait, a skill Morton prided himself on, one he tried to teach his family and his employees.

When Poliner's finally opened, Gershon wasn't around to see it. Cancer had already riddled his body but he didn't tell anyone until a week before his death. Morton was the first.

"I'm not sorry how things turned out," Gershon said on his deathbed.

Morton couldn't think of a response. Here was his friend, emaciated and about to die, and he was more determined to hold onto what had happened more than Morton was.

Suddenly, Gershon looked to the nightstand. "Take something out of there."

"I don't want to rummage through –"

"Just take it," said Gershon with more force than a dying man should have. "Please."

"What is it?"

"You'll see. There's only one thing in there."

Morton fished it out. He held it up and immediately wanted to put it right back where it had been. "I can't take this. It's yours."

"That's why you will. I don't have anyone else to give it to."

"What about your sister?"

"She doesn't want it. She never wanted anything from me. Better you have it."

After Gershon died, Morton would think about him often at first, than less so. He didn't want to dwell on what things would have been like had he lived.

This way, it was easier to forget. Easier to move forward.

In hindsight, the explanation Morton helped to concoct about Declan McGrady's disappearance was incredibly short-sighted. How could his boy not grow up with a serious chip on his shoulder, and a burning need to discover the truth about his father? With the connections Rory had built up through the kind of ferocity Morton knew well in the old man, it was only a matter of time.

How Morton could have forgotten his time would eventually be up, he didn't know. But no matter what Rory's reasons were, he couldn't destroy the restaurant.

He simply couldn't.

Morton heard the buzzer ring. Finally, it was time. Oddly, in carrying out this plan, he would remember Gershon more than anyone else.

It wasn't much longer to wait.

Morton opened the door and frowned.

"What the hell took you so long?"

The man—a boy, really—began to apologize. "Mr. Poliner, I'm so sorry, but I thought you said I should be here at 3 AM –"

"No, you're right. I'm just anxious."

"Not as much as me."

Morton had watched the boy grow up, beginning as an awkward teenage busboy to a more confident young man serving customers during his summers home from college. He'd returned home after graduation with a gift for entrepreneurial savvy. If Gershon's grandson couldn't save Poliner's, no one could.

They left the restaurant together, and Morton locked the doors for the last time. He wouldn't cry. He wouldn't show any emotion that this was the last time he would see it before it was taken away from him.

The boy kept a brisk pace until they reached the designated spot, deep in the middle of an abandoned park near Avenue D.

Then he stopped, and Morton did too.

"I can't believe I have to do this," the boy said, trembling.

"It's the only way."

"This is crazy. This is how I get to take over Poliner's? Why did I listen to you?"

"Because this way I protect myself. Do you really want Rory McGrady to demolish it? To give it to those clowns at Cervico to do what they please?"

"Of course not!"

"Then do it. This will be quick. It will be easy. Just follow my directions."

"What if something goes wrong?" asked the boy.

"Nothing will." Morton fished in his pockets. "But there are three things I have to take care of first." He held out the ring. "I should give this back to you. It was your grandfather's. He was a remarkable man and I am so, so sorry you never knew him."

The boy stared at the ring, awestruck, before putting it in his own pocket.

Morton followed step two of the plan, handing over his cash and pay slips. "Put these in a safe place. Better yet, burn them."

"Why?"

"People will look for them. But if they stay missing, the story will stick."

The boy said nothing.

"And lastly, when you go into the shop in the morning –"

"That wasn't part of the plan!"

Morton shushed the boy. "It is now. When you go, make sure Kelsey gets her drawing back. You know the one I'm talking about?"

The boy nodded, but not before a strange expression darted across his face. Morton understood. It would be another thing to regret.

He never thought it would end like this. He thought he would have had once last chance to say goodbye to his beloved grandniece, to tell Kelsey that someday, the restaurant would be hers if she wanted it. He thought he would have had more time to wrap up loose ends and keep others safely hidden.

Most of all, Morton thought his ending would be far quieter, far less violent.

But this was the only way to save Poliner's. And himself.

Morton looked up at the boy, who was shaking in terror that Morton refused to allow himself to feel.

"Stop it, Daniel. It'll be fine. Trust me."

The boy slowly raised the gun and fired.

Morton wouldn't have to wait anymore.

Afterword

"Twilight on Second Avenue" would never have been born had I not had dinner one night at the Second Avenue Deli and seen the poster on the front door: a smiling picture of Abe Lebewohl, the restaurant's founder, and a plea for information on his still-unsolved murder in 1996. Although the usual questions—what happened and why—bombarded my brain, what emerged was a desire to tell the story of the lengths a person would go to save something he'd worked so hard to create and that meant everything to him.

Ironically, just as I'd turned the story in, the Second Avenue Deli shut down in January—possibly forever—because of a rent dispute between Lebewohl's brother, Jack, and the store's owners. A spooky coincidence, no doubt, but I wonder what secrets lurk deep in the heart of the restaurant, waiting to be discovered.... –S.W.

THE BALLAD OF DAVEY ROBSON

RAY BANKS

Ray Banks (born 1977) has been everything from a double-glazing salesman and a croupier, right through to being a disgruntled office monkey. He is the creator of the Leith-born Manchester PI Callum Innes, who features in Saturday's Child *and* Donkey Punch, *both published by Polygon. He also wrote* The Big Blind, *which Ray says "some people liked." When he's not checking his prostate, he looks forward to the day when he's no longer an angry young man, but an angry old man. With a stick and all his own teeth.*

THE BALLAD OF DAVEY ROBSON
by Ray Banks

Davey Robson felt the carrier bag knock against the side of his leg as he headed towards the steps that led down to the Quayside. He pulled his anorak tighter around his torso as a cold gust of wind caught in the narrow space. The height of summer all around him, and he was the only one wearing a jacket. Not that anyone cared. People knew he was there, but avoided eye contact. These weren't his peers. These were the men and women who worked in the sandstone and glass office buildings that stared facelessly across the Tyne. Professional people, working people, earning people.

Not his kind of people at all.

Time was, Davey thought, he was just as flash as the fuckers down here. He didn't have to work six days a week to get it, either. Nah, all he needed was a good one-off and he'd be set for a couple months. But times changed.

Aye, didn't they just?

Davey found his bench, settled himself down with a creak in the joints and took a deep breath. Times changed, right enough. This rolling river used to be industrial. Used to transport coal and ships. Now it was a shit-colored artery in the middle of a dying city, despite what the fucking papers told him. Up the road, the new law courts. The other way, flats with names like St James Condominiums and Thirty Degrees North, with on-site health club facilities. False. All of it. As bland and manufactured as the music blaring from the bars down here. Pound-a-pint and mutton dressed as lamb on the karaoke machine.

He brought his bag up onto the bench next to him, laid one hand on top. Stared at the seven bridges, glowing in the evening sunlight. They reached over the Tyne, at once extending towards and pushing away Gateshead, as if the town was some drunk auntie. Newcastle had plenty to push away. The Baltic gallery and The Sage music centre stood proud, but they were the only things that did, south of the river.

Davey made this journey from the Sally up on City Road every evening. Tonight was different, though. Tonight was the night.

He smiled, fished in his pocket. Dug out his baccy tin and popped the lid. He started rolling a cigarette with yellowing fingers. He pulled at the loose strands from either end and stuck them back in his tin. Waste not, want not. Hard lessons learned those years spent at the hostel. You saved your money, you saved everything. You kept your head down and didn't piss about, didn't raise your voice. Then nobody asked you questions.

"Y'alreet, mate?"

Davey lit his roll-up, looked in the direction of the voice. Lad of about sixteen, maybe older. Wore a trucker cap with a hoodie, his hands balled up in the pockets of his trackie bottoms. Looked nervous, or just twitchy. Davey couldn't tell which. And he didn't care. He nodded, then turned back to the river.

"You got a tab there?" said the boy.

Davey thought about it for a moment. Then: "Nah."

"Howeh, I'll buy one off of you."

"Nah."

"You gonna give us your last drag then?"

The kid started bouncing on his heels. Out of the corner of his eye, Davey saw something hard in the kid's pants, and it wasn't his cock. He heard a faint click of metal against metal. Took a lungful of smoke and, as he exhaled, Davey said, "That a butterfly knife you got there, son?"

The lad narrowed his eyes and worked his mouth like he was chewing on something. Cogs whirring in his brain, the kid was thick as day-old pigshit. Just like the others Davey had seen littering the streets. Young, bold, vicious. The young dealer on the corner, shouting his wares for anyone to hear and not giving a shit.

"What d'you think you're gonna do with that?" said Davey. "You gonna stick an old man 'cause you want a fuckin' tab, is that it?"

"Give us a tab then."

"You don't get it, son. How's about you sack the hardcase shite and take a walk, eh?"

Davey turned to face him. The lad must have seen that cross-hatched scar on Davey's throat, keeping a week-old beard at bay. Davey had seen it enough in the mirror to know its effect.

"Aye, y'alreet," the lad said. His hands were out of his pockets, held up clean. "I get it."

"Good."

The lad tugged on the brim of his cap and took off. Davey watched him disappear, turned his attentions back to the river.

He didn't need company. Not tonight.

It was a while back, but Davey remembered everything. Hadn't lost his marbles yet.

Jimmy Cleghorn. A hardcase from Walker, used to run with his brother Brian. But when Brian went to Durham for a bus pass stretch, Jimmy needed someone else to run with, and Davey was daft enough to agree. He was already in his fifties then. Starting to feel the cold, not as quick as he used to be.

"Low Fell," said Jimmy.

"Post office?"

"Aye."

"Fuck's sake."

"Post offices are cream, Davey. You wanna rob a fuckin' bank, you go right ahead. I'll promise to write to you when you get put away."

"Fuckin' *post office*, though. How much money's gonna be in a post office?"

Jimmy showed his teeth. "Where d'you get your dole cashed, man?"

"That's just me."

"Nah. I been watching. The Low Fell one's the only place in twenty miles. All your locals go there to get their folding. And there's nae fuckin' jobs, is there?"

"Not unless you want to work in a call centre."

"So that's a lot of fuckin' dole."

In hindsight, he should have known better. Working with Jimmy Cleghorn was like shooting yourself full of rock salt. It wasn't fatal, but it sure as hell hurt like a bastard. And you couldn't trust the guy, especially without his brother to keep him in check. But Davey needed the cash, and he was fucked if he was going to go back to a day job, even if he'd been lucky enough to find one.

So they did over the post office, Davey on bag duty. The Ford Escort sat outside, its dodgy engine running. Davey kept one eye on the car, in case someone got the bright idea to nick it. A pistol that weighed a fucking tonne, bin liners in his pockets.

"ANYONE-GET-ANY-FUCKIN'-NOTIONS-THEY'RE-FUCKIN'-DEAD!"

And Jimmy let a cartridge go, a boom loud and vicious in the room. An old gadgie hit the deck, the fastest he'd ever moved in his life. Plaster dust rained on him. Davey straight for the windows, kicked at the side door. "Open the door, love."

It opened sharpish; a petrified woman with blue hair and the body of a thirty-year-old stood there with her mouth flapping. Davey chucked her the black bags. The pistol made his knuckles white. It was loaded, but more likely to blow his hand off than do damage to anyone else. He hoped he wouldn't have to use it.

Jimmy kept shouting. Davey couldn't make out the words over the ringing in his ears. He hadn't expected that blast from the double barrel. The women with the blue rinse took her sweet time filling the bags. Davey motioned with the pistol and his wrist ached. She started crying. Stopped what she was doing and broke right down.

"Howeh, just fill the bags, love," Davey said. "Chop chop."

Jimmy got over there in a few steps. She didn't notice him until he knocked her sideways with the butt of the double. Then she had a few seconds before she went under, eyes rolled back in her head. Jimmy grabbed at the bags, thrust the gun into Davey's hands. Said, "I'll get the car started."

Then he was gone. A memory.

And the car's engine was already running.

Davey held the guns for a full minute before he realized he'd been well and truly fucked.

He was tired enough by the time he managed to track Jimmy down. And the younger man running his mouth didn't help matters.

"Christ, Davey, howeh man. I didn't fuckin' - "

"Shut your trap, Jimmy."

"You do this, you're fuckin' *dead*, you hear me? Brian'll find out, man."

"Brian's in Durham nick. And I'm letting you off easy, marra."

What had the guy thought? That leaving him in the lurch was a way to make friends and influence people? Aye, Davey was getting old, but that was no reason to piss him around.

Jimmy hadn't expected it, more fool him. He'd spent most of the cash, hidden the rest on the Quayside. That's where Davey took him. Jimmy Cleghorn, hog-tied and gagged in the back of a stolen Micra. Davey wanted to nick a bigger car, but couldn't be bothered. After all, what was the point in making the turncoat fucker comfortable? He thought a ride in the boot was bad, just wait until he had the gun barrel digging into his scalp.

"What did you think was gonna happen, Jimmy?" Davey asked. "You daft cunt. Shoulda done the right thing and got the fuck out of the country."

Jimmy didn't answer; the gun blast already cut him short. Face down in the dirt, leaking blood and white meat.

Davey wiped the still-warm blood spray from his face. He tossed the pistol onto the back seat of the Micra, grabbed a shovel. He started to dig. It was still dark, the night sky clear. He could just about see what he was doing. Not that it mattered, really. It was only a shallow grave and this place was deserted. Old warehouses, wasteland. He'd thought about hefting Jimmy into the Tyne, watch the bugger wash out to sea. But there were too many things that could go wrong. Knowing his luck, Jimmy'd end up in Jarrow, scare the shit out of one of the original Marchers.

So a hole in the ground it was. He worked up a sweat, managed to get three feet down before he stopped, lit a cigarette. The smoke hurt his throat, but he needed the nicotine.

Cigarette clamped between his teeth, Davey grabbed Jimmy by the legs. That was as close as he wanted to get. Cleghorn had evacuated his bowels and bladder at the moment of death, and from the smell of him, he'd had more than a few square meals. Davey dragged the body a few steps, then watched it topple into the hole.

A leg stuck out, twisted against the earth. Davey aimed a kick and felt the bone crack under his foot. Then he pushed the limb into the pit.

Finished his cigarette and tossed the filter onto Jimmy's corpse. Let him burn. Where he was going, he'd better get used to the heat.

ƒ

Davey ground out the roll-up, breathed in fresh air. It didn't suit him, caught his lungs and provoked a coughing fit. He wasn't as fit as he used to be. The years he'd been at the hostel, he'd thought about Jimmy Cleghorn a lot. The guy had invaded whatever dreams he'd managed to have. Laughing at him for the way he'd ended up.

Aye, Jimmy *would* fucking laugh at that.

But then Jimmy didn't have much of a sense of humour. Jimmy was a saucer-eyed speed freak. Jimmy laughed at fucking clouds.

Old, man. You're just too fuckin' old.

ƒ

The night after he covered Jimmy with dirt, Davey went to The Sun In Splendour. He had the cash burning a hole in his pocket and he liked to drink. The pub he went to with a stacked wallet, it had the rep of slicing up students. He loved that. Made him feel like the old days, when he'd sit and sup with some of the hardest bastards this side of the Tyne.

Beer led to a whisky, the best stuff they had. Then the amber spirits kept calling. Davey got louder as the drink took hold. He started distributing the wealth, playing bigshot. Once Jimmy's brother found out about what happened, there'd be hell to pay. Davey knew that. He had time, but it was inevitable. The way he saw it, he might as well celebrate while he still could.

He didn't see the two lads. When he staggered to the toilets, they must have followed.

The blows were delivered low and hard. Davey cracked his head on the hand dryer. Ended up with him out on the street, ripped up and puking blood into the gutter, cursing God between heaves, cursing Jimmy Cleghorn too. The fucker was laughing at him from hell.

The lad with the crater face had taken a short blade to Davey's side. A butterfly knife, from what he remembered. And Christ, didn't his bowels feel greasy when he saw the blood. Not too deep, but deep enough to worry about. Davey kept one white hand on the wound, tried to keep the cold at bay. If he lost it, he'd bleed to death. This part of town, there'd be no ambulance. Not for a guy stinking of booze and howling at the moon. He was just another derelict. And he wept like a baby that night. Every time his knees gave way, every time he hit the ground, he'd cry. No room for self-respect when self-preservation takes over.

The Sally Army hostel was five minutes away. And as he stumbled through the doors, he praised the God he'd cursed. These people had to help him. They took him in. A poor homeless guy who'd been done over by thugs.

Davey had a home, but he couldn't go back. He was too feverish, sweating through the guilt. Jimmy Cleghorn had arranged that attack, he thought. Or the money was cursed. Or Davey was cursed. Something was fucked somewhere along the line.

He retched into a bucket placed by his bed. There was blood in the vomit.

He was dying, and he knew it. And he was dying because he deserved it. His own fault, running his mouth, robbing people. Payback. Playing younger than his years, it was bound to bite him in the arse. He never thought it would bite so hard, though.

Someone was saying, "It'll be alright."

Davey Robson didn't believe a word of it.

❦

Across the Tyne, drums started playing, a ferocious tribal beat lifting up into the sky. Part of The Sage's opening extravaganza. Soon there'd be fireworks. Davey smiled to himself.

He didn't die that night, even though he felt like it. He wanted to give up, just curl up and leave the world. There was nothing left for him. But once the people at the hostel cleaned him up and showed him his bed, he saw a way out. It was his sanctuary, and all he had to do was keep his head down.

Brian Cleghorn came out of prison two months ago. That's what Davey'd heard. By all accounts, Brian wasn't the same nutter who went in, but Davey wasn't about to take any chances. He was still invisible at the hostel. He'd given the woman a false name. He wasn't Davey Robson anymore. Now he was Harold White, Whitey to his friends.

He had a new life. But there was one thing left to watch. One more thing to make sure of.

When Davey read about the new music centre, his chest got tight. He had images of some dozy builder finding Jimmy Cleghorn in the ground. So he'd come down to the Quayside every day since, watched that eyesore being built from the foundation up. Watched the Quayside change, found himself growing old fast. The money he still had, the cash those two charvas hadn't taken, he kept it in a shoebox under his bed. He had mourned his old life, but then resigned himself to anonymity.

It was better that way. You learned to live without. You learned to take each day as it came.

He reached into the plastic bag, pulled out a bottle of beer and set it on the bench next to him. The first drink since The Sun In Splendour. He was going to enjoy this one.

"Davey."

He recognized the voice. The Cleghorns sounded the same. He didn't turn. "Give us a second."

Brian Cleghorn came into view. The guy had filled out. Happened to some blokes when they went inside – they blurred at the edges. Davey moved his bottle and Brian took a seat.

Silence between them, the drums subsiding into a million hearts beating.

"Y'alreet, Bri?"

"Not so bad."

"You look canny. Durham agreed with you."

Brian nodded.

"How'd you find us?" said Davey.

"I got a lad on the payroll. Lives down the corridor from you."

"You're not paying him enough then."

They both stared out at the Tyne. A crowd was forming outside The Sage. Middle-class music lovers, Davey thought. Invitation only. Looking to get as much of the free bubbly as they could.

"You kill him, Davey?"

"What d'you think?"

"I heard you did."

"If I killed Jimmy, I wouldn't be sitting here, would I?"

Brian took a deep breath. "If you didn't kill him, you'd still be Davey Robson." He stood up. "C'mon, got a car waiting."

Davey cracked the beer and took a long drink. The bubbles scratched at his throat. He wiped his mouth with the back of one hand, stifled a belch.

"Howeh, Davey. Don't be a fuckin' pain."

"I want to watch the fireworks."

"Fuck the fireworks. I'm being nice about this."

"Wait a second. They're gonna let them fly."

Brian turned as a rocket screeched into the sky, exploded in a fountain of stars. Another rocket joined it, then three more screamers. In the staggered purple dusk, Davey whistled, then said, "How's that, eh? No expense spared."

"Let's go, Davey," said Brian.

Davey got to his feet, raised the bottle as a toast to the last nail in the coffin. Took a swig. Shook his head. Then pitched the bottle into the Tyne.

Brian made sure Davey went first as they headed towards the waiting car.

Toasting a bloody firework display. His mind must have been shot.

It was time to put the old bastard out of his misery.

Afterword

"The Ballad Of Davey Robson" came about after watching the gradual construction of The Sage music centre on the Gateshead side of the Tyne in Newcastle - I work up the street. It was weird seeing that big silver witchetty grub being built, because there's an uneasy mixture of young professional riverside flats elbow-to-elbow with old council stock and the Sally Army hostel up the road. A definite tension in the air. As for Davey Robson, he's a direct Geordie relation of John Tormey's character Louie in Ghost Dog:Way Of The Samurai, *kind of a sad-sack ex hard man. In fact, I felt an affinity with all those guys. Fuck Lee Marvin, I want my tough geezers to apply pile ointment whilst singing Flavor Flav. Yeeeeaaaah, booooy. –R.B.*

SAY GOODNIGHT TO THE BAD GUY

DUANE SWIERCZYNSKI

Duane Swierczynski (born 1972) is the author of Secret Dead Men *(Point Blank Press) and* The Wheelman *(St. Martin's Minotaur), which was optioned for film by director Simon Hynd. His third novel,* The Blonde, *is due out this November. He's the editor-in-chief of the* Philadelphia City Paper, *and lives in that city with his wife, son and daughter.*

SAY GOODNIGHT TO THE BAD GUY
by Duane Swierczynski

He who follows in the wake of death
Risks all to gain little
Only his soul
—Ling Yuan, 2nd Century Chinese warrior/philosopher

Well I'll be thinking about that
when I'm pissing on your grave.
—Clint Eastwood, *In the Line of Fire*

The trip took barely two hours. Philly isn't far from New York. The two cities pretty much share New Jersey as a backyard.

Two commuter trains and five blocks later, I was staring at Cole Ford's front door.

It was a thick slab of stained wood with an opaque, diamond-shaped sheet of Plexiglas in the middle. Ford took his time answering. The first words out of his mouth:

"I've got company. Put down your bag and come meet Hilda."

I glanced past him, toward the kitchen, and saw the round form of a flower print dress. A flower print dress draped over a side of beef. Yowza.

"We're having liverwurst and beer."

The most remarkable thing about Cole Ford was how unremarkable he looked. Just another grandfather-looking guy, someone you'd blow by without a second thought, other than: *bad denture job.*

It looked like he had a boxer's mouth guard in there.

Ford's kitchen table was imitation woodgrain, and it was littered with warm cans of beer. Wax paper with thick stacks of sliced liverwurst and American cheese. Cigarette trays and loose ashes, twitching around from the breeze of the open kitchen window. There were also jar candles everywhere—two on the table, another three on the counter. They were all different scents, which made the kitchen smell like pumpkin-berry-pine, with a mellow note of baby powder.

"Lemme fix you a sandwich."

"I'm okay, Mr. Ford."

There was no way I could eat. Not with clashing scents in the kitchen. Beneath the baby powder was something else. Something *off.*

But Ford was already headed to his fridge.

"How are ya," Hilda said, drawing out every syllable, even though there were only three of them.

"Very good. Are you Mrs. Ford?"

"Oh my word," she said. "Me? And Jimmy?"

"Shut the fuck up Hilda," said Ford. "I told you, I've gotta talk to this kid for a while, and I don't want you opening your mouth for a while."

"Sorry, Jimmy."

"And light another candle. You're starting to stink again."

Hilda looked at me apologetically. "It's my bag. Ya know." She gestured to her side. "The doctors say it's supposed to be odorless, but…"

"If that's odorless, then I'm smelling the guy next door who shit his pants. C'mon Hilda. We're trying to eat here. Light a fucking candle."

My God.

Cole Ford.

I was actually here, in his kitchen.

⁊

The name "Cole Ford" will mean nothing to you unless you're a crime fiction junkie like me.

Cole Ford is the Holy Grail of the Hardboiled.

He wrote a story called "Two Bullets and a Bucket of Gasoline" which, as far as anyone knew, was the only story to ever appear under the "Cole Ford" byline. All we have by way of physical proof is the story itself: a 1,200 worder, accompanied by a sketch, inked in black and blue.

But oh, what a story.

Utterly modern in its concision; there was not a word you could add or subtract to the story without eroding its brilliance. Yet it was rich in violence and passion—a primal scream from the strangled throat of urban America that wouldn't sound out of place today.

Cole's harder-than-hardboiled voice cast aside skin and muscle and veins and nerves and cleaved right to the bone.

It was the Clash, circa 1954.

It was the H-Bomb in your den.

Nobody who read it fresh off the newsstand was ever the same again.

The impact on mystery fiction was immediate: Spillane said he wished he wrote it. MacDonald said he was dumbstruck by its audacity; the other Macdonald could only agree. Chandler, it was widely reported, was utterly ruined by it, and didn't write again until the dismal *Playback*. There's a letter from David Goodis to a Hollywood friend in which he mentions "Two Bullets and a Bucket of Gasoline," and then, in the very next paragraph, talks about moving in with his parents back in Philly to "get his life right again."

The genre, many hardboiled mystery critics now agree, was never the same after Ford's story appeared.

Little is known about Ford, and what we do know comes from Luther McCall, the legendary editor of the Golden Lion paperback line. He saw "Two Bullets," recognized its raw acid genius, and immediately set out to find Ford to commission a novel. No easy task, that.

McCall rang up John McCloud, *Manhunt's* editor, who said that Ford was a 29-year-old stumblebum who reportedly borrowed a department store typewriter—he filched some empty pages from the sales counter—sat down and banged out 1,200 words before security was summoned. Those 1,200 words, of course, were "Two Bullets and a Bucket of Gasoline," which Ford dropped off at the *Manhunt* editorial office at 545 Fifth Avenue in Manhattan. "I happened to be walking by the front desk and I saw Hal [Walker, managing editor] with his nose buried in a stack of pages," said McCloud. "Hal says to me, 'Jesus, Johnny, you've gotta read this.' And that was it. Ford showed up the next day, demanding cash, not even seeming happy in the least that he was going to be published, and then walked right out again."

Hal Walker told Luther McCall that Ford smelled like a taproom, so he started his search there: every taproom in the greater Manhattan area. Every day, McCall would take his egg salad or tuna or salami and onion in a brown bag that his wife Kirsten had packed him, and he'd drink exactly one glass of beer in a different bar, asking about Ford. Nobody'd heard of him… until nine weeks later, when McCall took a liverwurst and mustard into Jimmy's Corner at 140 West 44th Street— a hangout for boxing fans and down-on-their-luck prizefighters.

That's where I met McCall, just a few weeks ago. He insisted on taking me back there, where it began.

"We sat at this table," McCall said, "but I had to bribe him first. He wanted lunch. Come to think of it, he wanted two lunches. One to eat here in the taproom, one to take home with him. Later I found out, he didn't really have what you'd call a home."

McCall looked his age; he'd just celebrated his 80th birthday, and was still recovering from surgery where they installed a defibrillator. "Used to have a pacemaker," he said. "In case my heart slowed down. Now they put this thing in here to zap it if it goes too slow, or put the brakes on if it goes too fast. Two for the price of one."

I'd found him easily enough: McCall was listed. Lived in Queens.

The publishing industry had passed him by in the early 1970s; he later made a living doing porn paperbacks, two a week, $500 a pop.

He brought me one of them: *Doberman Rape Gang*, the title read.

"It's one of my better ones," he said.

McCall was surprised when I called him; even more surprised when he learned I wanted to talk about Cole Ford.

He insisted we meet right away.

"We sat here," he continued, "and I somehow convinced him that he could have all of the beer and sandwiches he wanted if he could sit down and write a novel. He said he didn't have no typewriter. I said I'd get him a typewriter. He said he didn't have no quiet places to write. I said I'd get him that, too, and enough sandwiches and beer to carry him though. He sat there quiet for a while, then asked how many. I told him, 'Golden Lion is big time, we can pay maybe $2,000 for a novel.' Actually, I could go as high as $2,500, but this was a first-timer—I wanted to leave myself some wiggle room. But then he says no, I mean, how many sandwiches per meal? Ford was an odd duck like that. He didn't like to sit down to less than two sandwiches per meal. Otherwise, he'd rather go hungry. Figure that."

My heart started racing. I'd never heard of a Cole Ford *novel*. It was too good to be true.

"Did he ever write the novel?"

McCall smiled, and when he smiled, his eyes seemed to close shut.

"He wrote it in my living room."

"You're joking."

It took another beer to draw it out of him—McCall was jazzed by my enthusiasm, and seemed to delight in delivering every detail as slowly as possible. But the fact was, Cole Ford wrote a novel called *Say Goodnight to the Bad Guy*.

The title, McCall claimed, was his.

"Ford moves in with us, me and my wife Kirsten, and first thing he says is, I can't live with no German. Now Kirsten had blonde hair, and she's blue-eyed, but it's not like she's the daughter of a Nazi war criminal. But Ford goes on and on about it, and every time he talks about Kirsten, he calls her 'that German wife of yours.' I tell him to get over it, and show him the couch and the spare typewriter. And his beloved sandwiches.

"Then he goes, 'Look, I don't have no ideas,' and I tell him, that's no problem, I've got a box of index cards full of story synopses—stuff we'd kick around the office, type out, and wait for somebody to hit a dry spell, and then we'd sell 'em one of these cards. I gave one to Ford, free of charge. He took one look, shrugged his shoulders, then started typing. You should have seen it. None of that tortured artist crap—no cracking his knuckles, or pouring a glass of wine, or rolling a cigarette. He attacked that page like a butcher who had a dozen dead cows on hooks, waiting to be processed."

Ford, McCall claims, would write during the day. McCall would edit his pages at night, and Ford would stay up all night running them through the typewriter again.

"Kirsten would complain about the noise, but Ford wouldn't say anything to me, other than grumble about my German wife, and how you could never trust a German wife. Always going on about the German wife, the German wife. Never mind that I'm German. And a little Scottish."

Two weeks later, Ford handed McCall a stack of pages and told him he was done, and he'd be needing his two grand.

"I looked at that stack, and he only had 56 pages done. I mean, to be fair, it *was* a complete novel, written in his special, no-bullshit way, but I couldn't bring something like that back to Golden Lion. People would throw tomatoes at me, trying to sell a pamphlet like this for a quarter. I told him, 'We need a little more.' He was not happy. I tried to show him a few places where the story could be expanded, deepened, but he just shook his head. 'The story's done, Luth, the story's just plain fuckin' done.' I couldn't get him to shake the notion."

"So what did you do?" I asked.

"I told him to write another novel, second in the series, because I was sure that Golden Lion would want his next book. He looked at me all funny, but I told him, 'Look, we never do this, but if you want write another one, I can tack a $500 bonus on top of that two grand, you get paid as soon as you type the last word.' I know it wasn't the nicest thing to do, but I was desperate. I'd already risked my marriage, not to mention my job, by going out on a limb for this guy. Not to mention all of the cold cuts Ford went through. You would have thought he was a sandwich junkie, they way he mainlined those bastards."

Five days later, Ford handed McCall another 56 pages. And, like the first 56, it was stone brilliant. The promise of "Two Bullets" in full bloom.

"I put the two together, and with a little smoothing over here and there, it made a 112-page manuscript. Not hefty by any stretch, but do-able at Golden Lion. And true to my word, I had his cash waiting for him."

My God. The novel existed. I had been bracing for the news that Ford had given up after 20 pages or so.

"What happened?" I asked. "Why was it never published?"

There was a cold gleam in McCall's eye. He was going to milk this for everything.

"Oh I'll tell you why," he said.

♪

What Luther McCall didn't know was that, a week before I'd called him, I'd tracked down Cole Ford.

His real name was Jim Taubman, and he had grown up in East Oak Lane—oddly enough, just a few blocks away from David Goodis and his parents. From what I could tell, Taubman's story was the oldest story in the book: rich son goes off to earn his fortune in New York, loses everything, and is eventually disowned by his parents. Becomes a bum.

But in this case, the bum wrote a 1,200-word story that changed mystery fiction forever.

And he also has an unpublished novel somewhere.

I found Cole Ford thanks to my worst enemy. VaultofEvil is his handle; I still don't know his real name. We bid on old issues of *Manhunt* and other crime pulps on eBay.

We once went up to $248 over a battered *Mike Shayne* that featured an early Richard Laymon story. A mag worth $15, tops, through a private seller.

That's how much I hate VaultofEvil.

(I won the *Mike Shayne*, at least.)

He also likes to gloat—which is another reason I hate him. So when he landed that December 25, 1954 issue of *Manhunt*, signed by one of the contributors, he emailed to brag. Who is it, I emailed back. Cole Ford, he emails. I'm stunned. So I shoot back something sarcastic: That nobody? VaultofEvil emails back: Hey, this Ford may be nobody, but how many signed *Manhunts* you got? Besides, I got it right from the writer himself.

It hits me: VaultofEvil has no idea who Cole Ford is.

Then it hits me again, this time with a backhand: Cole Ford is *alive*, and selling his own copy of *Manhunt* on eBay.

I check the listing: the seller is "JTaubman" in Philadelphia, PA.

A little detective work later, and I'm reasonably sure "James Taubman" is actually "Cole Ford."

Just two commuter trains and five blocks away.

I called to be sure. On the phone, Taubman seems to be hard of hearing, but admits the truth:

"Yeah, I wrote that."

I told him I would very, *very* much like to see him.

"Yeah, that would be okay."

49

ζ†

"Let's eat already," Ford was saying. "The liverwurst is getting warm. Have yourself a beer before we get started."

"I don't really drink," I said. "Or eat meat."

Ford was quiet for a moment. The very idea seemed to boggle his mind. "Well then I've got rabbit food in the basement. I'll give you a scoop of that. Come on, you fuckhead. Eat with me."

"Do you have any milk?"

"Not unless I'm serving White Russians."

Ford drained half of his warm Genesee Cream Ale in one long pull, paused to belch, then proceeded to finish off the sucker.

"We went to the center last week," he said, apropos of nothing, "and they had a roast beef special. All the roast beef you could eat, and a big jar of Jewish pickles. Those bastards were as big as a baby's forearm. The rolls were Kaisers. They had pepper, horseradish sauce, mayonnaise… the whole nine. But the horseradish was stuff from a jar. Real weak. May as well have been fucking mayonnaise."

Luther McCall hadn't been exaggerating. Cole Ford was still obsessing over sandwiches. But I needed to gently steer him away from the cold cuts and into the reason I came down here this morning. The thing that's keep me up nights, throwing blankets around the bed, mad with hope.

If Cole Ford/Jim Taubman still had a copy of his *Manhunt*, was it possible that he still had the original manuscript for *Say Goodnight to the Bad Guy* somewhere?

I could imagine the new trade paperback edition, complete with:

The heretofore-unpublished novel.

The story, "Two Bullets and a Bucket of Gasoline."

Short essays by Spillane, Block, Westlake, Crumley, Gorman, Connelly, Bruen, praising Ford's contribution to the genre.

A foreword by Luther McCall, explaining the "story behind the story."

An introduction by me.

A career-maker, if there ever was one.

"I thought the horseradish was *good*," Hilda said. "I don't like it too tangy."

"Ah you don't know fucking horseradish, woman. And hey, what did I tell you about your mouth?"

"Sorry Jimmy."

"Yeah, you're sorry. Everybody's sorry. And this kid here's not touching his sandwich."

I couldn't eat because the thousand questions bouncing around inside my skull. Couldn't come right out with the biggie:

Where's the novel? Show me now! Show me now!

I needed to ease up to it, ask where he'd been all of these years, to see if what Luther McCall'd told me was true.

That Cole Ford had gotten freaked out by the possibility of fame, and crept out of the house in the middle of the night with the manuscript of *Say Goodnight to the Bad Guy*—and, if McCall's estimates were right, the makings of two sandwiches' worth of cold cuts.

"I think he was scared," McCall had explained back at Jimmy's. "It must have finally hit him, how having that novel published would change his life. I knew it was a masterpiece. Kirsten, who read it, too, agreed with me. And I think Cole Ford was coming around to realize it, too. So he split. And absolutely broke my goddamned heart. I was never the same, as an editor, or a man, after that."

I told McCall about my plans to try to find Cole Ford, and he just smile-squinted, and said: "Good luck. Let me know if you find him."

Maybe that was the way to go.

Luther McCall's been asking about you, I could say.

There was a knock at the front door.

Ford had a liverwust sandwich halfway to his mouth. "Oh, who the fuck now?

⁁

It was Luther McCall, of course.

He'd followed me down from New York. Took the same train, even, I would later learn. I hadn't noticed him.

"Cole Ford, you smiling son of a bitch," McCall said, then raked his fist across Ford's face.

I saw blood jet from the old man's mouth.

"Oh my word," said Hilda.

Ford doubled over, coughed, and then spit his oversized dentures out onto his green shag carpet. He coughed again.

McCall had a sap in his wrinkled hand, and brought it down on Ford's back. The man jolted, then fell to his hands and knees.

"I've been waiting 50 years for this, you shitbird," McCall said.

The surreality of the events of the past 10 seconds had frozen me in place, but now I stood up from my kitchen chair and raced into the living room. "Mr. McCall," I said, "what are you doing?"

"I'll tell you what I'm doing," he said, bringing the sap down on Ford's neck in time with the *do*.

"Oh, fuck!" Ford cried.

"Oh my word," Hilda repeated.

"I'm giving this guy his precious fucking sand(*fwhap!*)wiches, courtesy my German fuck(*fwap!*)ing wife!"

"Stop it!" I said.

Ford was shaking on the floor by this point, his un-dentured mouth making little fishy kisses on the carpet.

McCall pointed the sap at me. "I didn't tell you the whole story, young man. Didn't want to tip my hand. You want to tell it, Cole? Oh, that's right, you're too busy bleeding out of your mouth. Better let me, then.

"The night this useless shitheel finished his book, we all did some celebrating. Opened up a bottle of Maker's Mark. Cole, me and my little German wife, in our apartment. I had too many and passed out in my bed. Got up around 3, thinking I'd fix myself a sandwich, get a little food to counteract the booze, and what do I see?"

I'd read enough 1950s Golden Lion novels to know exactly where this was headed.

In fact, this particular plot twist—the wife giving the comely stranger a blowjob on the family couch (though you couldn't say "blowjob" back then, you had to refer to it as "opening her lips wide to his passion" or some such euphemism)—featured in at least a half-dozen Golden Lion novels in the latter part of the 1950s. Some writers had even claimed that McCall had forced that particular plot point on them, even when it made no sense in their novel, such as a search-for-Inca-gold adventure story or a lesbians-in-the-college-dormitory potboiler.

McCall didn't have to finish. But he did anyway:

"I find this shitbird's *pen* in my wife's mouth!"

Another blow with the sap, this time on Ford's buttocks. Ford didn't react. Even the shaking had stopped.

Oh my no.

McCall breathed heavily, used his free hand to push his gray hair back in place. "By the time I pulled my revolver out of the closet, this little fucker had already hightailed it out of the window. He didn't have a stitch on, but he remembered to take his precious little manuscript with him. Oh yes he (*fwap!*)did."

He looked at me, trying for the sorrowful puppy look. Which was kind of ruined by the blood-encrusted sap in his hand.

"My Kirsten was never the same after that. Our marriage was never the same. She wouldn't come near my... near *me*, like that, ever again. Not until the day she died."

"That's because," Ford mumbled from the floor, "she could never find your shrimpy little dick."

A veiny fist launched up from the floor, and nailed Luther McCall in a place where he presumably hadn't been touched since 1954.

"Oh my word."

McCall's' 80-year-old frame bent in half. His legs shook beneath him, desperately trying to support his body weight. He looked like a flamingo on crack.

Then he fell on his ass.

Then he surprised us all by whipping the sap across Ford's forehead. I heard the unmistakable sound of a skull cracking.

But that didn't stop Ford. In fact, it kick-started the worst of the violence. The two men were relentless in their need to punish each other. I understood McCall's fury; Ford's anger—maybe he was just pissed off about being away from his sandwich too long—remained mysterious. Both went at it like they meant it. Glass shattered. Couch fabric ripped. Tables rocked. In the kitchen, a candle went airborne; a curtain caught fire. Years of dust fueled the flames. I made the mistake of trying to break up the melee, but received a sap blow on the ear, which shattered my hearing on one side and send me flying through a flakeboard door and down a flight of stairs carpeted with the thinnest, most threadbare material available. Every step *hurt*.

I must have been knocked senseless by the fall. I saw smoke pouring through the doorway at the top of the stairs. The fire burned fast and hot.

I rolled over. The brown and yellow linoleum blocks were cold beneath my hands and cheek. The entire right side of my head cycled through various forms of pain like a car alarm. I pushed myself up and tried to get my bearings. More smoke now. Upstairs was out. God, I hoped Ford and McCall (and Hilda) had the sense to continue their fight outside on the back lawn, or something. I needed to stand up. Prayed nothing was broken.

I used a table to pull myself up, and was relieved that I could stand on my own legs. I looked down.

At an old battered typewriter. Next to a newish looking Dell PC.

Cole Ford's writing desk.

The wooden ceiling a few week away was starting to buckle, but I couldn't leave now. Not until I…

Above the desks. Stacks and stacks of manuscripts, in varying degrees of yellow, pinned together with gold tacks through golden grommets. I reached up to pull one out and a pile fell to the desk. The title page:

LICK THE CORDITE OFF MY FINGERS
A novel by Cole Ford

I flipped to another one:

THOUSAND YEAR FUNERAL
A novel by Cole Ford

And another:

SHOT TO HELL
A novel by Cole Ford

There were dozens of manuscripts here, all gloriously short, hand-typed manuscripts. *Knock-down Drag-out. Two Dollar Pistol. Big Fat Cigar Cherry. One Hard Year. I've Got It All Worked Out. Gin Mill Cowboys. Nickel-Plated. Philly Tough. The Casual Killers. Trouble In My Town. The Black and Blue Dahlia. Giveadamn. The Black Sedan. Mile 332…*

That's when the ceiling above me gave out.

The fire felt like water from a shower, washing over me, cleansing me in a way I didn't think possible.

On the floor, my burning fingers wanted to keep flipping until they found it:

SAY GOODNIGHT TO THE BAD GUY
A novel by Cole Ford

The words danced in my mind's eye, and as I inhaled smoke I feverishly imagined that I'd found it, the original manuscript, two 56-page typescripts placed on top of each other, with penciled-in transitions by the legendary Luther McCall, and I held the manuscript to my chest even as firefighters blew out the glass brick tile of the basement and came in for me, lifted me up, got me out of there, placed an oxygen mask on my face.

†

It took weeks to get out of the hospitals; months of skin grafts before my face didn't frighten people.

I waited a little longer, then took two commuter trains and walked the five blocks again.

The house wasn't there, of course. Just a missing tooth in an imperfect smile: this average rowhome block in Northeast Philadelphia.

In my most painful moments of therapy I'd dreamed of finding a chapter, even a single page intact, perhaps shielded from the rampaging fires by an iron door, or a metal proof lockbox.

But there was nothing.

They'd even done a hasty job of filling the basement with some dirt to prevent the hole from becoming a neighborhood trash dump.

Cole Ford and Luther McCall had perished in the fire. I didn't mention the fight; neither did Hilda. She just told them about the candles, and her colostomy bag, and told them she was to blame for knocking a candle over into a curtain. "I'm very sorry," she told them.

She lived only a few blocks away. I stopped by to see her, see how she was doing.

Okay, that's a lie.

I stopped by because she was the only living connection between the noir dreamworld in my mind and the fading embers of its physical manifestation. Those Cole Ford novels. Lost forever. It seemed strange that something that took so much to create could be so easily snuffed out of existence; acts of destruction seemed to fare much better in this world. Violence was everywhere; creation didn't stand a chance.

Oh *fuck* how I wanted to read those novels.

Hilda was propped up in a chair, watching CNN on one of those console TVs that double as furniture.

"How are ya?" she said, a confused smile on her face.

"How are you, Hilda?" I thought about hugging her, but the smell was still there. She didn't have any candles going in here. Not without her Jimmy here to tell her to light them.

We made inane small talk for a while, with me mostly listening. I sometimes have trouble talking to old people. Our frames of reference are so off. It was easy gabbing with Luther McCall; we had common interests. Still, I tried.

"Hilda, I've been wondering," I said. "Ever read any of Cole's work?"

"Who?"

"Jimmy. Your Jimmy."

"Oh yeah, Jimmy was a storytella. I read everything in that basement of his."

"You did?"

"Oh my word, yes.

"What did you read?"

"*Giveadamn* was his best. Prolly the closest to 'Two Bullets.' You could see the years of pain in that one. I read it a dozen times, oh my word."

My blood jumped. "Did you ever read *Say Goodnight to the Bad Guy? His first?*"

"Read it?" she said, then laughed. "Oh my word. I could say that book by heart."

❧

That night I rented a car and drove to Target and bought a case of scented candles.

Afterword

This story was inspired by a short biographical sketch of William Cole, the mysterious author of "Waiting for Rusty," which appeared in Hardboiled: An Anthology of American Crime Stories, *edited by Bill Pronzini and Jack Adrian. Many senior citizens I know, God love 'em—all they talk about is food. –D.S.*

Policy

MEGAN ABBOTT

Megan Abbott's (born 1971) novel, Die A Little *(Simon & Schuster) was nominated for an Edgar Award for Best First Novel by the Mystery Writers of America. Her second novel,* The Song Is You, *comes out in February 2007 and centers around a true-life crime from Hollywood's Golden Age. Her nonfiction study,* The Street Was Mine: White Masculinity in Hardboiled Fiction and Film Noir, *was published by Palgrave Macmillan in 2003. She lives in Queens, New York.*

f

POLICY
by Megan Abbott

I *want the legs.*

That's the first thing I think. The legs are the legs of a 20-year-old Vegas showgirl, a hundred feet long and with just enough curve and give and promise. Sure, there was no hiding the ropy blue veins in her hands or the tugs of leathery skin framing the bones in her face. But the legs, they lasted, I tell you. They endured. Forty years her junior, my skinny matchsticks were no competition.

In the casinos, she could pass for 45. The low lighting, her glossy auburn hair, legs swinging, tapping the bottom rim of the tall bettor stools. At the track, she looked her age. The sunglasses, the wide-brimmed hat, the bright gloves, sure, but then there was the merciless sunshine, the glare off the grandstand. It hardly mattered, though. She was legend.

I never knew what she saw in me. *You looked like you knew a thing or two,* she told me later. *But were ready to learn a lot more.* It was a soft sell, a long sell. I never knew what she had in mind until I'd already had such a taste I thought my tongue would never stop buzzing. Meaning, she got me in, she got me jobs, she got me fat stacks of cash too thick to wedge down my cleavage. She got me in with the hard boys and I couldn't get enough. I wanted more. *Give me more.*

It was so easy. I did the books at Club Tee Hee, a rinky-dink joint owned by a friend of my old man. Straight out of Dolores Grey Business School, but I could make those digits fall in line and my fingers danced on the adding machine and when the manager, Jerome, asked me to cook the books, I did it. When he asked me to make him a fake numbers book for his single-action game, I did that too.

That was where I first saw her, heard all the stories told behind hands as she walked into the place. About the big gees and button men she'd tossed with back in the day, everyone from Dutch Schultz to Joey Adonis and Lucky himself.

She came every few weeks, sipping a club soda with a twist and counting Jerome's vig before she drove off in her Alpine White El Dorado to kick it upstairs. I figure she must've heard about the way I could work things, work things and keep my mouth shut about it. She knew everybody and everybody knew her and she plucked me out of that two-bit hootchy cooch and put me on the big stage, footlights up my dress.

I wanted more.

You gotta look the part, she said, surveying me up and down, my off-the-rack acid-green rayon number, shiny with wear. *You can't look like a kid eating dinner off a hotplate. You can't look like a table-hopping pickup either. We gotta believe there's nothing funny about big money in your hand.*

She showed me how to look like I belonged, tasteful picture hats, spare makeup. She took me to the big department store downtown, the one with all the mirrors and deep carpets. Bought me three fine suits—cream, oyster white, periwinkle blue. Skirts hit below the knee but still fit snug in the right places, because she was no fool. You had to play that angle too, get a second glance from the high rollers. *Honey, I got the legs, but your ass is your ticket. And that rack won't hurt either.*

She told me that my sugar-blonde dye job had to go. Don't want to stand out too much, don't want to be picked out in a big crowd. She came over one night, near one o' clock, to give me my first job, a run to the track the next day. Too late to go to the hairdresser, she did me herself, peeling off her doeskin gloves. I sat in a chair in front of the kitchen sink, leaned my head back far and she plunged her jagged-emerald-covered hands through my hair again and again, turning ratted blonde into smooth honey brown. I remember looking up at her, into her eyes, husk of creased skin hanging over them. Heavy lidded like a snake. *She's figuring something now*, I thought. *She never stops running the odds.*

She talked to me, low and cool, for hours, never losing her ramrod posture, never raising her voice above her near-whisper. She told me all I had to do was go down to the bullring and place dime bets on a few choice horses. Taking out the *Racing Form*, she went through the races and wrote "place" next to some horses and "show" next to others. *You don't want to hurt the odds, so never bet to win*, she said. *You spread the money around and bet to place and show and you get a return on investment at least 70 percent of the time. That's the stuff. More important, the dough gets cleaned and the tax men only see racetrack winnings.* She explained it all and made me tell it back to her to see if I understood. Oh did I.

From then on, I did whatever she told me. I knew if it wasn't for her, I'd be shaking my ass for more coin at the Tee Hee or still stuck with my head over the ledger, postponing the inevitable roll in the sack with the manager for a shot at a bigger paycheck. She saved me from all that. She turned me out and you never forget the one who turned you out.

But it wasn't made for forever. I didn't have her stuff.

Sometimes as we sat in her plush pink and gray living room I'd look at her under the milky cast of the brass wall sconces, look at her while she passed on words of wisdom (*You always want to know the strategy behind it, honey. You do things for them without knowing why, there's nothing in it for you.*) and I'd see what she must have been like back in 1929, bright-eyed, dewy-cheeked, slinging those gorgeous stems one across the other and making hay while times were good.

I'd look at her and I'd think about all the stories I'd heard. About how she carried a long-handled pair of bejeweled scissors in her purse when she collected in the rough parts of town, about the time an angry wife tried to run her over in her Cadillac outside her husband's betting parlor, about a stripper named Candy Annie who crossed her on some deal but, when Annie walked into the Ladies Room at the Breakwater Hotel in Miami three months later, she got her revenge with a straight-edge razor, gutting the stripper like a fish.

The favorite tale among the boys at Club Tee Hee was about a New Year's Eve party back in the Thirties where she shimmied with every hood in the place until one of them asked her to put her money where her mouth was. Story was, she threw her head back and laughed, saying, "I'll put my mouth where the money is," and made her way to every man in the room, on her knees. On her knees. Later, when one of the wives came up to her and called her a whore, she slapped the wife around, grabbed her by the hair and tugged her against her chest, asserting, "I'm the best damn cocksucker in this burg, and I got the rocks to prove it. Your knees have rubbed plenty of carpets, you rotten bitch. Where are your diamonds? Where are they?"

Later, when we were close like we were, when we could talk about these things, I asked her about the story and she looked at me like I was a goddamned fool. *That was Virginia Hill,* she said, stubbing out her cigarette. *Hillbilly tramp. I got better things to do with my mouth.*

And it was hard to imagine that much hot blood running through her. If she had a man in her life, I never heard tell. The job was the life. Four decades of carrying money, getting high rollers to place sucker bets, moving swag across state lines and adjusting odds for the boys working the policy racket all through the east side. *Butter and eggs lottery,* she called it, shaking her head. She herself was proud to say she'd never in her life laid down a bet on her own nickel. *I'm no chump. I know the odds. I make them.*

So, I wore the clothes, I did the jobs, I followed orders. All business. And no matter how many shiny-haired swains pressed against me, I never played around. When it paid, I went on dates with the high-stakes gees but never laid for one. *Be the lady,* she told me. *They beat their wives, they beat their whores. I never took more than three socks from one of these goons in all my years. That's why. Be the lady.*

But didn't you ever fall for one? I asked once, sucking on a swizzle stick and hoping for some sign of soft in the old lady, something beating under the finely pressed shantung suit. *Sure, kid,* she said, eyelashes grazing her cheeks. *There were a few. I lived this life, you know. But I watched myself and I never mixed business with anything else. There were men, but not these men. No. Straight men. Straight enough. Men who may not have lived by the book but lived by some book. In this life,* she said, *crossing these glorious gams, shimmering in the low light of the lounge, you can't let your guard down. If you can control yourself, you can control everyone else.*

But then there he was, as if on cue.

Before him, I'd never fallen for one before. Never bothered to look up for one that wasn't just a money clip to me. In all my girl years, I'd only rolled pro forma with high school boys, office boys, head knocking on adam's apples in backseats, mouth dry and raw. They never made me want more.

But he was the one. All black Mick hair and sorrowful eyes and sharkskin suits cut razor sharp. I could feel the way it was going the minute I saw him losing his shirt at blackjack. My palms itching, I rubbed them together. I could feel it everywhere, something sharp pulsing under my skin. *I'll crawl hands and knees for this one,* I thought. *I can feel I'm going to be on my hands and knees for this one.* He saw it on me too. He figured fast he had the upper hand. Things got awfully crazy right off. I couldn't help myself. I let him do whatever he wanted. Who was I to say no. There was nothing he could do that I didn't want. Not even that.

Never fuck up, she told me once. *That's the only rule.*

You've never made a mistake, not one, in all these years, I asked. Mixing up numbers, late to the track, one drink too many and you start talking too much to the wrong fellas?

She looked at me in that icy way of hers. Then, in a flash of the hand, she tugged open her crepe de chine jacket, buttons popping. There, on her pale, filmy skin, skeined over with thready wrinkles, I saw the burn marks, long, jagged, slipping behind her bra clasp, slithering down her sternum.

How, I started, my mouth a dry socket. *A state trooper pulled me over for speeding downstate,* she said, palm flat on her chest, patting it lightly. *Made me open the trunk, tapped the false bottom and found 60K in hot rocks, each one a fingerprint.*

But that wasn't your fault, I said. *I should have been more careful,* she said. *I learned the hard way. The boss then, the big one, he watched while one of his boys did it. Pressed me against a radiator until the smell made us all sick.*

I learned the hard way, she said, Now you've learned it easier. *You don't need this on your fine chest*, she said, fastening the mother-of-pearl buttons. *So don't fuck up, baby.*

I won't, I said. I won't. And I meant it.

⚶

I never let her see me with him those first weeks that it went on, hotter and crazier every night. I saw him after I finished every run, after I helped her look for hits, envelopes from all over the city spread across her glass coffee table. She always wore her gloves when she did it, not to hide her worn hands, not from me, but because she knew where the betting slips had been, grimy candy stores, shylock newsstands, back kitchens and bowling alleys. Her gloves, in one of a dozen shades of white, rose, pale yellow, danced along the envelopes, flipping over the slips, looking for the matches. She was so fast, and I was getting fast too. And I never told her about him. I knew what she would say. *You lost it, you little bitch. You lost it. You can't control yourself, you're of no use to me.*

One night, he ripped my $350 faille day suit from collar to skirt hem in one long tear. Fuck me, I was in love.

I didn't want her to know I'd lost it, all of it. I didn't want her to know I'd gone so crazy, and all for a sharpie, a piker racking up big losses every day, even when I told him how it worked, how he'd never make it that way, loading it all on one horse, one race. And how no one won on policy games for long. That's why they call it a racket. But he kept dumping it all, on overhead tips, bad tips, tips everyone knew were fixes. I dropped those tips. It was my job. They were all junk.

And I did everything to make sure she never saw him. I knew if she saw him, she would know I'd gone for him. I felt like it was all over me, all over my face, a spreading stain. The closest she got was an eyeful of the bruises on my thigh, an oval for each finger. Sliding across the bench seat of her El Dorado, my skirt rode up and she saw them through my stocking. She saw the bruises dotting my outer thigh in a perfect radial pattern.

Green, violet, raw, hot to the touch. My palms itched every time I looked at them.

Who did it, she said, tongue darting. *Who did it to you.*

I got caught in a turnstile, I said, shaking my head, tugging my skirt down.

She looked at me, flinty, hard. I found myself counting the faint lines crimping her deep crimson mouth. A line for every lie told to her by a two-faced shill like me.

I knew she didn't believe me. She knew how to read everybody, most of all me, who she'd made from scratch. She'd given me my poker face, molded it herself, so she knew it when she saw it.

Listen, baby doll, somebody hurts you and they don't get a second chance, she said, putting one gloved finger on my thigh until I winced. *You're mine. Roughing you up is roughing me up. And I don't let anyone rough me up. You're mine and someone puts his dirty paws on you they might as well be on me. You're my girl. I won't think twice.*

And I knew she meant it.

He and I, we'd been at it for a month or so when he threw me the curve. Guess I knew it was coming, could feel it in my gut even if I didn't let myself think it out loud. He knew what I did, he knew my job. He knew there was big green to be had if you were willing to veer from the script. He wanted me to veer, hard. He owed 75 Gs with a vig to send your eyeballs back into your head and he needed me bad.

His hands on me, what could I do. I wanted more.

Some tout passed him a tip and, as tips go, it didn't look half bad. Could be smart money. But what good did it do him with only two-hundred clams to stake. I'd give him all I had, but that still wouldn't get him the big pot he needed. Not even close.

Don't you see, he said. You're carrying a fat handbag to the track that day. Can the dime bets and let it all ride on Rum Tum Tiger in the third.

It was crazy and I let him know it. She'd have my neck for it and who knew what might happen to her.

So you don't do it, he said. Supposing, baby doll, you get mugged on your way to the track. It ain't no one's fault. Could happen to any slip of a girl who makes her way among sharpers and trouble boys.

His hand on my hip bone, my hip fast on the mattress. Fuck me, who knew I was so easy? Easy and a chump.

The next day, the big day, I started to lose my nerve. She'll never buy it, baby, I said. I wouldn't. But he said he had it all figured out. If I wanted, he could knock me one, make it look good. This sounded right.

You're going to have to put me in the hospital, I said.

He didn't pause a second before his fist came at me, a hard belt to the jaw that snapped my head back against the wall with an awful pop. I saw stars. Then, before I knew it, his left came at me, swiveling my head the other way, cheekbone cracking against the metal door frame. I thought I would be sick. I held my stomach with both hands.

Give me one more, lover, I said, chin raised, face hot, whole body shuddering.

The next one knocked me out.

❦

When she saw me on the gurney in the emergency room, her eyes widened. It was the first time I'd ever seen the whites of her eyes. Her jaw was trembling so slightly, like a violin string. So slight only I would notice. Because I'd never seen it any way but granite-still.

I'm sorry, I said. Feeling the gluey rush of the morphine. I'm sorry.

She almost placed one gloved hand on mine. It hovered there. She was showing me something, but just barely.

I told you about tails, she said. *About where you walk and when. What about the snub nose?*

They got me coming out of the car, I murmured. I don't know where they came from. They came from nowhere.

The nurse made me lean back. She talked about my contusions, my crushed cheekbone, the concussion.

I'm sorry, I repeated. You have to know. It will never happen again.

All right, she said, *I'll take care of it*. And reached down to the sheet that hung off the edge of the gurney. She lifted it with her gloved fingers, pulled it up my chest. I could hear her breathing, hear her thinking. *How am I going to play this with the big boys*. That's what she was thinking. *How'm I going to save my girl*.

Somebody played that dough, she said as she smoked a long, black cigarette. *All on one horse. Someone knew all about you*.

But that was it. She never said another word about it.

You get one, I said to myself. That was your one.

❦

As for him, he didn't pay off the shylocks. Instead, the next day, he bet it all on Gilded Lily in the fifth and lost it down to his last nickel. I came home, he'd pawned my mink hat, my platina fox coat, the longest string of pearls you ever saw. When I squawked, he jammed his fingers into my sunken cheekbone, knocked me down on the carpet and gave me one last farewell fuck that rubbed my back raw—all before skipping town for good.

Never again, I told myself, body torn to pieces. Here on out, I only bend for her. I only got ears for Mama.

Part of me wanted to come clean with her. But I kept my mouth shut. Rule number one.

That night, I dreamt of things happening to me, to her. Of faceless men in black cars running me down, of long blades and hinges of skin, of shotguns in my face and the smell of my own flesh against the radiator.

The next day, she phoned. She said, *You can't make any runs until your face heals and you stop looking like a two-dollar whore.* She told me she would have new jobs for me in a week or two. Until then, I'd have to lay low. But I'd been through a lot and she'd come over that night and take me out. She said not to worry. She'd taken care of things.

She came over at nine p.m., dressed head to toe in sharky silver. *I brought you something*, she said, lifting the garment bag in her hand. *You can wear this tonight.*

I asked her if there'd been any fallout from the bets that weren't placed. I'd heard from Jerome at Club Tee Hee that Upstairs wasn't happy paying off a higher return rate to bookies whose bets they'd covered as place and show. They weren't happy. And they were looking into things.

She looked at me and shook her head. *It's just a twist in a long seam, darling. Don't worry your black and blue head over it.*

And I let myself feel relieved. And she could tell. *You don't give me enough credit, baby*, she said. *You're my girl. I took care of it.*

Her garnet lips curled, slanted, something, something like a smile. The closest to a smile she came. I smiled back.

Now let's go celebrate, she said. *Toast your recovery. Let's paint the town.*

I said okay. I said I'd love to. I was hers. Mama.

We're going to dress you to kill, she said. *You gotta show 'em you're not down for the count.*

She unzipped the garment bag in one long stroke and the shimmering red dress gushed out. *With your fox*, she said. *It's meant to go with the platina fox.*

The fox was hanging in the window of Abie's Pawn Shop, but maybe I was starting to feel like I could get around it. I was starting to feel like things were going to hang straight. Something like relief.

The dress was shimmering, inviting me in. I slid out of my robe and I felt her hand touch my still-raw back as I stepped in. The neckline hung low, weighted down with heavy beading like scales against my chest. We walked over to the long mirror in the corner of the room. She stood behind me, six inches taller, that crown of titian hair and those narrow eyes.

This was me once, she said, as if to herself, as we looked in the mirror, her silver gloves laced across my collar bones. *I guess I'm a thousand years old to you, I've seen it all. But look. We're the same, We're the same. I made you. Sometimes it's as if I made you up inside my head.*

I didn't say anything. I watched the red panels splash against the silver of her suit. I didn't know what to say. My teeth somehow were clattering. I looked in her eyes, the lashy slits. Were those my eyes? Would they be? Those eyes, they knew everything. Everything.

I felt like we would be locked like this forever, pressed against each other, front to back, she with one sharp stiletto jutting between my stocking feet. The red dress tight across my breasts, my hips, her hands splayed across my throat. I should have seen it coming. I never was that bright.

She knew everything. Everything.

I hope he was worth it, she said, teeth glittering. *Was he worth it.*

Her arm came forward and I saw the straight razor in her gloved hand. She held it to one side of my throat. A curtain of blood fell.

Afterword

This story was inspired by the dazzling life of mob queen, courier and muse Virginia Hill, née Onie Hill, a.k.a. Virginia Norma Hall, a.k.a. Virginia Herman, a.k.a. Virginia Oney d'Algy, a.k.a. Virginia Gonzalez, a.k.a. the Flamingo. "I work where I want and when I want," she once said, "I don't dance for nobody." When the press tracked her down in Paris to inform her that her paramour, Bugsy Siegel, had been murdered in the home he bought for her, she told reporters, "It looks so bad to have a thing like that happen in your house." –M.A.

3-A

JENNY SILER

Jenny Siler (born 1971) is the author of five novels including Flashback, *a thriller set in Morocco, and* An Accidental American, *which will be published in early 2007 by Random House. Jenny has contributed to several anthologies, among them the infamous* Tart Noir *and more recently,* Greatest Hits, *a collection of stories about hit men and women. Jenny grew up in Missoula, Montana, and has lived and worked her way around the world as, among other things, a salmon grader, a grape picker, a furniture mover and a bartender. She and her family are currently living in Lexington, Virginia.*

3-A
By Jenny Siler

It was a perfect morning, cold and clear, the snow iridescent beneath the cloudless sky. Snow and more of it, relentless miles of fresh powder stretching up and back into the mountains, obliterating the landscape of the valley floor. Ed had been walking for some time—away from the others, he thought—so when he first saw Maggie he was surprised. She was wearing her brother's red wool cap, and for a moment Ed mistook her for him. But as she came closer he could see the tips of her brown hair and the curls that framed her face.

Later, this aspect of the morning would become the one thing Ed's lawyer would keep going back to, as if Ed had somehow been confused by Maggie's appearance, as if it was fear that had driven him to act. Of course this was wrong, but by the time the trial rolled around there was only so much they could do, and so Ed had let it stand. It was the one thing that had bothered him all these years. Not the time, for he was guilty after all. He had done what he had done, and in this respect he could hardly be angry for what had happened to him. But this other thing, he just couldn't let go.

Ed already knew what she was going to tell him, had known as soon as she'd asked Jim to pull the car over outside of Florence. They'd been passing a bottle of Pete's father's homemade whiskey around and everyone else took it as proof that Maggie just couldn't hold her liquor. But, watching her hunched over in the snow, retching up her meager breakfast, Ed had known, and had felt sick himself. And when she'd climbed shakily back into the car he'd turned his face away from her.

Maggie didn't say anything at first, just came quietly toward him, her shins breaking the snow. She could shoot as well as any of them, and usually enjoyed hunting, but that day she wasn't carrying a gun. Looking back, these final moments were the hardest for Ed to reconstruct. A year and a half after the trial was over Jim had come down to the prison asking about what had happened that morning, and even then, with the memory of it still fresh in his mind, Ed had been unable to say.

"We had words," he'd told his friend, finally, all he could offer him, and then they'd sat there together in the visiting room listening to the wind beat at the glass.

"Welcome to Aunt Susan's." The waitress smiled pleasantly and slid a menu from the side of the podium, then turned and started back through the dining room, motioning for Ed to follow. She was short and round, with a red smudge of a mouth and uncooperative hair. Sixty, Ed told himself, sixty-five, his younger sister's age, but sexy still, in the way that women who have to work at it can be. Though that could have been prison talking. You'll take what you can get that first night out, his last cellmate, an Indian kid from North Dakota who was already doing his third stretch, had told him.

It was a weekday, the mid-afternoon lull, and except for Ed's bus driver and some local kids camped out at a table in the back, the restaurant was empty. It was the kind of place a family would come, out for a ride on a Saturday, looking for a milk shake and a slice of pie. The kind of place Ed had looked for, back when he'd been hauling logs. Outside, a big wide porch with a chorus line of wooden rocking chairs, impatiens blooming in whiskey barrel planters. And inside, the odor of coffee and fryolator grease, walls cluttered with memorabilia, old newspaper clippings and black and white photographs. Pictures of Little League games and car washes and bowling victories. Fourth of July picnics and Homecoming parades.

A record of this town's life, Ed thought, scanning the walls as he followed the woman back through the dining room, trying to piece together all he'd missed.

"This okay, hon?" The woman stopped at a booth and set the menu down. She was wearing a pin on the pocket of her uniform, a tiny yellow ribbon curled onto itself.

Ed glanced around the room at the empty tables. There was a part of him that wanted to tell her, "no," that felt almost obligated to, just because he could, but he didn't. "Sure, doll," he said, and slid into the booth.

"Coffee?" she asked.

Ed winked. "Light and sweet, just like you."

She smiled awkwardly, as if she could tell what he was thinking, then turned and made her way toward the coffee machine.

Ed set his menu aside and glanced at the newspaper clipping that hung beside his table, the headline, TAKE THIS, JAPS! Beneath the headline was a grainy picture of a boy proudly displaying a giant ball of tin foil, and the by-line: *Johnny McCorkle on his way to the recycling center with a year's worth of Wrigley's wrappers.* Next to the article was a smaller photograph, a man in wrinkled fatigues with a cigarette in his mouth. In the background, a line of palm trees and a puff of smoke.

"Here you go, sugar," the waitress reappeared with Ed's coffee. She set the cup and a bowl of plastic creamers down on the table. "You know what you want?"

"Pie," Ed told her. "You got anything good today?"

She flipped Ed's menu over and tapped the back page with the tip of her pen.

Ed looked down at the elaborate photographs, a beauty contest of bouffanted confections. "What's Kahlua?" he asked helplessly.

"You know, like a white Russian." The waitress smiled, and her red lips parted to show a set of graying teeth. Gnaw-your-arm-off ugly, he heard the Indian kid say.

"Is it good?"

"Sure." She lowered her voice a notch, as if they were sharing some great secret, then pointed a chipped nail at an especially ornate creation, a marbled wedge piled with whorls of whipped cream and delicate chocolate curls. "But I like the Amaretto cheesecake, myself."

"Okay," Ed agreed.

"You'll like it. I promise." She smiled reassuringly and slid the menu out from beneath his fingers, then turned away and started toward the kitchen.

Yes, Ed thought, watching her go, imagining how it might be, the two of them back at her small house, her heavy breasts against his face, and the smell of her shampoo, something cheap and fruity. And suddenly he was reminded of another woman, years earlier, a waitress he'd known outside of Spokane, whose husband had been killed in the Pacific. A skinny red head with a little boy who'd sat in her car reading comic books while they screwed.

❧

There were five of them crammed into Jim Creeley's old Ford: Jim and Ed, Jim's sister, Margaret, and their friend from the mill, Pete Algren, and Pete's cousin, Carl. It was December 22nd and there was nothing on the radio but holiday music, Rudolph the Red-Nosed Reindeer and Silent Night.

Pete had brought a bottle of his Dad's homemade whiskey to warm up with and they were passing the bottle around the car, each person taking their turn. The road was a white tunnel in their headlights, the valley still dark around them. The moon was up, lighting the jagged teeth of the Bass Creek drainage from behind. East, over the Sapphires, there was the barest blue flush of dawn.

Margaret was sitting in the front seat with Jim, and Ed could see her face when she turned her head to take the bottle, her features caught in the lights of the dash, the muscles in her neck tensing as she brought the whiskey to her lips and drank. She was older than they were by a few years, a secretary at a dentist's office in town, with her own apartment. *Loose*, Ed's mother had said once, forcing the word out from between clenched teeth.

She finished drinking, then wiped her lips and turned in her seat. "Here, boys," she said, winking as she passed the bottle to Pete, and then suddenly something was wrong. "Pull over," she moaned, clamping her hand across her mouth.

Jim looked over at her. "You okay?"

She shook her head. "Pull over, goddamn it."

Jim hit the brakes and the Ford fishtailed wildly, sliding into the opposite lane before coming to a stop on the shoulder of the highway.

"Oh, God!" Ed heard Margaret say. "Oh, Jesus!" She fumbled with the door latch, then leapt out and staggered away from the car, down into the low ditch where the berm of the road fell away.

❦

Brussels, Ed told himself, emptying a sugar packet and two of the creamers into his coffee. One of those names the railroad used to give the towns they built. Spin the globe and point a blind finger. He hadn't seen the town driving in, figured he'd been on the wrong side of the bus for it and that it was down the hill a ways. He had only a vague recollection of the name from his high school days, but this was the other side of the state from where he'd grown up, and would have been too far to come for football games.

But a nice place, nonetheless, from what he could tell from the pictures. Far nicer than the ugly little mill town he'd grown up in. And the people, all healthy and attractive, smiling perpetually out from behind glass. Ed imagined them coming with their photographs and scrap book clippings, all chipping in to make the collection. Little Johnny McCorkle even, old now, but still with the same toothy smile.

Yes, Ed thought, a nice place, and suddenly he could see himself staying, maybe even getting a job at Aunt Susan's, coming in each day until this history became his as well. When he was younger he'd worked in the prison mess and he'd enjoyed the rhythms of the kitchen. He could learn to enjoy them again.

There was a burst of cruel laughter from the back of the restaurant and Ed glanced up in time to catch the kids staring at him. Hooligans, he thought, and not even that, small-town kids with too much time on their hands. But still, Ed checked himself instinctively, glancing down at his frayed jacket and faded shirt, the outfit he'd picked out that morning from the racks of donated clothes in the prison discharge.

A perfect fit, the old man in the discharge room had told him, and it had felt good then, the first time in all those years he'd seen himself

75

in something besides the standard denims. But now he was starting to wonder if he'd made the right choice.

✠

"Must be twenty below," Pete Algren remarked, breathing onto his bare hands, rubbing his palms together.

Jim nodded distractedly. Something, either reflex or genuine concern, had made them all get of the car, but now none of them knew quite what to do. For a moment Ed thought about going to Margaret, but then he realized what the gesture would mean, how the others would take it, and he stopped himself.

"Freeze your balls off cold," he agreed, wishing he could get back in the car, but not wanting to be the first one to do so.

Pete glanced nervously at his cousin. Carl was from California originally but had come up to Montana to go to school on the GI Bill. He'd lost a foot to frostbite during the Ardennes Offensive and everybody treated him like a hero, but Ed had never liked him.

Ed would have gone, of course, if he could have, had wanted to go just like everyone else, but because of his father's death he'd been given a hardship deferment—3-A, they'd called it. He'd spent the war years driving long hauls across the Idaho panhandle, trying to keep his mother and sisters fed and clothed.

"What?" Ed shrugged off Pete's stare and slid his cigarettes from his pocket, slapped the pack against this hand. "It's just an expression."

"You think she's alright?" Carl asked, with genuine concern.

"She's a tough kid," Jim said, but evidently this wasn't answer enough.

Carl turned and made his way down the embankment, half-slipping on his wooden foot, then walked to where Margaret was standing and put his hand gently on her back.

"What'd you have to go and say that for?" Pete asked, when Carl was out of earshot.

"Jesus," Ed told him. "Can't you give it a rest? You'd think he's a goddamn saint or something. It's a foot for christsakes." He looked down at Carl and Margaret. They stood unmoving for a moment, then Margaret straightened up and wiped her hand across her mouth. Carl said something to her and she shook her head in response.

And suddenly Ed understood. She was fucking him, he thought, watching the two of them struggle up the embankment together.

✠

"Keep it down or I'll throw your asses out of here!" Ed's waitress cast a fierce glance toward the table in the back and the kids sullenly obeyed.

She shook her head, then turned to Ed. "No manners," she apologized, setting his cheesecake on the table. "It's best just to ignore them."

Ed looked down at the brown slab in front of him, the meager smear of whipped topping. There was a crust around the edges of the slice, as if it had been sitting out for some time. It didn't look at all like the cheesecake in the photograph.

"Anything else, hon?" she asked. "More coffee?"

Ed shook his head and nodded awkwardly toward the wall, not wanting her to go. "It's an awfully nice collection," he remarked. "Whoever owns this joint must be a real history buff."

"You're kidding, right?" She tucked her tray under her arm and started to leave, but Ed stopped her.

"You must have your picture up in here someplace, too."

She smiled at him then, and this time there was nothing but pity in her face. "It's a chain," she explained. "You know, like the commercial: 'Welcome home to Aunt Susan's.'"

Ed looked at her blankly

The woman paused for a moment. "Don't you get it,? There's hundreds of these places, and no matter where you go they got the same pictures on the wall. They shipped a whole crate of them out here from Atlanta when we first opened."

But Ed still didn't understand.

"Jeez, hon," she said, finally. "How long you been in for?"

❦

"Isn't anyone going to say anything?" Margaret asked.

No one had spoken since they'd started on their way, but they were all thinking the same thing. They all came from big families—Jim and Pete each had four sisters and Ed had five—and they all knew what it meant when a girl got sick like that. Ed was happy that he'd stopped himself earlier, that he'd had the sense to stay up on the road with the others.

"I guess this just proves that dames can't hold their liquor, 'ey boys?" Jim said, slowing the car, turning off the highway and onto the narrow road that led to the reservoir. He glanced in the rearview mirror and laughed and the two of them, Ed and Pete, laughed nervously back. Carl was silent.

"Wisecrackers," Margaret said bitterly, fumbling a Camel from Jim's pack on the dash. "Can't any of you do better than that?" She lit the cigarette and took a drag, then hastily rolled down the window and tossed the unsmoked butt out.

"Disgusting," she muttered under her breath, and Ed wasn't sure whether she as talking about the cigarette or them or both.

Judy Garland's voice warbled over the radio, the static-clogged strains of "Have Yourself a Merry Little Christmas." Margaret reached for the dial, turned the volume way up.

When she slumped back in her seat Ed could see that she was crying.

♪

Ed took a bite of the cheesecake and felt it catch in his throat. It was gummy and thick, with a manufactured taste. He pushed his plate away and slid out of the booth.

"Everything okay, sugar?" his waitress asked.

"Fine," Ed told her. "Just fine." He fumbled in his pocket, took out the brown envelope they'd given him that morning. Seventy-eight dollars worth of savings, and a one-way bus ticket. "What do I owe you?"

The woman shook her head. "Don't worry about it."

"Well, I *am* worried," Ed said, trying to remember the prices from the menu. He slipped a five dollar-bill from the envelope and set it on the table. "I can carry my own weight."

"I wasn't suggesting otherwise," the waitress told him.

"Freak," Ed heard one of the kids say as he started for the door.

♪

It was daylight by the time they got to the reservoir. They left Margaret in the car and started down to the water, Pete and Carl and Jim heading together toward the north, while Ed looped southward. It wasn't unusual for them to split up like this, and neither Pete nor Jim said anything, but Carl made a big show of trying to convince Ed to stay with the group, and finally Ed had to get tough with him. Later, of course, this would look bad, but at the time Ed just wanted to be alone.

He walked for some time, not thinking much about shooting anything. Though the others must have been, for he could hear the occasional boom of a gun shot ricocheting undistorted through the cold air.

He'd been out for nearly an hour before he saw Margaret. At first he thought it was just a coincidence, that she'd gotten tired of sitting in the car and had gone out for some air, and that their paths had crossed. But after a few minutes, when it became clear to Ed that she was struggling to catch up to him, he stopped walking.

It seemed to take forever for her to come to him, picking her way through the drifts. She stopped within a few feet of him and stood there for a moment without speaking. She was breathing hard from the walk, and the tendrils of hair that tumbled out from beneath her brother's hat were gray with frost. At first Ed thought she was waiting for him to say something.

"It's okay," she said finally. "You don't have to worry. The baby's not yours, anyway."

Ed shrugged. Though they'd only been together a few times, Ed wondered how she could be so sure, but he didn't want to push his luck by asking.

She turned then, as if to go, but stopped and looked back at him, shaking her head incredulously. "Carl's offered to marry me," she said. "Can you believe it? Crazy kid."

❧

The first stop out, Ed thought. The first stop out from the prison and how many of his kind did they see? One a day at least. Those kids just waiting for the afternoon bus to roll off the exit so they could catch a glimpse of a prison freak.

Ed walked to the edge of the parking lot and looked out across the valley toward the barren rim of the mountains in the distance. Down the hill, where Brussels should have been, a handful of gray buildings huddled along the railroad tracks. A weathered grain elevator. A defunct service station. A half-dozen shacks suffering from prolonged neglect.

Fifty years, Ed realized. Fifty years he'd been gone. Twenty years since he'd seen his sister, since their mother had died and she'd been the one to come and tell him. She'd be closer to eighty-five by now, and the waitress, not her age, but her daughter's. And what did this make Ed?

❧

When exactly did you make the decision to shoot her? Ed's lawyer had asked him before the trial. It had seemed important at the time, the distinction between choice and impulse. The prosecutor made it

79

seem like Ed had decided before they even got to the reservoir, that this was why he'd gone off on his own. And even though this wasn't true, Ed had let it stand, had preferred this version of events to what had actually happened.

In reality, there had been no choice. Right up until the end, Ed had planned to let Maggie go. Even on the roadside, when it had first crossed his mind that the baby might be his, he hadn't thought to kill her. It was the other thing, what she said about Carl, that had made him do it. And even then, it wasn't a decision but simply what had to be done.

It was like that old movie with the people in the lifeboat, Ed had thought, looking back on it later, and the only question which one of them would survive. But this wasn't quite right, either. It was more like she had something on him, some vital piece of evidence, and this was the only way he could save himself.

⑪

"Hey, buddy!"

Ed turned his head to see the bus driver coming toward him across the parking lot.

"You okay, there?" the man asked.

Ed nodded in reply. He'd stepped out of the parking lot and was standing at the edge of the rocky embankment where the hillside dropped away toward the valley floor.

"No need to do anything drastic," the driver said, stopping several yards off, smiling nervously. A gust of wind barreled down the valley and the rocking chairs on the front porch of Aunt Susan's swayed in unison.

Ed glanced at the remnants of the town one last time, then stepped back onto the asphalt pad. "Just getting a better look," he told the man. "Not much to see, is there?"

"No," the driver answered, sounding relieved.

Though Ed could have told him there was never anything to worry about.

Afterword

It's true what they say: having a baby really does change everything. Before my daughter was born I was acquainted with Cracker Barrel, that ubiquitous chain of home-style restaurants, only tangentially, from the billboards that sprout up along every interstate highway in America. In my pre-child life, I had not yet come to appreciate them, as I do now, for their child-friendly service and consistently clean restrooms, and the piles of cheap gift-shop tchotkes with which my daughter can amuse herself for literally hours at a time. For a while my husband and I resisted the pull, but my daughter loves Cracker Barrel, and on an eight-hour car trip, whatever my daughter loves, we love too.

And yet, I've come to suspect that there is something dark and disturbing at work behind the log cabin façade and gentle white rocking chairs. Cracker Barrel is exurbia in all its grandeur. It is a choice we have made, and made gladly, to sacrifice the possibility of real quality for the promise of predictability. While Main Streets all across America wither from disuse and apathy, planned communities like Celebration, Florida offer an illusion of Mayberry living without all the nasty realities of life in a real small town. In the same way, Cracker Barrel and its counterparts promise the homey comfort of mashed potatoes and meatloaf without unpleasantries such as slow service or unclean bathrooms that a stop at a real country diner might possibly (God forbid!) entail.

But what strikes me most about these exurban cathedrals is the elaborately concocted myth they work so hard to perpetrate. Mementos of a "simpler time" are a staple of modern exurban culture, which is devoted not to America as it is today, but to a highly romanticized vision of what our country once was, and presumably, what it still might be. Step into any Cracker Barrel or Applebee's or Ruby Tuesday, and you will find the walls adorned with old photographs and newspaper clippings, weathered washboards and pieces of rusted farm machinery. The intent, of course, is to lend an air of localness and authenticity to these establishments, but in truth few, if any, of these items are actual local memorabilia, but are rather part of a kind of "nostalgia kit" shipped out from corporate headquarters.

Interestingly, this romantic myth of America past has gained added traction in the years since 9/11. This is not surprising, of course, since we are engaged in a war with no end in sight, and these kinds of myths are an integral part of the culture of war. Though in the culture of war our false sense of ourselves necessarily extends beyond simple nostalgia to shape our notions of valor and cowardice, good and evil.

In "3-A," the main character, Ed, comes face to face with these myths in all their absurdity when he visits one of these restaurants after spending fifty years in prison. Over the course of the story, Ed is forced to recognize his cowardice as he relives the events that landed him in prison in the first place and confronts what he and the world outside the prison walls have *become during the five decades of his incarceration.*

Though war makes only a few cameo appearances here, this story, to my mind at least, is very much about war, about the nature of fear and cowardice, and the stories we tell ourselves in order to justify the choices we make. It is my hope, and my intent as a storyteller, that we might be coaxed to confront some portion of our own cowardice as Ed confronts his. —J.S.

THE
NECKLACE

SEAN DOOLITTLE

Sean Doolittle (born 1970) is the author of four crime novels: Dirt, Burn, Rain Dogs *and* The Cleanup (forthcoming). *His short fiction has appeared in a variety of publications, including* The Year's Best Horrror Stories *and* Best American Mystery Stories. *Doolittle lives in Omaha, Nebraska with his wife and kids. Sean is cursed with the title of "nicest guy in mystery fiction."*

THE NECKLACE
by Sean Doolittle

"What a bunch of fucking assholes," Lonnie Kyle said.

I looked at him sitting there on my couch. Mid-thirties, balding ungracefully. Flab around the middle. Yellow teeth and dull mean eyes. I'd gotten word he might be coming, but I hadn't invited him. Counting introductions at the door, I'd known him not quite an hour.

"Do you have something against sick kids, Lonnie?"

"Who's talking about sick kids?"

"She is," I said.

He glared at the television, where a spokeswoman from the local children's hospital discussed an upcoming gala fund-raiser event. I'd turned on the noon news while he unfolded his plan on my coffee table.

"These rich pricks." He held his hands on either side of his face. "Oooh, look at us, we're all coming to town. Make way, suck our dicks. Whatever. Right?"

"I suppose I hadn't thought about it."

"Bunch of assholes. All the same, too."

I chuckled, just trying to be polite. "I'm sure I wouldn't know."

On the television, the spokeswoman lifted her hair, modeling a lavish diamond necklace over her plain, peach-colored sweater. 120 carats, she said, as the camera slowly tightened in on her throat. The strands followed the curve of her neck in dripping clusters, throwing fire under the bright studio lights. The desk anchors oohed and ahhed.

The necklace was valued at $1.2 million, the lady from the children's hospital said; it would be the featured lot of the charity auction to be held on Saturday evening. Some actress had worn the piece to the Academy Awards in February, where she'd presented an Oscar to somebody else.

So who knows where the bidding might end up? The anchors chuckled back and forth.

The spokeswoman from the hospital did her best to keep the tone on track. *Well, yes, high up there, we certainly hope.*

She was blushing, I noticed. As if wearing such a glamorous, extravagant item embarrassed her a little.

Or maybe it was the heat from the lights. She waited out the close-up, then used her hands to drape her hair back around her shoulders like a shawl.

"Bunch of assholes."

"I'm sorry," I said. "But I don't think I'm your man."

"What. Seriously?"

"Seriously."

His face fell. "It's a good plan."

The way I understood it, Lonnie had recently taken a job as night watchman for a rent-to-own outlet in midtown. Somehow he'd determined that the proprietor kept a foolish amount of cash on hand. Mr. Kyle suspected the man ran a sports book out of the store, possibly something else in the illegal line. He wasn't sure.

It didn't matter. All he needed was a skill man for the Mosler safe in the back office.

"I'm sure it's a good plan," I said. He'd drawn it by hand on a sheet of spiral notebook paper. "But it's a four-person job."

"Say what?"

"It's a four-person job."

"Shit," Lonnie Kyle said. "I'm already on the inside. I got security covered. You bust the safe. Why split it four ways?"

"Because it's a four-person job."

Even if it hadn't been, I'd already decided that I had no interest in working with Lonnie Kyle. And even if I'd had any, he was no kind of partner. I could tell that just by listening to him.

"Anyway," I said, "I'm not really working anymore."

"You're not working anymore."

"Not really."

He looked around the place. "Come on."

"I'm more or less retired," I said. "For several years now, I'm afraid."

"You're serious?" He stood up and took a few steps. "No offense, but this place. . .look, no offense, but this place is a shit hole."

It wasn't a shit hole at all. It was a very small one-bedroom apartment in a reasonable neighborhood. It was a clean building and the rent was fair.

"Not to mention, Pops, but you're getting up there." He gave me a once-over. "What are you, sixty? Sixty- five?"

"I'm seventy-two."

"Wow. Lot to show for it. Some retirement."

I shrugged. "I've got what I need."

"Man, you got a crappy sofa and about, like, a three-inch TV. How many jobs you think you got left?"

"That's what I've been trying to explain."

Lonnie Kyle was getting frustrated. I wasn't trying to frustrate him.

"Seriously," he said. "Don't you want a little more around you when you go out?"

"I'm seventy-two, Lonnie. Not ninety."

"Exactly. Don't you got any ambition? Hell, I'll carry your tools."

I smiled. "That's not the issue."

"Well, what?" He made a motion with his fist that I believe was meant to be inspiring. "No risk, no reward. Right?"

"I hear that's what they say."

"It ain't even hardly any risk. I'm telling you, I worked hard on this. It's a good plan."

Lonnie Kyle's plan wouldn't work, but I didn't know how to tell him that in a way he'd understand.

Bottom line, he was right. My ambition was low. I'm seventy-two, not thirty. This is what I have around me, and it's fine.

"I'm sorry," I said.

The news finished up with the woman from the children's hospital, their final segment for the half hour. They signed off with another close-up of the necklace, valued at 1.2 million, but worn by a famous actress to the Oscar awards.

Lonnie Kyle had gotten the idea that he'd be taking no for an answer. His shoulders slouched. He sighed heavily and stared at the television screen, sullen, as though he were suddenly looking at everything he'd never have.

All at once, his eyes flickered.

"Hey." He raised his face to me. "Hey."

"Yes?"

He went to the window, swept up in a thought. He opened the blinds with two fingers, looking down through my apartment window at the shared back lot below.

"That's the Channel 5 building over there. Isn't it?"

"It is."

"You live right behind the news station."

"I do."

"The news was just on."

I could almost imagine the sound of the gears grinding in Lonnie Kyle's head. I hoped I didn't see where this was going. But I was afraid that I did.

"The lady who was just on TV." He pointed at the television. Then he pointed out the window. "Is in that building right now."

"I suppose she is," I said. "But son. . . ."

He was already out the door.

Lonnie Kyle ran by me so fast that he created a draft. The rush of air lifted the creased, wrinkled, coffee-stained sheet of notebook paper he'd left behind. The paper floated gently to the floor in his wake.

I stood there a moment, taken aback. Then I shook my head and went to the same window where he'd been standing.

In a minute I saw Lonnie Kyle burst from the exit door of my building on the ground level, one floor below. He shoved his hands into his pockets and slowed himself to a casual walk. He strolled across the lot, toward the back of the Channel 5 building.

I sighed, stooped, and picked up the sheet of notebook paper from the floor.

This, I could have told him. *This is exactly why your plan wouldn't work.*

✝

There's a good deal of young money in this town. More than you'd think, if you didn't know.

People don't dream of retiring here. It's just another medium-sized city tucked away in flyover country: half a million people, Midwestern values, relatively high employment and relatively low crime. Not much of a thrill if you like mountains or coasts.

Unless you're the type who follows finance, in which case you'd probably know about Harmon Beale.

Harmon Beale is the founder and CEO of Morton Kliner Inc., a holding company that started in textiles thirty years ago, diversified broadly, and is now worth billions. Beale himself is about my age. He's known for living modestly, steering a straight ship, and for speaking only when he has something to say. There's a surprisingly large club of people around here who follow the man like an oracle.

As well they probably should. Beale made them all millionaires.

Each year in April, Morton Kliner hosts an annual shareholders meeting here in town. Gates, Buffett, The Donald—they've all been known to come in for the festivities. The local businesses all roll out the red carpet. There's a golf event and a charity dinner and general hubbub for two or three days.

According to the lady from the children's hospital, the necklace was designed and created locally by Creighton Munger of Warrenstein's Fine Jewelry and Gifts. Warrenstein's, a Morton Kliner subsidiary, had donated the one-of-a-kind piece for sale. Proceeds from the auction would benefit the construction of the hospital's new oncology wing.

I wanted to shout: *She's not wearing it!*

For heaven's sake. She wouldn't even be carrying it.

I don't know why I followed Lonnie Kyle. I certainly didn't owe him a thing. The fact that he clearly carried some sort of deficit was

89

none of my concern.

But I did feel a little bit sorry for ruining his day. He'd run out of my apartment without the childish schematic for the rent-to-own job he'd worked so hard on.

And for whatever reason—I've spent some time thinking about it, and I'm still not sure why—some simple part of me looked at Lonnie Kyle, saw a 30-something dreamer with dim prospects, a young man already half gone to seed, and hated to see the poor sorry lummox make a fool of himself in broad daylight.

By the time I traced his path out of my building, Lonnie Kyle had taken position against a Dumpster on the far side of the parking lot. He loitered there, hunkered in the shade of the garbage bin, watching the back door of the television station.

It was a fine spring day: fragrant and sunny, quite warm for April. What did he think?

Did he really believe she'd come strolling outside in the million dollars worth of diamonds he'd just seen her wearing on live television?

Did he not see the two men in plainclothes walking toward the glossy black Town Car parked fifty feet from the same door? The men were chatting and one of them laughed. The other carried a hardshell security case.

The woman from the children's hospital emerged from the building before I'd made it halfway across the lot. Middle-aged, a nice figure, that peach-colored sweater with a charcoal skirt. Medium heels.

I thought about yelling out a warning, but it was too late. Lonnie Kyle had already made his move.

He met her at a dark gray sedan and spun her around. His hands went to her neck and fumbled there.

The woman screamed like a wildcat. They grappled only a moment before she stomped his instep, drove her knee into his balls, and blasted him in the eyes with pepper spray.

Now Lonnie Kyle screamed, doubling over in pain. He clawed at his face.

The woman bolted. She practically dove into her car. She started the engine, dropped into reverse, and punched the gas.

The Warrenstein's escort on the driver's side of the Town Car started running the moment he heard the woman from the children's hospital scream. His right hand disappeared beneath his sport coat.

Purely out of habit, I'd already sized them up. Retired cops, both of them. The one carrying the hardcase limped when he walked, and he looked too young to be retired. I assumed he'd been sidelined by some sort of injury.

When the woman's back bumper caught Lonnie Kyle in the hip,

the second escort slammed his door and ran after his partner, favoring his bad leg, locking the Town Car over his shoulder with a remote key.

Lonnie Kyle disappeared beneath the back end of the sedan. His head met the bumper, then the parking lot. It sounded like a coconut hitting pavement; I could hear it from where I stood.

The shudder of the impact kicked the woman's apparent panic into overdrive. She craned over her shoulder, frantically searching for her attacker. The sedan's reverse lights blinked off, and she gunned the car forward.

Then backward.

Forward again.

Lonnie Kyle was caught beneath the axle. The car dragged him several feet in each direction. Finally, the back tire rolled over his head, leaving his limp, twisted body in a heap.

It was horrid. All the while, the armed security escorts from Warrenstein's shouted at the windows of the sedan, wildly gesturing for the woman to stop, only scaring her more.

It wasn't until she finally did stop that I noticed where I was standing:

Next to a temporarily abandoned Lincoln Town Car with a $1.2 million diamond necklace locked inside.

And the windows down.

It was warm for April. Had they purposefully left the car this way?

When the woman screamed, had their police instincts simply overridden their experience as jewel escorts?

Was it possible that neither of them, having once carried badges, took their current job very seriously?

It had taken approximately nine seconds for the entire scene to unfold. The woman piled out of her car and into the arms of the escort who had left the security case behind. When she saw Lonnie Kyle's rag doll body behind her car, face down in a spreading black pool, she went hysterical.

Others—passersby, employees leaving the building for lunch—began to converge on the scene. In approximately three more seconds, pandemonium would reign.

The station had exterior cameras. Somebody had just begun snapping photos with their cellular phone. People were probably looking out windows by now.

More people appeared. The chaos at the center of the parking lot became a vortex, drawing every watt of attention in the area. The first escort knelt by Lonnie's body, making the 911 call. The second escort still had his hands full of screaming spokeswoman.

I had those three seconds to evaluate my small corner of the situation to the best of my ability.

I sprinted away from there, hips stiff, my old knees crackling, clutching the case to my chest like a two-bit criminal.

∯

"I don't know a thing about jewelry," I said. "But I read a funny story about Harry Winston once."

"Who?" The police chief looked concerned.

But Creighton Munger smiled. Warrenstein's master jeweler spread his thin fingers on the table top. "I'd enjoy hearing it."

"Yes," said Harmon Beale. "By all means."

So I told them the story of a colossal diamond that had been discovered somewhere in Africa in the 1930s. According to historical record, Harry Winston, the famous jewel man, had purchased the freak stone through a London boutique.

According to legend, nobody could decide on the best way to transport the rock to the States. They discussed chartered airplanes. Caravans. Armed bodyguards.

In the end, Winston mailed the invaluable stone to himself for 64 cents postage.

"I always wondered if that story was true."

Creighton Munger's careful eyes twinkled like the stones in the necklace I'd returned to him. In ten more years he'd walk with a stoop. I could tell by looking at him.

"The Jonker Diamond," he said. "726 carats in its rough state."

I grinned. "Is that right?"

"Oh, indeed."

"Do you suppose it really happened that way?"

He smiled back. "It's one of my favorite stories."

For the past hour, I'd told them another story. I started with the truth: I do in fact live in the apartment building that I own, which shares a parking lot with the broadcast station for Channel 5 news.

The rest was a bit of a reach, but age makes you trustworthy. When you're young and full of snap, everybody assumes you're trying to get something over on them. Once you reach grandfather territory, even the skeptics give you the benefit of the doubt.

I told them that I'd been looking out my second-floor window when I saw a man attack a woman in the parking lot. During the confusion, I'd seen another man run away from Warrenstein's Town Car with a black case in his arms.

I told them that I'd hurried to my bedroom and watched from the window there. I told them I'd seen the second man deposit the case in

92

the Dumpster behind my building as he fled.

"Not a bad move," the police chief had said. "No garbage service until Monday. Plenty of time to come back."

Harmon Beale said, "I don't suppose the decoy intended to be run over by a car."

They took my photograph, to compare against the evidence they'd collected so far.

I didn't believe they'd find anything worth examining. Old men don't run like anybody they might have captured on their tapes, or in their witness accounts.

I should know. I was so sore that I'd practically hobbled into the room.

And I look quite different when I shave my beard and take off my eyeglasses. My grandkids like the beard, so I'm already impatient to grow it back.

For the time being, the lines in my face are even deeper than I remembered. Even without the whiskers, I could pass very easily for the seventy-one year old landlord that I am.

Morton Kliner, Inc., by way of Warrenstein's Jewelers, paid me $5000 as a gesture of appreciation for the return of the charity necklace.

The theft added zest to the anecdotal value of the piece, which sold for just over $4 million to a hotelier from Florida.

I donated half my reward money to the hospital foundation. Not because I felt that I owed them. They'd already done fine on the deal, through no particular doing of their own. We're still talking about sick children.

After a half day's legwork, I slipped $1500 into a plain white envelope and dropped it through the mail slot of the Warrenstein's man who had lost his job over the incident. I included the business card of an independent security firm that had recently lost an employee.

The remaining thousand dollars I used to pick up the equipment I thought I'd need. I tapped three guys I'd used before, good and reliable boys, and we did Lonnie Kyle's rent-to-own.

Lonnie had been right: it was more or less a solid plan. I gave the guys an even split, and we went home with fifty grand apiece.

The following Monday, I used the proceeds from the rental store job to purchase one Class A share of Morton Kliner, Incorporated. Down $400, trading at $49,789 per share.

The purchase improved my holdings in the company to a grand total of 274 shares. I've been acquiring a little at a time for years now, ever since Morton Kliner went public at $1200 per share. Lately the stock isn't performing like it used to, but I still buy when I can.

One of these days, I'll probably sell.

People with short memories criticize Harmon Beale for being too old, too cautious, unwilling to take the big risks. I suppose I take the long view.

I read about Lonnie Kyle's burial in the paper. *Sparsely attended,* it said. I wonder if anybody besides the reporter showed up.

Afterword

"The Necklace" was one of those stories that started out as one thing and ended up being another. I'd already accepted—with gratitude—this editor's invitation to appear in these pages, but I honestly didn't know I was writing this story for Damn Near Dead *until it was finished.*

Later, I came to recognize the obvious probability that I'd had this anthology's fundamental underlying themes in mind the whole time. Funny how the mind starts to go... —S.D.

PART TWO:

DUFFERS AND BACHELORS

FATHERS AND SONS

CHARLES ARDAI

Charles Ardai (born 1969) is the Edgar and Shamus-nominated author of Little Girl Lost *(under the pen name "Richard Aleas"); his short stories have been selected for* Best Mystery Stories of the Year *and* The Year's Best Horror Stories. *He is also the founding editor of Hard Case Crime, in which capacity he has had the pleasure of publishing work by authors such as Madison Smartt Bell, Lawrence Block, Stephen King, Ed McBain and Donald E. Westlake. Charles is insanely well-read. Go ahead. Try to stump him.*

†

FATHERS AND SONS
by Charles Ardai

The hospital room stank of latex gloves and recirculated air. Dorian could smell the damp antiseptic scent from the last time the room was mopped. The background hum of quiet motors was punctuated by the beeping of the old man's IV machine, metering out drips of whatever the hell it was they were pumping into his veins. Dorian closed the door gently behind him.

His father's head turned. There was gauze on his neck, covering a patch of mottled purple skin. Two thin tubes ran under the gauze and into his neck. What they were for he didn't know. Keeping his father alive. That's what it was all for, wasn't it?

The old man didn't talk, didn't say anything, just stared. When he finally spoke, he was hoarse, quiet, tentative. "Dori'?" he said.

He came forward, put his hands on the old man's arm, felt how thin, how fragile, he was. "Yeah, Pop."

"How…?"

"The doctor called me. Said I'd better come."

"But Dorian…" The effort of talking took an enormous amount out of him, you could see it.

"I gave him my cell number, so he could reach me."

"You shouldn't've."

"I had to, Pop. I had to know how you were."

"Mickey could've—" He coughed. "Could've got it out of him. You shouldn't've…"

"Sh," Dorian said. "Sh."

"Dori'…Mick wants you *dead*. You understand? *Dead*." He coughed again. It was horrible to watch. His sunken chest shook under the loose gown. His eyes closed.

"Don't worry about Mick, Pop. You just worry about yourself. You gotta be strong."

"I'm worried about you," the old man said. "Mick never forgave you for…" His voice trailed off. They both knew what he'd never forgiven him for.

"I can take care of Mick, Pop."

"No you can't." The words were quiet, but it was like he was trying to shout. The veins on either side of his father's neck stood out and his head, completely hairless now after all the chemo, shook with the

effort. He sank back into the bed. "Mick blames you for his son."

"I'm telling you, Pop, Mick's..." Dorian's voice caught. "Mick understands. We've talked, he said it's okay. He doesn't want a war."

The old man started to cry. His mouth hung open and the tears flowed down his face. Dorian looked away. When it was over, he leaned over the side of the bed and used a corner of the sheet to wipe his father's face.

"You could never lie to me," the old man whispered. "You're a bad liar."

"I'm not lying, Pop."

"Mick would...never say that. Never. Not about his son."

"He didn't say that it was *okay*. But, you know, it was like that—"

"Tell me the truth. Tell me what happened."

"Nothing happened, Pop—" The old man's fingers tightened around his wrist. Where the strength came from Dorian didn't know, but it was like a clamp pinching tight, pulling him down toward the bed. "Honest, Pop."

"Tell me..." He winced as some invisible pain came and went. "The truth."

"All right," Dorian said, shaking his hand free. "All right. I just didn't want to agitate you, the way you are now. It's not good for you."

"What," the old man said. Then after a few shallow breaths: "Happened."

They looked at each other, the old man and his son, and then Dorian looked away, started pacing, walked to the foot of the hospital bed and back. "You know where I was staying, Pop, right? At the apartment on Ludlow? By the warehouse?"

His father nodded. His eyes, Dorian thought, looked fearful. His father, who'd never been afraid of any man, of anything. The police held him in that basement on Mott Street for two days, beat him bloody, and the day he came out, he looked every man in the eye, even Mick, and you knew he was one hundred percent in control, they hadn't broken him. And now – now he had tubes going into his neck and his eyes were full of fear.

"Ever since I came back to the city, I didn't go out on the street, I didn't call anyone, just like you said. Julie was bringing me food. You remember Julie, right? Charley's girl, the one with the thing on her lip? You remember."

His father didn't respond, just waited for him to go on.

"But then Dr. Batoon called. On my cell. I wasn't going to answer, but I saw it was him, and you know, I couldn't...what am I supposed to do? It could've been an emergency, you could've had another stroke or something."

The old man was shaking his head slowly, side to side.

"He said your condition was bad, that if I wanted to see you alive I had to come now. That's what he said, Pop. So I told Julie to get the car, pull it up to the loading entrance and I'd get in the back seat, ride covered up under a blanket. I was careful. I was, I'm telling you, there's no way Mick could've found out—"

"The doctor," his father whispered.

"That's right," Dorian said. "The fucking doctor. Sold me out. Mick was in the alley with his man Danny, you know, with the eyepatch—"

"Jesus." He said it soft as a prayer.

"—and when I went out there, Danny's got one arm around Julie's neck and a Glock to her temple, and Mick's standing there leaning on a cane and he says...Pop, are you sure you want me to—"

"Yes. Yes. Goddamn it, yes."

Dorian shot a glance at the closed door, then lowered his voice. "He said, 'First I'm gonna kill your girlfriend and then I'm gonna kill you. And only because I respect your father, only because I've known him seventy-four years and he saved my life twice when we were growing up, I'm gonna give it to you fast and clean rather than the way you deserve.'"

The old man winced.

"I told him, I said, 'You're all wrong, Mick. To begin with, Julie's not my girlfriend, she's Charley's girl,' but he didn't listen. He nodded at Danny and Danny shot her in the head."

"Christ..."

"I still had the door open, so I ran back in the building and up the stairs and down the hall to the front. Meanwhile, Danny's coming after me, shooting off round after round, and I'm ducking and dodging and praying. Somehow I make it out the front door without getting hit. And would you believe there's a cab pulling up right outside to let somebody off?

"But the woman inside still has to pay. I try to pull her out but she starts yelling, and by the time I get her out, Danny's caught up with me. He puts the gun in my back, apologizes to the woman and the cabbie, very polite, and he pulls me back into the building."

There was one chair in the hospital room, a heavy, uncomfortable armchair with purple upholstery on the seat and the back. Dorian dragged it over next to the bed. He sat down in it and took his father's hand in his own. It weighed nothing, like a piece of paper.

"Mick made me let them into the apartment. They sat me on the couch and Danny stands over me with the Glock and Mick says, 'I just want to know one thing, when my son was dying, what did he say to you?'

"So I say, 'I'll tell you if you let me go,' and he says, 'No, you'll tell me, period,' and I say, 'Well, in that case he didn't say anything, he just died,' and Mick nods at Danny." Dorian took a deep breath. "Danny puts the Glock in my face, I mean right there, I can *smell* it, and I know, he's gonna do it, he's really gonna shoot me, same as he shot Julie. The only thing I can do is play for time, so I start making some shit up, how Michael talked about Mick at the end, how he said, 'Tell my father I love him,' you know, anything I can think of, and I'm thinking *There's no way he's going to buy this*, but Mick tells Danny to back off. So I keep talking. Telling him how Michael's lying there, you know, crushed under the truck, and he's saying he wants his mother to know this and his sister to know that, and it's all bullshit, Michael was killed instantly, but you know, whatever he wants to hear, I'm telling him. And all the while I'm edging over to the end of the couch where I've got a gun stashed, under the cushion."

He looked at his father's face. The old man looked flushed. "Pop, really, you don't need to hear this. I mean obviously I made it out – I'm here, aren't I? Let it alone."

His father tried to say something, couldn't get it out, and crooked his fingers, jerked them toward himself in a *Come here* gesture. Dorian leaned over, brought his ear close to the old man's mouth. The voice was small, the words squeezed out with great effort and great care. "Tell me...what happened. I want...to know."

"I shot him, Pop. I shot him, I got my hand on the gun and I pulled it out and shot him, one-two-three, one in the belly and then two in the head. This was Danny, I mean. Then when he was down I kicked the Glock under the couch and told Mick I was leaving and I walked out and I jumped on the 7 train and came here, and—what, Pop? I'm telling you, that's what happened, what are you...?" The old man was straining to say something but it wasn't coming out and tears were welling up in his eyes. It was a horrible thing to see, to stand there powerless and watch your father fight just to fucking breathe. "What, Pop? What?"

"You're lying to me. You're lying." There was practically no sound to it at all, just air, the ghost of speech, the thinnest sound he'd ever heard. Tears were running down the old man's face and now, damn it all, Dorian felt them on his own cheeks, too. "He'd never..." the old man said, straining. "You couldn't... He'd've had...his own gun. And even if he didn't...he'd've gone for Danny's...followed you here...he'd be waiting right outside that door..."

"Pop," Dorian said, "don't—please don't—"

"You killed him, didn't you," the old man whispered, "you killed

Mick, you shot him too, don't lie to me..."

"Yes!" Dorian shouted. He was bawling. "Yes, I did, Pop, I did, I'm sorry, I know Mick was your friend, but I had to, don't you see, I had to come here, I had to see you, I had to, you needed me..."

His father lifted one of his paper-thin hands and patted the back of Dorian's clenched fist. His eyes closed.

"You're a good boy," he whispered. "Mick shouldn't've tried to... kill you...his son...a man's son...you don't..." He winced again, a bad one this time. "I'll tell him...when I get there..."

The old man fell silent. His hand stopped moving. But Dorian sat with him, watching the sheet rise and fall over his ribcage, watching the dangling IV bag slowly drain into him, listening to the hum and the beeps and all the other slow impersonal sounds of death's approach. The room was cold – why the fuck are hospitals always so goddamn cold? – and his father's hand felt colder still. Batoon had sounded sure that this would be it, that he wouldn't live through the night; and though when Dorian had seen Mick standing there in the alley he'd thought it had all been a set-up, sitting here now, he knew Batoon had been telling the truth. How long can a man go on fighting when all that's left of him is bones and tears and barely enough breath to speak?

Dorian sat holding his hand, and didn't notice at first when the sheet's slow rise and fall ended, when the pale pink skin of the old man's hand grew slowly paler and then waxy white. When eventually he did notice it, he stood, kissed the old man's forehead, and left the room.

The corridor outside ran past a pair of vending machines and a waiting area crowded with empty benches. An old man sat on one, his liver-spotted hands gripping the rubber handle of his cane. He stood with some difficulty as Dorian slowly approached, helped to his feet by the younger man standing beside him. The old man looked at Dorian with a sad expression; the younger man with the severe features just stared at him coldly out of the one eye not covered by an eyepatch.

"Thank you," Dorian said.

"Your father was a good man," Mick said. "I did it for him, not for you."

He put one hand on Dorian's shoulder and steered him toward the elevator. As he walked, Dorian felt the point of Danny's gun pressing through the fabric of his shirt against the base of his spine.

Afterword

I originally came up with the idea for this story when Lawrence Block approached me to contribute to an anthology he was editing called Manhattan Noir. *At the time, I was commuting back and forth fairly frequently from Manhattan (where I live) to Flushing, Queens, where my 92-year-old grandmother was trying desperately to recover from a broken hip and the infections that had developed in its wake. She was being shuttled back and forth from hospital to rehab center and back again as her condition alternately improved and worsened, and from talking with her doctors, I knew they felt she didn't have much time left. But she was a tough woman. She'd grown up in Europe between the wars, she'd survived the Nazis and the Communists, she'd come to New York in 1957 with a young daughter and no money and had somehow managed to carve out a decent life for herself and her family, and now, by god, she wasn't going to let go without a fight. So she kept fighting and I kept riding the long, long 7 train to the end of the line.*

And it was on one of those long, long train rides that I found myself thinking about how my grandmother must feel, trapped in her hospital bed; she'd lived in Manhattan for more than forty years and she'd loved it, but now she knew she'd almost certainly never see it again. I thought, Wouldn't that be interesting for a book called Manhattan Noir, *if the story weren't set in Manhattan at all but instead took place just outside and were about someone longing to go there but knowing it's in vain, like Moses doomed never to set foot in the promised land? I thought: What if you had an old man in a hospital bed, and his son comes to visit him, and the whole thing is the son telling his dying father a story about things that happened to him earlier the same day in Manhattan. The story the son tells wouldn't even have to be true—just a story calculated to make the old man feel a little better on his deathbed...*

And that's where "Fathers and Sons" came from, or at least it's the germ of the idea. The story obviously changed a lot from original concept to final execution, and not necessarily for the better (isn't that always the way?). In particular, at some point the Manhattan element stopped being central to the concept—so I wrote another story for Larry's collection and filed this idea away, with no particular notion of when or where I might ever use it. And then, out of the blue, Duane came to me with the idea for Damn Near Dead. *Serendipity? Fate? Who knows? But I had the idea ready to go, and the story followed within days.*

As for my grandmother...on April 16, 2005, having outlived her sis-

ter, her husband, her daughter (my mother), and most of her other blood relatives, by six decades in many cases, Martha Gordon died. Her final months were inspiring and awful.

This story is dedicated to her memory. —C.A.

DUFFERS
OF THE
APOCALYPSE

VICTOR GISCHLER

Victor Gischler (born 1969) is the author of four novels, including the Edgar-nominated Gun Monkeys *and his most recent* Shotgun Opera. *His work has been translated into French, Italian, Japanese and Spanish. While at the University of Southern Mississippi, Gischler earned his Ph.D. in English. That and a buck eighty will get him a cup at Starbuck's. He lives in the wilds of Skiatook, Oklahoma with his wife Jackie and son Emery. He's never met a video golf machine he didn't like.*

DUFFERS OF THE APOCALYPSE
by Victor Gischler

You wouldn't think somebody could get killed that way, but I saw it. I guess that's not true. But I did *hear* it, the unmistakable *thwock* of a golf ball striking skull. Knock a guy for a loop, sure, but kill him? What are the odds? We didn't even know at first, the three of us standing there on the tee box.

Pete Dexter and I had watched Tony DeLuca crush one. It had shot left, low and fast like a cruise missile hugging the ground, and we'd heard it hit. I thought it had smacked a tree trunk.

"You'll have some trouble getting out of there," Pete said. "Trees." He stepped up, groaned as he bent and stuck his tee in the ground, placed an orange Top Flight on it. Pete was tall, stork-like and stooped, age pushing his narrow shoulders together.

Tony was still standing there, posing for a picture, driver cocked in frozen follow-through, watching the stand of trees like his ball might still bounce out. "Shit." He was a fat guy in a purple jogging suit, rogue strands of black hair combed over and fooling nobody. His face hung heavy with chins. He finally stepped back to let Pete have his shot.

"Let me show you how it's done." Pete swung his three-wood, all loose jointed and pointy elbows. He made good contact, and the ball flew high, came down soft in the center of the fairway a hundred and fifty yards away. "I think I can put it on in three from there."

My turn. I stood on the tee, looked down the length of the fairway. The grass was green, and the sky was blue. There was no way you could tell I was grinding and tumbling and sliding to the end of the world. The end of my particular world anyway. I teed up a Pinnacle, and the wind kicked up. That's what wind did in Oklahoma. It kicked up and blew you down.

I hit the ball into the dry, cold November air but didn't see it land, went to one knee instead, the spasm in my gut worse than it had been in a while. I clenched teeth to keep a moan from getting out.

"What's with you?" Tony asked.

"Nothing. My shoe's loose." I undid the laces and tied them up again. Slowly. The spasm passed, and I suddenly felt my age, so tired, like my bones would shatter and scatter in the wind like sticks. I stood, felt a little dizzy but forced a smile. "Not bad." My ball had rolled a few yards past Pete's.

""Nice shot," Pete said.

"Let's find mine." Tony was already in his cart.

"I'll help you look." I got into my cart.

All three of us each had our own cart. Almost everyone in the retirement community surrounding the golf course had a cart, even those who didn't play. It was a convenient way to get around, the golf course, the pool, the general store, community center and Dotty's the little bacon and eggs diner almost out to the highway. Some people even took their carts to the Methodist church down the road a bit. Not me. God and I weren't speaking.

I pulled ahead because my cart was fastest. After thirty years in the U.S. Army motor pool, I couldn't help but take a wrench to anything with wheels. My cart got about three or four miles per hour than most of the others. So anyway, that's how I got to Tony's ball first and found the body.

⛳

Here's what I want you to know about me. My name's Roscoe Carter, and I'm not a bad guy. I don't do things the wrong way. I drive the speed limit. I pay taxes on time. I got a new cordless phone, and you're supposed to charge it a full twenty-four hours before using it. Those are the instructions. I don't know what happens if you don't charge it the full twenty-four hours, and I don't want to know. Rules protect us.

But when you can't use protection anymore, when you don't need it, those rules start to seem sort of random, and you start feeling like you've been living in a little, narrow rut, and it's only taken certain doom to open your eyes wide.

So you start playing it loose.

I'm not a bad guy. I'm only reacting the way you'd react too if the whole world had shifted under your feet.

⛳

When I came around the low mound, I saw him in the sand trap. He'd made a pile of himself falling down, butt sticking in the air, thick as hell horn rim glasses off to the side. His mouth hung open. A deep black and purple bruise between his eyes. I looked around, saw Tony's Titleist ten feet away, and put two and two together. I was out of my cart and on the way over to him when Tony's and Pete's carts came up behind two seconds later.

"Oh, shit," Tony said. "I'm gonna get sued."

I knelt beside the guy, touched his shoulder.

"He okay, Roscoe?" Pete called.

I shook my head. "Nope."

"I am gonna get sued," Tony said. "Shit, shit, motherfuck, hell."

Pete unzipped a pocket in his golf bag, fished out a cell phone. "You want me to get an ambulance?" We lived in a retirement community, the land of broken hips and strokes and backs thrown way, way out. The paramedics had been so many times, the ambulance could drive itself.

Tony said, "I know that guy. It's Freddy what's-his-name. The retard with the lazy eye who helps the groundskeeper and does odd jobs for everyone." There was a rake three feet away, evidence he'd been raking the trap.

"When he comes around, ask him if he wants an ambulance," Pete said. "I've got it on speed dial."

I shook my head and laughed. That's right, I laughed. It was all so fucking ridiculous. "You don't understand. This guy's a goner."

A long second of uneasy silence. The wind blew dead leaves past us.

"Bullshit," Tony said.

Pete asked, "So you don't want the ambulance then?"

"Will you fucking shut up about the ambulance." Tony waddled up to the body, squatted down next to me. "Check him again."

I touched his throat and then his wrist. "No pulse."

"Fucking shit."

Pete stood right behind us now, peered at the body like it was a roadside attraction. It wasn't real to him yet. "What happened to him?"

"I think Tony killed him with his golf ball."

"Oh, like hell. You can't kill a guy with a golf ball."

I pointed to the purple bruise, the deep imprint of the dimples where the ball had hit. "That's your Titleist over there, right?"

"Shit!" Tony smacked a fist into his palm. "Stupid soft-headed retard. Who gets killed by a golf ball?"

I pointed at Freddy's corpse. "This guy."

"Better call the police," Pete said. "Got them on speed dial too."

"Wait a minute." Tony stood, made *calm down* motions with his fat hands. "Just hold on. Let's think about this."

"What's to think about?" Pete said. "It was a freak accident."

"Just wait."

Pete shook his head. "I'm calling the police."

Tony snatched the cell phone out of Pete's hand.

"Hey!"

"No cops."

"Why not?" I asked.

"I haven't had good luck with cops," Tony said.

Tony had come out of the East three years ago with a Brooklyn accent and a truckload of ugly furniture. There had been talk about him, but there was always talk about everyone. That's what old men did over checkers or a drink of whisky, talk and talk and talk the past back to life like any of it mattered.

It was more than talk now.

"We can't just leave him lying there," Pete said.

Tony looked side to side. Nobody around. "Why not?"

Pete's eyes widened. "Please say you're joking."

"I'm not fucking joking," Tony said. "Look, I hired this guy last week to wash and wax my Lincoln and he scratched it. I screamed at him in front of the whole neighborhood, said I was gonna fucking break his neck. He wanted to get paid for the work, and I told him to fuck off. He shouted at me, and I said if he ever raised his voice like that again I'd fucking kill him. Like a half dozen people heard me threaten the guy."

Pete was shaking his head. "It was just an argument."

"Listen to me, Pete. I've had some incidents in the past. Never mind the details. Let's just say the cops won't be giving me the benefit of the doubt, you know?"

"This is nuts," Pete said. "It was an accident."

"Fuck accidents. I'm not risking it."

Pete turned his back on Tony, pleaded with me. "Roscoe, help me talk sense into him."

I'd only been half listening to them bicker. Mostly, I'd been standing there looking at Freddy get cold in the howling Okie wind. What was it that the golf ball had knocked out of him? What spark or intangible puff of mist? What did a soul look like, and how could it just turn a guy off by slipping out of a nostril or an ear hole or an anus? Would a soul even stand a chance, floating around out there in this wind? Freddy didn't look dead or broken. He just looked deflated, like somebody could come along and pump him up again and he'd be just fine.

Tony said, "Try to see it from my point of view. Calling the cops ain't gonna bring him back, and it's gonna cause hassle for us."

"Jesus," Pete said. "You can't just—"

"Let's cover him up," I said.

Pete blinked. "What?"

I grabbed the rake, began raking sand up against Freddy's body.

"Yeah, that's good," Tony said. "That's the idea, Roscoe. I'll help."

He tried shoveling sand onto the body with his six iron. When that didn't work too well, he dropped to his knees, started scooping sand with his hands.'

"This can't be happening." Pete said.

After a few seconds Pete got down beside us and scooped sand. I knew he'd cave. He'd been counting on me to be sober and sane and help him against Tony. A month ago, I'd have been on his side. Now I didn't feel anything, not remorse for Freddy nor any guilt in burying him. I didn't even feel like I was doing Tony a favor.

There was only the cold wind and sand under my fingernails and dead meat, and if God were watching He didn't have jack shit to say about it.

⚑

Later that afternoon, I sat in my recliner and watched something on TV. I'm not sure what, a blur of lights and talking heads. Pete and Tony had slunk home, probably trying to figure some way to get comfortable with their shame. I'd stayed and finished the round, shot nine over par. By the eighteenth hole the wind had gotten so bad it even blew the putts off line.

I washed down a pill with a swig of warm Johnny Walker. Sweat on my forehead. The gut pain seared and a twisted and wormed its way in and out. The pill made me loopy and the whisky didn't help, but there was nothing else for it. I took another pill. They didn't work fast enough. You could measure the rest of my life with less than half a calendar, count it out in hours and minutes. Maybe four months. Something like a hundred a twenty days. Three hundred and eighty meals. How many holes of golf?

I cursed God for every minute I wasted in the recliner waiting for the pain to pass.

The doctors had tried to explain, as if understanding in stark technical terms would make me feel better somehow. I didn't know what cancer looked like, but I imagined it like a black weed, a thorny vine growing through my guts, twisting around my stomach and liver and kidneys, twisting and squeezing and choking.

The one in my head I imagined differently, a fleshy wad with worms growing out of it, eating their way into different chunks of my brain. It didn't hurt like in my guts, but sometimes little parts of the day would go missing, like scenes edited out of a film.

I didn't want to spend my last days talking to the police. I didn't want the golf course closed down because it was a crime scene. And I didn't want anyone shedding tears over a dead groundskeeper when I was dead on my feet right in front of everyone. Where were my tears?

114

I wasn't asking for any. I just wanted my life for a few more months. I would eat junk food and pain pills and drink whisky and wake up in the morning and play golf and damn the universe and everyone in it.

❦

My eyes popped open. The TV was off, no lights. The world outside was red, glowing hellish in the open windows. The wind had increased yet again, branches and debris flying past the windows. I had the sudden sensation the house was slowly turning, spinning like a lazy merry-go-round.. It just seemed that way because of all the stuff flying past the windows, and the pills and the whisky and my head light as a feather.

I stood, wobbled, stumbled into the kitchen. The interior of the house glowed like hot blood, the red-orange sun near the horizon pulsing like hate through the hazy, smoky sky. I was hallucinating, dreaming I was in hell.

The kitchen light didn't work. I pulled the little battery-powered radio out of the junk drawer, found an A.M. news station. Storms had dropped out of the north. Fierce winds gusting up to seventy miles an hour had blown down a number of power lines which had ignited grass fires. They swept across the eastern part of the state.

I wasn't hallucinating. I was just in Oklahoma.

I stumbled and fumbled and rumbled back through the dark, hell-red house, made it into the living room just as the front door flew open and slammed against the wall, the black outline of a figure against the bloody sky.

I yelped and stepped back. Fear. I'd forgotten for a second I was dead already.

"Roscoe?" A tentative voice. "I'm sorry, Roscoe. I knocked, and I guess you didn't hear me. I tried the door, and the knob flew out of my hands." Wind raged through the house,

"Close the door, Pete."

He came in, closed it behind him. "What's happening?"

"Radio says storms. Power line started grass fires."

"'Come with me to talk to Tony."

"No. You want some whisky?"

"Are you even listening?" he asked.

"You're burning daylight," I told him. "Now have a drink of whisky or fuck off." I handed him the bottle.

"I don't get a glass?"

"That's for pussies."

"Jesus, Roscoe. You've changed." He titled the bottle, took a good swig, coughed and sputtered some of it over his lips. "Been a while since I had a good, stiff drink. My doctor says—"

"To hell with your doctor."

He nodded, took another swallow. "This thing with Tony isn't right. We've got to come clean. I called him, and he yelled at me. He said stool pigeons don't last long in the joint. Who's he think he is, Jimmy Cagney?"

Pete handed the whisky back to me, his hand coming out of shadow, the amber liquid catching the hell light from the window. It looked like he was handing me a bottle of fire. I took it and drank.

"Come with me, and we'll talk to him," Pete said. "Please. I like living here. I don't want the board to revoke my lease."

"Not my problem." I shut my eyes as tight as I could and took a double-swig of the Johnny Walker.

When I opened my eyes again, I was on the toilet, pants around my ankles. It took me a few seconds to realize this, sitting in the pitch dark. Somehow I'd lost track of Pete and the time and my whisky bottle. The worms had eaten the footage. Scene deleted.

I wiped my ass and went to bed.

❦

I awoke in the wee hours, the wind still blowing Oklahoma off the map, windows rattling, the roof and walls vibrating like they'd all fly apart. I wasn't sure if it were a dream or not.

Take me to Oz you hellish zephyr son of a bitch!

❦

I went to the garage in the morning and worked on my golf cart. I wanted it to go faster, spend less time between holes. Play through at light speed. Rocket cart. I washed down a pain pill with coffee, opened the garage door and went outside. The wind had died away some but not much.

I noticed the cars right away. You don't see many cars in the neighborhood because everyone gets around in the golf carts, but there were a lot of cars in driveways and on the streets. People running around with suitcases.

My next door neighbor Naomi Zoller was making good time toward an SUV in her walker.

"What's the word, Naomi?" I called.

"My son's up from Denton to take me out of here," she said.

116

"Didn't you hear?"

"Hear what?"

"The fire went through Moss Point, burnt up fifty houses. It's coming this way. You gonna leave soon, I hope."

"Nope. No place to go." I didn't have a son from Denton or anyone from anyplace else either. All I had was a set of Ping irons and a tee time.

I went back into the garage and loaded the bag onto the cart. I put a fresh whisky bottle up front and some tees and a new box of balls. I had eighteen to play. I drove the car out of the garage, paused in my driveway. The sky was thick with smoke. I could smell it now. It reminded me of camping.

The commotion at the end of the street caught my attention, a cop car with lights blinking and an ambulance. Right in front of Pete's house. Two guys carrying a body out on a gurney, sheet pulled up over the face.

Oh … shit.

Suddenly Tony was next to me in the cart. Fat son of a bitch gasping for breath like he'd just run a mile. He had on a Sooners ball cap, pulled low down over his eyes. Mirrored sunglasses.

"Drive," he said.

"What the hell are you talking about?"

"I shot Pete. Jesus, oh God. I didn't mean—" He seemed like he was getting ready to cry. "We started arguing, and I tried to make him understand … he wouldn't fucking stop and listen to me. I've got to get out of here. Drive me over to Dotty's, and I'll call a cab."

"Get out of the cart."

"I'd drive myself, but the ambulance is blocking the road. Christ, I think I see a cop heading for my front door. Shit"

"I said get the fuck out."

He poked something into my ribs. "And I said drive."

I looked down. A nickel revolver with a short barrel.

I started driving, made the turn at the other end of the street toward the golf course. Every second the air grew darker with smoke.

"I said take me to Dotty's Diner," Tony said.

"They won't look for you on the golf course. Let's play a round."

"Are you crazy? Turn it around."

"Nine," I said. "Let's just play nine."

"Fucking turn it around!" He jabbed me again with the revolver.

I got the cart up to full speed, maybe thirty miles per hour after my adjustments. Maybe thirty-five. Then I slammed on the brakes. Tony pitched forward, almost flung out of the cart. He dropped the revolver, and it clattered at my feet. I leaned over and shoved him out of the cart.

He landed with a fat thud on the cart path, and I stomped the accelerator. I looked back, saw him running after me and sucking for breath.

I kept driving, reached the clubhouse in two minutes. The guy who operated the pro shop ran out and loaded a computer into a Jeep. I cast my glance past him and saw flames sweeping across the driving range.

I popped a pill, drowned it with a swig of whisky. "I have a tee time," I yelled. I picked up the revolver, stuck it in my waistband.

"Are you nuts, old man?" He got into the Jeep and sped off.

The wind shifted and the smoke came so thick I could hardly see the clubhouse thirty feet away. I turned the cart toward the first tee.

I took another swig of whiskey, teed up the ball. No time to jerk around. I hit it hard, and it flew down the middle of the fairway. Two hundred and fifty yards at least. A good start.

Tony erupted from the smoke, lumbered toward me. "We've got to get out of here. The fire."

I pulled the revolver, pointed it at his face, and he froze. "Get lost."

He left back the way he came, eyes wide with terror.

I played the hole then the next.

The fire crept along on all sides, wind constantly blowing and shifting, the smoke burning my eyes.

Then the worms struck.

I was near the eighteenth green, the fire barley twenty feet away, my eyes watering, snot pouring from my nose. I coughed. I looked down, saw the revolver tight in my fist. I looked back and saw Tony half in and half out of my cart. I ran to him, saw the bullet holes in his chest. He must have tried to take the cart, tried to flee the inferno like I should've been doing.

I bent to grab his shoulders and haul him out of the cart when I caught site of my scorecard. I blinked, looked again, did the math to be sure. I was three under par. I checked the green, squinted through the smoke. My ball was maybe nine or ten feet from the hole. If I sank the putt, I'd hold the course record for men over sixty-five. I grabbed my putter, but the shin-high flames ate up the fairway between me and the green.

I jumped into the cart and powered through the fire, parked the cart right on the green. I took another swig of whisky and climbed out, holding my putter. Wind blew ash and dust around me. Fire circled the green.

I stood over the putt, tried to imagine how I'd gotten here, what I must've done to negotiate the water on seven, how I could have possibly birdied the big par five. I'd never know. The worms had taken it all.

The green was in flames now, so much smoke between me and the hole. I was putting on faith. I struck the ball, followed through. My pant legs burned.

I couldn't see the hole anymore. But I heard it, the plonk of the ball finding the bottom of the cup.

God had told Noah he'd never destroy the world by water again. Next time it would be fire. Say what you will, but the Old Man tells the truth.

Burn, baby, burn.

Afterword

Duane's timing was perfect. When he asked me for a Damn Near Dead *story, I was just wrapping up my novel* Shotgun Opera. *In* Shotgun, *the protagonist Mike Foley is also a senior citizen, a gunman who's been hiding out for forty years and has to come out of retirement. So I was already in the right frame of mind to think about a hero with some miles on him.*

But I wanted to do something slightly different for "Duffers..." I didn't want him to be a detective or a hit man or a former FBI agent or whatever. Those guys would probably make for interesting stories, but I wanted to talk about the regular guy who'd reached that age when he was supposed to be having a well-earned rest, but instead, fate throws him a curve ball. Life itself can be noir enough without thugs on our asses. —V.G.

DAPHNE MCANDREWS AND THE SMACK-HEAD JUNKIES

STUART MACBRIDE

Stuart MacBride (born 1969) has scrubbed toilets offshore, project managed multimillion pound IT projects, run his own graphic design company, failed the interview to become a funeral director, dressed up as a woman for money, and asked people: "Do you want fries with that?" For a bit of a change he now writes grisly crime novels set in Aberdeen—oil capital of Europe. His first novel, Cold Granite, *was nominated for Best First Novel by the International Thriller Writers; his second,* Dying Light, *will appear in May from Harper Collins (UK) and August from St. Martin's Press (US).*

DAPHNE MCANDREWS AND THE SMACK-HEAD JUNKIES

by Stuart MacBride

Half past eight on a cold autumn evening and Sergeant Dumfries had his feet up on the reception desk, a mug of tea in one hand, a copy of the Oldcastle Advertiser in the other. Reading about the hunt for little Lucy Milne. The lobby door clattered open, letting in a howling gale, setting the posters flapping on the notice board. He sat upright with a sigh, put the newspaper away and plastered a professional smile on his face. An old lady with a walking stick was wrestling a tartan shopping trolley in through the heavy wooden doors. She had a little Westie terrier on the end of an extendible leash, barking happily as bright-orange leaves tumbled in around the old woman's ankles, twirling about the police station lobby like demented highland dancers.

"Can I help you with that, madam?"

She flashed him a smile. "No, no we'll be fine." There was something familiar about her, but Dumfries couldn't put his finger on it. Five foot two, overweight, grey-brown overcoat, tartan headscarf, granny boots, face like a wrinkled cushion… With one last tug she got the trolley inside, letting the lobby door slam shut. For a moment the swirling leaves hung in the air, before slowly drifting to the linoleum floor.

She trundled her shopping trolley up to the reception desk and peeled off her headscarf, revealing a solid mass of grey curls, hairsprayed within an inch of their life. "Dear, oh dear," she said, giving a little shiver. "What a dreadful evening! I was saying to Agnes this morning – we always have tea in the Castlehill Snook: they do a lovely fruit scone – and I was saying how the weather seems so much worse this year. I remember when—"

Dumfries stifled a groan as she wittered on – just his luck to get stuck with an old biddy in for a bit of a chat. "So," he said, making sure his fixed smile hadn't slipped, "What can I do for you madam?"

She stopped talking and studied at him for a moment. "Norman, isn't it? Norman Dumfries?"

"Er…" He shifted uncomfortably in his chair. "Yes?"

"Who would have known you'd turn out so tall! You were such a wee lad at Kingsmeath primary – see I told you eating your greens would do you the world of good."

And that's when it clicked. "Mrs. McAndrews, thought I recognized you!" This time Sergeant Dumfries's smile was genuine. "How you been?"

"Not too good Norman," she said, leaning forward and dropping her voice to a conspiratorial whisper, "there's a naked man in my shed, and I think he's dead."

❦

While most school dinner ladies were waxing lyrical about the exotic delights of custard crèmes and garibaldi biscuits, Daphne McAndrews had remained steadfast: as far as she was concerned it was homemade shortbread or nothing. Humming happily she arranged some on the tray, next to a fresh pot of tea and six mugs, and carried it out the back door.

The police had set up a pair of huge spotlights, training them on the shed at the bottom of the garden, making the wasp-chewed wood glow. The rest of the garden was shrouded in darkness, the trees groaning and creaking in the buffeting wind. Daphne tottered carefully down the path, trying to keep the tea things from blowing away.

The shed door was propped open and half a dozen men dressed in those white plastic over-suit things they wore on telly, were poking about inside. It was a big shed, Bill's pride and joy, but she'd barely touched it since he'd gone, just dusted from time to time. It was comforting to know that there was something of him in here: in a grey urn at the back, next to the little wooden fire engine he was working on before he died.

"Is everyone ready for a nice cup of tea?" she asked, stepping over the threshold and closing the door behind her, shutting out the wind.

Someone span round and stared at her. "You shouldn't be in here!"

"Oh, wheesht. My Bill used to say that all the time, but a bit of shortbread always made him change his tune."

"No, you don't understand, this is a crime scene." He flapped his hands in the direction of the naked young man, sprawled against the far wall, under the shelf with Bill's urn on it, wearing nothing but a pair of argyle socks.

"It's not a crime scene, it's Bill's shed. Now stop being silly: time for tea." She started pouring. "Beside, it's not like I haven't seen a naked man before. And as a dinner lady, you get used to being around death. One lump or two?"

"Err…" He looked around at his companions, but no one came to his rescue. Policemen were just like little boys: you had to be firm, stand your ground, and not let them get away with anything. Cheeky monkeys. He cleared his throat and stared at his shoes for a moment, before saying, "Two please."

The shortbread was going down a treat –she wasn't a leading light of the Women's Rural Institute for nothing – when the shed door banged open again. A small pause and then someone roared, "What the hell's going on in here?" It was a man with a moustache and a thunderous expression. "Sergeant, this is supposed to be a crime scene, not a bloody tea party!" The policeman with two sugars blushed and apologized, the words coming out in a shower of crumbs. The newcomer's head looked like it was about to explode. Shouting and swearing he dragged the policemen out into the back garden and shouted at them some more. Going on about trace evidence and shortbread crumbs and disciplinary hearings… Then he noticed Daphne was still in the shed, sipping her tea.

"YOU!" he said, flinging a finger in her direction, "Get back in that bloody house!"

✠

A nice WPC was sent in to take her statement. "Don't worry about DI Whyte," she said, as Daphne opened a tin of Pedigree Chum Senior, "he's going through a bit of a divorce at the minute."

Daphne gave a haughty sniff and scraped a solid tube of chicken and heart into a clean dish. "If my Bill was alive today…" But he wasn't, so there was no point even thinking about it. She put the dish down on the floor, and whistled. "Come on darling, din-dins!" An old, yellow-white Westie dog clattered into the kitchen, little stumpy tail going at twenty to the dozen. He had Mr. Bunny, his favorite, tatty old squeaky toy, clamped in his jaws.

"Oh, he's so *sweet*!" The WPC beamed. "What's his name?"

Daphne reached down and ruffled the fur between her boy's ears. "This is Little Douglas. Bill named him after my father, on account of the family resemblance. He's going to be fifteen in February. Aren't you Wee Doug, aren't you? Yes you are! Yes you are!" He gave a cheerful bark and stuck his nose in the dog food.

"Can you tell me when you found the dead man in your shed Mrs. McAndrews?"

"Hmm? Oh, it was…" Daphne frowned in concentration. "Coronation Street. That blonde lassie was having an affair with the Asian chap and I was thinking I could really do with a nice cup of tea. So I waited for the next advert break and went through to make one. Only before I turned on the light I saw this naked woman running climbing over the back fence. And I thought—"

"Wait, you saw a naked woman? Not a naked man?"

"Oh yes, when you work in a school canteen you get to know the difference. Anyway she was clambering over the fence, and I got Wee Doug and we went out and he was very brave, weren't you? Mummy's little soldier. He's very protective you know. Anyway, I saw the shed door was open and I went to close it and there he was. So I got on my overcoat and went to the police station and reported it."

"Why didn't you just dial 999?"

Daphne shook her head sadly. Young people these days. "My dear, reporting a dead body isn't like ordering a pizza. Some things you just have to do in person."

¢f

The Castlehill Snook was nearly empty at half past ten on a Tuesday morning – just a middle-aged couple in the corner, bickering over a map – so Daphne and her best friend Agnes McWhirter had no trouble getting their usual table by the window overlooking the Castle car park. A large coach from Germany was disgorging tourists in front of the pay and display machine, all of them clutching little Scottish flags and plastic bags from the Woollen Mill. The sky was the color of warm slate, wind making the tourist's cagoules whip and snap as they tried to get round the Old Castle ruins before the rain came on.

Daphne unclipped Wee Doug's lead and let him snuffle about the tiled floor; by the time the waitress arrived with the cake trolley, he was curled up beneath a chair. Snoring.

Agnes ordered her usual fruit scone, but Daphne shocked everyone, even herself, by asking for a slice of Battenberg instead. "Are you feelin' OK?" asked Agnes, staring aghast at the slice of yellow and pink sponge. Taking a deep breath Daphne told her about the dead body in her shed, the naked woman clambering over the back fence, and what that nice Sergeant Norman Dumfries had said when she'd called in past the station first thing this morning.

"Fancy that!" said Agnes, pouring the tea. "Naked drug addicts in your shed!"

"I know, I'm that mortified." Daphne shuddered, took a bite of her Battenberg and chewed suspiciously. It wasn't like her to entertain baked goods involving marzipan. She fed the rest to Wee Doug.

"They were probably having kinky, drugged-up sex. That's what these people do you know, get high and indulge in filthy sex games: it was in the Sunday Post. Mr. McAndrews would *not* have liked that!"

Daphne nodded, her husband had been as conservative in the

bedroom as she was in the biscuit department. He would never have asked her for a fig roll when there was perfectly respectable shortbread available.

"Of course, they're all at it." Agnes tapped on the window. On the other side of the castle car park a ragged figure was trying to sell copies of 'the Big Issue' magazine to the scurrying German tourists. "Drug addicts the lot of them. 'Junkies' – they're everywhere these days, it was in the Sunday Post. I tell you, Oldcastle's getting more like that 'Los Angeles' every day. Next thing you know there'll be drive by shootings and prostitutes on every street corner!" She nodded sagely and the first drops of rain speckled the teashop window, getting heavier and heavier, sending the tourists scurrying back to their bus. The scruffy figure watched them in silent resignation then tromped away into the downpour.

⚡

The shed was filthy by the time the police were finished with it, covered in fingerprint powder, nothing put back in the right place. Dressed in her 'Sheep of Scotland' pinny and yellow rubber gloves Daphne scrubbed and polished and tidied until it was all good as new. She stood back and examined her handiwork with grim satisfaction – there was a lot to be said for a clean shed. She frowned. Bill's urn didn't look right.

It was a medium urn, because her husband had been a medium man. His remains would have looked short-changed in a large urn, and buying a small one would have meant leaving bits of him at the crematorium. And you never knew which bits they'd be, would you? The last thing she wanted was to get up to heaven and find Bill was missing a leg, or a hand. Or his gentleman bits. He wouldn't like that. She picked the urn off the shelf and squirted it with furniture polish, buffing it up with a yellow duster until it… the lid was loose. With trembling hands she unscrewed it all the way.

⚡

Daphne had never felt more like a drink in her life. Not even when Bill died. Sitting at the kitchen table she poured herself a stiff sweet sherry, threw it back and poured another one. "Oh Bill!" His urn sat on the tabletop in front of her. A big scoop of his ashes were missing. Someone had stolen bits of her husband… Wee Doug padded back and forth under the table, his claws clickity-clacking on the linoleum,

128

whimpering. He knew his mummy was upset.

Biting her bottom lip Daphne screwed the top back on the bottle. Wallowing in self-pity wasn't going to do Bill any good. If she wanted justice, she was going to have to get off her backside and do something about it. It was what Bill would have wanted.

❦

Rain clattered against the cobbled street, shining like beads of amber in the yellow streetlight as Daphne trudged along Shand Street, heading back up Castle Hill to the teashop, pulling her tartan shopping trolley behind her. Wee Doug's nose poked out through a tiny opening in the top, sniffing the cold night air for a moment, before sensibly ducking back down again, out of the rain. The teashop would be closed, just like all the other shops she passed on her way up the hill, their windows glowing, but lifeless. Like the empty streets. "That's because everyone with an ounce of sense is indoors!" she told herself, stopping for a moment to rest. It was hard going and her hip was beginning to complain. Dampness seeped in through the seams of her old raincoat, her left boot squished as she walked, and her glasses were all fogged up. Sighing she leant on her walking stick and thought about turning round and going— A noise.

She froze, struggling to locate the sound over the rain drumming off her plastic headscarf. Nothing. She turned up her hearing aid, but it didn't make any difference. Probably just her imagination playing tricks... And then she heard it again, someone singing and swearing softly to themselves.

Slowly Daphne crept up the road, pulling the trolley with her, scanning the empty shop doorways on either side. A wee cobbled close disappeared off between the knitwear place and the kilt shop, the little alleyway roofed off by a hairdressers on the first floor. It stretched away into the darkness, a link between the towering sandstone buildings on Shand Street and the dour brick of Mercantile Road. Gloomy and forbidding. That's where the noise was coming from.

Plucking up all her courage, Daphne stepped into the alley. It was dark in here, the streetlights on Shand Street barely making a dent in the shadows, but she could just make out a figure, huddled in a doorway, a grubby pink blanket pulled round his shoulders, sitting on a pile of flattened cardboard boxes. The flare of a match and she saw his face as he lit a scrawny, hand-rolled cigarette – bearded, dirty. Not the man who'd been trying to sell the 'Big Issue', but as Agnes said, they were all drug addicts. He was probably doing drugs right now, chasing the rabbit, or whatever it was called. Straightening her shoulders she marched right up and said, "Excuse me?"

The man didn't answer, just kept on swearing away so she poked him with her walking stick.

"I said, excuse me."

He squealed and scurried backwards into the wall, jittering and twitching, watching her suspiciously. "What you want?" His eyes glittered in the dim light like a snake.

"I'm looking for a woman."

The man leered. "You wanna them big fat lesbians?" She poked him with her stick again. Hard. "Ow! Cut it out!"

"This particular woman was in my shed last night, with a young man. She took someone… something of mine and I want it back!"

There was a silence as the man stared at Daphne, probably undressing her with his eyes, these drug addicts were all alike. Sex mad. "So…." he said leaving his doorway, the filthy pink blanket still wrapped around his shoulders, smelling of urine and Marmite. "You gonnae make it worth my while like?"

Daphne blushed, sex mad – she knew it. Quickly she rummaged in the damp pockets of her raincoat and came out with a half-empty bag of mint imperials. "Would you like a sweetie?"

He reached out and snatched the bag. "Got any money?"

"Manners!" Daphne bristled. "What would your mother say if she—" He shoved her aside and she slipped, clattering down onto the cold, wet cobbles, grunting in pain. Oh God – what if she'd broken her hip?

"Where's your purse?" He loomed over her, digging through the pockets of her raincoat, sniffing anything he found, before hurling it away into the rain-drenched night. Handkerchief, lipsalve, hairgrips, the tatty old tennis ball Wee Doug liked to chase in King's Park. Then her house keys. Grinning he held them up to the light. "Brilliant." He stuffed them in his pocket. "Now where's your bloody purse?"

Daphne raised a shaking hand and pointed at the tartan shopping trolley. The junkie rubbed his hands and unzipped the top compartment. A grumpy growl rumbled out and the filthy smile fell from his face: "What the hell's this?" Swearing he kicked the trolley's wheels out from under it, sending it flying, spilling Wee Doug out into the gutter. Ignoring the Westie's indignant barks, he rummaged inside the trolley. Mr. Bunny was hurled out into the night, closely followed by a plastic bag full of rolled up plastic bags and a spiral bound notebook covered in shopping lists. Wee Doug scurried off after his squeaky toy as the man grunted, "Ya beauty…" and settled back on his haunches to rifle through her handbag.

Gritting her false teeth, Daphne pulled herself to her knees, laddering her support stockings on the rough alley floor as she struggled upright, trembling with rage. Her walking stick was lying in the gutter; she grabbed it. "Did your parents never teach you any MANNERS?" It was a good sturdy walking stick, a shaft of tempered oak and a thick handle carved from a Stag's antler. It made a satisfyingly wet thunking sound as she battered it off the man's head.

He yowled and she hit him a second time. Harder. He tried to say something, but she swung the handle into his face – something went crack and teeth flew, so she did it again: his cheekbone cracked. And again: his left eye spurted blood. And again: he got his hands up in time to shield his face and she heard finger bones snap. Again, and again and again...

Daphne lent back against the wall, puffing and panting, one hand clutching her aching chest. Wondering if she was about to have a heart attack. The man lay on his side, curled into the foetal position, not moving. Wee Doug sniffed the back of the drug addict's head then cocked his leg and peed on it. When he was all done he picked up Mr. Bunny, trotted over and sat in front of Daphne, little tail wagging away sixteen to the dozen, happy as could be.

It took her while to calm down, but eventually the pain in her chest subsided and her breathing returned to normal. She wasn't going to join Bill just yet.

She jabbed the horrible man with her stick, forcing him over onto his back. His face was all swollen and puffy, misshapen, covered with blood, a flap of skin hanging loose on his forehead. Leaking out into the cobbles. He gave a little cough and a small plume of red sparkled in the dim light. She prodded him in the chest and he groaned. "I asked you a question, young man: who was the naked woman?"

He said something quite rude and Daphne battered the head of her walking stick off his knee. It wasn't quite a scream, wasn't quite a moan, but it sounded painful. "Who was she?"

He was crying now, tears and snot mixing with the blood and dirt. "I don't... I don't know..."

"You're lying." She hit him again, right on the ankle joint.

"Oh God no! Please! I don't know!" Sobbing, rocking back and forth on the ground, covering his head with his arms. "Please..."

Daphne scowled and counted to ten. So much for plan A. "If you don't know: who does?"

"I don't... Aaaaaagh!" It was the elbow this time "Please! I don't..." Ankle again. "Aaaaaaagh! Colin! Colin'll know! He sells stuff. He'll know!"

She smiled. "And just how do I find this 'Colin'?"

Daphne had never been in a public bar on her own before – it wasn't the sort of thing a respectable lady did – but she owed it to Bill. Screwing up her courage she marched through the doors of the 'Monk and Casket', a seedy looking place at the bottom of Jamesmuir Road. It was mock Tudor on the outside, but inside it was all flashing gambling machines, vinyl upholstery and sticky floors. It wasn't a busy pub, just a handful of men and women, looking somewhat the worse for drink at half eleven on a Wednesday night.

Stiffening her courage she hobbled up to the bar, taking her shopping trolley with her, and ordered a port and lemon. And a medicinal brandy – her hip was still sore and she was soaked through after walking all the way here from Castle View.

The bartender was a big hairy man with earrings and a missing front tooth. He leant forward and whispered, "We've actually called last orders, so I can't legally serve you," then slid her drinks across the bar. "If you'd like to make a donation of two pound fifty to the lifeboat fund: that would be OK by me." Wink, wink. Blushing, Daphne thanked him and slid the money into the orange plastic lifeboat sitting on the bar.

"I'm looking for a man." She said.

The barman smiled. "Sorry, Darling, I'm married."

"No, a man called 'Colin'. Do you know him? Someone told me he'd be here."

Silence from the hairy barman, and then, "Are you sure you're looking for Colin? Colin McKeever? Crazy Colin?"

Daphne nodded, looking around the bar, trying to see if anyone looked like a 'Crazy Colin'. It wasn't a big place: just a handful of tables, some framed photos of the local football team, the pinging, chattering fruit machines, and a single door leading off the room marked *Toilets, Telephone And Function Suite*. The customers were as seedy as the pub: a pair of over-made-up women cackling away in the corner with their alcopops; a fat man with a beard hunched over a pint of stout; two suspicious looking types in black leather… "Is he the one in the hat?" She pointed at an unusual, weasely-looking man with long black hair and a baseball cap, sitting on his own.

"No, that's Weird Justin. Crazy Colin's upstairs with Stacy. Now, why don't you finish up your drink and I'll call you a taxi, OK? A nice old lady like you doesn't want to have anything to do with the likes of Colin McKeever."

A small flutter of excitement – he was upstairs with a woman! Maybe it was the one from the shed? "Of course, of course." She downed her brandy in a single gulp, then did the same with the port and lemon. "I'll just nip off to the loo…" Grabbing the shopping trolley's handle she pushed through the door and into a stinky corridor. A door on either side said *Gents* and *Ladies*, but right at the far end was a set of stairs with a small plaque hanging over it *To Function Suite*. Daphne took a deep breath, and started hauling the shopping trolley up the stairs.

One floor up and the sticky linoleum gave way to sticky carpet, with just enough room at the top of the stairs for Daphne to catch her breath. Unrecognizable 'music' thumped through from the other side of a battered wooden door. Why did no one know what a tune was anymore? When this was all over, she was going to go home, put on some Barry Manilow and get herself a nice cup of tea.

She turned her hearing aid down to low and opened the door to the function suite. It was about the same size as the bar downstairs, but more neglected. Ancient chairs lined the walls, fold-away tables piled in one corner, a mirror ball hanging from the ceiling, glittering over the small wooden dance floor in the middle. A man and woman rocked slowly back and forth, shambling round to the 'music'. She had her arms wrapped around his shoulders, he had his hands on her buttocks. Kneading away like he was making bread.

The current song bludgeoned its way to a halt and then another one, equally dreadful, started. There was one of those 'Boom-Box' things sitting at the side of the dance floor, so Daphne marched straight over and turned the horrible machine off. Blessed silence. The man stopped rearranging his girlfriend's underwear and scowled. He wasn't the most attractive of men – thin and short, with a scabby little beard thing, spiky hair and glasses. But he looked like a Colin. "What the hell did you do that for?" He let go of his partner, but she continued to dance, shuffling round and round in the absence of music, on her own.

Daphne squared her shoulders. "I want my Bill!"

"I've not sold you anything."

"Don't you play games with me, young man. Your hussy broke into my shed and she stole my Bill! I want him back."

Crazy Colin looked back over his shoulder at the dancing woman. "You saying Stacy's kidnapped someone?" He laughed as Stacy tripped over her own feet and tumbled to the floor. She made an abortive attempt to get back up then gave up, sprawled on her back in the middle of the dance floor, like a dead starfish. "You've got to be kidding – she couldn't tie her shoelaces unsupervised. You got the wrong girl, Grandma."

"I said I want him back!"

"Nothing to do with me, Grandma. You got a problem with Stacy you take it up with her…" He grinned. "After I've finished like." He started to take off his shirt. "You wanna watch? No charge."

Oh… my… God… he was getting undressed! She didn't want to have to see some strange man's private parts! She hadn't even liked looking at her husbands. "I don't want any trouble; I just want my Bill back."

"Bill, Bill, Bill, Bill, Bill," He turned his back on her, unfastening his belt.

Daphne hurried back to her shopping trolley and unzipped the top, lifting out Wee Doug. He yawned and looked around the room, then sat down and had a bit of a scratch. Daphne pulled herself up to her full five foot two inches and pointed an imperious finger at Crazy Colin as he unbuttoned his fly. "Go on, Wee Doug, KILL!"

Wee Doug looked up at her, then at the end of her finger. Daphne tried again. "Kill!" Still nothing. She grabbed Mr. Bunny from the shopping trolley and hurled it at the undressing man. The toy rabbit landed right in the crotch of Colin's trousers as he tried to get them down over his shoes. Wee Doug growled, his little feet scrabbling on the wooden floor, not going anywhere fast until suddenly his claws got purchase and he was away, tearing across the dance floor like a dog half his age. Barking.

The man span round at the noise, eyes wide. He grabbed the waistband of his trousers and hauled them up, which was a mistake as Mr Bunny was still trapped in there – his two ragged ears sticking out of the man's fly at groin level. With a final happy bark Wee Doug leapt and clamped his jaws onto Crazy Colin's crotch. There was a high pitched scream.

Daphne took a firm grip of her walking stick and went to shut him up.

❦

Shaking, Daphne washed the blood off her hands and face with cold water and bitter-smelling hand soap in the ladies' lavatory. Wee Doug was sitting up in the shopping trolley happily – the reclaimed Mr Bunny looking none the worst for his adventure in a strange man's trousers – watching as she stuck the head of her walking stick under the tap, the water turning pink as Crazy Colin McKeever's blood slowly rinsed away.

"No one knows…" She told herself. "No one knows…" Not even the girl – she was comatose the whole time. Couldn't have seen anything. Couldn't have— A knock on the toilet door and she almost shrieked.

"Hello?" It was the bartender, sounding concerned. "Are you in there?"

Oh God, he's found the body! "I… I…"

"You OK? You've been in here for ages."

"I… I'm fine." She looked at herself in the mirror. He doesn't know. No one knows. "Just a jippy tummy."

"That's your taxi."

She nodded at her reflection and plastered on a smile, then opened the bathroom door, taking Wee Doug and the tartan shopping trolley with her. "Thank you," She said, trying to keep the tremble out of her voice as he helped her out through the front door and into the cab.

"You take care now." He stood in the street, waving as they drove away.

𝆑

It was a rumpled Daphne McAndrews who slouched into the Castlehill Snook at quarter to eleven the next day. She'd slept badly, even with a quarter bottle of sweet sherry inside her, knowing that they'd put her in prison for the rest of her natural life. The police would find Colin McKeever's body and do all that scientific stuff you saw on the telly. And they'd know it was her. Provided the nasty man who'd tried to steal her purse in the alley hadn't already reported her for thrashing him. She couldn't bring herself to use the walking stick today, not now it was a murder weapon, and her hip ached.

Daphne collapsed into the chair opposite Agnes and looked sadly out the window at the Castle car park. Determined not to cry.

"You feelin' OK Daphne?"

She just shrugged and ordered a fruit scone and a big mug of coffee. When the waitress was gone, Agnes leaned forward and asked, in her best stage whisper, "Did you hear about the murder?" Daphne blanched, but Agnes didn't seem to notice, "Beaten to death," she said, "a drug-dealer – in a pub! Can you believe it?"

Daphne bit her lip and stared at the liver spots on the back of her hands. "Did… Do they know who did it?"

"Probably one of them gangland execution things. If I've said it once, I've said it a thousand times: Oldcastle's getting more like Los Angeles every day. I tell you…" She launched in to a long story about someone her Gerald used to go to school with, but Daphne wasn't listening. She was wondering when the police were going to come for her.

𝆑

The patrol car pulled up outside the house at half past seven. At least they hadn't put the flashing lights and sirens on. She'd have died of embarrassment if the neighbours had seen that. She'd spent the day cleaning the place until it sparkled: no one was going to say she went off to prison and left a dirty house behind. With a sigh Daphne climbed out of Bill's favorite chair and answered the front door. It was Sergeant Norman Dumfries, the little boy who wouldn't eat his greens. She ushered him through to the kitchen and put the kettle on. Just because he was here to arrest her, there was no need to forget her manners.

"Tea?" she asked as he shifted uncomfortably from foot to foot.

"Err... Yes, that would be lovely." Adding, "Thank you." as an afterthought.

She made two cups and put them on the kitchen table, along with a plate of shortbread, telling Sergeant Dumfries to help himself. "Err..." he said, looking sideways at Bill's urn, still sitting on the tabletop from last night. "I'm afraid I've got something very awkward to tell you—"

Daphne nodded. There was no need to make it hard on the boy, he was doing his best. "I know."

He blushed. "I'm so sorry, Mrs. McAndrews."

"You're only doing your job, Norman."

"I know, but..." he sighed and reached into his police jacket pocket. This was it, he was going to handcuff her. The neighbors would have a field day.

"It's all right," trying to sound calm, "I won't put up a fight."

He looked puzzled for a moment, before bringing out what looked like a little plastic freezer bag. It was see-through, and full of grey powder. "We, em... the man you found in your shed had..." he stopped and tried again. "We did a post mortem on him yesterday. He died because he'd injected himself with... Err..." He held up the bag. "We had to take a sample to make sure. I'm sorry Mrs. McAndrews." Gently he picked Bill's urn off the table and tipped the contents of the plastic bag inside.

"Oh God."

"I'm sorry Mrs. McAndrews. We think they were already under the influence of drugs when they broke into your shed to fool around. They discovered Mr. McAndrews remains and... Well, the man had residue in his nasal passages and his lungs, so it looks like they tried snorting the... ah... deceased. When that didn't work the man tried injecting. And then he died." It was silent in the kitchen, except for the sound of Wee Doug snoring. "I'm sorry Mrs. McAndrews."

She grabbed Bill's urn and peered inside. It was nearly full. "Did they both...? You know?" Sergeant Dumfries nodded and Daphne frowned. She wasn't sure she liked the thought of Bill being inside another woman, and Bill would certainly not have been happy about being inside a naked man.

"Anyway," Sergeant Dumfries stood, "I have to get back to the station." He looked left and right, as if he was making sure they were alone. "Just between you and me," he said in a conspiratorial whisper, "we've got a drugs war on our hands! One bloke got worked over right outside the kilt shop last night – said it was a gang with baseball bats – and the next thing you know some drug dealer gets battered to death! Mind you, at least we've got a witness to that one."

Daphne covered her mouth with a trembling hand, the girl: she was unconscious! She couldn't have seen anything – it wasn't fair!

Norman helped himself to a piece of shortbread. "We found this doped-up woman at the scene," he said, in a little spray of crumbs, "who swears blind some huge hairy bloke with a Rottweiler, kicked the door down then bashed the victim's skull in with a pickaxe handle." He shook his head in amazement as Daphne went pale as a haddock. "I know," he said as she spluttered. "Miami Vice comes to Oldcastle, how bizarre is that?" Sigh. "Anyway, better make sure you keep your doors and windows locked tight. OK?"

When he was gone, Daphne sat at the kitchen table, trembling. "Drug War". She let out a small giggle. The giggle became a snigger, then a laugh, and ended in hysterics. She'd gotten away with it. Wiping her eyes she pulled Bill's urn over and peered inside. There was only about a teaspoon missing. What would that be – an ear, a finger, his gentleman's bits? He'd miss them, even if she wouldn't...

With a smile she ripped the edge off a couple of teabag and poured the powdered leaves in. At his age he'd never know the difference.

Afterword

I have to admit that I've never really read a 'cosy' before, but I kind of fancied writing one. A nice little story about an old lady, and her wee dog, who solves a crime. And beats someone to death. Something with drugs and violence in it. Maybe a bit of sex too. 'Cosy Noir' – that's what I wanted to do.

And so Daphne McAndrews was born. I like her: she's got that vicious streak that comes with being married to the same person for thirty years. And she does make some damn fine shortbread. – S.MacB.

Daphne McAndrews's Homemade Shortbread

> *1lb butter*
> *1lb white flour (plain)*
> *8oz Semola (fine ground semolina)**
> *8oz caster sugar*
> *Salt*

1. Cream the butter and sugar together in a bowl. Add the flour, Semola and a pinch of salt and mix until it looks like breadcrumbs.

2. Tip it out onto a clean work surface and kneed into a ball – shouldn't take too long or it'll go tough and nasty – then roll into a thick sausage-shape. Wrap your dough in clingfilm and chill it while the oven heats to 190.C

3. Slice the sausage into disks about a half inch thick and bake for 15 to 25 minutes on a lightly buttered, non-stick sheet until they're a nice and pale gold.

4. Take them out of the oven and dust them with more castor sugar, leave them to cool for 10 minutes, then transfer to a wire rack.

* If you can't get it, rice flour will do, but you have to hang your head in shame.

THE LAST BACHELOR OF NORTH MIAMI

JASON STARR

Jason Starr (born 1966) is the author of Cold Caller, Nothing Personal, Fake I.D., Hard Feelings, *the Barry Award-winning* Tough Luck *and the Anthony Award-winning* Twisted City. *His next novel,* Lights Out, *is due from St. Martin's in September 2006. He lives with his wife and daughter in Manhattan. It is widely agreed that Jason has the best hair in all of mystery fiction.*

f

THE LAST BACHELOR OF NORTH MIAMI

by Jason Starr

I was in the kitchen, looking into the dining room through the pass through at Tessie, who was sitting at the dining room, watching a soap opera—she called it "her show"—on the little black-and-white set. I was thinking how, even with her teeth in, she looked like hell and how I couldn't stand the sight of her anymore.

"I'm going to the club," I said.

She was staring at the set and didn't hear a word I said. How many times did I have to turn up her goddamn hearing aid?

"I'm going to the club!" I shouted.

Her head started to turn, like she thought she heard something, maybe a little birdie tweeting outside, but she kept staring at the TV.

I had to limp into the living room with my bad hip and my bad leg and lean right in front of her and say, "I'm going to the club," and she said, "What?"

"The club," I said. "I'm going to the club."

"Again?" she said.

"What again?" I said. "It's morning. I didn't go yet today."

"So? You went yesterday."

"What, I can't go two days in a row?"

"Stop yelling."

"I have to yell. I talk, you can't hear a goddamn word I say!"

"You want to go to the club, go to the club."

"I am going. I wasn't asking you, I was telling you!"

I started toward the door then stopped, said, "Aw, Christ," realizing I'd forgotten my Marlin's cap. It was supposed to be a scorcher today and I couldn't go outside without it. So I had to go all the way across the condo into the bedroom to get it. By the time I got the cap and made it back to the front door I was exhausted and felt like I needed a rest. But like I hell I would. I just wanted to get out of there as fast as possible.

⁂

I wasn't going far anyway. I just had to get to the elevator in the middle of the condo, take it down one level, and then go about twenty more yards to Pearl's apartment. It took me about ten minutes to get there.

I rang the bell, knowing it would take her awhile to get to the door. She'd had two hip replacements and needed a walker. She also had stomach cancer that kept coming back and a lot of other crap wrong with her. Didn't we all? I had so many pills I was supposed to take I didn't know what the hell I was treating anymore. And the doctors down here, they didn't care if we lived or died. They just gave out pills and collected money. The weren't doctors; they were drug dealers.

Sometimes Pearl had a home attendant come over, but I knew she didn't have one today, Wednesday. Or was today Thursday? I had no idea and you know what, my dear Scarlett? I didn't give a damn.

Finally, Pearl opened the door.

"How's it going, baby?" I said and laid a big one on her.

I didn't know what it was about women—why some did it for me and some didn't. If you saw Pearl walking down the street you might think she was no different than every other leathery, wrinkly old bag in North Miami Beach. Maybe you'd think she didn't look much different from Tessie. They both had they white hair up in a bun and they both had thick glasses and they were both fat. But to me Pearl was the hottest dish in Florida. I'd turned ninety-six last year, but when I was around Pearl, I swear to God, I felt seventy-five. She wasn't a spring chicken herself—she'd turned ninety-one last year—but she just had it, whatever the hell "it" was. Sure, part of it was fantasy; I knew that. She had pictures around her condo, of her from the '50s and she was a knockout back then, let me tell you. Tessie was good-looking in her day too, but Pearl had pin-up girl looks. She had the acid-blonde hair and the pointy brassiere and those great hips. What the hell happened to hips anyway? Now you see the young girls at the Broward Mall or wherever and they're straight as a board, no curves anywhere. It had to be all the exercises they did and those goddamn diets.

But, yeah, Pearl used to be the real thing all right. She reminded me of the broads I used to know back in the day, when I had my pad on West Ninety-sixth in Manhattan. I was a ladies' man back then, what they used to call a bachelor before bachelor meant gay. I just didn't want to get tied down, that was all; I liked my freedom, I liked being on my own. I knew a lot of girls back then, fast girls, and I had me a time all right. I never had kids and I didn't get married for the first time till I was fifty-two, and when Brenda died I swore I wouldn't get married again. And I kept my word for a long time too. When I moved down to the Florida, back in the '80s I was in heaven. I was a single, good-looking widower around dozens of horny widows. Was I thinking about marriage? Like hell I was. I could still get it up back then too. Yeah, sometimes I'd go through three, four broads a week—picked them up and put them down like bowling pins. Then, in the early '90s, my medical problems kicked in. I had the bypasses, the cancers removed, and I felt like I needed some companionship. Tessie was always nice to me and took care of me and I knew she wanted to get hitched so I figured, What the hell? Little did I know that less than a year into it I'd already start to feel tied down and want out. And now it had been nine years. Nine, but it felt like ninety.

At the door, Pearl was kissing me back and I pulled her close to me, feeling her sagging breasts up against my chest, trying to imagine what they would've felt like when they were big and pointy back in the day. Then she pulled away when I tried to slip my tongue into her mouth.

"I don't have my teeth in," she said.

"Who cares?" I said and tried again.

But she pulled back and said, "Oh, stop it, Jack," and went into the kitchen.

Following her I said, "Let's go to bed, baby."

I wasn't looking to have a roll with her. Ten, fifteen years ago, I would've for sure, but I couldn't remember the last time I'd had a hard-on. Maybe it was five, six years ago in the middle of the night when I was in bed with Tessie–lot of good that did me. I used to use all the devices—the pumps and whatever—and Viagra, but nowadays nothing helped. Besides, the way my heart was, the doctors told me that sex could kill me. But I still liked getting naked with Pearl, touching her all over, even spending a little time below the belt, if you get my meaning. Hell, it was better than nothing, right?

"I can't do this anymore, Jack," Pearl said.

Jesus Christ, why did women have to be so temperamental? If this were 1950, I would've slapped some sense into her. But you weren't allowed to do that nowadays, thanks to all that women's lib crap. I really felt sorry for young guys today, I really did—having to let their women dish it out and having to just stand there and take it.

"What the hell can't you do?"

I was trying to hold back my anger, but my blood pressure was probably going through the roof and my face was probably bright pink.

"This," she said. "All this going around, behind Tessie's back. I feel so bad about it."

"To hell with Tessie," I said.

"She's your wife, Jack."

"You never gave a damn about that before."

"I do now."

"Why?"

"Because."

"Why because? That's the problem with you women. You think too much."

"She's my friend and I don't want to hurt her."

"Stop with that crap," I said. "What is it? Did they change your medication or something?"

"I'm serious, we have to stop."

Again, I wanted to slap her around. Pearl was the type who'd been slapped around before; I knew she was. Then I thought, what the hell? and I did it. It wasn't a hard slap—with the arthritis in my elbow and shoulder that was impossible—but it caught her right on her left cheek and it made a nice sound. It served its purpose, that was for sure.

She took it well, too. Like a woman with class. She wasn't crying and she didn't even look hurt. She knew she deserved it, that she'd been out of line. And it shut her up—that was the best part.

"We're not stopping anything," I said.

"I don't want to stop," she said. "I love you."

"If you love me keep your mouth shut and stop complaining or there's more where that came from."

She liked when I talked to her like that. I could tell. She was the old-fashioned type of broad who knew her place and liked to be put in it. That was why I liked her so much.

"Of course I want to keep seeing you," she said. "But not like this."

"Then like how?"

"I want us to be together. Really together."

"All right, and how the hell am I supposed to do that?"

"Divorce Tessie."

I thought about it a good five seconds then said, "All right, that's what you want me to do, I'll do it."

"You're gonna do it? Just like that?"

"Why not?"

"She loves you."

"You want to be with me?"

"Of course."

"Then shut up, take your clothes off, and get into bed, baby."

She was the old-fashioned type all right. She did exactly as she was told.

❦

Of course the last thing I wanted to do was hurt Tessie, but I had no choice. Yeah, Tessie had been good to me, and she was loving and caring and all that crap, but what did I care? A guy had to take care of himself sometimes, right?

I decided I'd get it over with as soon as possible and I knew the best way to do it. I'd broken up with hundreds of broads over the years. The trick was to get it done quick, not dilly around. You had to just rip off the Band-Aid. It was better that way, limited the pain.

That night, after Tessie put dinner down on the table and we started eating, I said, "Look, it's over, all right?"

That was the way to do it—just lay it on them, nice and clean.

"What?"

Jesus, I didn't have patience for this hearing aid crap.

"It's over!" I yelled. "I'm leaving you for Pearl!"

She heard me loud and clear, but she looked confused, maybe hurt. But that wasn't my problem.

"What do you mean?" she said, her eyes getting moist. "What're you—?"

"Look," I said, "I don't mean anything personal by this, see? I think you're a swell broad and all, but I wanna be with Pearl and that's it. I'm gonna pack my stuff and move into her place. I'll get a lawyer to work out all the paperwork with Social Security checks and whatever. Sorry it had to end this way, but that's just the way it is, baby."

Yeah, I handled it perfectly all right, like a knockout punch in the first round. The screwy old bat didn't know what hit her.

The rest of the night she was in bed crying a lot and she was on the phone with her kids down in the city. I hated seeing her like that, I honestly did, but what the hell was I supposed to do, stick around being miserable just to make some broad happy? That wasn't my style—never had been, never would be. I didn't try to talk to her at all because I knew it wouldn't do any good. When women got upset there was no stopping them.

I packed a valise. I didn't have much stuff. I'd always kept my life that way—light. I had some pictures of my nieces and nephews and their kids and other stuff like that I wanted to take along, but I figured I'd get a maintenance guy to pack up that crap for me eventually.

As usual I had to get up to pee about a dozen times, but besides that I slept well. Tessie wasn't in bed with me. She spent the night in the living room, crying like a goddamn baby, and in the morning she was still there.

"Get over it already, will ya?" I said.

I took a shower and got dressed. Then I wheeled the valise out through the living room and headed toward the front door. I was thinking about my new life with Pearl, how great it would be to eat some new cooking for a change, when I felt the pain in my back. I'd had a heart attack once, a mild one, and that's what I thought was happening—something with my heart or my lungs. I hit the floor hard and my bad hip went, making a loud snapping noise, and then I saw all the blood. I still didn't know what was happening—I thought I was hemorrhaging or something. Then I looked up at Tessie, holding the big bloody knife.

"You think I'd let you walk out of here?" she said. "You two-timing bastard."

She took another swipe at me with the thing. This time she only grazed me. I tried to get up. I wanted to take that knife away from the crazy old broad, teach her a lesson she'd never forget but, God damn it, I couldn't move. Hell, I couldn't even breathe.

Afterword

This story was inspired by years of visits to my grandmothers' condos in North Miami and Fort Lauderdale. And the voice is my grandmother's current husband Max all the way through. —J.S.

LAST RIGHT

ZOË SHARP

Zoë Sharp (born 1966) spent most of her formative years living on a catamaran on the northwest coast of England. She opted out of mainstream education at the age of twelve and wrote her first novel at fifteen. She turned to writing crime after being on the receiving end of death-threat letters in the course of her work as a photojournalist, and this led to the creation of her no-nonsense ex-army-turned-bodyguard heroine, Charlie Fox. Zoë is finishing her sixth novel in the Charlie Fox series, Second Shot.

LAST RIGHT
by Zoë Sharp

The youth arrived like a peasant, hitching a ride on the flatbed of a rusty pickup truck to the end of the driveway - two bales of straw, a goat, and an iPod, his traveling companions.

The guards watched him walk the last half-mile in, shouldering his rucksack and trudging between the citrus trees, his feet kicking up the dirt into the shimmer of the hot dry air. They took lazy beads on him with their rifles, and joked with each other about whether they should shoot him before he reached the main gates, just to relieve the boredom.

It was only when he drew nearer that they recognized his face, despite the simple clothes, and they shivered at the thought that they had even contemplated killing Manuel de Marquez's son, just for sport.

They had the gates opened before he'd reached them and he walked straight through without acknowledgement or thanks, as though it had never occurred to him that things would be otherwise. He demanded to be taken to his father and had barely skirted the two bullet-proof Mercedes parked near the fountain before old Enrique hurried out to greet him, taking the youth's hand in both his own and gripping it fiercely, his rheumy eyes filling.

"Julio!" he said. "We feared you would be too late."

"The old bastard's still alive then?"

Enrique tried to look shocked but couldn't quite bring it off. "Your father is dying," he said, quietly, as though afraid of being overheard.

Julio laughed and it wasn't a pleasant sound. "He's been dying for years. Why the hurry now?"

"He's near the end. I think he has been hanging on, waiting for your return."

The youth shook his head. "More likely that he's bargaining with the devil over the terms of his admission."

"The priest is with him."

Julio turned in sardonic surprise as the pair mounted the front steps.

"You've managed to find another man of God who will stand his blasphemy?"

Enrique shrugged. "Priests," he said. "It is their calling."

Julio's amusement backed and died. "For any that try to save the

152

soul of my father," he said, icy, "it's more like a penance."

✝

They had placed the old man in a room on the ground floor, where it was cooler in the heat of the daytime. Mats had been laid on the tiles outside the door, so that the footsteps of those passing would not disturb him. The bodyguard at the doorway nodded to Enrique and roughly took Julio's rucksack from his shoulder, dropping it onto an antique table and burrowing through the contents with his huge hands, like a mole tunneling into soft earth. When he could find nothing that resembled a weapon, he handed it back and jerked his head for them to continue. Enrique stepped back with a small smile, an incline of his head that said, *You're on your own. Good luck!* and Julio pushed open the door.

Manuel de Marquez had withered in the weeks since his son had last seen him, and the smell in the dimness of the room was of a body already fallen into decay, forced to keep functioning by an iron will and a meanness of spirit that would have dismayed any but those who knew him well.

Already he had outlasted the most optimistic prognosis. Some said it was purely out of spite. But they said it in whispers, with one eye cast over their shoulder, even so.

For no one could argue the fact that Manuel de Marquez was an evil man. He'd made a life's work of it. There were rumors that he'd shot the doctor who had first diagnosed the cancer and such was his reputation that no-one doubted it might be so. Even now, dying, he had one bodyguard outside the room and another within, standing in the corner opposite the doorway like a column of rock. Julio had known Angel since he was a child and had never seen the man smile.

As he entered, de Marquez opened one yellowed eye and focused on his only son, ignoring the murmuring of the elderly priest on the far side of the bed. The man never paused in his incantations, the familiar Latin phrases threading past his lips as easily as the beads of the rosary slid between his gnarled fingers.

"So, you've come to watch me die, have you?" de Marquez said. The voice was clogged, rasping, every syllable dragged up from the depths of sodden lungs before it could be jettisoned into the musty air.

"I've come for truth, if you can still remember what that is," Julio said, and the old man saw the echo of his wife in the young man's haughty dignity. "The truth about my mother."

The old man closed his eyes briefly. "She left," he said. "Twenty years ago. She left and never came back. Never thought about her husband or her son again."

"How can you be so sure?"

De Marquez gave a hollow laugh, gasping as his breath staggered in his throat because of it. "Do you see her here, in this room? Weeping by my bedside? No. She was faithless as a whore. I should have known it from the day I married her."

The youth paced, quick jerky steps of anger, to the shuttered window by the priest's chair, and back to the doorway. The old man shut his eyes again, as if just to watch the movement was too tiring. He heard the boy stop, the slight grate of his boots on the tiles as he turned.

"So why did you marry her?" Julio asked and the humility in the tone made de Marquez stay the harsh retort that had formed ready on his tongue. He weighed the possibilities with care, a man who had made it his business to never apologize and never explain. He opened his eyes and stared at his son and wondered if, in some corner of his soul, he owed the boy the full story.

No, probably not.

"She was a great beauty," he said, grudging. The gurgle in his chest marked the festering of his body, a sound like a blocked drain and just as rancid. "She bewitched me, cast a spell like no other. It was a kind of madness. I would have done anything to have her." He made a rumble of self-disgust. "And in the end, when there was no other way, I grew desperate enough to put a ring on her finger."

The boy paced again, over to the mumbling priest and back again, the bodyguard's eyes never leaving him.

"And was she happy?"

"Happy!" de Marquez scorned. "What's happy? For a while she was obedient and willing—what else is a wife? She had no family and I gave her family. Within a year she had fallen with child. She had a son. What more could I ask for?"

"What *did* you ask for?"

"Loyalty," the old man said, his lip curling. "It was a busy time. We were building up our interests across the border. I was away a good deal." He paused, gasping a little again, his breath hissing like steam. "She grew bored and then she grew secretive, and that's when I knew."

"Knew?"

"She had taken a lover."

The words were ripped out of him, raw, and left to bleed between them in the stinking room.

"Where was your proof?" Julio demanded with the same lift of his chin that *she* had always used. How, de Marquez wondered, did you inherit a gesture from a parent you hadn't seen for twenty years and could no doubt barely remember?

"She withdrew herself from me for a time, as though she couldn't bear my touch. And she never had enough money. I gave her a generous allowance, but she always came back for more. Eventually, I had Angel follow her."

Julio turned to glance at the silent bodyguard in the corner, but the big man showed no sign of reaction as his name was spoken. My mother, Julio thought, must have been blind not to have noticed such a tail. Perhaps by that time, she didn't care . . .

"And Angel brought you your proof?" he said aloud, skeptical.

"She went to Ciudad Juárez and waited for a man who crossed the border from El Paso," de Marquez said, his face coated with a slimy sweat that oozed from his pores. "He was young, handsome. The two embraced. They took a hotel room together and for the whole of that afternoon and all through the night they never left it. What more proof did I need?"

"So tell me, Father," Julio said, coldly. "Did you kill her, or did you have Angel do it for you?"

For a moment the accusation spread across the room like a fishing net cast across the water, unfolding in flight and hanging suspended in the air. De Marquez stared. Even the priest stumbled over his words, frowning, as though he'd never had cause to falter before. Only the bodyguard remained totally impassive.

Then the net dropped, the moment passed, and de Marquez laughed, a sluicing wash of sound. He lifted one shriveled hand from the sheet as if to admonish, only for it to flop back again, without strength.

"She came home, unharmed," he said, but his eyes had turned sly.

"Not so the man she met," Julio said. "He was found beaten to death in an alleyway, two days later, wasn't he?"

His father allowed his paper-thin eyelids to flutter closed, hiding behind them. *How could the boy know this?*

"Is that where you've been all this time? Digging through the slums of Juárez? What did you hope to find there?"

But the youth ignored him, speaking instead to the silent bodyguard. "It was a shame you didn't do some digging of your own, Angel," Julio said softly, "before you murdered him." He spun back to the old man lying in the bed. "His name was Julio, just like mine," he said. "Ah yes, I see the surprise in your face, and the worry that, maybe, my mother took her lover sooner than you realized, hmm? That maybe I am not your son after all?" He snorted, tossed his head like one of the Andalusian horses de Marquez had kept before the sickness had wasted him too far to hold the reins.

"She chose the name," de Marquez whispered, remembering, jaw clenched tight. "And every time she spoke it she must have been flaunting *his* name in front of me. The name of her—"

"Her brother," Julio said.

De Marquez felt the jolt of it like a barb in his chest, flooding his failing heart, forcing the blood to cascade through his ruined vessels at a rate that could not be sustained. He gripped the bedclothes with his bony hands, overwhelmed by the roar of his own blood. *Her brother?*

"She had no family," he said, but heard the doubt leaching through his voice as he spoke the words. "If she lied to me…"

"She believed them lost to her, but she never gave up hope."

"So how were they so miraculously found?" the old man demanded, his voice like a whip. "You expect me to believe in fairy tales?"

"Her brother contacted her. He wrote a letter. He wanted to meet her, at the border. She sent him money."

"Fabrication," de Marquez snapped, but he was trembling badly. "Conjecture. She told me nothing of this."

"She did not want to incur your anger, expose you to embarrassment, if their claims turned out to be false," Julio said. He was very still now, almost poised, and his voice was low. "So she made her excuses to you and she traveled alone to Juárez and she met with him."

"And they spent the night together in a hotel room," de Marquez said, bitter. "That is not how brother and sister behave."

"She wanted somewhere private where they could talk and not be disturbed," Julio said. "They had much to talk about. They shared a room, yes, but not a bed."

"You cannot possibly know—"

"I spoke to the maid who serviced the room - as *he* should have done," Julio said, turning reproachful eyes on Angel. "When she walked in the next morning they were still talking together, she told me. The bed had not been slept in. My mother was weeping. 'Look,' she said to her. 'I have found a brother, an uncle for my son.' She never forgot the joy on my mother's face."

De Marquez swallowed, his throat suddenly arid as the desert, and did not trust himself to speak.

"So she came back here, to you, her heart filled with happiness. She had found her family. Her mother was long dead, but she at least had her brother, Julio; and her father was still alive. She had her proof - a locket, a picture of her father as a young man that had been worn by her mother, and now passed on, And what did *you* do?"

Julio stalked closer to the bedside and stared down at the wizened form of his father. For the first time, Angel moved forwards, his steps a quiet scrape on the tiles, like a giant rock being slid out of its position. Julio threw a contemptuous glance at him.

"You murdered her, in your jealousy. You didn't listen to her explanation, did you? You struck her down." He jerked his head towards Angel. "Did *he* help you hide her body? Do her bones lie at the bottom of a well somewhere, or is she here?" He stamped his heel on the tiles, making the old man start. "Eh, you look guilty, old man. She's right here, isn't she? Under the dirt floor of your wine cellar, perhaps? Even in death you hated to let her stray too far out of your sight."

Silence fell like dusk. Even the priest had ceased to mutter his prayers.

"What's done is done and cannot be undone," de Marquez said, weary. He shrugged and met the piercing glare of his son's gaze with the suspicion of a defiant smile hovering on his thin lips. "What else is it you want from me? Apology? Regrets? You won't get them. If you wanted to send me to my grave tormented by what I've done, well the fate of my wife wasn't the best or the worst of it, by any means. What do I care if he was her brother, after all? She still lied to me about where she was going. To me!" He paused, collected his breath and his temper only with enormous effort, and said, with calmer scorn, "She deserved to die."

Julio erupted with a suddenness that surprised his father, jumping forwards, hands outstretched. The bodyguard, Angel, seemed to move much more slowly by comparison, but he reached the youth before he'd taken more than two strides, pinioning his arms, lifting him as though he was a child, swinging him towards the door.

De Marquez could still hear the boy cursing and struggling along the corridor outside, louder as the second bodyguard came to Angel's aid.

The priest made a noise that sounded like a sigh. Slowly, as though his bones were hurting, he got to his feet and crossed the room to close the door quietly, dulling the sounds of the struggle, his prayer book and his rosary swinging from his fist.

De Marquez didn't move except for the labored rise and fall of his chest as he drew in shallow splashy breaths. There was a burning in his lungs now, a prickling to his vision, and a secret writhing fear that the end was close and he was not prepared to meet it.

"So, father, it seems you've heard my last confession, after all," he said, wheezing, his eyes flitting over the man's shabby cassock as he approached the bedside. "And are you prepared to grant me absolution."

"The Lord rejoices over every sinner who repents, my son," returned the priest.

By the time Angel had Julio calm enough to return, the priest was once again folded neatly into his chair by the shuttered window.

"The strain was too much for him, but he went quietly, in the end," the priest said as they stared at the dead man. The bodyguard crossed himself.

The priest rose, was almost at the doorway before Julio asked him, "Tell me, father—did he find peace?"

Turning, the priest paused and then said, "As much as he was able to."

ꟷ

A week after his father's death, Julio de Marquez ordered the excavation of the wine cellars. The bones that were found there were of a woman in her late twenties. She had been shot, just once, through the back of her skull and buried naked save for an old tarnished silver locket, the chain still around her neck.

Enough money changed hands for the local authorities to turn a blind eye as Julio took the remains of his mother north, to El Paso, to a little churchyard near the Franklin Mountains where he finally laid her bones to rest alongside her own mother, and her murdered brother.

Afterwards, when the earth had been shoveled in onto the coffin and Julio stood alone by the graveside, looking down, he heard a voice behind him:

"Thank you for bringing her home, my son."

Without turning, Julio said, "Was it worth it? Just to shorten his life perhaps by a few hours?"

"I believe in an eye for an eye. He took both son and daughter from me. It was only right that he should go before his time. Besides, if I hadn't finished him off, you would have done so yourself, and what kind of a man would I be if I didn't want to save my only grandson from eternal damnation?"

Julio turned at last, to see the man who'd been taken for a priest, now wearing a good suit and a black tie as a mark of his respect for the occasion.

"Besides anything else," the old man said, dredging up a tired smile. "What does it matter? I'm damn near dead myself."

Afterword

This wasn't the story I intended to write for this anthology. I wanted to expand on the character of Walt, the retired FBI guy from my Charlie Fox book, First Drop. *But Walt just wasn't talking to me when I needed him, and I kept getting this picture in my head of a darkened room with an old man dying and a priest by his side. And before I knew it, the rhythm of the prayers had stuck there, like a really bad song that you just can't help humming all day after you've heard it. Sorry.*

Incidentally, I blame my grandmother for my life of crime. She was the one who gave me a copy of an old Leslie Charteris 'The Saint' book - which I still treasure - when I was about nine. Up until then Black Beauty *was more my line. —Z.S.*

FUNERAL FOR A FRIEND

SIMON KERNICK

Simon Kernick (born 1966) loose series of four London-based crime thrillers have received much critical acclaim, with the London Independent describing his first novel, The Business of Dying, *as the crime debut of 2002. The books feature corrupt cops, violent hitmen and mercenaries with murky pasts. And they're the good guys! His fifth novel is standalone thriller called* Relentless.

FUNERAL FOR A FRIEND
by Simon Kernick

There's always the low murmur of whispered conversation at a funeral. The men, unsmiling, acknowledge each other with terse nods and stiff handshakes; the women kiss and hold one another in tight embraces, as if somehow the strength of their emotion will protect them from a similar fate. It won't. The end, I can tell you from experience, is lurking round every corner.

I'm pleased with the turnout today, though. I didn't think that I was that popular. I am, or was, a pretty brutal man. But I was powerful, too, and power tends to attract followers, I suppose.

I'm looking for one man in particular, but so far he's conspicuous by his absence. Most of the people have already taken their seats, and we're only five minutes away from the 2.30 start time. The door to the church opens, but it's not him. It's Arnold Vachs, my former accountant, here with his wife. Creeping unsteadily down the aisle, like the bride at an arranged marriage to King Kong, he's small and potbellied with the furtive air of a crook, which is very apt, since that's exactly what he is. His wife—who's a good six inches taller and supposedly an ex-model—definitely never married him for his looks. But Arnold Vachs earns big money, and that makes him one hell of a lot more attractive.

Finally, with one minute to go, the man I'm waiting for steps inside. Tall, lean and tan, with a fine head of silver hair, he looks like an ageing surfer who's suddenly discovered how to dress smart. It's my old blood brother, Danny O'Neill, looking a lot younger than his sixty years, and as soon as I see him, I'm transported back four decades, right to the very beginning.

The year was 1967, and I'd just come back from a twelve month stint in Nam. I was still a kid, barely twenty, with the remnants of an unfinished High School education, and no job or prospects. The difference between me and every other Joe was that I was a killer. A few months earlier, our unit had been caught in an ambush in jungle near the border with Laos, at a place called Khe Sanh. We were forced to pull back to a nearby hill and make a stand while we waited for the copters to come and pull us out. Nine hours we were on that hill, twenty-nine men against more than three hundred. But we stood our ground, took seven casualties—two dead, five wounded—and cut down more than forty Gooks. So, when I came back home, I'd lost any innocence I might have had, and pretty much all my fear, too. I was a new man. I was ready to embark on my destiny.

I teamed up with another vet called Tommy 'Blue' Marlin, and Tommy's friend, Danny, who'd also served in Nam, in the 51st Airborne. The three of us went into business together. And our profession? I'd call us Financial Advisors. The cops, though, they preferred the more derogatory term of bank robbers.

We liked to hit small-town outlets. The money wasn't as good as the Big City branches, but the security was minimal to the point of non-existent, and the staff tended to be too shocked to resist. We'd walk in, stockings over our heads, and I'd put a few rounds from my M16 into the ceiling, so everyone could tell we were serious, before pointing the smoking barrel at the employees. They always got the message, and filled up the bags we provided like they were ODing on amphetamines.

Sometimes we'd hit the same bank twice; sometimes we'd hit two places on the same day. But you know what? Nobody ever got hurt. In nineteen raids, we never had a single casualty. It was an enviable success rate. Problem was, it all changed when the cops decided to poke their noses in.

The target was a branch of the Western Union in some nowheresville town in north Texas. We'd been scoping it on and off for a couple of weeks and knew that the security truck came to pick up the takings every second Wednesday, just before close of business. That meant hitting the place early Wednesday afternoon for the best return. Everything went like it always did. Blue waited outside in the Lincoln we were using as a getaway car, while Danny and me rushed inside, put the bullets in the ceiling, and started loading up with greenbacks. But while we're doing all this, a cop car pulls up behind the Lincoln because it's illegally parked. The cop comes to the window and tells Blue to move the car, but just as Blue—being a good, dutiful citizen—pulls away, the cop hears the gunshots, draws his own weapon and goes to radio for back-up. He's still got the radio to his ear when Blue reverses the Lincoln straight into him, knocking him down. The cop's hurt but still moving, so Blue jumps out of the Lincoln and puts three rounds in his back while he's crawling along the tarmac towards his radio. Problem is, this is the middle of the day and there must be a dozen witnesses, all of whom get a good look at our man.

Two minutes later and we're out of the bank with more than twenty grand in cash, only to see the corpse of a cop on the ground and no sign of the getaway car. Blue's lost his nerve and left us there. Lesser men would have panicked but Danny and me weren't lesser men. We run down the street to the nearest intersection and hijack a truck that's sitting at a red light. The driver—a big, ugly redneck—gets argumentative but a round in his kneecap changes all that, and we turf him out and start driving.

We're out of town and out of danger long before the cavalry arrive, but the heat's on us now. A dead cop is a liability to any criminal. His buddies are going to stop at nothing to bring the perps to justice, but me and Danny figure if we give them the shooter then maybe we'll be less of a target.

Two days later, we track down Blue to a motel on the New Mexico/ Texas border. He's in the shower when we kick down the door and, as I pull back the curtain, he begs for mercy. Just before I blow his head off, I repeat a phrase one of the officers in Nam used to say: *To dishonor your comrades is to deserve their bullets.* He deserves mine, and there are no regrets.

Danny and I both realize that with Blue's death, the armed robbery game's probably not one for the long term. We've made a lot of money out of it, getting on for half a million dollars, most of which we've still got. So, we do what all good capitalists do: we invest, and what better market to invest in than dope. This was the tail-end of the Sixties, the permissive decade. The kids wanted drugs, and there weren't many criminals supplying it, so Danny and I made some contacts over the border in Mexico, and started buying up serious quantities of marijuana which we sold on to one of our buddies from Nam— Rootie McGraw—who cut the stuff up into dealer-sized quantities and wholesaled it right across LA and southern California. One hell of a lot of kids had us to thank for the fact they were getting high as kites for only a couple of bucks a time. It was a perfect set-up and as more and more people turned on, tuned in and dropped the fuck out, so the money kept coming in. And Rootie had a lot of muscle. He was heavily involved in one of the street gangs out of Compton, so no one fucked with our shipments.

Rootie's in the church now, dressed in black from head to toe, looking the height of funereal fashion, but he was always a snappy dresser. He might be pushing seventy with a curly mop of snow-white hair, and just the hint of a stoop, but the chick with him would have difficulty getting served in the local bar and you know what they say: *You're only as old as the woman you feel.* This girl's a beauty too, with a skirt so short she could hang herself with it. A couple of people give her dirty looks, including my long-term mistress, Trudy T. Trudy's always been a good woman—we had something going on and off for years— but she's turned a little bit conservative ever since she found the Lord a couple of years back, and I think she's forgotten what a wild one she was in her day. Seeing that miserable look on her face now, I want to pipe up and remind her of that home-made porno movie we made on the 8 millimeter back in the mid Seventies—the one in that hotel room in Tijuana where Trudy was on her hands and knees snorting lines of coke off the flat, golden belly of a nineteen year-old Mexican whore while I brought up the rear, so to speak. Religion, I conclude, has a lot to answer for, although I sympathize with Trudy for wanting to hedge her bets now that the end's a lot nearer for her than the beginning.

Talking of coke, that's what really made us. There was money in marijuana—no doubt about it—but it was nothing compared to what could be made trading in the white stuff. By the end of the Seventies, we were bringing close to a thousand kilos a year into the States, using Rootie's distribution network to market it to the people, and clearing ten mill in straight profit. We could have got greedy but the thing about Danny and me was that, first and foremost, we were businessmen. We pumped our profits into legit businesses—construction, property and tourism, in the main—and eventually we were able to pull out of the smuggling game altogether.

Just in time, as it turned out. Within months Rootie got busted and, because he showed loyalty and refused to name the people he was involved with, he got shackled with a 15 to 25 sentence, and ended up serving 12.

It served as a good lesson to Danny and me. Always be careful. And we were. We built up an empire together—one that was turning over thirty million dollars a year—and we staffed it with men and women who showed us the same loyalty that Rootie had shown. We were a success story. I can look back and claim, with hand on heart, that I truly made it, and you can see that by the numbers of people in this church today. Three hundred at least. Friends, employees, lovers. Lots of lovers. Trudy T was one, but I've always been a man with appetites—they used to call me the Norse Horse, back in the day- and there were plenty of others. Row 6, to the left of the aisle sits one. Claire B was a movie star once upon a time, with the kind of perfect good looks made for the silver screen. She's eighty years old now and used to call me her toyboy. We had a lot of fun together, and that's why she's weeping quietly into her white handkerchief now while an old geezer, who must be close to a hundred, puts a wizened arm round her shoulders.

I scan the room and see Mandy H—a former Vegas showgirl I had a fling with back in the summer of '79—beautiful once, now cracked and hardened with age, her face as impassive as an Easter Island Statue as she stares straight ahead; then there's Vera P who took up with me for a while in the late eighties, after the death of her husband, a man who was one of my longest serving employees. She was lonely and I was horny, a combination that was never going to work, but I guess I must have had some effect on her because she's sobbing so ferociously it's making her hair stand on end. And the service still hasn't even started yet. I should be impressed but I'm forgetting it already as I catch sight of Diana, as regal as an Ice Queen, sitting right down at the front.

Diana. My wife; my widow; my one true love—still as beautiful in her fifty ninth year, as she was the day we met on a snowy New York afternoon, twenty-five years ago. I was in Central Park for a business meeting with one of our Manhattan-based partners that I didn't want anyone snooping on. Not only because we were talking details that weren't entirely legal, but also because we were giving the guy a bit of a beating on account of the fact that he'd been cheating the organization. I'd just broken a couple of his fingers and was leaving him to two of my most trusted men to finish off, when as I came out from behind some bushes, I saw her gliding along the path in my direction—this gorgeous willowy blonde with a fur hat perched jauntily on her head and a little dog on a lead—and this cool, languid look in her eye. Man, I knew straight off, I had to have her. Within an hour, we were sharing cocktails. Within three, we were sharing a bed. Inside a month, we were man and wife. I'm nothing if not a fast worker.

I always wanted kids, but Diana couldn't have them. That's why there are none here today. It doesn't matter. We had each other, and for me, that was good enough. Everything had come up roses. The money was rolling in; the cops could never touch us; and I was married to the woman of my dreams.

Life was good. All the way up until last month it was good.

And then it all went wrong and twenty-five pounds of plastic explosive placed on the underside of my Mercedes Coupe, directly beneath the driver's seat, ended the life of Francis Edward Hanson, aged fifty eight: lover, friend, businessman and killer.

A homicide investigation started right away, and there are currently plenty of suspects, but no one who really stands out. We'd killed or bought off most of our rivals years ago. The two homicide cops are in here now, sitting at the back of the church, trying without success to blend chameleon-like into their surroundings. They're wearing cheap suits and furtive expressions and they couldn't really be anything else. One or two of the guys turn and give them the look. No one in our organization likes the cops.

The service lasts close to an hour. It's too long really, especially in this heat. They sing my favorite hymn: Cat Stevens' "Morning Has Broken," and I remember I once amputated a man's leg to that particular song, which brings a smile; and Danny does a reading from one of the psalms. I've never believed in a Supreme Being, I've seen too much injustice for that. But I've always hoped there was some sort of afterlife—somewhere you can kick back and take it easy—and I'm pleased to announce that there is one, and that so far it looks like it might be pretty good.

And then it's all over. My coffin moves effortlessly along a conveyer belt to the right of the pulpit and disappears behind a curtain. In keeping with my express wishes, my remains are to be cremated rather than buried. The cops aren't too happy about this—you know, seeing their evidence go up in smoke—but they've finished with my body now, so they haven't got any grounds for refusal. There's a final bout of loud sobbing—mainly from the women—and then the mourners file slowly out into the furnace-like heat of a New Mexico afternoon.

I see Danny move close to Diana. They talk quietly. It looks to the untrained eye as if he's offering her comfort and condolences, but I know better. His hand touches her shoulder and lingers there a second too long, and they walk through the graveyard together, continuing their conversation. Several people turn their way, with expressions that aren't too complimentary, but they don't care. Danny's the boss now and I'm reminded of that old English phrase: *The King is dead. Long live the King.* Life goes on. I'm the past. Like it or not, for these people, Danny's the future.

Except he isn't.

There's going to be a Wake back at the ranch that I've called home for these past twenty years. They've got outside caterers coming in and it sounds like it'll be a huge party. I'm only pissed off I can't attend. And look at this: Danny and Diana are traveling back there together. They ought to be more careful. The cops are going to get suspicious. But they seem oblivious.

Diana gets into the passenger seat of Danny's limited edition, cobalt-blue Aston Martin. I've always liked that car. He gets in the drivers side and then, three seconds later: Ka-Boom! There's a ball of fire, a thick stream of acrid black smoke, and then when it finally clears, a burnt out chassis with four spoked wheels, and very little else.

People run down towards the site of this, the second assassination of a member of our organization in the space of a month. They want to help, but there's nothing they can do. Trudy T—she of Christian faith and Tijuana hotel rooms—lets loose this stinging scream that's probably got every dog in a ten mile radius converging on the church, and the two cops shout for everyone to keep calm and stay put, one of them already talking into his radio. They are roundly ignored.

I just keep walking, ignored by the crowd, knowing that my disguise, coupled with the plastic surgery I've recently undergone, means that no one will have recognized me.

Now that I've got my revenge, it's time to start my new life. I always trusted Danny, and I think that's been my problem. I don't know when his affair with Diana started, but I guess it must have been a while back. Me and her haven't been so good lately and this has been the reason why. I think it was a bit much that they wanted to kill me, though, and make it look like an assassination. Not only is it the worst kind of betrayal, but it was stupid, too. How did they think I wouldn't find out about it? Maybe love makes us all foolish.

Anyways, I did find out. A friend of Rootie's knew the bombmaker and it didn't take much to get him to tell me when he was going to be planting his product under my Merc. Diana's got an older brother—her last living relative, but a guy she rarely sees. His name's Earl and he lives alone. At least he did. He's dead now. Being roughly my height and build was a bit unfortunate for him. I had him killed—just to spite her—and his body planted in the Merc on the morning that I was supposed to die. Rather than being ignition-based, the bomb was on a timer (something the cops'll probably work out eventually, not that it'll do them much good), and when it went off, tearing the corpse into a hundred unrecognizable pieces, everyone simply assumed it was me who was dead in there.

Not wanting to give anyone the chance to disprove this theory, I disappeared off the scene, having already opened bank accounts in false names and bought a house for myself in the Bahamas. Only thing was, I couldn't resist coming back to watch my own funeral and, of course, see the bombmaker's talents put to work for a second time. And it was a nice bonus, too. Getting both of them at once. Saves me tracking down Diana later.

As I get in my own car, and leave the scene of carnage behind, I think back to the friendship Danny and me had, and it makes me a little melancholy that it had to end like this. Like the time with Blue, though, I don't have any regrets. Danny knew the score. It had been banged into him from our earliest days.

To dishonor your comrades is to deserve their bullets.

And now he's had mine.

I think that if he wasn't splattered all over the sidewalk, he'd probably approve.

Afterword

Funerals were what influenced my choice of story for this anthology. Unfortunately, I've attended a few over the years, and on those occasions where I've been sat in the church amongst the dozens, scores, sometimes hundreds, of mourners, listening to the church representative talk about the life of someone he never knew, I've found myself wondering what it would be like to attend my own sending-off. I imagine myself casting a careful eye over the attendees, seeing who's weeping, and more importantly, who isn't. And so that's what happens with my central character. He attends his own funeral, during which he comments on the various mourners and their relationship to him, and in doing so, gives the reader a view into his colourful and nefarious criminal life and, most importantly, how it came to such an abrupt and violent end. —S.K.

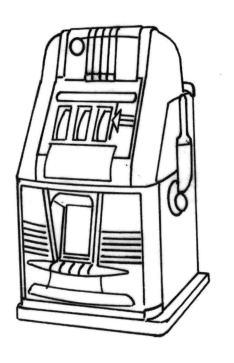

PART THREE:

KILLERS AND CONS

THE KILLER
BESIDE ME

ALLAN GUTHRIE

Allan Guthrie (born 1965) sent this short bio: "Last anyone heard, Allan Guthrie was alive and writing." That's typical of the Edgar-nominated author of Kiss Her Goodbye, *who lives in Edinburgh with his wife Donna. It's why his friends call him "Sunshine." His next novel,* Hard Man, *is due out in both the U.K. (Polygon) and U.S. (Harcourt) early next year.*

ƒ

THE KILLER BESIDE ME
by Allan Guthrie

"**W**e're long past our sell-by date." Trevor switched his grip on his cane. He'd been clutching it hard for ages now and his hand was clammy. What were the bastards up to, taking so long to get here?

"Bollocks," Harry said. "We've got a good couple of years in us yet. We've defied the odds so far. I'm looking forward to old age. Has its perks. You can spit on the floor and beat nosey children with your cane."

"But after a while," Trevor said, "you'll get tired of lying in a pile of your own shite."

"Or somebody else's."

"What're you saying? If anything, you'll lose control of your bowels before me."

"At least I can still get it up."

"Fuck you. Anyway, that's not what I mean. Just making a point," Trevor said. "We shouldn't be here. Not at our age."

"Fuck, we're not in our seventies yet. Don't write us off. I can see the day when we'll need special adult undergarments. I long for that day."

Trevor didn't move. He couldn't, not without his brother's help. The settee was too deep. A faded old two-seater, that's the best the fuckers could come up with. Stuffed out of the way in a room that was some kind of cleaning room. A hoover, mop in a bucket, stink of furniture polish. The bank manager had had to move a cardboard box full of rubber gloves and dusters before they'd been able to sit down. When he left, he'd locked the door behind him.

Where the fuck were the police?

Trevor said, "I once gave a blind man a blow job, you know."

"You did not."

"Did."

"Not."

"You were asleep."

"Shite."

"You were."

"I'd have woken up."

"You were drunk. Paralytic."

"Then you must have been too."

"You can't hold your drink. Anyway, it's true. Back at Aggie's—"

"I don't want to hear about it."

"Well, I'm telling you."

"I'm not listening." Harry started singing. But he couldn't drown out Trevor's voice. Especially after Trevor started shouting. Harry gave in, asked, "What happened?"

"He wondered into the bedroom by mistake. I heard him scuffling around, banging into things. I put on the light." Trevor adopted a high-pitched voice. "I spoke like this," he said. "Made him think he'd walked into a lady's room. Completely fooled him."

"But why?"

"For fun."

"No, why did you blow him?"

"He asked. Completely up front about it. And I felt sorry for him."

"That's fucking disgusting."

"A selfless act," Trevor said. "Some might say it was noble."

"Wonder what he'd think if he knew you were male."

"He'll never find out."

"I could tell him."

"But you don't know who it is."

"Bet I can guess."

Trevor said, "How the fuck?"

"How many blind people stayed at Aggie's?"

"Three. At least."

"One was a woman, so it wasn't her. So there's a fifty-fifty chance of me getting it right."

"Well, I'm not going to tell you."

"But I know, anyway."

"No way."

"Do too."

"Ah, away and shite, you old fuck."

The two old men were silent for a while. The sound of traffic seeped through the walls behind them.

"Who was it, then?" Trevor asked.

"Not telling."

"You don't fucking know. You were asleep. You don't remember it. So how can you know? You can only guess."

Harry shrugged. Well, as much as he was able to. "This conversation is over."

"Fine."

"Yeah, fine."

"Good."

"Well, shut up."

"I will."

"How did you turn out gay, anyway?"

"I'm not fucking gay."

"You gave a blind man a blow job."

"So?"

"That's pretty gay."

"You think so? How do you explain Edna, then?"

"Okay, so you're bisexual."

"At least I'm sexual."

"What's with you today? You've done nothing but pick on me from the minute we woke up."

Silence.

"The surgeon's in town."

"Huh?"

"The surgeon." Trevor stared at Harry's annoying blank face. "*The* surgeon. *Our* surgeon."

Harry looked away. "Shut up about that. It's not happening. You want to end up like Carslaw, back in '98?"

"Don't remember him."

"Yeah, you do. Big guy. Talked about cars all the time?"

"Vaguely."

"Went into hospital for a hip replacement," Harry said. "Never saw him again."

"Died?"

"Escaped. Outran the bastards, him and his dodgy hip."

"Yeah?"

"Course not, you thick twat. He went under the knife. Didn't have the heart for it. Went to sleep and never woke up. You don't remember?"

"Nope."

"Jesus. Maybe you're senile already."

"Fuck off."

"Can't speak to you. Don't know why I bother."

Trevor said, "Leave me alone then."

"I will."

"Give your pecker a tug."

"You sure you don't want to?"

"Fuck off, you dirty bastard."

"Well," Trevor said, after a while, "I expect an apology at the very least."

"For?"

Trevor crossed his arm over his chest. Said nothing.

"Huh?" Harry said. Shook his head. "Okay, I'm sorry I said you were gay."

"Not that. I don't care about that."

"Thought you wanted an apology."

"I do. But not for the gay remark."

"Well, what, then?"

"What do you think?"

"Fuck's sake, how am I supposed to know?"

"Take a wild guess."

"No," Harry said. Thought for a minute. "Nope. Nothing."

Trevor looked him in the eye.

"Well, maybe," Harry said. He looked down at his hand. He was better with his hand than Trevor was. Maybe because Harry was right-handed.

"Say it."

Harry sighed. "The robbery? Us ending up here?"

"Great fucking guess. You're a fucking genius."

"Sarcasm's unbecoming."

"Oh, but robbing a fucking bank without telling me is okay?"

"Didn't think you'd mind."

"Like I had any choice."

"You knew about the gun."

"Yeah, but how was I supposed to know what it was for?"

"What'd you think it was for?"

"I dunno. Self-defense?"

"Oh, yeah. You really believed that."

"Lots of kids about, what're they called, hoodies. You know they'll fuck us over, pair of old codgers like us, joined at the hip. Anyway, that's what you said."

"I lied. You always know when I lie."

"Not this time."

Silence. "So, you're claiming you had no idea? Not even an inkling?"

"That's right."

"Up until what point?"

"What do you mean?"

"At what point did you realize what was going on?"

"Once you got the gun out and said, 'Everybody freeze. This is a robbery.'"

"Pretty fucking cool, that."

"No, it wasn't. You're not cool. You'll never be cool. It's not even a proper fucking gun. You're retarded."

"Speak for yourself."

"Thanks, I will."

"So what's going to happen now?"

"Dunno. They'll fetch the police. And they'll probably come and handcuff us. Lead us off to some pokey room somewhere in a police station and bombard us with questions." Trevor paused. "I'm going to tell them the truth."

"Which is?"

"I was coerced into it."

"Coerced? Cofuckingerced? I hate it when you know words I don't. How do you do that? I've never seen you so much as pick up a dictionary."

"You *forced* me to do it. That better?"

"Suit yourself. Doesn't bother me what you say."

"You'll back me up."

"I will?"

"Sure. You know it's the truth."

"But why should I?"

"Because you don't want to go to prison."

"What's you getting off with it got to do with me going to prison?"

"Everything. Think about it."

Pause.

"Well?"

Harry said, "I'm thinking."

"Nothing clicked?"

"If I'm guilty, they'll send me to prison."

"Yeah. But if I'm innocent, they can't send me to prison. So how do they arrange that, short of an operation?"

"Ah, I'm with you. Fucking nice."

A key scraped in the lock. Harry and Trevor got to their feet. Took a well-timed joint effort. A difficult operation, but they'd had lots of practice. They waddled forwards a couple of steps as the door opened. A young guy in a suit walked in tucking his bleached blonde hair behind his ear.

"Hi," Harry said. "You're the manager, right? I'm Harry. This is Trevor. Nice bank you've got. Don't like this room much, though. Smells like a summer breeze."

The bank manager ignored Harry, looked at Trevor.

Trevor said, "I'm innocent."

He nodded. "It's clear you weren't a willing participant. I could see you trying to get your brother to put down … this." He held up the gun. "Whatever it is."

"I was coerced." Trevor looked sideways at Harry.

"Don't you mean co-*arsed*?" Harry said. "Fucking cockjockey."

"So can I go?"

The bank manager said, "That may be problematic."

"But I'm innocent."

"I dare say." He pulled a face. "You'll have to wait for the police to decide."

"I want to go home."

"That's too bad."

"Harry can stay."

"That's impossible. Even if I could let you, it's physically impossible."

"But you've no right to keep me here."

"You have to stay till the police get here." The manager tucked his hair behind his ear again. "I have every right to insist on that."

"You're fucked," Harry said. He started laughing. "I robbed your bank. I pulled out my gun and waved it around and threatened people with it and there's fuck all you can do because I'm a Siamese twin and my brother's innocent."

"I thought," the bank manager said, "that the correct expression was 'conjoined twin'."

"To you," Harry said, "it is."

Trevor lashed out with his cane, struck the bank manager on the temple.

"Oh," Harry said. "Nice fucking shot."

"Thanks," Trevor said. The bank manager was sprawled on the floor. He groaned. "After three," Trevor said.

Together the conjoined twins lurched out of their seat. They bent over and Trevor picked up the gun. "You okay?" he asked the bank manager.

The bank manager opened his eyes, saw the gun in Trevor's hands, flinched.

"Know what it is?" Trevor said. "Humane killer. Used for killing livestock. Place the weapon to the animal's forehead like this." He placed the gun to the bank manager's forehead. "And then when you pull the trigger, it fires a steel bolt into the animal's brain."

The bank manager said, "No. For God's sake."

Trevor shrugged, straightened up. He turned, smiled at Harry. Placed the gun to his brother's forehead and pulled the trigger.

Harry jolted. A red circle beauty-spotted his brow. Blood began a slow trickle downwards. His eyes closed.

Trevor dropped the gun. "Jesus," he said.

Harry slumped to the side, dragging Trevor sideways. They fell on the floor, landing on top of the bank manager.

The bank manager cried out. Trevor struggled to get his wind back, then said, "Sorry."

No point trying to get back to his feet. That was an impossibility now.

The bank manager struggled out from beneath them, sat with his back to the wall, hugging his knees. After a while, he relaxed, gently massaged his temple. He moved forward, slowly, eyes on Trevor. Then he examined Harry. "You've killed him," he said. He picked up the gun, stared at it.

"Yeah," Trevor said. "Can you call an ambulance? Tell them they'll need to perform an emergency separation on a pair of conjoined twins. And they'll need to do it now. There's a number in my back pocket. They'll need to phone it. It's the number of a surgeon who can perform the operation."

"You planned this?"

"Harry would never agree to the op. Too risky."

"So you did agree to the robbery? You weren't as innocent as you claimed?"

"I'm admitting to nothing. Just call for an ambulance. And get the surgeon. He's in Edinburgh at the moment. But he's on standby." Trevor paused. "Hurry. I think I'm going into shock."

"What if I refuse?"

"No matter." Trevor was short of breath. "The police'll bring an ambulance with them. Where are they?"

"Ah, Trevor," the bank manager said. "You really believe a couple of geriatric Siamese—forgive me—*conjoined* twins having a public argument constitutes a serious enough threat for us to call the police?"

"But my brother asked for your money."

"And you told him to be quiet."

"But he waved his gun around." Trevor glanced at the humane killer in the bank manager's hand.

"And you took it off him and gave it to a teller."

"So, what are you saying? You didn't call the police?"

"Nope. No police." He paused. "No ambulance." He walked towards the door.

"Fuck," Trevor said. "I won't survive longer than a couple of hours on my own. Harry's dead. Don't you understand what that means?"

The bank manager turned in the doorway, said, "I understand completely."

"Come on," Trevor said. "What kind of a sadistic fuck are you?"

"I'm a bank manager." The door closed.

Afterword

I was once a bank manager. Like all my writing, "The Killer Beside Me" is autobiographical. —A.G.

TENDER MERCIES

JEFF ABBOTT

Jeff Abbott (born 1963) is the author of eight novels, including his latest thriller, Panic, *which was nominted for Best Novel by the International Thriller Writers, and his forthcoming novel,* Fear. *Jeff is a three-time nominee for the Edgar Award, a two-time nominee for the Anthony Award, and a past winner of the Agatha and Macavity Awards. Jeff's short stories have been anthologized in collections such as* Best American Mystery Stories *and* The World's Finest Crime and Mystery Stories. *If Jeff were to have Sean Doolittle killed, the title "nicest guy in mystery fiction" might be his.*

TENDER MERCIES
by Jeff Abbott

Lionel Dupuy was often invisible these days, but it didn't bother him. He had been intelligent and handsome his entire life so it always came as a gentle shock to him that, at seventy-five, few people seemed to truly notice him any more.

But in his difficult and important work, invisibility was often an advantage. Today's job was standard; he walked into the soft cool of the nursing home, wrinkling his nose at the antiseptic smell that never quite covered the twin odors of urine and sweat, nodded politely to the bored staffer at the desk, and kept his eyes firmly ahead and fixed on the turn in the hallway.

"Sir?" the staffer called.

Damn, he thought. Today he'd drawn Miss Alert and Helpful. He leaned on his cane and turned, kept the smile on his face, blinked hard as though his eyes needed to focus. "Yes?"

"May I help you?" The staffer had a bright, easy smile; a pretty girl.

"Oh, I'm just heading down to room 404. See my friend Willie Todd."

"Oh, okay," the staffer said. Lionel turned back around and continued his slow progress down the hall. That was the secret; mention a name and a room number and dress in tweed and if you were old, you were set. It took a bit of checking on the client's side but as long as you were specific—*get me the name and room number of a patient who's asleep most of the time for camouflage*—the client usually delivered and you could stay invisible.

He went past room 404, glanced in at the dozing Mr. Todd, and went down to room 400.

Mr. Flint was asleep, too, snoring while a soap opera played on the television, and Lionel eased the door shut.

"Mr. Flint?" he called.

Snore.

"Okay, then," Lionel said gently. He couldn't help himself; he scanned the corkboard above the man's bed. He thought these boards were a rehearsal for a tombstone. Life, summarized in film, cork, and thumb tacks. Nearly every patient had them and Mr. Flint's was typical—high school graduation photos of grandchildren, with smiles full of bright promise; yellowed photos going back decades, of Mr. Flint with a woman Lionel guessed to be Mrs. Flint; Mr. Flint with

188

his four grown children, two boys, two girls, in family snapshots at weddings and birthdays. No one ever took photos at funerals, Lionel realized for the first time.

He wondered if anyone would take a photo at Mr. Flint's funeral. Probably not. Who wanted mementos of sorrow?

He checked the man's breath: steady. Flint was just napping heavily. So Lionel turned the cane around, eased the rubber tip off, slid the capped syringe free. The needle was from a manufacturer in Switzerland that prided itself on the narrowness of its gauge and the cleanness of the injection. He found the injection site the client said would be there—a healing needle mark on Flint's arm from an IV he'd had two days ago.

Lionel plunged the needle home and pressed the syringe's injector.

Mr. Flint opened his eyes, opened his mouth, and went silent and still.

"There, there," Lionel said. "It's been a good life, hasn't it? You deserve a better ending than suffering, friend." He took Mr. Flint's silence, not broken by breath, as agreement.

He removed the needle, upended it back into his hollow cane, and put the rubber tip back on the cane's end. He glanced again at the corkboard; he wondered which of the children had hired him to ease their father to heaven. He guessed it was the youngest son, who wore hair in a greasy ponytail and favored black turtlenecks. A sensitive artist who didn't want a father to suffer through years of Alzheimer's. Or perhaps a rotten ingrate who couldn't wait to get hands on a father's life insurance.

It didn't matter. Mr. Flint was at long-earned peace. Lionel wiped the light switch and the doorknob clean with a handkerchief his niece had given him and headed slowly back down the hall. He smiled at his sleeping alibi, the Mr. Todd who would never know that he came, and at the bright-smiled staffer who glanced up from her tabloid to say good-bye.

❧

Lionel took pride in his business model. Many of his clients referred each other to him. He always used a voice scrambler on the phone. He only accepted cash. No one knew his real name. He suspected they didn't even know that he was the same age as his victims; he considered that a secret business advantage.

After the Flint job, he collected the remainder of his ten thousand from the drop site—a locker at the Fort Lauderdale bus terminal—and went home. He didn't need the cane to walk and he left it in the car. He washed his hands, cracked open a beer, and took a long drink standing at the window.

Every job made him feel sad. You couldn't backtrack and fix things in life you had left undone, and when you got so sick that living was a limbo, then those undone things hung over your head like a weight ready to fall. Whatever undone business Mr. Flint had was beyond worry now. It had been a kindness, a tender mercy, no matter the family's motive.

His phone rang. He kept two lines in the house and one was the business phone. He opened a drawer, slipped the voice scrambler on the receiver, and answered. "Yes?"

"Um, yes, I want to speak to Mr. Grimm."

It was his working name. He thought Mr. Reaper was just a bit too depressing. "This is Mr. Grimm."

"Ah. Okay. Well. I have a problem," the voice continued. "I hope you can help me."

"I hope so, too."

"My uncle. . .he's had a good life. But he's not in the best of health. His mental facilities are fading. I can't bear to watch him go crazy."

"I understand. My fee is ten thousand. Half up front, half on completion of the mercy." He never called it a hit. He thought the term inaccurate; he never struck anyone.

"It won't. . .hurt him?"

"No."

"Okay." The man breathed a sigh of relief. "That's such a load off my mind. Thank you."

"All right. What's your uncle's name?"

"Lionel Dupuy."

Lionel said, after a moment's shock, "Could you spell that last name for me?"

⚐

When he hung up the phone—having accepted the contract on himself—he went back to the window and picked up his beer. It had no taste. He poured it down the sink and brewed a pot of Marine-strong coffee.

He had three living relatives, all children of his dead sister, and he wondered which of the greedy bastards wanted him gone. Scott was a divorced lawyer in Atlanta, and only wrote at Christmas with the latest accomplishments of his über-wonder teens, who apparently could score touchdowns, achieve Eagle Scout, and win debate tournaments simultaneously. Garry worked at an Orlando theme park

190

as a dancing zebra character named Stripey. Jill was a Miami newlywed, a chef who'd married a prominent restaurateur named Brad. Jill and Brad always invited Lionel for Thanksgiving and Christmas, which Lionel appreciated even though he rarely accepted the invitation.

Garry, he decided. The voice didn't sound like Garry's quiet rasp but he'd been to acting school, he could disguise his voice well enough where Lionel wouldn't see through the deception. Garry was the one most likely in financial straits. Dancing zebras presumably did not pull down large salaries, and Garry liked to bet on ponies; they'd gone to the race tracks together a lot last summer.

He would watch the bus terminal tomorrow, see which of his supposed loved ones showed up to make the deposit.

It didn't seem possible; Scott, Jill, and Garry had all sat on his knee, opened Christmas presents he'd given them, come to his door for advice and shelter when they bickered with their mother.

He drank his coffee, felt a tightness in his chest that he knew was disappointment. He had money after a lifetime of doing quiet favors for powerful people, and now he had a nice specialty that still brought in cash and let him sleep soundly at night. His nephews and niece thought he was an importer of fabrics and pottery from South America; he dressed well, he drove a nice car, his mortgage was paid off. The kids were his heirs; he'd told them all a couple of years ago last Thanksgiving, when he had his will drafted. So any of the kids might believe there was a sizeable inheritance ripe for the taking, even when divided by three. He thought better of them. And the nerve, suggesting that Lionel was crazy: that offended him as much as the contract.

He considered his options. If he confronted the guilty party, Lionel would tip his hand about knowing of the plot, which meant he was Mr. Grimm, which meant, surprise, surprise, kids, your uncle is a hired killer. That would be dicey; he could not trust them to keep his secret if he was already a target for murder. If Lionel didn't confront Guilty Party, and he remained alive, then Guilty Party would wonder what had happened to Mr. Grimm. Worse, if he declined the work, Guilty Party might hire another contract killer to finish the job. Someone young and spry and wielding a knife or gun.

He clicked on cable, surfed to a vintage film channel. He still loved the old movies of his childhood. The world was truly no simpler then, its supposed innocence was a myth, but it looked simpler. Sometimes you needed to look for the solution of least resistance.

Halfway through a World War II melodrama, Lionel realized there was only one way to solve his problem.

41

The next morning he sat in a cafe inside the bus terminal, sipping awful coffee, wearing heavy glasses; false, yellowed teeth; a gray beard that wasn't his, and a floppy hat. He was a slender man, and he wore shoulder pads in a too-big jacket. He didn't want any murderous relatives to recognize him.

At least not yet.

He'd left simple instructions for his newest client. The key to locker 1411 would be left taped in an envelope under the small metal shelf in the pay phone stall under the third phone from the left. Proceed to the locker; leave the first half of the payment and the information: where Lionel Dupuy lived, worked, ate; any medical condition that could be leveraged in the mercy, and so on. Lock the locker and tape the key under the first phone closest to the ticket counter and then leave the terminal. Failure to leave immediately would result in forfeiture of the money and a bullet in the ass (Lionel always laughed when he said this part, so the client was never sure if he were joking or not, and he wanted the client to be nervous enough not to linger to try and catch sight of him).

He could see, from his vantage point, the locker, the phones, and the entrance. Now he waited. He didn't watch the doors; he didn't watch the phones. He kept his gaze close to the locker. It might be a long wait and instead of a newspaper he held a thick copy of a Greek translation of *War and Peace*. He thought the Greek letters on the cover would discourage casual conversation from other patrons and better, he could pretend not to understand much English if he encountered a determined extrovert waiting for a bus.

Forty minutes into his vigil, he saw a hand open the locker. Not one of the kids. A young woman, attractive, in her early twenties. She wore a hooded, cream-colored sweat suit and fat-lensed dark glasses. She stuck a thick manila envelope into the locker, shut it, went to the phones, pretended to make a call as she taped the key back under the phone. She hung up after ten seconds and glanced over her shoulder. His eyes went back to the Greek text as her gaze flicked across him. He counted to twenty and then glanced up as he tongued a fingertip and turned a page. She was gone and then he spotted her, going through the front doors.

Guilty Party had a co-conspirator. He followed the woman.

He stepped out into the parking lot in time to see her get into a waiting silver Mercedes and roar away. Mud obscured the license plate; he said "well, well" in impressed surprise. He turned and went back into the terminal.

She'd followed his instructions to the letter. The money, the information on his life and habits, the key were all there. He tucked the envelope inside his pocket and drove home. He examined the bills—they didn't appear to be marked.

I really only have one choice, Lionel thought. *I'll have to kill myself.*

᚛

Two days later he sat at the kitchen table, waiting for his murderer to appear.

He'd made one phone call two hours ago and said into his scrambler: "It's done."

"It is?" Guilty Party asked. Lionel thought—hoped, rather—he heard regret surging in his murderer's voice.

"It is."

"Painless?"

"I forgot to ask him if it hurt," Lionel said.

"You said it would be painless."

"It's not my job to make you feel better about your decision." Lionel kept his voice steady.

"I suppose not. You'll have the rest of your money tonight."

"The locker key will be under the pay phone, same as last time."

"Thank you. My family. . .we thank you. It was a mercy."

"I could tell," Lionel said, "that your uncle Lionel was a pretty used up guy." He hung up. But he didn't go rushing off to the terminal to see if the young woman in the Mercedes showed up again to deliver the rest of the payment. He turned out the lights and sat at the coffee table, a Beretta in his hand, waiting.

᚛

It took five hours. Lionel almost fell asleep. Finally a timid knock rapped at the door. Lionel opened his eyes in the dark. Another knock. Another knock, then a question asked low against the door frame, for the benefit of any neighbors with their hearing aids turned up: "Uncle Lionel? You okay?"

He waited. They all had keys, of course. It was what family did.

Lionel yawned through two more knocks, another low call of his name, then the key slid into the door.

He raised the gun, cocked it, put on a smile in the dark. He didn't feel seventy. He felt twenty, ready to slap down the world when it got in his way.

The door opened and the outline of a young man stood against the dim light of the hallway for a moment before he shut the door behind him. Darkness again, and silence, except for the scratch of fingers groping the wall, searching for the wall switch.

The lights flicked on. Brad—Jill's husband, the restaurateur—stood blinking at him.

"You were probably planning on screaming," Lionel said, "when you found my body. I'd forget that notion."

Brad stood frozen. A weak smile twitched on his face. "What's with the gun, Uncle Lionel?"

"Someone has to come discover my body. The faster you do, the quicker my will's in probate. I didn't think you'd waste a whole day."

He tried the smile again. "I don't understand."

"Mr. Grimm does," Lionel said, and let the name sink into Brad's shock. "Is Jill with you?"

"No," he said after a moment.

"She know about this?"

"No, sir."

"Good. Put your hands on your head."

"You can't be serious."

"Serious as a stroke."

Brad, after a moment, obeyed.

"Hiring a contract killer is a felony, son."

Brad swallowed and found his bluster. "You can't prove anything."

"Your Mr. Grimm had a tape in his pocket of your phone conversation. I bet one of them fancy FBI computers'll be able to tie your voice right back to you."

"Where's Mr. Grimm?"

"Dead. In the back bedroom. He tried to shoot me up with a needle and I shot the bastard."

"You. . .shot him."

"Self-defense. And I doubt any jury would convict me for shooting you, since you hired him."

"You're wrong. You're crazy. We've all thought you were losing your mind. . ."

"Please. I have twice the brain power you do and several times the guts. I want to know why you wanted me gone. If you deny it, if you lie, I'll shoot you dead. Unvarnished truth. It's your only hope."

Brad swallowed. "The restaurants. They're failing. Jill and I needed a cash infusion—or we could lose it all. I know I can make the restaurant work, I just needed the cash to tide me over. . ."

His life. Ended for a restaurant, a room with tables and chairs and mediocre food and hundreds of unimportant conversations and dirty plates and wine-kissed glasses.

"Tell me about the hot little number who ran your errands at the bus station."

Brad's mouth worked in silence.

"Mr. Grimm had a digital camera, too."

"She's just a. . .friend."

"Jill know about her?"

"No, sir."

"Jill doesn't know much, does she?" Shame, too, his niece was a kind and sweet woman who deserved better.

"No, sir." He sounded miserable.

"I appreciate your honesty," Lionel said. "I don't suppose you ever thought of asking for a loan from me."

"You might say no. I'm sorry, I'm so sorry."

"We got to sort this out, Brad. Like men. You won't do Jill much good in a jail cell. Or in bankruptcy court. I don't want her miserable. So I'm going to help you out of the jam you're in."

Brad nodded, seeing light at the end of his tunnel, relief on his face. "What are you going to do?"

Lionel put down the gun; it was empty anyway. "Bring me my cane, would you? Let's go for a walk and a talk and figure out how to solve this problem."

✦

"Had he shown signs of being suicidal?" the policeman asked Lionel the next day.

"No. . .but he was deeply upset." Lionel glanced out the window, past the path that went out over the waterway where Brad's body had been found in the predawn hours, drowned. "We argued. He wanted money from me. He told me his restaurant's in awful shape. I said no. Not a loan, at least, but maybe I could buy in as a partner. As a steadying, mature hand. I truly wanted to help him and my niece. But it wasn't what he wanted to hear, he was desperate, he went crazy, lost his temper. He raised his hand to me. . .but then he stormed off."

The detective frowned at the stooped, fragile old man. "I'm very sorry for your loss. Mr. Dupuy."

"Thank you. . .I just can't believe he's gone. I have to call his wife and tell her, that's going to be hard."

"I know you'll be a comfort to her, sir."

Lionel leaned on his cane and gave a mournful, bittersweet smile to the policeman. "Yes. Family is a mercy, isn't it?"

Afterword

My inspiration was simple: write about an old guy who kicks ass. Lionel wrote himself—he appeared in my head, full-blown, camouflaged behind the stereotype of a harmless old man but commanding an iron nerve. I fully suspect he'll be back in another story or appearing in one of my novels—Lionel is not one for retirement. –J.A.

PROS AND CONS

DONNA MOORE

Donna Moore (born 1962) lives in Glasgow, where she has a thrilling dual career as a mild-mannered pension consultant by day, and an unemployed superhero by night. For relaxation she listens to Dean Martin and The Ramones, watches screwball comedy and film noir, and enjoys salsa, cha cha cha and merengue—despite having two left feet. Her debut novel, …Go To Helena Handbasket, was published this year by Point Blank Press,

PROS AND CONS
by Donna Moore

Barry Sheehan looked at the sparkling diamonds around the wrinkled throat of the woman in front of him and surreptitiously adjusted his y-fronts. Wealth always gave him a hard-on and these two auld bitches were dripping with it. It wasn't so much the wealth itself, as the idea of separating it from its rightful owners. In this case La Contessa Letitzia di Ponzo and her sister Signora Teodora Grisiola.

Sheehan smiled at the two frail old dears in front of him and thought how easy this was going to be. He considered his smile to be the deal-clincher. He'd practiced it in front of the bathroom mirror, and convinced himself he looked like Cary Grant, when in reality he looked more like a constipated ferret.

"Well Mr. Sheehan," the Contessa adjusted the diamond necklace with a liver-spotted hand, "I think you will do very well as our chauffeur." Her Italian accent was light and soft. It reminded Sheehan of some actress in an old black and white film he'd seen on video when he was last in Mountjoy Prison. "If you would like to come back tomorrow in the morning, we will have ready a uniform for you and you can drive us out to Fairyhouse Racecourse to meet some of our potential clients."

Sheehan's interest was piqued. "You ladies are interested in horseracing?" He patted the crumpled Racing Post in his pocket. Things were looking better and better. The chance to drive a Daimler, a shot at stealing some rather fine diamonds, and a day at the track.

"Gambling? No." The Contessa made a moue of distaste and her silent sister looked shocked at the thought, raising a jeweled hand to her throat as if to cross herself. "But we have an interest in fine thoroughbreds, yes. Now Mr. Sheehan. I will see you out. I apologize for the lack of etiquette, but we haven't yet got around to hiring a butler." She picked an almost invisible speck of dust off her suit — Hardy Amies, dress designer to the Queen —and Sheehan stood up. He'd been dismissed. Fighting the dual temptations of bowing to them and nutting them he allowed the Contessa to usher him to the door of the Georgian townhouse that she and her sister were currently calling casa.

🎸

Back in the Drawing Room, the Contessa stood at the window and watched Sheehan strolling up Lower Leeson Street towards St Stephens Green. Her sister looked at her curiously. "Well, Letty, will he do?"

"He's a dodgy, rat-faced, little wanker who wouldn't know the word 'honesty' if it gave him a lap dance and bit him on the arse. He's perfect." Her accent was now more Isle of Dogs than Island of Venice. "Didn't he remind you of that punter you had in the 60s, Dora? The politician who liked you to dress up as a milkmaid and squeeze his udders? Assistant to the Assistant of the Minister of Agriculture, Fisheries and Foods wasn't he?"

Dora giggled. "Old Marigold? Yes, but I do hope Mr. Sheehan doesn't want me to slap him on the buttocks and hit him with a fly switch. I'm getting too old for that sort of thing."

Letty removed the diamond necklace and threw it down on the table, rubbing her neck. "That cheap tat is giving me a rash. Did you see Sheehan fixing his beadies on it?" She pulled a packet of Rizlas and a pouch of tobacco out of her fake Chanel handbag and expertly rolled a cigarette one-handed, lighting it with a Zippo displaying a Hell's Angels emblem and the motto "Live Fast, Die Young." She groped under the chintz cushion of the settee for the bottle of tequila she had planked there earlier, and opened The Racing Post which, just a couple of minutes ago, had been in Sheehan's pocket. She still had all the old skills.

Just plain Lettuce and Dora Huggins—ex-high class hookers, ex-brothel madams, ex-pickpockets,-drunk rollers and -petty criminals—had moved up in the world.

🎸

Sheehan leaned against the Daimler in the private enclosure at Fairyhouse and watched Ireland's rich and famous swarm around his new employers like bluebottles around diamond-encrusted shit. Gobshites. He had to admire the Italian pair though. Their scam was a good one. From what he'd observed today they were selling certificates of part ownership in thoroughbred horses. 50,000 euros a share. The women had the right patter, references from top names in the horseracing world, the backing of Lord This and Duke That. Most of all they were fluently talking the language of the greedy bastards drooling all over them. The language of cold, hard cash.

"A 25% to 30% return in 3 months," the Countess was saying

in her clipped, lightly accented tones, as she tapped out strings of numbers on the slim laptop computer on the table in front of her. "Guaranteed. The stud fees on their own are worth a fortune in income. Why, the Duke of Chalfont was able to restore the family seat in a year from his returns. 200,000 euros, Mr. Kavanagh? Certainly. Just give me your bank account details and we'll effect the transaction immediately."

These rich tossers might not be able to recognize a hoor with the clap when they saw one, but Sheehan certainly did. He'd made a fair packet from this sort of scam himself until he'd gone to jail for it. His was on a smaller scale of course, but Sheehan recognized the signs. He'd sold dodgy TV advertising (he'd even got a film student friend to film a couple of fake adverts—and they'd made a porno while they were at it; Sheehan was rather proud of his starring role—OK, it was a short fuckin' fillum and it was all wobbly cameras and badly dubbed sound, but they'd got the money shot and that was the main thing). He'd guaranteed his investors a 30% return every 60 days. And, of course, he'd made sure to deliver to the first few investors. They spread the word and all the other suckers signed up. Needless to say, the other suckers never got their promised returns. Or their capital back as it happened. It was risky, and you had to have balls to pull it off. For a while Sheehan had managed to juggle those balls in the air as he robbed Peter to pay Paul, but eventually the whole thing had collapsed like a drunken sailor, and Sheehan hadn't managed to disappear before the Gardai came a-calling.

Sheehan narrowed his eyes and ground out his cigarette under the heel of his boot. He was decked out in his new green and gold uniform—knife-edge creases in the trousers, gold buttons shining, black boots polished to within an inch of their life. He was hot, uncomfortable and he'd nearly lamped the auld bitch one when she gave him the uniform. Green and gold? He was a Unionist all the way. Green and feckin' gold? If it hadn't been for that insult he might have stuck with his original plan of heisting the diamonds. Now he was going to make this job really worth his while. Sheehan had a grudging admiration for the aul wans. But it wasn't going to stop him relieving them of some of the cash. It would be like taking candy from a baby.

❦

"Well Dora, how much have we made?" Letty put her feet up on the rented Georgian table in the drawing room, popped the cork of a magnum of Dom Perignon and opened a packet of pork scratchings.

Dora entered the final few numbers into the laptop. "Just short of 4 million euros. Not too shabby." She opened one of the miniature bottles of Tia Maria that she'd stolen off the trolley on the EasyJet flight over from Luton the week before, clinked it against the bottle of champagne in Letty's hand and knocked it back.

"Piece of piss, Dora. Piece of piss." Two enormous trunks were open at Letty's feet, each of them half full of clothes. "I checked the flight to Rio. We need to be at the airport in an hour or so. Sheehan should be back in a few minutes to drive us."

"And here I am, *ladies*." Sheehan lounged in the doorway, a smile on his thin lips.

Letty dragged herself back into Countess mode, removed her feet from the table and gently placed the half empty champagne bottle down, burping in a ladylike manner as she did so. "Ah, Sheehan, please could you take these trunks to the car."

"Oh, I don't think so. I think you and I and Dora here need to have a nice wee chat, about an equitable sharing of the proceeds of your day at the races. It's only fair after all."

He moved to where Dora had been sitting and turned the laptop round to face him. "4 million euros, eh? And what are two auld bitches like yerselves going to do with 4 million euros? A nice old peoples' home should set you back a couple of thousand at the most. I might let you have 10,000 or so, just so you can keep yourselves in Rich Tea Biscuits."

Letty jumped up from the sofa and took a couple of tottering steps towards him. Sheehan picked up the plane tickets lying next to the laptop and laughed, as Letty and Dora stared at him wide-eyed and open-mouthed, dewlaps quivering in unison.

"And yez think yez are heading off to Argentina with your ill-gotten gains?"

"Brazil," muttered Letty, as she regained her composure, hefted the half empty magnum of champagne, and swung it at the back of his head with as much vigor as she'd once used to whip politicians and High Court judges into submission in her previous career. "Rio de Janiero is in Brazil you stupid fucking little twat." She dropped the champagne bottle onto Sheehan's rat-like face as he lay on the floor staring blankly upwards. As the bottle smashed his nose Letty said "That'll teach you, you little wanker" and wiped her hands on her skirt.

※

Colm O'Neill knocked on the door of the Georgian Townhouse, his home-made collecting tin in hand. If he'd chosen to use his IT degree wisely he could have had a future. But he didn't like to get up in the morning so, instead, he'd printed out some imposing looking business cards and brochures for a charity proclaiming itself 'The Holy Sisters of Perpetual Misery' and spent his afternoons fleecing Dublin's tourists and residents alike of the odd 20 euros. Just enough to get himself a wee carry-out from the offy and a couple of ounces of the finest cannabis from his dealer in Gardiner Street.

An elderly lady opened the door and looked at him calmly, a smaller woman fluttering behind her like a stressed-out moth. Quickly sizing them up – the well-cut suits, the jewels adorning their necks and fingers, the general aura of wealth, Colm decided to go for broke. "Howya ladies. I'm collecting for The Holy Sisters, and wondered if you'd be after sparing 50 euros for a good cause?" He rattled his tin to tempt them.

"Certainly young man, do come in." The non-fluttering woman opened the door wider and he stepped into the hall. Two huge old-fashioned trunks and several smaller bags were in the hallway, coats draped over them. "You've just caught us on our way out. We're waiting for a taxi to take us to the airport." The woman looked at him appraisingly for a long moment and then rummaged in her handbag. Pulling out a large wallet she gave him a hundred euros. "A fine strapping young chap like you—I wonder if you'd do us a small favor. Would you take these two trunks here to the dump? We just... don't have the time. And although they're on wheels they're terribly heavy and my sister and I are not as young as we used to be. It's just some old papers and old clothes that we don't want."

Colm practically snatched off her hand to get to the 100 euro note. "Sure, and whyever not."

"I just need to put a couple more things in." The woman disappeared into a room to the left, came out a couple of minutes later and slid a fat envelope into a compartment at the side of one of the trunks.

Colm lifted the handle of the brown trunk. She was right. It was heavy. Maybe he should ask for 200 euros. Still, there might be something inside worth having—he didn't want to appear too greedy. "Have a lovely trip ladies. And thank you. The Sisters of Perpetual Misery will bless you."

❦

Letty and Dora sat in Business Class with their feet up, watching 'Oceans Eleven' on the screen in front of them as they sipped their champagne on the flight to Rio.

Dora smiled happily. "Letty, that nice young man is going to open

204

the trunks, isn't he dear?"

"Of course he is Dora. He won't be able to resist."

"What do you think he'll do when he finds those nicely packaged portions of Mr. Sheehan?"

"I have absolutely no idea. But hopefully the 10,000 euros I also put in the trunk will offset the horrible shock." Letty studied George Clooney on the screen as he scammed the Las Vegas casino out of a fortune. "Dora, do you know if they have casinos in Rio?"

Afterword

When I grow up, I want to be just like Aunt Abby Brewster or Aunt Martha Brewster in Arsenic and Old Lace. *They're sweet, gentle, huggable...and murderous. I've long found them two of the loveliest old dears and have wondered what they would be like if updated for the 21st century. Then I saw a TV program telling the true story of elderly ex-hooker who conned gullible rich people out of small, and sometimes large, fortunes. And she did it using nothing more than sheer brass neck. And there I had it: Arsenic and Old Whores. –D.M.*

STEPPING UP

MARK BILLINGHAM

Mark Billingham (born 1961) is the author of a series of novels featuring London-based DI Tom Thorne, the latest of which is Buried. *He has been shortlisted for five CWA Daggers, won the Sherlock award for the creation of the Best British Detective, and, in 2005, won the Theakston's Old Peculier Award for Crime Novel of the Year. Though feeling far from damn near dead, and still not discounting the possibility of a top-level soccer career, there are worrying signs. He has started to yell at complete strangers that pop songs don't have a tune and complain that his children treat the house like a hotel. He remains in some doubt that he is still getting away with wearing an earring.*

†

STEPPING UP
by Mark Billingham

I was never cut out to be the centre of attention. I never asked for it. I never enjoyed it.

Some people love all that though, don't they? They need to be the ones having their heads swelled and their arses licked; pawed at and fawned over. Some people are idiots, to be fair, and don't know what to do with themselves if they aren't smack in the middle of the fucking action.

Of course, there were times when I *did* get the attention, whether I wanted it or not. When things were going well and I won a title or two. I got it from men *and* women then, and you won't hear me say there was anything wrong with that. Blokes wanting to shake your hand and tarts queuing up to shake your other bits and pieces, well nobody's complaining about that kind of carry on, are they?

But *this*, though…?

The doctor had been banging on about exercise, especially as I was having such a hard time giving up the fags. It would help to get the old ticker pumping a bit, he said. Get your cholesterol down and shift some of that weight which isn't exactly helping matters, let's face it. You used to box a bit, didn't you, he said, so you shouldn't find it too difficult to get back in the swing of it. To shape up a little.

Piece of piss, I told him, then corrected myself when he smiled and straightened his tie.

"Cake, I meant. Sorry, Doc. Piece of cake."

I don't know which one of us I was kidding more.

I got Maggie's husband, Phil, to give me a hand and fetch some of my old gear out of the loft. We scraped the muck off the skipping rope and hung the heavy bag up in the garage. I thought I would be able to ease myself back into it, you know? Stop when it hurt and build things up slowly. Trouble was it hurt all the time, and the more I tried, the more angry I got that I'd let myself go to shit so badly; that I'd smoked so many fags and eaten so much crap and put so much booze away down the years.

"It was mum's fault for spoiling you," Maggie said. "If she hadn't laid on meat and two veg for you every day of her life, you *might* have learned to do a bit more than boil a bleeding egg. You wouldn't have had to eat so many take-aways after she'd gone…"

Once my eldest gets a bee in her bonnet, that's it for everyone. It was her that had nagged me into going to the doctor's in the first place, getting some exercise or what have you. So, even though the boxing training hadn't worked out, the silly mare had no intention of letting the subject drop.

One day, in the pub with Phil, I found out that I wasn't the only one getting it in the neck.

"Help me out, for Christ's sake," he said. "She won't shut up about it, how she thinks you're going to drop dead any bloody second. Just do *something*."

"Snooker?"

"Funny."

"Fucked if I know, Phil. There's nothing I fancy."

I'd told Mags I wouldn't go jogging and that was all there was to it. I've been there, so I know how that game works; shift a few pounds and fuck up your knee joints at the same time. Tennis wasn't for the likes of me and the same went double for golf, even though a couple of blokes in the pub had the odd game now and again. The truth is, I know you have to stick at these kind of things, and that's never been my strong suit. I had a talent in the ring, so I didn't mind putting the hours in, and besides, I had more…drive back then, you know? Day after day on a golf course or a sodding tennis court, just so I wouldn't look like a twat every time I turned out, didn't sound much fun.

Plus, there weren't that many people I could think of to play with, tell you the truth…

"There's a class," Phil said. "Down our local leisure centre. One night a week, that's all."

"Class?"

"Just general fitness, you know. Look it's only an hour and there's a bit of a drink afterwards. You'll be doing me a favor."

"Hmmm." I swallowed what was left of a pint and rolled my eyes, and that was it. That's how easily a misunderstanding happens and you get yourself shafted.

I should have twigged a couple of weeks later when Maggie came by to pick me up. On the way there I asked her where Phil was, was he coming along later and all that, and she looked at me like I'd lost the plot. See, I thought it was *his* class, didn't I? A few lads jumping about, maybe a quick game of five-a-side and then a couple of beers afterwards. When I walked out of that changing room in my baggy shorts and an old West Ham shirt, I felt like I'd been majorly stitched up. There was Maggie, beaming at me, and a dozen or so other women, and all of them limbering up in front of these little plastic steps.

A fucking *step* class. Jesus H…

And not just women, either, which didn't help a great deal. There were a couple of men there to witness the humiliation, which always makes it worse, right? You know what I'm talking about. There were three other fellas standing about, looking like each of them had gone through what I was going through right then. An old boy, a few years on me, who looked like he'd have trouble *carrying* his step. A skinny young bloke in a tight top, who I figured was queer straight away, and a fit-looking sort who I guessed was there to pull something a bit older and desperate.

Looking around, trying my hardest to manage a smile, I could see that most of the women were definitely in that category. Buses, back-ends, you see what I'm getting at? I swear to God, you wouldn't have looked twice at any of them.

Except for Zoe.

I met her forty-odd years back, when I was twenty-something and I'd won a few fights; one night when I was introduced to some people at a nightclub in Tottenham. Frank Sparks was doing pretty well himself at that time, and there were all sorts of faces hanging about. I wasn't stupid. I knew full well what was paying for Frank's Savile Row suit and what have you, and to tell you the truth, it never bothered me.

There weren't many saints knocking around anywhere back then.

Frank was friendly enough, and for the five or ten minutes I sat at his table, it was like we were best friends. He was one of those blokes with a knack for that, you know? Told me he was following my career, how he'd won a few quid betting on me, that kind of thing. He said there were always jobs going with him. All sorts of bits and pieces, you know, if things didn't work out or I jacked the fight game in or whatever.

I can still remember how shiny his hair was that night. And his teeth, and the stink of Aramis on him.

She was the sister of this bloke I used to spar with, and I'd seen her waiting for him at the back of the gym a few times, but it wasn't until that night in Tottenham that I started to pay attention. She was all dressed up, with different hair, and I thought she was an actress or a stripper. Then we got talking by the bar and she laughed and told me she was just Billy's sister. I said she was better looking than any of the actresses or strippers that were there guzzling Frank's champagne, and she went redder than the frock she was wearing, but I knew she liked it.

I saw her quite a bit after that in various places. She started going out with one of Frank Sparks' boys and wearing a lot of fancy dresses. I remember once, I'd just knocked this black lad over in the fourth round at Harringay. I glanced down, sweating like a pig, and she was sitting a few rows back smiling up at me, and the referee's count seemed to take forever.

❦

You just get on the thing, then off again; up and down, up and down, one foot or both of them, in time to the fucking music. Simple as that. You can get back down the same way you went up, or sometimes you turn and come down on the other side, and now and again there's a bit of dancing around the thing, but basically…you climb on and off a plastic step.

I swear to God, that's it.

Maybe, that first time, I should have just turned and gone straight back in that changing room. Caught a bus home. Maggie had that look on her face though, and I thought walking out would be even more embarrassing than staying.

So, I decided to do it just the once, for Mags, and actually, it didn't turn out to be as bad as I expected. It was a laugh as it goes, and at least I could do it without feeling like it was going to kill me. It was a damn sight harder than it looked, mind you, make no fucking mistake about *that*. I was knackered after ten minutes, but what with there being so many women in the class, I didn't feel like I had to compete with anyone, you know what I mean?

Ruth, the woman in charge, seemed genuinely pleased to see me when I showed up again the second week and the week after that. She teased me a bit, and I took the piss because she had one of those microphone things on her ear like that singer with the pointy tits. They were *all* quite nice, to be honest. A pretty decent bunch. I'd pretend to flirt a bit with one or two of the women, and I'd have a laugh with Anthony, who didn't bang on about being gay like a lot of them do, you know?

Even Craig seemed all right, to begin with.

The pair of us ended up next to each other more often than not, on the end of the line behind Zoe. Him barely out of breath after half an hour; me, puffing and blowing like I was about to keel over. The pair of us looking one way and one way only, while she moved, easy and sweet, in front of us.

One time, he took his eyes off her arse and glanced across at me. I did likewise, and while Ruth was shouting encouragement to one of the older ladies, the cheeky fucker winked, and I felt the blood rising to my neck.

I remember an evening in the pub with Maggie and Phil, a few weeks in, and me telling Maggie not to be late picking me up for the class. To take the traffic into account. She plastered on a smartarse smile, like she thought she'd cottoned on to something, but just said she was pleased I was enjoying myself.

It only took one lucky punch from a jammy Spaniard for everything to go tits up as far as the fighting was concerned. I had a few more bouts, but once the jaw's been broken, you're never quite as fearless. Never quite as stupid as you need to be.

Stupid as I had been, spending every penny I'd ever made, quick as I'd earned it.

With the place I was renting in Archway, the payments on a brand new Cortina, and sweet FA put by, it wasn't like I had a lot of choice when it came to doing door work for Frank Sparks. Besides, it was easy money, as it went. A damn sight less stressful than the ring anyway, and I certainly didn't miss the training. Your average Friday-night drunk goes down a lot easier than a journeyman light-heavyweight, but the fact is, I couldn't have thrown more than half a dozen punches in nearly a year of it. I was there to look as if I was useful, see, and that was fine. Like I said before, I was happier in the background and I think Frank was pretty pleased with the way I was handling things, because he asked me if I fancied doing a spot of driving.

And that's when I started seeing a lot more of her.

She wasn't married yet, but I'd heard it was on the cards. Her boyfriend had moved up through the ranks smartish, and was in charge of a lot of Frank's gambling clubs. Classy places in Knightsbridge and Victoria with cigarette girls and what have you. She used to go along and just sit in the corner drinking and looking tasty, but some of these sessions went on all night, and she'd always leave before her old man did.

So, I started to drive her.

I started to ask to drive her; volunteering quietly, you know? There were a couple of motors on call and we took it in turns at first. Then, after a few weeks, she asked for me, and it sort of became an arrangement.

In the image I still have of her, she's standing on a pavement, putting on a scarf as I indicate and drift across towards the curb. She's clutching a handbag. She waves as I pull up, then all but falls into the back of the Jag; tired, but happy as Larry to be on the way home.

In reality of course she was thinner, and drunker. Her eyes got flatter and the bleach made her hair brittle, and she was always popping some pill or other. That crocodile handbag rattled with them. The smile was still there though; lighting up what was left of her. The same as it was when I looked down through the ropes that time and saw her clapping.

When I felt as though I was the one who'd had the breath punched out of me.

How bloody old am I?

It's a fair question, but I don't suppose it really matters. *Too* old, that's the point, isn't it? Too old to smoke and not worry about it; to put on a pair of socks without sitting down; to think about running for a bus.

Too old to feel immortal…

Like you'd expect, it was mostly Diet Coke and fizzy water in the pub afterwards. I had orange juice and lemonade myself, for the first week anyway, but Zoe drank beer from the off.

Ruth didn't give a monkey's what anyone did once the class was over, but there was one woman who didn't approve; who clearly enjoyed having another reason to dislike Zoe. She was glaring across at her from an adjoining table, one night a few weeks in, and I was giving it the old cow back with bells on.

"Maybe she's jealous because she secretly fancies you," Zoe whispered.

I pulled a face. "Christ, don't put me off me pint!"

She really enjoyed that one. Her laugh was low and dirty, and it still amazes me really, to think of it coming out of a mouth like hers. A face like that.

"She's just dried-up and bitter," I said. "Hates it that she's doing this to try and change how she looks, or what have you, while others don't really have to."

Zoe smiled, leaned a shoulder against mine. "Some people just don't know how to have fun, you know? Think their bodies are temples and all that."

"My body's more of a slaughterhouse these days," I said.

She enjoyed that one too. It felt fantastic to make her laugh. We shared a big packet of crisps, which really wound up the old bag on the next table. She left early, while Zoe and me and a few of the others stayed until they rang the bell, same as always. Ruth and Anthony were giggling by the jukebox, and Maggie kept an eye on me from a table near the door, where she sat clutching her mobile phone, waiting for Phil to come and pick the pair of us up.

"Why *do* you come?" I asked her. "It's not like you need to lose weight or anything. You seem pretty fit…"

She leaned a shoulder into mine. "You're sweet."

"I'm just saying."

She took another swig from her bottle. "I'm lazy," she said. "I need to make myself do things, get out and do something a bit off the wall, you know? Anyway, it's a laugh, don't you reckon?"

I did reckon, and I told her.

"I work in a stupid office," she said. "The people there are all right I suppose, but I don't want to see them after work or whatever. I think it's good to meet people who aren't anything like you are. People with different lives, you know? I tried a French class, but it was too hard, and the teacher was a bit stuck-up. This is much better. Much."

She had a voice it was easy to listen to. She certainly wasn't posh, but there wasn't really an accent either. Just soft and simple, you know?

"What about you?" she asked.

I said I was basically there to keep Maggie happy, and to try and get at least some of the old fitness back. I mentioned that I used to box a bit and she said that she could see it. That it was in the way I carried myself.

I had to hide my face in my glass, and I'd all but downed the rest of the pint by the time the blush had gone away.

"Someone needed a drink," she said.

There was a burst of high-pitched laughter from Ruth and Anthony, and when I looked across, I could see that Maggie had gone from a smartarse smile to something that looked like concern.

I went up to get the two of us refills, and exchanged nods with Craig who was deep in conversation with the woman behind the bar. He was smoking which made me deeply fucking envious. If Maggie hadn't been sitting by the door, I might well have ponced one.

"Enjoying yourself?" he said.

When the barmaid went to fetch the drinks, Craig span slowly round and leaned back against the bar. He looked across at Zoe for a minute, more maybe, then turned to me. His face said 'I *know*, I couldn't agree more, mate. But look at *me* and look at *you*.'

Or he might just have been asking me to pass the ashtray.

Oh fuck it, who knows?

ff

Her old man had a place in Battersea, on the edge of the park. There was a night I was driving her back from one of Frank's casinos, down through Chelsea towards Albert Bridge, when she started asking me all manner of funny questions.

"Do you actually like any of them, though? Are any of them really your mates if you think about it?"

The gin had slowed her up a little. Thickened her voice, you know?

"Any of who?" I said.

She jerked a thumb back towards where we'd come from. "That lot. The boys. They're just people you work with, aren't they? Just blokes you knock around with, right, and I don't suppose any of them give a toss about you, either. Wouldn't you say?"

I shrugged and watched the road. It wasn't like I'd never heard her talking bollocks before. Next time she spoke, her voice had more breath in it, and she kept saying my name, but that's something else people do when they've had a couple, isn't it?

"It's just London, right?" she said. "Frank doesn't own stuff anywhere else, does he?"

"I don't know. I don't think so."

"I don't think so either."

"He's been up north on business, definitely. Manchester..."

"It was only a few times," she said. "Just to meet people."

"Birmingham as well. I drove him to the station."

"He was just looking though, that's what I heard. Nothing came of it. It's all here really, don't you reckon?" She said my name again, slow with a question in it. Wanting me to agree with her. "Everyone's here, aren't they?"

I heard a song I knew she liked come on the radio and I turned it up for her. That girl who did Eurovision without any shoes on. I was waiting for her to start singing along, but when I looked in the rear-view I could see that her eyes were closed.

Her head was tipped back and her mascara was starting to run.

Things really started to go pear-shaped the time Zoe turned up looking like she did and Craig didn't turn up at all.

I hadn't admitted it to myself, not really, that the two of them were seeing each other outside the class, but I had to stop being stupid and face facts when I saw her walk in like that. It was like I suddenly knew all sorts of things at once. I knew that they'd got together, that everyone else had probably sussed it a damn sight faster than me, and I knew exactly what had happened to her face.

In class, I stepped that bit faster than usual. I stamped on and off that bastard thing, and it was automatic, like I could do it all day and I wasn't even thinking. Ruth said how well I was doing and when Zoe smiled at me, encouraging, I had to look away.

Afterwards, she didn't turn towards the pub with the rest of us, and when I saw that she was heading for the car-park, I moved to go after her. Maggie took hold of my arm and said something about getting a table. I told her I'd be there in a minute, to get one in for me, but she didn't look very happy.

I tried to get a laugh out of Zoe when I caught her up; made out like I was knackered, you know, from chasing after her, but she didn't seem to really go for it. "Do you not fancy it tonight then?" I said. "Not even a swift half?"

She was fetching her car-keys from her bag. Digging around for them and keeping her head down. "I've got an early start in the morning," she said. "New boss, you know?"

I nodded, told her that one wasn't going to hurt.

She caught me looking, not that I was trying particularly hard not to. It was like a plum that someone had stepped on around her cheek, and the ragged edges of it were the color of a tea-stain. There was a half-moon of blood in her eye.

"I didn't know there was a cupboard open and I turned round into it," she said. "Clumsy bitch…"

"Shush…"

"I actually knocked myself out for a few seconds."

"Listen, it's all right," I said.

"What is?"

"Come and have one quick drink," I said. "Who am I going to share my salt and vinegar crisps with if you don't?"

It was as though she suddenly noticed that my hand was on her wrist, and she looked down and took half a step back. "I'll see you next week."

"Look after yourself." It came out as a whisper. I didn't really know what else to say.

She pressed the button on her car-keys and when the lights flashed and the alarm squawked, I saw her jump slightly.

In the pub, I couldn't blame Maggie for being off with me. I sat there with a face like a smacked arse, and I couldn't have said more than three words to anyone. After half an hour I'd had enough, and I asked her to call Phil, get him to fetch us early. That didn't go down too well either because she was having a laugh with Anthony, but I just wasn't in the mood for it.

As we were leaving, Ruth raised her glass and said something about me being her star pupil.

Zoe didn't turn up at all the following week.

❦

We were driving, same as always. Seemed like, when it came to being close or what have you, that was the only time we ever really saw each other. Me in the front, her in the back.

"Go slowly, will you?" she'd said when she got in.

Obviously I was going to do what she wanted, right, and it was raining like a bastard anyway, so it wasn't like I could have put my foot down. Still, I wanted to get back to her place as quickly as I could. Don't get me wrong, I hated it when she got out of the car, hated it, but lately I'd taken to stopping somewhere after I'd dropped her off; soon as I'd got round the corner sometimes.

I'd pull over in the dark and sit quiet for a minute. Reach for a handkerchief. Throw one off the wrist, while I could still smell her in the car.

Sounds disgusting, I know, but it didn't feel like it back then.

I drove, slow like she wanted along the Brompton Road and down Sydney Street. Staring at the jaguar leaping from the end of the bonnet; the road slick, sucked up beneath it.

When I turned up the radio to drown out the squeak of the wipers, she leaned forward and asked me to switch it off.

Pissing down now. Clattering on the roof like tacks.

"There's people been talking to me," she said.

"What people?"

"They've been going over my options, you know?"

"What options?"

"The choices I've got."

I looked in the mirror. Watched her take a deep breath when she saw that I didn't understand.

"Billy's fucked up," she said. "Silly bugger's really gone and dropped himself in it."

Her brother. My ex-sparring partner. Always had been a bit of a tearaway.

"What's he done?" I asked. Prickles on my neck.

"He went for some flash Maltese fucker with a knife..."

"Jesus."

"Didn't really do him too much harm, but they'll happily bump it up to attempted murder. Put him away for a few years unless I decide to help."

I knew who she was talking about now. Coppers were the same as anyone else at the end of the day. There were plenty of stupid ones, but enough of them with brains to make life interesting.

"There's only Billy and me," she said. "The bastards know how close we are."

She started to cry just a little bit then. I went inside my jacket for the handkerchief I'd be using later on, but she'd already pulled one out from her handbag. I'd heard the pills rattling as she rummaged for it.

I was taking us over the bridge by now. Gliding across it. The lights swung like a necklace up ahead and the rain was churning up the water on either side of me.

"It's not like I know a fat lot."

"Fat lot about what?" I said, but it was obvious what she was banging on about.

"Frank. Frank's business. All that."

All that.

"Obviously they think I know something." She raised her hands, let them drop down with a slap on to the leather seat. "Maybe I know enough."

Course she did; she wasn't stupid, was she? Enough to get her little brother out of the shit and herself slap bang in it.

I wanted to slam on the anchors and stop the car right there on the bridge. To reach into the back and shake her until her fillings came loose. I wanted to tell her that her brother was a pissy little waster, and that she shouldn't be such a daft bitch, and to say absolutely fuck all to anyone about fuck all.

I was the one that kept my mouth shut though, wasn't I? The one who just gripped the wheel that little bit tighter and maneuvered the car like I was on my driving test. Checking the wing mirrors, hands at ten to two, watching my speed.

"I need to go away," she said.

Ten to two. Both eyes on the road...

"Somewhere abroad might be best. Somewhere hot, near the sea if I get a choice, but it might not have to be that far. Maybe Scotland or somewhere. I've tucked a bit away and I'm sure I can make a few bob later on. I can type for a kick-off."

Slowing for lights. No more than a mile away from the flat on the edge of the park. Checking the mirror and feathering the brake; moving down through the gears.

"I just don't feel like I can do it on my own, you know? That's the only bit I'm scared of, if I'm honest. It's pathetic I know, relying on someone like that, but the thought of nobody being there with me makes me feel sick, like I'm looking over the edge of something. I don't mean sex or whatever, but that's not out of the question either. It's mostly about having someone around who gives a toss, do you know what I mean?"

Waiting for the amber, willing that fucker to change.

"Someone who worries..."

She said my name, and it felt like I had something thick and bitter in my gullet.

Neither of us said anything else after that, but we were only five minutes away from the flat by then. The silence was horrible, make no mistake about that, but it just lay there until it sort of flattened out into something we were both willing to live with. Until she asked me to turn the radio back up.

When we pulled up, I got out to open her door, then climbed back *in again quick without saying much of anything. When I looked up she was standing there by my door. She had an umbrella, but she never even bothered getting it out; just stood there getting pissed on, with the rain bringing her hair down, until thick strands of it were dead and dark against her face.*

She was saying something. I couldn't hear, but I was looking at her mouth, same as always.

I thought she said : "It doesn't matter, Jimmy."

Then she put the tips of two fingers to her lips and pressed them against my window. They went white where she pressed, and I could still see the mark for a few minutes after I drove away.

I didn't stop the car where I normally did. Just kept going for a bit, trying to swallow and think straight. I drove up through Nine Elms and pulled in a mile or so past the power station.

Sat there and stared out across the shitty black river until it started to get light.

⚔

Craig looked confused as much as anything when I walked round the corner. Grinned at him. It was half way through the morning, and him and a couple of older women in blouses and grey skirts had come out the back entrance of the bank for a crafty smoke.

"All right, mate?"

"Ticking along," I said. "You?"

It must have been there in my face or the way I spoke, because I saw the women stubbing out pretty long fag-ends, making themselves scarce. Neither of them so much as looked at him before they buggered off.

Craig watched his colleagues go, seemed to find something about it quite funny. He turned back to me, taking a drag. Shook his head.

"Sorry, mate. It's just a bit strange you turning up here, that's all. How d'you know where I worked?"

"Zoe must have said, last time she came to the class, you know?"

Something in his face that I couldn't read, but I didn't much care.

"How's she doing, anyway?" I said.

"Er, she's good, yeah."

"It was a shame she stopped coming, really. We were all saying how she made the rest of us work a bit harder, trying to keep up."

"She just lost interest I think. Me an' all, to be honest." Then a look that seemed to say they were getting their exercise in other ways, and one back from me that tried and failed to wipe it off his face.

It was warm and he was in shirt-sleeves. I was sweating underneath my jacket so I slipped it off, threw it across my arm.

"Are you feeling OK?"

"I'm fine," I said.

"You've gone a bit red."

I nodded, looked at the sweat patches under his arm and the pattern on his poxy tie.

He flicked his fag-end away. "Listen, I've got to get back to work…"

"Right."

"I'll say hello to Zoe, shall I?"

"How's her face?"

That took the smile off the fucker quick enough. Put that confused look back again, like he didn't know his arse from his elbow.

"It's fine now," he said. "She's all gorgeous again."

"Nasty, that was. Not seen many shiners worse than that one. Door wasn't it?"

"Cupboard door."

"Yeah, that's what's she said."

"She forgot it was open and turned round fast, you know? Listen—"

I was just looking at him by now.

"What?"

I knew I still had *that*. You never lose the look.

"What's your problem?"

Breathing heavily, a wheeze in it. For real some of it, like the red face, but I'd bunged a bit extra on top, you know. Laid it on thick just to get his guard down.

"I think maybe you ought to piss off now," he said.

I bent over, suddenly; dropped the jacket like I might be in some trouble. He stepped across to pick it up, like I wanted him to, which was when I swung a good hard right at his fat, flappy mouth.

❦

I never had her in the car again after that night. Only saw her a couple of times as it goes, and even then, when she looked over, I always found something fascinating in the pattern on the carpet or counted the bits of chewing gum squashed onto the pavement.

Spineless cunt.

She went away some time after. I suppose I should say I was told she went away. It's an important distinction, right? Told like there was actually nothing to tell, but also like there wasn't much point me asking about it again or wasting any money on postcards.

A few years ago we were having a meal, me and one of the lads I used to knock about with back then. You have a curry and a few pints and you talk about the old days, don't you? You have a laugh.

Until her name came up.

He was talking about what he thought had happened and why. Wanted to know what I thought had gone on; fancied getting my take on it. You used to know her pretty well, didn't you, he said. That's what I heard, anyway. You used to be quite close to her is what somebody told me.

I had a mouthful of ulcers at that time. It was when my old girl was suffering, you know, and the doctor reckoned it was the stress of her illness that was causing it. Ulcers and boils, I had.

When he mentioned her name the first time, I started to chew on a couple of those ulcers. Gnawing into those bastards so hard it was making my eyes water, though my mate probably thought it was the vindaloo.

You used to be quite close to her, he said.

I bit the fuckers clean out then, two or three of them. I remember the noise I made, people in the restaurant turning round. I bent down over the table, coughing, and I spat them out into a serviette.

That more or less put the tin lid on our conversation, which was all right by me. My mate didn't say too much of anything after that. Well, we'd been talking about what was happening with me and my old lady before, and when he saw the blood in the napkin, maybe he was confused, you know, thought I was the one with the lung cancer.

§

It wasn't the best punch I ever threw, but it made contact and I concentrated on the blood that was running down his shirt-front as he swung me round and pushed me against the wall.

"What the fuck's your game, you silly old bastard?"

I tried to nut him and he leaned back, his arms out straight, holding me hard against the bricks.

"Take it easy."

I thought I felt something crack in his shin when I kicked out at him. I tried to bring my leg up fast towards his bollocks, but the pain in his leg must have fired him right up and his fists were flying at me.

It was no more than a few seconds. Just flailing really like kids, but Christ, I'd forgotten how much it hurts.

Every blow rang and tore and made the sick rise up. I felt something catch me and rip behind the ear; a ring maybe. Stung like fuck.

I swore, and kept kicking. I shut my eyes.

My fists were up, but it was all I could do to protect my face, so I can't have been doing him a lot of damage.

But I was trying.

When the gaps between the punches got a bit longer, I tried to get a dig or two in, just to keep my fucking end up, you know? That was when the background went blurry, and his face started to swim in front of me, but as far as I'm concerned that was down to the pain in my arm. It had bugger all to do with any punishment I might have taken.

The fucker hit me one more time, when I dropped my fists to clutch at my arm. It was all over then, more or less. But it was the pain in my chest that put me down, and not that punch.

Not the punch.

⟨⟩

There's always a *something* that gets you from one place to the next, right? That you're chasing after in some way, shape or form. Granted, some people are happy enough to let themselves get pissed along like a fag-end in a urinal, and yes, I know that some poor bastards are plain unlucky, but still…

OK, then, to be fair there's *usually* a something. For me, anyway, is all I'm saying. If I'm centre of attention right now, for all the wrong reasons, it isn't really down to anyone else, and I'm not going to feel sorry for myself.

That's more or less what I tried to say to Maggie and Phil when they came in, but they were in no fit state to listen, and I don't think I made myself very clear.

Fuck, they're *at* me again…

Loads of them, and I thought there was supposed to be a shortage. Poking and prodding. Talking over me like I'm deaf as well as everything else.

It's not pain exactly.

It's warm and wet and spreading through my arms and legs like I'm sinking into a bath or something. They've got those things you see on the TV out again, like a pair of irons on my chest. Like they're going to iron out my wrinkles.

Now they're going blurry either side of me, same as that fucker did when I was punching him. The sound's gone funny too.

And clear as you like, I can see her face. The stain around her eye and the purple bruise. The hair lying dead against her cheek in the rain.

Music as I step up and step up. Some tuneless disco rubbish while I'm sneaking looks at her in that tight leotard thing and Ruth bawls at me through her stupid microphone.

As I step up off the beach. With the sea coming up on to the sand behind me. Noisy, like the sigh of someone who's sick of waiting for something.

Stepping up on to the hot pavement, where she's stood waiting with a drink. That mouth, and her hair darker now and she looks magnificent. And we lean against each other and drink sangria at one of them places where you can sit outside.

The music's still getting louder, so I ask them to turn it up.

That song she likes on the radio.

The bird with the bare feet.

"I wonder if one day that, you'll say that you care.
If you say you love me madly, I'll gladly be there..."

Afterword

I got the idea for the story waiting for a flight home from Chicago airport, no more than a day or two after Duane had asked me if I'd write something. I'd love to say that Jimmy's story came to me fully formed, but it was probably no more than a bad pun and an old song, which is usually more than enough.

I've always enjoyed tales, in books and on film, about the old stager who gets one more shot; about the acid of regret and the balm of redemption. More basically, I also like good jokes about old people. I laugh, same as most people, at gags involving various mental and physical faculties failing. I laugh, nervously, knowing very well that I might be laughing at the same joke a few short years down the line, unable to remember my second name, or needing to change my underwear afterwards.

Growing old, gracefully or otherwise, has always seemed to me to be a mixture of the comic and the tragic: arthritis and bad dancing; senility and cat food. The image of a hard case reduced to step-aerobics seemed both sad and funny enough; like a good place to start a story about a man's chance to be a better old fool than he had been a young one.

The day after I finished "Stepping Up", I was browsing in a charity shop and found an original 45 of the song that Jimmy remembers: "Puppet On A String" by Sandie Shaw. It was only 25 pence and though it was scratched and in a tatty sleeve, I felt compelled to buy it. It seemed like a nice way to round things off, and the perfect thing on which to spend most of the fee I'd been paid for writing the story.

That's the other thing about getting older. You worry about money more... —M.B.

FEMME
FATALE

LAURA LIPPMAN

Laura Lippman (born 1959) is the author of the Tess Monaghan series and two critically acclaimed standalones, Every Secret Thing *and* To the Power of Three. *She lives in Baltimore. Her 11th novel,* No Good Deeds, *will be published this summer. The editor is happy that Laura didn't order his legs broken after forcing her to reveal her birth year for this anthology.*

FEMME FATALE

by Laura Lippman

This is true: There comes a time in the life of a beautiful woman, or even an attractive one with an abundance of charm, when she realizes that she can no longer rely on her looks. If she is unusually, exceedingly self-aware, the realization is a timely one. But, more typically, it lags the physical reality by several years, like a thunder clap when a lightning storm is passing by. One one thousand, two one thousand, three one thousand, four one thousand . . . boom. One one thousand two one thousand three one thousand four one thousand five one thousand. Boom. The lightning is moving out, away, which is a good thing in nature, but not in the life of a beautiful woman.

That's how it happened for Mona. A gorgeous woman at 20, a stunning woman at 30, a striking woman at 40, a handsome woman at 50, she was pretty much done by 60 – but only if one knew what she had been, once upon a time, and at this point that knowledge belonged to Mona alone. A 68-year-old widow when she moved into Leisure World, she was thought shy and retiring by her neighbors in the Creekside Condos, Phase II. She was actually an incurious snob, who had no interest in the people around her. People were over-rated, in Mona's opinion, unless they were men and they might be persuaded to marry you. *This is not my life*, she thought, walking the trails that wound through the pseudo-city in suburban Maryland. *This is not what I anticipated.*

Mona had expected . . . well, she hadn't thought to expect. To the extent that she had been able to imagine her old age at all, she had thought her sunset years might be something along the lines of Eloise at the Plaza – a posh place in a city center, with 24-hour room service and a concierge. Such things were available – but not to those with her resources, explained the earnest young accountant who reviewed the various funds left by Mona's husband, her fourth, although Hal Wickham had believed himself to be her second.

"Mr. Wickham has left you with a conservative, diversified portfolio that will cover your costs at a comfortable level – but it's not going to allow you to live in a *hotel*," the accountant had said a little huffily, almost as if he were one of Hal's children, who had taken the same tone when they realized how much of their father's estate was to go to Mona. But she was his wife, after all, and not some fly-by-night spouse. They had been married fifteen years, her personal best.

"But there's over two million, and the smaller units in that hotel are going for less than a million," she said, crossing her legs at the knee and letting her skirt ride up, just a bit. Her legs were still quite shapely, but the accountant's eyes slid away from them. A shy one. These bookish types killed her.

"If you cash out half of the investments, you earn half as much on the remaining principle, which isn't enough to cover your living expenses, not with the maintenance fees involved. Don't you see?"

"I'd be paying cash," she said, leaning forward, so her breasts rested on her elbows. They were still quite impressive. Bras were one wardrobe item that had improved in Mona's lifetime. Bras were amazing now, what they did with so little fabric.

"Yes, theoretically. But there would be taxes to pay on the capital gains of the stocks acquired in your name, and your costs would outpace your earnings. You'd have to dip into your principle and, at that rate, you'd be broke in—" he did a quick calculation on his computer – "seven years. You're only sixty-eight now—"

"Sixty-one," she lied reflexively.

"All the more reason to be careful," he said. "You're going to live a long, long time."

But to Mona, now ensconced in Creekside Condos-Phase II, it seemed only that it would feel that way. She didn't golf, so she had no use for the two courses at LeisureWorld. She had never learned to cook, preferring to dine out, but she loathed eating out alone and the delivery cuisine available in the area was not to her liking. She watched television, took long walks, and spent an hour a day doing vigorous isometric exercises that she had learned in the late-60s. This was before Jane Fonda and aerobics, when there wasn't so much emphasis on sweating. The exercises were the closest thing that Mona had to a religion and they had been more rewarding than most religions, delivering exactly what they promised – and in this lifetime, too. Plus, all her husbands, even the ones she didn't count, had benefited from the final set of repetitions, a series of pelvic thrusts done in concert with vigorous, yogic breathing.

One late fall day, lying on her back, thrusting her pelvis in counterpoint to her in-and-out breaths, it occurred to Mona that her life would not be much different in the posh, downtown hotel condo she had so coveted. It's not as if she would go to theater or museums; she had only pretended interest in those things because other people seemed to expect it. Museums bored her and theater baffled her – all those people talking so loudly, in such artificial sentences. Better restaurants wouldn't make her like eating out alone, and room service was never as hot as it should be. Her surroundings would be a considerable improvement, with truly top-of-the-line fixtures, but all that would have meant is that she would be lying on a better quality carpet right now. Mona was not meant to be alone and if she had known that Hal was going to die only fifteen years in, she might have chosen differently. Finding a husband at the age of 68, even when one claimed 61, had to be harder than finding a job at that age. With Hal, Mona had consciously settled. She wondered if he knew that. She wondered if he had died just to spite her.

ff

There was a Starbucks in LeisureWorld plaza and she sometimes ended her afternoon walks there, curious to see what the fuss was about. She found the chairs abominable – had anyone over 50 ever tried to rise from these low-slung traps – but she liked what a younger person might call the vibe. (Mona didn't actually know any young people and had been secretly glad that Hal's children loathed her so, as it gave her an excuse to have nothing to do with them or the grandchildren.) She treated herself to sweet drinks, chocolate drinks, drinks with whipped cream. Mona had been on a perpetual diet since she was 35 and while the discipline, along with her exercises, had kept her body hard, it had made her face harder still. The coffee drinks and pastries added weight, but no more than five or six pounds, and it was better than Botox, plumping and smoothing Mona's cheeks. She sipped her drink, stared into space, and listened to the curious non-music on the sound system. It wasn't odd to be alone in Starbucks, quite the opposite. When parties of two or three came in, full of conversation and private jokes, they were the ones who seemed out of place. The regulars all relaxed a little when those interlopers finally left.

"I hate to intrude, but I just had to say – ma'am? Ma'am?"

The man who stood next to her was young, no more than 45. At first glance, he appeared handsome, well put together. At second, the details betrayed him. There was a stain on his trench coat, flakes of dandruff on his shoulders down the front of his black turtleneck sweater.

Still, he was a man and he was talking to her.

"Yes?"

"You're . . . someone, aren't you? I'm bad with names, but I don't forget faces and you – well, you were a model, right? One of the new wave ones in the 60s, when they started going for that coltish look."

"No, you must think—"

"My apologies," he said. "Because you were better known for the movies, those avant garde ones you did before you chucked it all and married that guy, although you could have been as big as any of them. Julie Christie. She was your only serious competition."

It took Mona a second to remember who Julie Christie was, her brain first detouring through memories of June Christie, but then landing on an image of the actress. She couldn't help being pleased, if he was confusing her with someone who was serious competition for Julie Christie. Whoever he thought she was must have been gorgeous. Mona felt herself preening, even as she tried to deny the compliment. He thought he was even younger than she pretended to be.

"I'm not—"

"But you *are*," he said. "More beautiful than ever. Our culture is so confused about its . . . aesthetic values. I'm not talking about the veneration of age as wisdom, or the importance of experience, although those things are to the good. You are, objectively, more beautiful now than you were back then."

"Perhaps I am," she said lightly. "But I'm not whoever you think I was, so it's hard to know."

"Oh. Gosh. My apologies. I'm such an idiot—"

He sank into the purple velvet easy chair opposite her, twisting the brim of his hat nervously in his hands. She liked the hat, the fact of it. So few men bothered nowadays and, as a consequence, fewer men could pull them off. Mona was old enough, just, to remember when all serious men wore hats.

"I wish you could remember the name," she said, teasing him, yet trying to put him at ease, too. "I'd like to know this stunner that you say I resemble."

"It's not important," he said. "I feel so stupid. Fact is – I bet she doesn't look as good today as you do."

"Mona Wickham," she said, extending her hand. He bowed over it. Didn't kiss it, just bowed, a nice touch. Mona was vain of her hands, which were relatively unblemished. She kept her nails in good shape with weekly manicures and alternated her various engagement rings on the right hand. Today it was the square-cut diamond from her third marriage. Not large, but flawless.

"Bryon White," he said. "With an 'o,' like the poet, only the 'r' comes first."

"Nice to meet you," she said. Two or three seconds passed, and Bryon didn't release her hand and she didn't take it back. He was studying her with intense, dark eyes. Nice eyes, Mona decided.

"The thing is, you could be a movie star."

"So some said, when I was young." Which was, she couldn't help thinking, a good decade before the one in which this Bryon White thought she had been a model and an actress.

"No, I mean now. Today. I could see you as, as – Catherine, the Russian empress."

Mona frowned. Wan't that the naughty one?

"Or, you know, Lauren Bacall. I think she's gorgeous."

"I didn't like her in that movie with Streisand."

"No, but with Altman – with Altman, she was magnificent."

Mona wasn't sure who Altman was. She remembered a store in New York, years ago, B. Altman's. After her first marriage, she had changed into a two-piece going away suit purchased there, a dress with matching jacket. She remembered still, standing at the top of the staircase in that killingly lovely suit, in a hound's tooth check of fuchsia and black, readying to throw the bouquet. She remembered thinking: *I look good, but now I'm married*, so what does it matter? Mona's first marriage had lasted two years.

Bryon picked up on her confusion. "In *Pret a Porter*." This did not clear things up for Mona. "I'm sorry, it translates to—"

"I know the French," she said, a bit sharp. "I used to go to the Paris collections, buy couture." That was with her second husband, who was rich, rich, rich, until he wasn't anymore. Until it turned out he never really was. Wallace just had a high tolerance for debt, higher than his creditors as it turned out. Mona didn't leave because he filed for bankruptcy, but it didn't make the case for staying, either.

"It was a movie a few years back. By Altman. The parts were better than the whole, if I can be so bold to criticize a genius. The thing is, I'm a filmmaker myself."

Mona hadn't been to a movie in ten years. The new ones made her sleepy. She fell asleep, woke up when something blew up, fell back asleep again. "Have you—"

"Made anything you've heard of? No. I'm an indie, but, you know, you keep your vision that way. I'm on the festival circuit, do some direct-to-video stuff. Digital has changed the equation, you know?"

Mona nodded as if she did.

"Look, I don't want to get all Schwab's on you—"

Finally, a reference that Mona understood.

"But I'm working on something right now and you would be so perfect. If you would consider reading for me, or perhaps, even, a screen test . . . there's not much money in it, but who knows? If you photograph the way I think you will, it could mean a whole new career for you."

He offered her his card, but she didn't want to put her glasses on to read it, so she just studied it blindly, pretending to make sense of the brown squiggles on the creamy background. The paper was of good stock, heavy and textured.

"In fact, my sound stage isn't far from here, so if you're free right now—"

"I'm on foot," she said. "I walked here from my apartment."

"Oh, and you wouldn't want to get in a car with a strange man. Of course."

Mona hadn't been thinking of Bryon as strange. In fact, she had assumed he was gay. What kind of man spoke so fervently of models and old-time movie stars? But now that he said it – no, she probably shouldn't, part of her mind warned. But another part was shouting her down, telling her such opportunities come along just once. Maybe she looked better than she realized. Maybe Mona's memory of her younger self had blinded her to how attractive she still was to someone meeting her for the first time.

"I'll tell you what. I'll call you a cab, give the driver the address. Tell him to wait, with the meter running, all on me."

"Don't be silly." Mona clutched the arms of the so-called easy chair and willed herself to rise as gracefully as possible. Somehow, she managed it. "Let's go."

❦

She was not put off by the fact that Bryon's soundstage was a large locker in one of those storage places. "A filmmaker at my level has to squeeze every nickel until it hollers," he said, pulling the garage-type door behind them. She wasn't sure how he had gotten power rigged up inside, but there was an array of professional-looking lights. The camera was a battery-powered videocam, set up on a tripod. He even had a "set" – a three-piece 1930s style bedroom set, with an old-fashioned vanity and bureau to match the ornately carved bed.

He asked Mona to sit on the padded stool in front of the vanity and address the camera directly, saying whatever came into her head.

"Um, testing 1-2-3. Testing."

"You look great. Talk some more. Tell me about yourself."

"My name is Mona—," she stumbled for a second, forgetting the order of her surnames. After all, she had five.

"Where did you grow up, Mona?"

"Oh, here, there and everywhere." Mona had learned long ago to be stingy with the details. They dated one so.

"What were you like as a young woman?"

"Well, I was the . . . bee's knees." An odd expression for her to use, one that pre-dated her own birth by quite a bit. She laughed at its irrelevance and Bryon laughed, too. She felt as if she had been drinking

Brandy Alexanders instead of venti mochas. Felt, in fact, the way she had that first afternoon with her second husband, when they left the bar at the Drake Hotel and checked into a room. She had been only 35 then, and she had let him keep the drapes open, proud of how her body looked in the bright daylight bouncing off Lake Michigan.

"I bet you were. I bet you were. And all the boys were crazy about you."

"I did okay."

"Oh, you did more than okay, didn't you, Mona?"

She smiled. "That's not for me to say."

"What did you wear, Mona, when you were driving those boys crazy. None of those obvious outfits for you, right? You were one of those subtle ones, like Grace Kelly. Pretty dresses, custom fit."

"Right." She brightened. Clothing was one of the few things that interested her. "That's what these girls today don't get. I had a suit, a one-piece, strapless. As modest as it could be. But it was beige, just a shade darker than my own skin, and when it got wet . . ." She laughed, the memory alive to her, the effect of that bathing suit on the young men around the pool at the country club in Atlanta.

"I wish you still had that bathing suit, Mona."

"I'd still fit into it," she said. It would have been true two months ago, before she discovered Starbucks.

"I bet you would. I bet you would." Bryon's voice seemed thicker, lower, slower.

"I never let myself go, the way some women do. They say it's metabolism and menopause—" oh, she wished she could take that word back, one should never even allude to such unpleasant facts of life – "but it's just a matter of discipline."

"I sure wish I could see you in that suit, Mona."

She laughed. She hadn't had this much fun in ages. He was flirting with her, she was sure of it. Gay or not, he liked her.

"I wish I could see you in your *birthday* suit."

"Bryon!" She was on a laughing jag now, out of control.

"Why can't I, Mona? Why can't I see you in your birthday suit?"

Suddenly, the only sound in the room was Bryon's breath, ragged and harsh. It was hard to see anything clearly, with the lights shining in her eyes, but Mona could see that he was steadying the camera with just one hand.

"You want to see me naked?" she asked.

Bryon nodded.

"Just . . . see?"

"That's how we start, usually. Slow like. Every one has his or her own comfort zone."

"And the video – is that for your eyes only?"

"I told you, I'm an independent film maker. Direct to video. A growing market."

"People pay?"

Another shy nod. "It's sort of a . . . niche within the industry."

"Niche."

"It's my niche," he said. "It's what I like. I make other films about, um, things I don't like so much. But I love watching truly seasoned women teach young men about life."

"And you'd pay for this?"

"Of course."

"How much?"

"Some. Enough."

"Just to look? Just to see me, as I am?"

"A little for that. More for . . . more."

"How much?" Mona repeated. She was keen to know her worth.

He came around from behind the camera, retrieved a laminated card from the drawer in the vanity table, then sat on the bed and patted the space next to him. Why laminated? Mona decided not to think about that. She moved to the bed and studied the card, not unlike the menu of services and prices at a spa. She could do that. And that. Not that, but definitely that and that. The fact was, she had done most of these things, quite happily.

"Let me make you a star, Mona."

"Are you my leading man?"

"Our target demographic prefer to see younger men with the women. I just need to get some film of you to take to my partner, so he'll underwrite it. I have a very well-connected financial backer."

"Who?"

"Oh, I'll never say. He's very discreet. Anyway, he likes to know that the actresses are . . . up to the challenges of their roles. Usually, a strip tease will do, a little, um, self-stimulation. But it's always good to have extra footage. I make a lot of films, but these are the ones I like best. The ones I watch."

"Well, then," Mona said, unbuttoning her blouse. "Let's get busy."

ff

Fetish, Mona said to herself as she shopped in the Giant. *Fetish*, she thought, as she retrieved her mail from the communal boxes in the lobby. *I am a fetish.* This was the word that Bryon used to describe her "work," which, two months after their first meeting, comprised four short films. She had recoiled at the word at first, feeling it marked her as a freak, something from a sideshow. Niche had been so much nicer. But Bryon assured her that the customers who bought her videos were profoundly affected by her performance. There was no irony, no belittling. She was not the butt of the joke, she was the object of their, um, *affection*.

"Different people like different things," he said to her in Starbucks one afternoon. She was feeling a little odd, as she always did when a film was completed. It was so strange to spend an afternoon having sex and not be taken shopping afterward, just given a cashier's check. "Our cultural definitions of sexuality are simply too narrow."

"But your other films, the other tastes you serve—" Mona by now had familiarized herself with Bryon's catalog, which included the usual whips and chains, but also a surprisingly successful series of films that featured obese women sitting on balloons – "they're *sick*."

"There you go, being judgmental," Bryon said. "Children is wrong, I'll give you that. Because children can't consent. Everything else is fair game."

"Animals can't consent."

"I don't do animals, either. Adults and inanimate objects, that's my credo."

It was an odd conversation to be having in her Starbucks at the LeisureWorld Plaza, that much was sure. Mona looked around nervously, but no one was paying attention. The other customers probably thought Mona and Bryon were a mother and son, although she didn't think she looked old enough to be Bryon's mother.

"By the way," Byron produced a small stack of envelopes. "We've gotten some letters for you."

"Letters?"

"Fan mail. Your public."

"I'm not sure I want to read them."

"That's up to you. Whatever you do – don't make the mistake of responding to them, okay? The less they know about Sexy Sadie, the better. Keep the mystery." He left her alone with her public.

Keep the mystery. Mona liked that phrase. It could be her credo, to borrow Bryon's word. Then she began to think about the mysteries that Bryon was keeping. If she had already received – she stopped to count, touching the envelopes gingerly – eleven pieces of fan mail, then how many fans must she have? If eleven people wrote, then hundreds – no, thousands – must watch and enjoy what she did.

So why was she getting paid by the job, with no percentage, no profit-sharing? God willing, her health assured, she could really build on this new career. After all, they actually had to make her look older, dressing her in dowdy dresses, advising her to make her voice sound more quavery than it was. Bryon had the equipment, Bryon had the distribution – but only Mona had Mona. How replaceable was she?

ɛʃ

"Forget it," Bryon said when she broached the topic on the set a few weeks later. "I was upfront with you from the start. I pay you by the act. By the *piece*, if you will. No participation. You signed a contract, remember?"

Gone was the rapt deference from that first day at Starbucks. True, Mona had long figured out that it was an act, but she had thought there was a germ of authenticity in it, a genuine respect for her looks and presence. How long had Bryon been stalking her, she wondered now. Had he approached her because of her almost lavender eyes, or because she looked vulnerable and lonely? Easy, as they used to say.

"But I have fans," she said. "People who like me, specifically. That ought to be worth a renegotiation."

"You think so? Then sue me in Montgomery County courts. Your neighbors in LeisureWorld will probably love reading about that in the suburban edition of the *Washington Post*."

"I'll quit," she said.

"Go ahead," Bryon said. "You think you're the only lonely old lady who needs a little attention? I'll put the wig and the dress on some other old bag. My films, my company, my concept."

"Some concept," Mona said, trying not to let him see how much the words hurt. So she was just a lonely old lady to him, a mark. "I sit in a room, a young man rings my doorbell, I end up having sex with him. So far, it's been a UPS man, a delivery boy for a florist, a delivery boy for the Chinese restaurant and a young Mormon on a bicycle. What's next, a Jehovah's Witness peddling the Watchtower?"

"That's not bad," Bryon said, pausing to write a quick note to himself. "Look, this is the deal. I pay you by the act. You don't want to do it, you don't have to. I'm always scouting new talent. Maybe I'll find an Alzheimer's patient, who won't be able to remember from one day to the next what she did, much less try to hold me up for a raise. You old bitches are a dime a dozen."

It was the old bitches part that hurt.

ɛʃ

When Mona's second husband's fortune had proved to be largely smoke and mirrors, she had learned to be more careful about picking her subsequent husbands. That was in the pre-Internet days, when determining a person's personal fortune was much more labor intensive. She was pleased to find out from a helpful librarian how easy it was now to compile what was once known as a Dun & Bradstreet on someone, how to track down the silent partner in Bryon White's LLC.

Within a day, she was having lunch with Bernard Weinman, a dignified gentleman about her own age. He hadn't wanted to meet with her, but as Mona detailed sweetly what she knew about Bernie's legitimate business interests – more information gleaned with the assistance of the nice young librarian—and his large contributions to a local synagogue, he decided they could meet after all. He chose a quiet French restaurant in Bethesda and when he ordered white wine with lunch, Mona followed suit.

"I have a lot of investments," he said. "I'm not hands-on."

"Still, I can't imagine you want someone indiscreet working for you."

"Indiscreet?"

"How do you think I tracked you down? Bryon talks. A lot."

Bernie Weinman bent over his onion soup, spilling a little on his tie. But it was a lovely tie, expensive and well-made. For this lunch meeting, he wore a black suit and crisp white shirt with large gold cufflinks.

"Bryon's very good at . . . what he does. His mail-order business is so steady it's almost like an annuity. I get a very good return on my money, and I've never heard of him invoking my name."

"Well, he did. All I did was make some suggestions about how to—" Mona groped for the odd business terms she had heard on daytime television—"how to grow your business, and he got very short with me, said you had no interest in doing things differently. And when I asked if I might speak to you, he got very angry, threatened to expose me. If he would blackmail me, a middle-class widow with no real money, imagine what he might do to you."

"Bryon knows me well enough not to try that," Bernie Weinman said. After a morning at the Olney branch of the Montgomery County Public Library, Mona knew him pretty well, too. She knew the rumors that had surrounded the early part of his career, the alleged but never proven ties to the number runner up in Baltimore. Bernie Weinman had built his fortune from corner liquor stores in Washington D.C., which eventually became the basis for his chain of party supply stores. But he had clearly never lost his taste for the recession-proof businesses that had given him his start –liquor, gambling, prostitution. All he had done was live long enough and give away enough money that people were willing to forget his past. Apparently, the going price of redemption in Montgomery County was five million dollars to the capital fund at one's synagogue.

"Does Bryon know you so well that he wouldn't risk keeping two sets of books?"

"What?"

"I know what I get paid. I know how cheaply the product is made and produced, and I know how many units are moved. He's cheating you."

"He wouldn't."

"He would – and brag about it, too. He said you were a stupid old man who was no longer on top of his game."

"He said that?"

"He said much worse."

"Tell me."

"I c-c-c-an't," Mona whispered, looking shyly into her salad nicoise as if she had not made four adult films under the moniker "Sexy Sadie."

"Paraphrase."

"He said . . . he said there was no film in the world that could, um, incite you. That you were . . . starchless."

"That little SOB."

"He laughs at you, behind your back. He practically brags about how he's ripping you off. I've put myself in harm's way, just talking to you, but I couldn't let this go on."

"I'll straighten him out—"

"No! Because he'll know it was me and he'll – he's threatened me, Bernie." This first use of his name was a calculated choice. "He says no one will miss me and I suppose he's right."

"You don't have any children?"

"Just step-children, and I'm afraid they're not very kind to me. It was hard for them, their father remarrying, even though he had been a widower for years." Divorced for two years, and Mona had been the central reason, but the kids wouldn't have liked her under any circumstances. "No, no one would miss me. Except my fans."

She let the subject go then, directing the conversation to Bernie and his accomplishments, the legitimate ones. She asked questions whose answers she knew perfectly well, touched his arm when he decided they needed another bottle of wine, and although she drank only one glass to his every two, declared herself unfit to drive home. She was going to take a taxi, but Bernie insisted on driving her, and accompanying her to the condo door, to make sure she was fine, and then into her bedroom, where he further assessed her fineness. He was okay, not at all starchless, somewhere between a sturdy baguette and a loaf of Wonder Bread. She'd had worse. True, he felt odd, after the series of hard-bodied young men that Bryon had hired for her. But this, at least, did not fall under the category of fetish. He was 73 and she was 68, passing-for-61. This was normal. This was love.

Bryon White was never seen again. He simply disappeared, and there was no one who mourned him, or even really noticed. And while Bernie Weinman was happily married, he had strong opinions about how his new mistress should spend her time. Mona took over the business, but had to retire from performing, at least officially, although she sometimes auditioned the young men, just to be sure. Give Bryon credit, Mona thought, now that she had to scout the coffee shops and grocery stores, recruiting the new talent. It was harder than it looked and Bryon's instincts had been unerring, especially when it came to Mona. She really was a wonderful actress.

Afterword

I heard about senior citizen porn on the Howard Stern show. Didn't everybody? At any rate, "Blue Iris" was a regular guest and they played clips from some of her films. I thought it rather nifty. I grafted it onto the infamous "Coco" scene from the movie Fame, *but my character is much, much tougher than wimpy little Coco. I like stories about women who prove to be unusually resourceful.* —L.L.

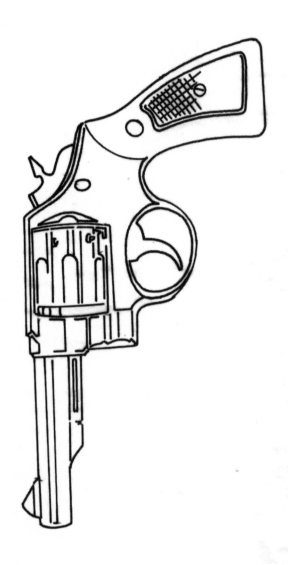

PART FOUR:

GUNS AND GEEZERS

PAYOFF

STEVE BREWER

Steve Brewer (born 1957) is the very tall author of 14 books, as well as a humor writer whose weekly column, The Home Front, runs in newspapers all over the country. Brewer's latest novels are the standalones Whipsaw, Bank Job, Boost *and* Bullets. *Among his other novels as the comic Bubba Mabry private eye series; a new Bubba hardcover,* Monkey Man, *is scheduled to be published in fall 2006. The first Bubba Mabry novel,* Lonely Street, *is currently in development by Hollywood filmmakers.*

PAYOFF
by Steve Brewer

He who hesitates is fucked.

Stop to think, to consider how you're not as young as you used to be, how your reflexes are slower or you don't move so well anymore, and it's already too late.

Eddie knew all that. So when he lost his temper, he didn't waver. He strode across the busy saloon, slipping the .38-caliber Smith & Wesson out of his hip pocket, and jammed its stubby barrel up the loudmouth's left nostril.

Eddie was a good foot shorter than the square-jawed college boy. He'd never been tall, and he seemed to shrink another inch every year he lived past seventy. His pants rode higher these days and the cuffs of his flannel shirts were loose around his wrists. But he still was powerful through the chest and shoulders—where it counts—and he drove his free hand into the younger man's breastbone, pinned him against the wall.

"Listen, punk," Eddie said. "I may be seventy-seven years old, but there's not a damned thing wrong with my hearing. You've been mouthing off since you strutted into this place. Calling me 'Q-Tip' because of my white hair. Calling me an 'old fart.' Making noise about how I should give up my table to you and your frat brothers."

The punk's three friends were behind Eddie now. He didn't like that, but there was no help for it. They wouldn't make a move as long as he had a bullet aimed at their buddy's brain.

"I've been coming to this bar for fifty years. The rules never change. First come, first served. Right, Mac?"

Eddie could see Mac out of the corner of his eye. The beefy bartender watched them, no expression on his square face. The only sign he was paying attention was that he'd stopped his perpetual wiping of the bar with his gray rag.

"That's right," Mac said. "Long as you're buying drinks, you've rented the table for the night."

Eddie nodded. "Now if you don't like those rules, you should find another place to drink. But if you're gonna come in here, where us old farts hang out, then you show some respect. Understand?"

The red-faced kid nodded as best he could with a gun up his nose.

Eddie took the revolver away. Blood trickled out the offended nostril. Some on the barrel, too. He wiped the muzzle on the guy's white shirt, making a lopsided red "X" right above his heart.

Then he stepped back. If the punk wanted to make a move, now would be the time. But he kept his hands at his sides, his eyes on the pistol that Eddie held close by his waist. He jerked his head toward the exit, and he and his friends went out into the chilly autumn night, casting fierce glances over their shoulders at Eddie, who watched until they were out of sight.

A couple of the other "old farts" clapped a few times. Eddie didn't acknowledge them. He turned to the bar, where Mac was pouring him a shot of the Irish.

"Taking a chance there, Eddie," Mac said. "They might call the cops."

"What the cops gonna do? Arrest me? I ain't scared of jail. Hell, at my age, prison beats a nursing home. In stir, I know who I can trust."

"Who would that be?"

"Nobody."

Mac nodded. "I'm glad you didn't shoot him, Eddie. We would've had to replace the wallpaper."

Eddie knocked back the whiskey, which made his eyes water. "Sorry to run off customers, Mac. But I couldn't listen to that shit anymore."

"We don't need their business. We ain't proctologists."

The bartender poured him another drink.

"I'll take this one back to my table."

Mac cocked an eyebrow. "Think it still belongs to you?"

Eddie looked over at his table, saw a girl sitting in the chair opposite the one where his brown jacket was draped. She was young enough to be his granddaughter, maybe twenty-three, about the age of the boys he'd run off. She dressed all in black. Had hair too matte-black to be natural, chopped short around her ears, which were studded with too many silver earrings. Too much makeup, too. Good posture, though, sitting straight, staring at Eddie's chair like the RCA Victor dog, waiting for him to return.

He shrugged at Mac and walked over to the table, sat down. "Where'd you come from?"

"Back there." She gestured vaguely toward the rear of the bar.

The place was narrow and deep, squeezed between a bakery and a pawnshop, a typical neighborhood saloon. The neighborhood was changing, though, "gentrifying," and unfamiliar faces kept popping up among the aging regulars. Eddie had been in the back earlier, visiting the men's room beyond the shadowy booths, but he hadn't noticed this girl. And he should've noticed. Despite the black clothes and the butchered hair and the macabre makeup, she was a looker.

Christ, would he never outgrow it? Eddie kept thinking he'd get too old to ogle young women, but the urge never went away. All that firm flesh. Lipstick and flashing eyes and hope.

"And you just decided to join me?" he said.

"I saw what you did. I was coming this way, going home, when you pulled out the gun."

Eddie's cheeks warmed. He'd known people were watching when he rousted those college kids, but most of the customers were ex-cons and small-timers, drunks and losers. Guys who'd turn a blind eye. Knowing this girl had seen him lose his temper was, well, it was embarrassing.

She fiddled with a silver ring on her thumb. She wore rings on most of her fingers, and the nails were painted black. Jesus, these kids. Every day's freaking Halloween.

She made her hands sit still, and met his gaze. Her eyes were startling, the palest blue he'd ever seen, the eyes of a wolf. Eddie felt something flop in his chest. Aw, hell.

"I need," she began, but the words caught in her throat, and she had to take a deep breath to start over. He tried not to stare at the swell of her breasts under her black T-shirt.

"I need someone killed."

Eddie looked around the saloon. No one seemed to be listening, but Frankie Matteucci, the aging fence who usually held forth at the far end of the bar, was staring at them. He looked away when Eddie met his eyes.

Eddie turned back to the girl, found her frankly sizing him up. Made him feel itchy.

"What are you, drunk?"

She shook her head. "I had a couple, but I know what I'm saying."

"What's your name?"

"Lucy." The name didn't fit her, but maybe that was the idea. More youthful rebellion.

"Well, Lucy, you've got the wrong guy. I'm no killer."

"You've got a gun," she said. "You clearly know how to use it. Weren't you ready to shoot that guy a few minutes ago?"

"Just putting a scare into him."

"I heard what you told the bartender. Prison or a nursing home. You don't have much to lose."

"That doesn't mean I want to spend my last few years locked up. Killing somebody? That's 'no possibility of parole' for a guy like me. I may not have many years left, but I'd rather not spend them behind bars—"

"Nobody says you have to get caught."

He couldn't believe what he was hearing. He tipped up the whiskey, felt its heat hit the bottom of his stomach. He caught Mac's eye, held up his empty to signal for a replacement.

"Something for you?" he asked the girl.

She shook her head. Said nothing while Mac's plump barmaid ferried the drink to the table. When they were alone again, Lucy murmured, "I have money."

"Yeah? How much?"

"Ten thousand dollars."

Eddie kept his face blank. Ten grand could solve some pressing problems. Pay off his ever-growing bar tab. Get him out of debt. Maybe let him move out of the cramped room he'd called home for the past few months—a mildewed "efficiency" with a shared bath down the hall, worse than a goddamned cellblock.

"Where'd you get that much money?"

"I inherited it." Something in his look must've given him away because she narrowed her spooky eyes. "It's all I've got, so don't ask for more. But I'll give it to you if you'll do this thing for me."

"Must be important, you're willing to spend your last dime on it."

"It's a matter of life or death."

Her intense expression hadn't changed, though Eddie thought she'd just slipped over into melodrama. "Matter of life or death." Shit, wasn't everything?

He leaned closer to her. "Who is it you want killed?"

"You'll do it?"

Eddie cackled and sat back, shaking his head.

"You're priceless, darling. You think you can just walk into a bar and wave money at an old man and get a murder?"

"I'm desperate."

He sipped his drink, staring at her. The color rose in her cheeks, and he thought she'd be beautiful if she scrubbed her face and washed that dye out of her hair.

"How do I know you're not a cop, setting me up?"

"I could say the same about you," she said.

"Hell, if I was a cop, I would've retired twenty years ago. I'd be living out my days in splendor, sucking on the tit of a government pension. But I worked the other side of the street, pulling heists and hijackings. Spent half my life in the pen. Now look at me. Barely making ends meet. Spending my Social Security on whiskey."

Disappointment showed on her face. She'd thought she had a live one, which is why she'd approached him. That, and the gun. Which, as a convicted felon, he wasn't even supposed to possess. If it hadn't been for those loudmouths—

"Sorry," she said. "My mistake."

She scooted back her chair and stood up.

"Hold on, darling," he said. "Maybe we can work something out."

Her eyes darted around the bar. Eddie looked, too, and he could see what she was thinking: Too many people paying attention to them now.

She pulled a pen out of her pocket, flipped over a cardboard Budweiser coaster on the table, and wrote on the back.

"Offer's good until this time tomorrow." She slid the coaster across the table toward him, then turned on her heel and left.

He looked at the number she'd written, chuckling and shaking his head. He tucked it in his pocket before he summoned the barmaid.

🐟

The next afternoon, Eddie knew something was up before he even reached the saloon. He was still down the block when he saw Frankie Matteucci barrel out the door, flushed and muttering. Frankie turned away and hurried up the busy street.

Eddie desperately needed some hair of the dog. He entered the dim saloon and saw Mac, in his fresh white shirt, towering behind the bar like a lighthouse.

"Hiya, Mac." Eddie unzipped his jacket, settling onto a stool before he caught the bartender's glum expression. "What's the matter?"

"It's the owner, Eddie. He went on the warpath today."

"He heard about me running off those punks?"

"No, it's your tab. No more credit until it's paid up."

Eddie felt like Mac had thrown a bucket of cold water over him. "You know I'm good for it. Soon as my check comes—"

"Boss says no more credit for anybody."

"Just one then. Christ, I got a headache that would kill a—"

"Sorry, but it's cash up front."

Eddie's temper flared. "Are you shittin' me? As much money as I've poured into this place over the years? I was buying booze here before you were born!"

Mac nodded his big head. "I know. I feel real bad."

Eddie sprang off the stool. "Forget it then! I'll take my business elsewhere."

He stomped outside. Bright sunshine needled his eyes. Belching trucks and honking taxis grated on his ears. Jesus, he needed a drink. Eddie dug through his pockets, trying to turn up enough cash to buy a bottle. He'd get the cheap stuff, fucking rotgut, take it back to his room—

Something in his jacket pocket. A cardboard coaster. He pulled it out and read the phone number.

Eddie met the girl outside his building that evening, though an icy wind had kicked up and clouds crowded the skies. He didn't want her to see the shithole where he lived. Didn't want her seen going in and out, in case the cops questioned his nosy goddamned neighbors. Not that Eddie expected cops. Hell, he didn't know what to expect. Better to play it careful.

She drove up in a little Japanese car, black of course, with a crumpled fender. Beeped her horn. The wind snatched at his jacket as he hurried along the sidewalk. He climbed into the passenger seat, the pistol gouging his hip.

Lucy slammed the car into gear and screeched out into traffic. Eddie reached back over his shoulder, fumbling for the seat belt.

"I brought half the money," she said by way of greeting. "It's in that bag by your feet."

Eddie restrained himself from reaching for the folded-over paper sack. Five grand. Right there by his scuffed black shoes. God almighty.

Lucy wore less makeup tonight. She looked softer, more feminine, without it, which seemed backward to him. But those piercing eyes were the same.

"You wanta stop somewhere?" he asked. "Get a drink?"

"No. I don't want to be seen with you. That's the best thing we've got going for us. Nobody knows about the connection between us."

"What about everyone who saw us in the bar last night?"

"I'd never been in that place before. Most of those guys were half in the bag. They wouldn't recognize me again."

She'd clearly given this some thought. Felt like she was way ahead of him, manipulating him.

"Don't get too cocky," he growled. "I still haven't agreed to do this."

She gave him a sidelong glance.

"It'll be easy," she said. "You just walk up, pop him and walk away. Toss the gun in the river. The cops'll never trace anything back to you."

"Who says I'm willing? I don't know this guy. Does he deserve to die?"

Lucy snorted. "No one deserves it more."

She steered the car onto a dead-end street lined by red-brick buildings three stories high. Spindly elms, already stripped of their autumn leaves, poked up from the sidewalk.

"That's it right there," she said as she pulled the battered car to the curb. "Ground floor. Third door from the corner."

Shades were drawn over the apartment's two front windows. The colored lights of a TV danced behind one. The other bore a rusty stain. While he watched, the silhouette of a man passed and disappeared.

"Who is this guy?"

"My brother-in-law," she said through clenched teeth. "The bastard."

"He's family? And you want him killed?"

She turned to face Eddie, impaling him with her eyes.

"My sister's been married to this bum for four years. He beats her. He mistreats her. He won't work. He deals drugs."

"A scumbag."

"That's right. But she won't leave him, even when both her eyes are blackened and she has to eat through a straw. He's gonna end up killing her."

"And you can't stand by and let that happen."

"She called me the other day, wanting money. They're broke and he owes some very bad people. So they're desperate. And how does Mel—that's his name, Mel—how does Mel plan to come up with the money? He wants to turn her out, make her a street whore. And that's a death sentence. I can't let it happen."

"Can't you get her away from him?"

"I've tried. Last time, he said he'd kill me if I came around here again. Now, when I want to see her, I have to meet her somewhere. Or I park down the street like this and call her on my cell phone."

"He lets her go?"

"Usually, he's so drunk or stoned, he doesn't even know she's left. But it's risky. She gets home when he's in a mood, and it means another beating."

"Christ."

"So you see, mister, Mel's got to go. I've thought about it, and there's no other way. I'd gladly do it myself, but everybody knows how much Mel and I hate each other. I'd be the first suspect. And my sister would never forgive me. But if you do it—"

"I got you," he said. "No connections."

Eddie stared out the windshield at the brick building, watching the windows, hoping for another glimpse of the man inside. He wondered how big he was, how tough. Not that it mattered. Son of a bitch wasn't bulletproof.

"See that hill, down at the end of this street?" she said. "That's a levee. The river's just the other side."

Eddie nodded. The brush-covered levee was only two blocks away, where the street dead-ended.

"You shoot him, walk down there, throw the gun in the river," she said. "That's very important. The cops can do tests on guns. It's the one thing that could get you in a jam."

He knew she was right, though he hated to go without a gun, even for a little while. But he could get a new one. Frankie Matteucci usually had a piece or two for sale. With ten thousand dollars, Eddie could buy a goddamned arsenal.

"Turn the corner, walk back to Chester," she said. "There's a bar. You can be indoors having a drink before the first cops even get here."

She put the car into gear and made a U-turn, headed back toward the well-lit thoroughfare.

"I'll call my sister," she said. "Take her out somewhere nice and public. Make sure we're seen. By the time I bring her home, it'll all be over."

Eddie nodded. It was a good plan. Why did it give him the creeps?

His voice sounded ragged as he said, "When do you want to do this?"

"Tomorrow night."

⚔

Best thing about the next day was the look on Mac's face when Eddie paid his tab in full. Three hundred and sixty dollars. In cash. Fanned out on top of the bar.

Before Mac touched the money, he was reaching for the Irish, ready to pour a new drink, but Eddie shook his head.

"Nope. I told you, I'm taking my business elsewhere from now on."

As he turned to leave, Mac said, "Come on, Eddie."

"So long, Mac."

Take a while to find another bar where he felt so comfortable, but that was okay. He had money to fund the search. And another five grand on the way.

⚔

That evening, Eddie went to Mel's neighborhood earlier than planned. The weather was still lousy, churning gray clouds and a slicing wind that kept folks indoors. He squatted in the weeds on top of the

255

levee, his back to the swift black water, a cap pulled low over his eyes, and watched as Lucy picked up her sister. The sister didn't look much like her—skinny and nervous, with shoulder-length brown hair—but from what Lucy had said, she'd suffered a tough life so far. Takes the juices right out of a woman.

The sister climbed into the passenger seat, and she and Lucy hugged each other tightly, long enough that the emotion made Eddie look away. He'd grown up in an orphanage, never had any siblings. What must it be like, he wondered, to have that sort of connection to another person?

Once they were safely away, he walked to Chester Avenue and the bar Lucy had mentioned. The place was a dump, but it had what he needed. Liquid courage. He tossed back a shot, then lingered over a second, giving Lucy and her sister time to get far away and establish an alibi.

His skin crawled as he returned to the apartment building. He turned up his collar as the first drops of rain spat down past the naked trees.

Eddie took a deep breath before ringing the doorbell. The moment seemed unreal, like a scene in a movie. One of those gloomy cops-and-robbers matinees he loved when he was kid. The shadows and the wind and the rain and the portentous moment.

He pushed the doorbell with the thumb of his left hand. His right was in his jacket pocket, wrapped around the revolver.

The door flung open and the man inside winced at the icy wind. Mel was a rangy cracker with an unlit cigarette dangling from cruel lips. He wore a sleeveless T-shirt, and he'd spilled something down the front of it, might've been red wine. His ropy arms displayed colorful tattoos—snakes and panthers and assorted other wildlife, a fucking zoo. Mel narrowed his eyes as he looked down on Eddie.

"What do you want, old man?"

Making it easier for him. "I've got a message for you."

"What message?"

Eddie didn't hesitate. He pulled the pistol from his pocket and jabbed it into Mel's midsection and pulled the trigger. Mel crumpled over, clutching his stomach, as if he'd been punched in the gut rather than pierced by hot lead. He staggered backward, the cigarette falling from his gaping mouth.

"Your wife says good-bye."

He shot him again, in the chest this time, and Mel slammed backward onto the floor. The second shot seemed louder, not muffled against Mel's body, and lights came on next door. Eddie pulled Mel's door closed and walked hurriedly toward the river.

Cold sunlight slanted through the blinds when Eddie woke the next morning to somebody tapping on his door. He'd fallen asleep in his clothes the night before, and they were as crumpled on the outside as he felt on the inside. He got to his feet, his head pounding, and staggered over to the door.

Lucy stood in the hall, though it took him a second to recognize her. She'd washed the black dye out of her sandy hair. She wore no makeup, and she was dressed in jeans and sneakers and a cloth jacket. She looked *normal*.

"What are you doing here?"

"Unfinished business."

Ah. The rest of his money. Not the way they'd agreed she'd deliver it, but he gestured her inside. He checked the empty hall and closed the door.

He tucked at his shirttail as he turned to face her, but froze when he saw the little semi-automatic in her hand, pointing at his belly.

"What the hell?"

"Step away from the door, mister."

Eddie felt a flutter in his chest. Last night's guilt and booze, today's shock. A wonder his old heart could take it. He did as he was told, moving toward the bed. Maybe he could sit a second, gather his wits.

"That's good," she said. "Right there."

"What's this all about?" he demanded. "I did what you wanted."

"That's right, you did. Good job, too. Mel's dead. The cops were there all night, but they don't suspect me."

"Or your sister."

A little smile curled her lips. "She's not my sister."

Eddie could feel his mouth hanging open. He clamped it shut.

"She's my lover," Lucy said. "And she's all mine now. Thanks to you."

Took a second for that to sink through Eddie's booze-fogged brain. But once it did, his temper sparked.

"So it was all bullshit?" he said. "None of that story was the truth?"

"Most of it was true. Just not the sister part. Mel was a bad man. He hurt her. He got what he deserved."

Eddie felt dizzy. His eyes roamed the room until they settled once again on her little black gun.

"What about me?" he said. "Is this what I deserve?"

She shrugged, like it didn't matter. Which pissed him off more.

"I'm the last link, right?" he said. "Get rid of me, and there'll never be anything to tie you to Mel."

"Something like that," she said.

Eddie's anger erupted, and he spewed curses. Lucy calmly waited him out. When he ran out of breath, she said, "That money I gave you. Where is it?"

"Wait a goddamned minute. I earned that money. Fair and square."

She gestured with the pistol. "You won't be needing it. I want it back."

"I spent a lot of it already."

"On what, liquor? That's why I can't leave you walking around, mister. You're an old boozehound. Eventually, you'll let something slip."

Eddie shook his head and said, "I never would." But he could see she wasn't buying it. He let his shoulders sag in resignation. Fuck.

"Money's under the mattress," he said.

She looked at the rumpled bed and made a face. She didn't want to go near the wrinkled linens and the old-man smell.

"Get it," she said.

Eddie shuffled over to the narrow bed in his bare feet. He slid his hand under the mattress, feeling around, until he found the butt of his new revolver, the one he'd bought off Frankie Matteucci with Lucy's money.

He wheeled, sliding the revolver out from under the mattress, thumbing back the hammer, bringing the gun around to point at Lucy's lupine eyes.

She'd relaxed a little because she thought she had the situation under control. Thought the old drunk would hand over the money and peacefully take his dose of death. Now, when things took a sudden turn, she wasn't prepared.

She hesitated.

Eddie didn't.

Afterword

Some of my favorite crime novels are the hard-boiled Parker stories by Richard Stark/Donald E. Westlake. When I set out to write a story for Damn Near Dead, *it was with this thought: What would a guy like Parker, a no-nonsense survivor of a heist man, be like if he lived to his seventies? He'd be a guy like Eddie, a tough old bird who's surprised that he beat the odds this long. –S.B.*

GEEZER TRICKS

CHARLIE STELLA

Charlie Stella (born 1956) is the critically-acclaimed author of Eddie's World, Jimmy Bench-Press, Charlie Opera *and* Cheapskates *and his new one,* Shakedown *(available in June), has received two *starred* reviews (Kirkus and Booklist). His first screenplay,* Fountain Avenue, *goes into production in August of 2006. Charlie lives in Brooklyn with his wife, the lovely Principessa. And he's way, way into the Average White Band—like some people are into the Dead.*

f

GEEZER TRICKS
by Charlie Stella

"**I** come here the mornings to make sure you okay," seventy-two-year-old Alfred Jenkins told seventy-seven-year-old Chriselda Weber. "You acting depressed lately got me to worry. You getting jealous, it ain't right."

Chriselda's eyes were wet from crying. She had been diagnosed with cancer a few weeks ago. Earlier this morning she had been staring at the faded internment numbers the Nazi's had tattooed on her right arm more than sixty-five years ago and thinking about the family she had lost to the Holocaust.

"What we have is fine," Alfred told her. "We company for each other once and now we friends."

Alfred and Chriselda had once been lovers. Lately, he had been affectionate with another woman where they worked. He assumed her melancholy had to do with jealousy.

"You need to let go," he added.

Chriselda sniffled before waving him off. She was a big woman of German descent. Her accent was still strong. "Vhat you are talking about, old man?" she asked. "You *Verlieren Ihres Verstandes*, eh? You are losing your mind. I am not crying for you, *blind*."

Alfred tilted his head to one side. "You calling me names again?"

"Dummy. *Blind* is dummy. Sometimes is what you are, eh?"

They were sitting in her kitchen. In another few minutes they would have to leave for work. Alfred pointed to the clock above the sink.

"You coming or you gonna be late again? New boy don't like it you're late. You give him an excuse, he'll fire you."

Chriselda waved the warning off. "New boy is *blind*, too."

Alfred stood up to leave. "I see you later," he told her.

"Please," Chriselda said.

❦

She showed up for work more than an hour late and was warned she would be fired the next time it happened. A few hours into the shift, using her most seductive phone voice, Chriselda asked the caller,

"Vat you got for me? Somesing big?"

"Something big, indeed," the caller said. "It's my good morning special, Fraulein."

"Ah, *guten morgen speziell*, I like zhat. How big zis mornink?"

They had been on the line a little over two minutes. The caller was a regular the women had nicknamed Pacman. They had started an internal pool to see who could keep him on the line the longest.

"Big enough to hurt, my little Eva," he said.

"Oh, I like zat, too. And you are packing for me, eh?"

"I am indeed."

"You are my Pacman, yes?"

"I am your Pacman, baby."

"Oh, it is sooo big. Can I touch it?"

"Please do."

Chriselda paused a moment to stall the conversation. "Ah, mine *Gott!*" she finally gasped. "Is too big!"

"It not even hard yet, baby. The snake still half asleep."

"I can't get my hand around it."

Chriselda spotted a roach crawling across a corkboard covered with yellow post-it reminders to keep the callers on the line for as long as possible. She had yet to keep Pacman on the phone longer than seven minutes.

"Why don't you get down there and take a closer look?" he told her.

"Oh, yes, *danke*. Oooh, I need both hands."

Chriselda saw Zora Lee Williams coming back from the bathroom and pointed at the roach. The slight black woman with short, blonde-colored hair used a *People* magazine to slap the bug off the corkboard.

"Now lick it," Pacman said.

"Oh, ya, may I?" Chriselda asked. Her eyes were following the path the roach had taken since it hit the floor. When it was close enough, she stepped on it.

"Oh, it's sooo good, mmmmm, ya," she crooned.

The caller was getting worked up. "Oh, baby, yeah, I like that."

"Mmmm, ya, is goot. So goot. Oh, Pacman, I vant you to give it to me today. I vant your big snake inside little Eva."

Zora pointed to her wristwatch. Chriselda held up five fingers. "Oh, mine *Gott*," she said. "I can hardly fit you in my mouth. Oh, *Gott!*"

"Come on, bitch, open that mouth. Get it all in there."

Chriselda feigned choking sounds. "I can't. Oh, *Gott*, I can't. Is too big!"

"Bigger than Adolf?"

"Ah, ya, much bigger. Adolf is *kleines*. Adolf is tiny. Is tiny *mit* the *kleines* balls, too, ya."

"Open wider!" Pacman yelled. "Wider!"

Chriselda gurgled on her end of the line. She rolled her eyes when she heard the caller starting to moan. "No, vait!" she yelled. "Shtop. *Anschlag*. Vait!"

A series of grunts were followed by a long growl.

"Pacman!" Chriselda yelled. "*Anschlag*! Vait!"

The line went dead. Chriselda looked at her watch and noted the time in her log. "Six minute putz," she said.

Zora was standing outside her cubicle now. "Ruby had him up to ten Monday morning," she said. "Nine-thirty-one, to be exact, but he got charged for the ten."

"Ruby doesn't have accent," Chriselda answered. "He talks Hitler, he goes. I can't shtop him."

Zora set her hands on her hips. "Ruby know how to slow him down, girl."

Upset at the mention of her office rival, Chriselda said, "Is *unsinn*. Nonsense."

"Ruby leads him away from where he wants to go," Zora continued. "He say this, she say that. Ruby plays Pacman. Gets him to stay seven minutes minimum every time."

Chriselda waved Zora off. "Is *unsinn*. He says Hitler, he can't shtop."

"I'm not gonna argue. Next time she gets Pacman, you listen in, see how she do."

"Bah," Chriselda said.

Alfred had just stepped inside the office. He carried a box of Dunkin Donuts to the kitchen.

"*Guten Morgen*," he told Chriselda.

"*Guten Morgen* yourself," said Chriselda, still upset at Zora's mention of Ruby.

"Morning ladies," Alfred announced.

"Morning," Zora said.

"Morning, fool," another woman said.

"That you, Ginny?" the old man asked.

"Never you mind," the woman replied from one of the cubicles. "Just bring me a coconut and an old fashion after you settled."

"Yes, ma'am," Alfred said.

He saw Chriselda was still watching him. He winked at her from the kitchen. Chriselda did her best to frown through her blushing smile.

In the afternoon, Zora, Virginia and Ruby had their drinks at the diner on Ralph Avenue. It was just after four o'clock. It had been a long day. They needed to be at work again early the next morning. They had been told things were about to change at work. They were waiting on Alfred to join them with the details.

Virginia was drinking a Rum and Coke, her fifth of the day. She had recently turned sixty-seven. She was a thick woman with a full head of gray hair she refused to color. Between sips of the drink, she talked about outsourcing and how they would all be replaced by "some bitches wearing head scarves with those dots in the middle of they heads."

Ruby had recently turned sixty-six-years of age, but looked much younger. She was of Bermudian decent, tall and graceful, and had the bluest of eyes. Ruby had been with the office a few months before her co-workers learned she was a lesbian and still sexually active. They teased her about taping the sex she had with her partner and replaying it for the perverts who called rather than talking to them and making it all up.

Now she sipped a Mint Julep while trying to assuage Virginia's latest concerns, but the big woman wasn't hearing it.

"You call the bank, the insurance companies, they all picking up the phones in India somewhere," Virginia said. "They don't be answering phones here anymore. How these fools calling us gonna know the difference who they talking to?"

Zora had been sipping her Brandy Alexander while searching the sports pages of the Daily News for the next day's entries at Aqueduct. "There's the accent, for one thing," she said without looking up from the newspaper.

"Oh, yeah, and when's the last time you talked to one of them Indian bitches?" Virginia said. She had turned on her bench seat and nearly knocked Ruby off one side. "Sorry, girl," she said.

"I don't talk to nobody I don't have to," Zora said.

"Unless they working the OTB."

Zora waved Virginia off. Ruby chuckled.

"Point is," Virginia continued, "you call and they try and fool you, say they name is Mary or Laverne or Roberta. The men call themselves American names, too. They real name is Singh, like the men drive the yellow cabs here."

"Those are legal operations," Ruby added. "I mean, we're legal, too, but not like banks and insurance companies. Know what I mean?"

Virginia said, "All I know is they making changes, it can't be good. They can get anybody to answer the phones for the fools we talk to and if they can get them for half what they paying us, they like to do it.

Then we eating pet food like too many our age. This job keep us alive. Can't afford to lose it."

Ruby didn't see the point in arguing. "Alfred will be here soon enough," she said. "Hopefully he'll have some answers."

"The fool better be here soon," Virginia said. "Or I'll be hungover tomorrow morning."

Ruby looked across the table just in time to catch Zora rolling her eyes. Both women chuckled.

❦

In the parking lot outside the diner, thirty-two-year-old Joey Fina offered Alfred Jenkins a hit from his joint.

"No thank you," the elderly man said.

"Makes you hungry?" Fina asked.

"Makes me stupid," Alfred said.

Fina had inherited the phone sex business from his father, a made man with the Vignieri crime family who had recently killed himself rather than turn state's evidence. The underboss of the family had subsequently assigned the business to the dead wiseguy's son as a show of respect and an enticement for others within the ranks to remain loyal.

Fina had some ideas he said he wanted to share with Alfred. "For the sake of business," he said. "Let me know what you think."

The old man had worked as security for the women who worked the morning and afternoon shifts. He also ran errands and kept the place clean. He'd been there more than fifteen years and earned less than two hundred dollars a week. Alfred had seen a lot over the years, but Joey Fina was scary stupid and exceptionally rude.

He nodded at the young wannabe gangster. "I'm listening," he said.

"These old broads my father has answering the phones," Fina said. "Any of 'em, you know, do more than that?"

"I'm not sure I know what you asking."

"They make dates? You know, on the side like. Take a little action for themselves."

Alfred had heard about Joey Fina from his father when the old man made his weekly stops. Ralph Fina was "concerned for his son," he used to tell Alfred. "The kids today, they think its all fun and games. They watch too much television and play too many videogames. They don't know how to talk to people."

The old man had been hard, but respectful. Alfred missed his politeness.

"I can't say for the shifts other than the ones I'm there for," he told Joey Fina, "but there's none of that going on mornings into the afternoons. Not that I know of."

Fina had just taken another hit from his joint. Alfred wondered if Fina had even heard his answer.

"You ever get a gum job from one of them?" the younger man asked. "I'll bet that's something worth paying extra for."

Alfred didn't laugh. It took Fina a few moments to realize he had spoken out of turn.

"Hey, no disrespect intended," he said. "I'm sure you like the old ladies and all. I'm sure they're nice people, but I'm just wondering could they make some extra money for us and themselves. If they did, you know, take some action on the side. It's probably an untapped well, senior citizen hookers."

Fina pointed to his head. "See, I'm all the time thinking about stuff like that. You'll have to get used to it, my man. I'm always thinking about ways to make the green."

Alfred was wondering how the hell Joey Fina had outlived his father.

"Anyway, there are a few things I want to change at the office," Fina added. He lowered his window, took one last hit on the joint, then tossed it out.

It was cold outside. The frigid air sent a chill through Alfred's body. He was grateful when Fina brought the window back up.

"First off, I want to put some of the old ones on with the younger ones," Fina said. "You know, as supervisors like. They're at it the longest. They can work the other shifts, one to each, and I'll move some of the younger ones up to the mornings for whoever supervises that shift, and then I got experience working round the clock, see?"

"The older women won't like it," Alfred said. "Neither will the young ones."

"Fuck what they like. It's a business, my man. I'm talking change for the sake of progress here."

Alfred said, "They've been working those shifts for years. It's been profitable, too. No need to change something isn't broken, son. That's what your daddy used to say."

"Yeah, well, my daddy is dead now and I'm not your son, okay?"

The old man remained silent.

"The other thing is office supplies," Fina added. "I'm not running a charity, no matter what my father did. Tell them, all of them, they got to anti up from now on. No more coffee on the house. No more donuts for free. They want free food let them sign up the meals on wheels bullshit. I'm running a business, not a charity."

Alfred frowned.

"That a problem?" Fina asked.

"They won't appreciate it."

"I don't give a fuck what they appreciate. They appreciate a paycheck, they'll get used to it fast enough."

"That it?" asked Alfred after a moment.

"You sure they aren't working the jamokes call in?" Fina asked. "'Cause if they were and they wanted to turn tricks for the office, I can work something out." He smiled again. "I can pay for their coffee, for one thing. Maybe even meals."

Alfred suppressed what he was thinking.

"Don't mention any of this to them yet," Fina said. "Encourage it, you want. Suggest it even. They go for it I'll give you a percentage, but don't tell them what I'm thinking yet. Let them sweat it out for now, our talk."

Alfred waited for more.

Fina said, "That's it."

The old man got out of there.

✄

Chriselda had joined the women and ordered Alfred a beer before he got there. He nodded at her before taking his first sip.

"Well?" Virginia said.

"I won't dignify what that boy had on his mind," Alfred said.

"Geezer tricks," Virginia said. "I knew it, the motherfucker."

"What did you know?" Zora said. "You thought it was outsourcing. That's all you talking about, outsourcing."

"I knew it was something," said Virginia.

"We still have jobs?" Zora asked.

"I believe so," Alfred said.

Zora slipped him a piece of the newspaper she had cut from the Daily News. She had circled names of the horses she wanted him to bet for her the next day. She nodded at Virginia, Ruby and Chriselda.

"I'll see ya'll in the morning."

"Five dollar double?" Alfred asked.

"One way," said Zora, handing him the money.

"Night, Zora," Ruby said.

"*Gute nacht*," Chriselda said.

Virginia remained silent until Zora was gone, then said, "God bless her. Woman doesn't have a care in the world."

"She is preoccupied," Alfred said.

"I envy her," Ruby said.

Virginia made a face. "The hell for? 'Least you got somebody."

"She has us," Ruby said. "We all have each other to talk to."

"You have Alfred to talk," said Chriselda with a little bitterness.

Alfred frowned at her.

"Zora can ignore the details," Ruby went on, "especially the stuff that makes the rest of us nervous. I admire that."

"She got the disease is what she got," Virginia said. "She like to be crazy with those horses."

Ruby looked to Alfred and smiled. He winked at her. Virginia saw their exchange. So did Chriselda. She excused herself and headed for the bathroom.

"You two crazy," said Virginia when Chriselda was gone. "Everything a big joke. Smile and a wink. You like to make that girl crazy, old man."

Ruby put a hand on one of Virginia's. "It's just our way of playing, girl."

"You playing and she hurting," Virginia said.

"Chrissy bring that on herself," Alfred said. "She got no reason to be jealous."

"That's what you say," Virginia said. "You don't know what she feel. You too busy sucking on your beer."

"Alfred and me just talk," Ruby said. "She needs to get over that."

"Easier to say than do," Virginia said. "She like the fool, lord knows why."

"She's feeling lonely," Ruby said. "I can understand that."

"Then stop your winking and such in front of her," Virginia said. She pulled herself off the bench seat. "I got to go the toilet. Ya'll can talk about me now."

Ruby frowned as the big woman wobbled away.

"Maybe we should stop fooling," she said to Alfred.

"It's just playing," he said. "Chrissy too needy is all. She get over it."

"Well, there gonna be any problems at work? What the man say?"

"That boy just anxious to prove himself."

"What did he propose?"

"He don't know what he's saying."

"I'm not that fragile, Alfred."

The old man needed to sip more of his beer first. "What Virginia said earlier. I told him it wouldn't play."

"He really that ignorant?"

"Plus some."

"What else he say?"

"Wants to break up the shifts. He might try before he learns it won't work."

"Break up the shifts how?"

"Spread you ladies around. Wants to call you supervisors so you can watch over the younger ones. He knows some of them are making dates. That happens everywhere, but he too young to know he can't stop it."

"He thinks we'll squeal on women desperate enough to turn tricks?"

"What he wants to think."

Ruby finished the last of her third drink of the night. "Anything else?"

"Wants to cut back on office supplies. Don't wanna pay for the coffee and snacks. Wants you all to ante up, he said."

"Good lord."

"He won't last long. He gonna lose this business one way the other, but it might be tough until he do."

"And then it might not be there when he's gone."

Alfred smiled. "Now you sounding like Ginny."

Ruby said, "Might be she's right."

⧋

The one bedroom apartment where the office was located had been partitioned off with separate cubicles where each of the women worked the phones. There were five booths, a tiny office for security, and the kitchen area for breaks and meals.

This morning Joey Fina was in early to talk to each of the older women his father had hired going back ten years. When he first arrived, he found Alfred waiting outside the building. The old man was there to tell him about a death in Ruby Anderson's family and that she wouldn't be in the next few days.

Fina had merely nodded at the news. He handed Alfred a five dollar bill for coffee and an egg sandwich, then headed inside.

Half an hour later, after he'd had his breakfast and was settled behind the small desk, he had Alfred send in "the German broad."

"You vanted to see me?" asked Chriselda from the door.

"Sit," Fina told her. He lit a cigarette as she did so. "You want?"

"I don't shmoke."

Fina set the cigarette in the ashtray. "You German or Jew?" he asked.

"Both."

"Really? When you come to America?"

"After the war," Chriselda said.

Fina nodded. "I never understood that, what happened there. Yous didn't fight back. Jews, I mean. In the camps. Yous outnumbered the guards. Yous just took it."

270

Chriselda huffed.

"You lose anybody?" he asked.

"Everyone."

"Sorry. How'd you get away?"

It was a difficult memory for her. She and her twin sister had been hiding in the basement of a neighbor's house when soldiers came searching for them. Her sister had given herself up to save Chriselda. She was executed later the same day.

"I survived," she told Fina now. "Vhat I am here for, please?"

Fina grabbed the cigarette and took another puff. This time he held onto it.

"I'm sorry about the woman lost somebody," he said, changing subjects.

"Ruby," Chriselda said. "Was her lover died."

"Really? How old is Ruby?"

"Sixty-six."

"And she's still getting some? God bless."

Chriselda coughed from the smoke.

"I have plans I discussed with Alfred," Fina said. "You're the only white one in the mornings. You can cut out the lateness, I'd like to—"

"I'm not to supervise."

"Grandpa told you?"

"Alfred is friend."

"He's also an employee."

"He doesn't vant for trouble."

"He still works for me."

Chriselda waved at the smoke. Fina ignored her.

"What if it meant your job, supervising?"

"I find somesing else."

"You quitting?"

"I don't say that."

"You don't supervise, you might as well quit."

Chriselda shrugged.

"It's something to think about," Fina added.

"You're short *mit* staff now because Ruby is out. You vant I'm to leave now?"

Fina smiled. "I can wait."

"Is that all?"

"Well, not really. I wanted to ask one more thing, kind of get a feel for what I'm thinking."

"Geezer tricks?"

Fina leaned forward. "He said that, too?"

"He doesn't have to. It's something a fool vood think."

"What if I could find the clientele?"

"Then you'd need to find hookers, too."

Now Fina chuckled. "You're the feisty one, huh?"

"I can go?"

"Sure," said Fina, finally crushing out his cigarette. "Can you send the fat one in?"

Chriselda was already out of the chair and had started for the door. She stopped and turned. "The fat von?" she asked. "You need to learn to talk, eh?"

Fina smirked. "Sorry I don't know her name," he said.

"Virginia," Chriselda said.

He dismissively waved at the door. "Just show up on time."

⁂

"That's two people feeling it today," Virginia said. "Ruby and Alfred."

They had met for a drink at the diner on Ralph Avenue again. Alfred had been there earlier having dinner. Joey Fina had fired him shortly after the second shift of girls arrived.

"Alfred was my fault," Chriselda said. "Boy asks me how I knew vhat he asks."

"Ain't nobody's fault," Alfred said. "That boy can't help himself. He trying to be his daddy."

"Well, someone should slap his face," Virginia said. "His daddy went and kilt himself. The boy should think twice about wanting that."

"That boy don't have a lick of sense," Zora said. "Firing Alfred for what? At what he was paid? Cost twice that much to replace him."

"Everybody knows I just took that job to be around you fine ladies," Alfred joked.

"Because you a fool," Virginia said.

"It vasn't right," Chriselda said. "I should call you after he talks to me."

Alfred ignored her. "Anybody hear from Ruby?"

"She left a message," Virginia said. "She taking it hard sounds like."

"They've been together a few years, her and her woman," Alfred said. "She loved that girl."

"People die," Chriselda said. "I'm sorry to say, but it happens."

Alfred shook his head at the remark.

"She still gonna need us," Virginia said. "Gonna need you, especially, old man. Lord knows why, but she liked to talk with you. She know you fired?"

Alfred saw Chriselda fidgeting at what Virginia had said. "I didn't tell her," he said.

"Well, she'll be even more upset when she hears it, so wait till she back before you do."

"I got one of her customers today," Zora said, trying to ease the tension. "While Chrissy in with the boy."

"Pacman?" Chriselda asked, trying to go along with it.

"The big snake hisself."

They both chuckled.

Zora went through her routine from earlier. "Easy, baby," she said with a breathless voice, "you too big for me. My God, you tearin' me up!"

"I think about what they paying with credit cards and it make me want to choke," Virginia said.

"Makes me want to use my own telephone," Zora said.

Alfred toasted the idea with his beer.

"I'd do it, too, except you know that boy would just go make more trouble than it's worth," Zora added.

"True that," Virginia said.

"Listen to Ginny, talking like a street boy," Alfred joked.

"Never you mind how I talk, fool," Virginia said.

"Don't mind me, girl, it's the beer," the old man said. "It's my third today."

"Third my fat ass," Virginia said.

The table, except for Chriselda, shared the laugh. "I take care of punk," she said when it was quiet again.

"Take care how?" Virginia asked.

"Don't vorry. I know a geezer trick."

The woman smiled. Alfred stared until Chriselda turned away from him.

"What we should do is approach that Russian man came around soon as the boy's daddy got scooped up," Zora said. "We made a deal with him, Alfred still have his job."

"We can still do that," Virginia said. "Talk to the man and try to survive."

"I say I take care," Chriselda repeated.

Virginia pointed a finger at Alfred. "Tell truth now, she that mouthy in the sack?"

"Shh your business," Chriselda said.

The table fell silent a moment before it erupted with laughter. The old man looked to Chriselda. She turned away from him.

Joey Fina had spent the night drinking and was sleeping it off in his car on Ralph Avenue when Chriselda met with the Russian men on the same street, half a block from the building where the office was located.

Chriselda sat in the back of the Buick and struggled to close the door. When she finally managed to slam it shut, she sarcastically thanked the two men up front for their help.

The driver remained silent. The man in the front passenger seat asked her what she wanted.

"Vhat I tell you two veeks ago," she said. "A gun."

"What you want gun for?"

"None your business."

"What kind of gun?"

"Gun to shoot. Small, I can fit in purse."

"A twenty-five?"

"I don't know numbers. Small."

The short man held up a Walther PPK.

"How much is?"

"Five hundred. Another fifty for ammo."

"Bullets?"

"Another fifty."

"You load for me, make to shoot?"

Both men chuckled.

"Yes or no?" Chriselda asked. "I have vork today."

"I make ready to shoot," the short man said.

Chriselda pulled the money from her purse. She showed the short man the cash, but held her hand out for the gun first.

"*Mit* the bullets, eh?" she added.

He popped the clip, showed her it was loaded, then slipped it back in and racked the slide.

"You going to rob us?" he asked before handing her the gun.

"Don't be putz," she said.

"Putz?"

She huffed and he handed her the gun. Then she handed him the money.

"I get out myself," she told them.

❦

Chriselda tapped on the driver's side window with the butt of the Walther until Joey Fina opened his eyes. He let the window down without noticing the gun.

"What is it?" he asked through a yawn.

She showed him the gun. "Give me vallet."

Fina smirked. "You fuckin' kiddin' me?"

"Now, I'm late for vork."

"Oh, yeah? How's this? Now you're fired from work."

Chriselda frowned. "Little putz," she said. "Give me vallet."

"Yeah, right, fuck you, ya' old cunt."

Chriselda shot him in the forehead. She waited for his body to slump over before leaning in the window and shooting him again, this time behind his left ear.

❦

She was a few minutes late for work. She had managed to recover more than three hundred dollars of the money the gun and ammunition had cost her. She had also brought a box of Dunkin donuts for the girls to snack on until lunch.

Zora was busy looking over the racing charts in the Daily News. Virginia was busy with a client on the phone, telling him she liked "to do a man nice and slow before he lost control and did his business prematurely, so you stay with me, baby, hear?"

Ruby was still away mourning the loss of her lover. Chriselda was surprised to find Alfred sitting in the tiny office.

"Vat you are doing here?" she asked him. "Boy fires you yesterday."

"Waiting on you," Alfred said.

"Vy?"

"I didn't like what you said last night. Got me to worrying."

"Vhat is to worry?"

"I stopped by your place this morning. You not there."

"I'm busy. I'm here now, eh?"

"You out the apartment early and late now."

"I said I'm busy. Vhat, you are boss now?"

"No, like I said, I was worried."

She waved him off. "Bah, you vorry for nothing."

"So, where were you?"

"*Mit* my lover, okay? Much younger than you."

Alfred frowned.

Chriselda said, "Vhat? Vhat is your business?"

"What you do, girl?"

Sirens sounded outside the building. Chriselda slowly opened her purse. When the sirens grew louder, she set the cash and the gun on the desk.

"Buy flowers for Ruby," she said. "Give rest to the girls."

Alfred took both her hands and was about to speak when

Chriselda shook her head.

"*Sprechen Sie nicht,*" she said. "Shhh, don't say."

Afterword

My grandfather on my mother's side, Pietro Telese, died from emphysema but it took the disease 77 years. He had one lung probably the last ten years of his life and continued smoking until the morning he died in his sleep. Whenever he would cough during those last ten years and I was around, he'd say: "Char-leh, it won't'a be longa now." Grandpa Pete was pure love and my true godfather. (I took his name at my confirmation. Carmelo Pietro Stella.) —C.S.

REQUIEM FOR MOE

REED FARREL COLEMAN

Reed Farrel Coleman (born 1956) was born and raised in Brooklyn, NY. He began writing poetry in high school and turned to crime fiction after college. His sixth novel, The James Deans, *was nominated for the Best Paperback Original Edgar Award. He is also the editor of the short story anthology,* Hardboiled Brooklyn. *His stories and essays have appeared in or will appear in* Dublin Noir, Plots With Guns, Wall Street Noir, Brooklyn Noir 3, Fuck Noir, These Guns for Hire *and* Crimespree Magazine. *Executive Vice President of the Mystery Writers of America, Reed lives on Long Island with his wife and two kids.*

REQUIEM FOR MOE
(A Moe Prager, Jack Taylor Variation)
by Reed Farrel Coleman

He appeared at the Brooklyn store one day, stepping out of a cloud of his own cigarette smoke; a tattered old genie coming out of the lamp. A genie, mind you, in a cheap blue suit and expensive brown shoes.

"Can't smoke in here," I said, not recognizing him at first.

"Moe, isn't it?"

"Do I know—"

I stopped myself and squinted through my glasses. While I didn't quite know him, we'd met once, maybe fifteen years before on the streets of Tribeca in front of the building where Pooty's had stood. Pooty's was a scruffy watering hole that had once been home to the best jukebox in the city, the place where I first fell deeply in love with my wife to be. Now Pooty's was gone and my wife to be is my wife that was. The genie was an Irishman, from Galway, as I recalled, an ex cop like myself and like myself a man who, in younger days, took on the odd private case.

"How are you?" I held my hand out to him.

Ignored it. Too busy crushing his cigarette out on the hundred and fifty year old broad plank flooring we'd just had restored and resurfaced. His role as fireman complete, he took my hand.

"Ah, it's good to see you, pal."

"I never did get your name all those years ago."

"Jack," he said as if the single syllable explained the history of the world and then some.

"Just Jack?"

"Why, will it not do?"

Said

"It will have to."

"Practical man, Moe. We've no use for practical men in Ireland. A country full of priests and poets. Piss on the streets of Galways and you'll catch the next five Yeats with the spray."

"I'll take your word for it."

"You'd be the first."

"So, what can I do for you, Jack? A bottle of Jameson?"

Said

"For fuck's sake, is there like a neon sign on me forehead?"

"No, just guessing."

"I've given up the drink, Moe."

"Jack, not to bust your balls, but this *is* a liquor store."

"I'm here for you, not for the drink. It's hard for me to confess, but I need your help."

"Help? How can I help you, Jack?"

"I'm looking for a cat."

"A cat?"

"Jesus, is there like an echo in here? Don't you still work cases?"

"I'm an old man."

"Bollix! It's in your blood."

"At my age the only thing in my blood is blood and thanks to the drug companies it's not even that. Besides, lost pets was never my beat."

Said

"Not that kind of cat, Moe."

"What, it escaped from the zoo? Somehow I don't picture a gimpy old Jew and crooked old Irishman chasing tigers through the streets of Brooklyn Heights."

"Not that kind of cat either."

"Maybe I didn't pay close enough attention in school. Am I missing something here or is there another kind of cat?"

Ignored the question

"When does your shift end?"

I checked my watch. "Two hours."

"We'll talk then."

The genie was gone. His crushed cigarette the only evidence he'd been there at all.

Old men don't cotton to cemeteries, particularly at night. Too much like visiting the house that's being built for them. *A house warming and I didn't even bring cake!* But a cemetery is where Jack brought me or, more specifically, where he had me drive us. And he could pick 'em, let me tell you. This was one of the big, old cemeteries in Cypress Hills, the one where Houdini had yet to escape from and one that played a sad role in my very first private case.

Although the place made me uncomfortable, it was hard to deny the majesty of the grounds. It was all very nineteenth century and early twentieth, when people built marble mausoleums and erected mighty headstones to please the god of Abraham. As we made our way through the narrow paths between the graves, Jack muttered and tsk-ed.

"What is it?" I asked.

"The greatest sin in Ireland is to let a grave go unattended. Your house can fall down around your ears and look like complete shite, but to let a relative's grave fall into disrepair. . ."

"This is an old cemetery, Jack. Most of these people's relatives are themselves dead."

He crossed himself as if it hurt to do so. Said

"Here we are."

Pointed at a lonely grave rimmed in very low, but neatly trimmed hedges. The headstone was an unassuming block of gray polished granite with the top beveled. The inscription was on the surface of the bevel beneath the Star of David.

ANNE BAUM
BELOVED DAUGHTER, MOTHER, ANGEL
BORN JAN 3, 1960 DIED JUNE 1, 1988

Atop the grave itself were the windblown stems of a hundred dead roses and several grimy statuettes and plaques. One of the filthy busts was a small white, blue and black porcelain bust of Edgar Allan Poe.

"Do you know the writer K.T. Baum?"

"The mystery guy?" I asked.

"The same. This is his daughter's grave. Run down by a drunken driver."

"Jesus!" Funny how Jews from Brooklyn say Jesus all the time. "I have a daughter myself. I don't know what I would have done if–"

"Let's not think of it, Moe. Life is burden enough without the added weight of imagined sorrows."

"You're right, of course. So what are we doing here?"

"Baum is a friend. As I don't possess many, I treasure the ones I do."

"But that still doesn't explain–"

"Look at the grave."

I obliged. He lit up, lifting a heavy silver Zippo to the tip of a cigarette; the genie once again supplying his own magic smoke.

"These are the awards he's won, I take it."

Said

"Fella, you take it right."

I knelt down to get a closer look at the grave, my arthritic knees creaking like an old coffin lid. Now I noticed what Jack had hoped I would see.

"Something's missing." I pointed to a clothes iron-shaped depression in the grass atop the grave. "The cat?"

"The Silver Whisker. About yea big." Jack held his bony hands eight or so inches apart. "Of equal height and near twenty pound of silver."

"Why do you suppose the thief took the cat and not the others?" Jack said

"Who can know the mind of a ghoul? Liked cats better than Poe. Wanted to melt down the silver, maybe."

"Maybe. Baum must be pretty old by now."

"Old and dying. Lung cancer's marking his days. Doctors said he should be dead going on two years now. Finally won that damn cat. Think the chase kept him above dirt. The thing had tasked him his whole career. Every award he'd ever won he dedicated to Anne, then placed it upon her grave. Now he can have his peace."

I considered that kind of peace as I was close to experiencing it myself. How much peace was there, I wondered, in endless sleep if you never woke up to appreciate it? I wondered if these were just the kinds of ruminations that drove ancient humans to create the gods that created them. I wondered if heaven was just waking up again? Old men do a lot of wondering.

❦

Baum's house was a big old Victorian in the Ditmas Park section of Brooklyn, a block or two in from Beverly Road. Jack had assured me it would be fine to stop by the house to chat with the dying author.

"The jumble of medicines keep him up all hours. He'll enjoy the visit."

We were greeted at the door by an odd gray woman. What I mean to say is that she was both older and younger than her age. There was an underlying prettiness, almost girlishness beneath her sixty-ish years and silvery hair. And no amount of years could hide the burn of her green and gold-flecked eyes, but she carried herself and the weight of the world with her.

"Gilda Baum, meet Moe Prager."

Jack had told me in the car that Gilda, Anne's younger sister, had years ago appointed herself to the position of caretaker. Not only did she help manage her father's writing career, but had done nursing courses in order to help manage his medical care as well.

Her handshake was steel.

"He's upstairs waiting for you, Jack. He knew you'd come."

"I'll go have a word with him, Moe. Then you can come on up."

Gilda showed me into the library. It was an impressive thing to behold: handcrafted walnut bookshelves from the parquet floors to the twelve foot high cornice molding that rimmed the mural painted on

283

the plaster ceiling. The mural was done in the pre-Raphaelite style. In it, a lovely woman with an imperfect nose, long white neck and cascades of red tresses floated on a raft of reeds downriver. Her arms were folded across her ample white bosom, the hint of a nipple peeking through her long delicate fingers.

"That's Annie," Gilda said matter-of-factly. "Dad had it done the year she was killed."

"Beautiful."

"That she was. Let me show you dad's other pride."

Gilda looped her arm through my crooked elbow and guided me to the other end of the library. There on display was a collection of old leather bound books and manuscripts in Lucite cases. I could make out some of the titles.

"It's a world class collection of Poe, O'Henry, Henry James. . ." she said proudly. "Annie loved O'Henry in particular. Any story with an ironic twist was meat for her. She was easily pleased."

There was an air of resentment in Gilda's voice, an understandable one. Tragic death makes giants of the mortal. I'm sure Baum had loved Anne before the accident, but because the love had turned unavoidably one-sided, he had made her into a kind of goddess. That couldn't have been easy for his other daughter. It must have been particularly difficult now with her father's impending death.

"I'm sorry," she said. "I've been rude. Can I get you something to drink?"

"Scotch on the rocks."

Her face lit up. She walked me into a room just off the library. It was an office of some sort and there was a lovely liquor cabinet against one wall.

"Dewar's okay?" she asked.

"Perfect."

"This is my office," she said as ice clinked into the glasses.

"You write too."

"Yes, but not detective stories like Dad. I do more scholarly work."

She handed me the hand blown tumbler. We toasted with a shrug and sipped.

"So, what do you make of the missing cat?"

"What do you mean 'What do I make of it?'" Gilda was almost defensive.

"I'm sorry. I didn't mean to–"

"No, no, I should apologize, Mr. Prager. It's been a rough several years with Dad and all. Frankly, there's never been an easy day for him since Annie was killed."

"I can only imagine."

"Let me go and check on Dad and Jack."

She scurried out of the room. I looked around, snuck a look at the ultra thin screen of Gilda's Micro Apple 90. I also picked up the book she had left open on her daybed. I put the book back where I found it and headed back to where I had been standing when Gilda had left the room.

"They'll be only a few more minutes. Dad loves Jack. They met in Galway years and years ago, in the 03 or 04. Jack had just lost a little girl of his own, I think. They were both feeding the swans down by the quay and seemed to hit it off."

"Gilda, do you mind if I tell you a story about my family?"

"No, go right ahead." The smile on her face belied the uneasiness in her voice.

"My dad was a failure in business and he equated that with being a failure as a father. I had an older brother, Aaron. Aaron was the best brother and such a devoted son, but his devotion to my dad was—"

"I'm sure this is all very interesting, Mr. Prager, but—"

"Moe."

"Moe then. But I really don't see what this has to do with—"

"Yes you do, Gilda. You see that it has everything to do with the missing cat. I had a peek at your computer and your reading material. Humor an old man by letting me finish. So, as I was saying, Aaron's devotion to my dad became a quest of sorts. He spent much of his own life trying to convince my dad he hadn't been a failure at all. Even after my father had passed away, Aaron tried convincing him. The business Aaron and I owned, the one I now run with the kids and grandkids, is a manifestation of Aaron's futile quest. Your father's dying. Painting leaves on a vine or stealing a silver cat off your sister's grave won't save him. Let him go, Gilda. It's his time. It's your time. It's almost mine."

She broke down, resting her head on my shoulder. Half a century of tears, grief, and sorrow seemed to pour right out of her. Jack walked in on the scene. Said

"I'm going outside for a smoke."

❦

Jack had been right about the weight of the damned cat statuette. The thing had quite a bit of heft to it. Gilda stayed downstairs as I brought the Silver Whisker up to show her dad. She had confessed the whole plot to me. . . well, most of it, anyway, when her crying had quieted down. She had stolen the cat in the hope of keeping her dad alive just a little longer.

She so desperately wanted him to see that she was everything that Anne had been, maybe more. She had done everything else she could think of, yet she could never compete with Anne's memory. Gilda knew it was a crazy thing to do and doomed to fail as everything else had failed, but. . . What she had neglected to tell me was that she, not her father, had written the book that had won the Silver Whisker. I don't know exactly how I knew that. I just did.

When I entered the bedroom, silver cat in hand, K.T. Baum was dead. Apparently, he knew it all, too. I placed the statuette near his right hand and left.

❦

I couldn't seem to find Gilda when I went back downstairs. I let myself out. I couldn't blame Gilda for wanting time alone. She had too many years of emptiness and self-deception to deal with in one night.

But Jack was gone too. When I stepped out into the cool black air of the Brooklyn night, all that remained of Jack Taylor on the planks of the wrap-around porch was a crushed cigarette butt and wisps of pungent cigarette smoke. *Whoosh!* The genie had gone.

❦

"Grandpa Moe," I heard a little boy's voice coming out of the genie's smoke. "Grandpa Moe."

"Sssshhh, honey, Grandpa is very sick," I heard my daughter Sarah say, her voice cracking slightly. "He needs to rest."

"But–"

"No buts, Aaron. God, you're just like your Great Uncle Aaron, may he rest in peace."

"I'll take over, Sarah," I heard my kid sister Miriam say.

"Where's Jack?" I said, my throat dry, my voice thin as a hair. I had trouble focusing my eyes. I saw the world through heat waves coming off hot tar and it smelled like a hospital.

"Take it easy, Moe. Rest. You really need–"

"Miriam, for chrissakes! Where's Jack?"

"Who's Jack?"

"Jack! Jack Taylor. Where's Jack Taylor?"

"I'll be right back."

The door opened and closed. That much I could make out. Then it opened and closed again.

"He's asking for someone we don't know, someone none of us

know," Miriam was near frantic.

"It might be the drugs," a man's voice explained. "It might be the cancer. At this point, it's impossible to know. Just sit with him and call the family in."

"Miriam," I called to her in a whisper."

"What is it Moe?"

"No silver cats for me, okay?"

"Okay," she said, though only I understood.

Then I went to sleep.

Afterword

In Ireland, so I'm told, it's a compliment to be called an old soul. Though young at heart, Ken Bruen's soul is old and fierce. The same can be said of his writing. I've always had an affinity for his Jack Taylor and am constantly inspired by Ken and Jack. The roots of my story are traceable to them both. —R.F.C.

HAS ANYONE SEEN MRS. LIGHTSWITCH?

COLIN COTTERILL

Colin Cotterill (born 1952) is the author of a brilliant detective series set in Laos after the communist takeover. The first two novels, The Coroner's Lunch *and* Thirty Three Teeth *are available; with a third on its way. He has taught in Australia, the U.S., and Japan, and has lived in Thailand, on the Burmese border, and in Laos. In the past, he has worked for UNICEF and local non-governmental agencies to prevent child prostitution and to rehbilitate abused children. Colin would like to encourage you to get involved in the Books for Laos project (www.colincotterill.com/bfld1.htm).*

HAS ANYONE SEEN MRS. LIGHTSWITCH?

by Colin Cotterill

"**H**as anyone seen Mrs. Lightswitch?" Siri asked even though he was alone in the concrete room. When he opened the freezer door, the cold air had briefly tingled his bushy eyebrows, but within seconds the draught was consumed by the oppressive heat of August.

The freezer in the Mahosot Hospital morgue was twenty-four inches wide, seven feet deep, and a yard high. Its French designer must have had a kneeling gnu in mind when he put it together, because all that upward space wasn't worth a tin kneecap to a human corpse. Unfortunately, the People's Democratic Republic of Laos didn't have any gnus, dead or alive. After the endless drought of that rainless season in 1977, there wasn't much wildlife to be had any more. They were hungry times. Even the street dogs were starting to look over their shoulders. The communist regime wasn't yet two years old but already it had been able to mismanage the country towards hardship. The three million people, who had been too slow to flee across the Mekhong to Thailand, had learned to be frugal and resourceful. And perhaps the most resourceful of them all was Dr. Siri Paiboun, the national and only coroner. At seventy-three, the snowy-haired little man had mastered every clever subterfuge to squeeze value out of what humble pickings were available.

To maximize the wasted space in the freezer, Dr. Siri had created a bamboo litter that formed a shelf and allowed two bodies to occupy the area at the same time. Without it, he could probably have piled four bodies one atop the other like sandbags – five with a bit of a squeeze – but that wasn't a particularly professional approach to forensic science. Siri admitted he wasn't much of a coroner, but he did have standards. Keeping his corpses in presentable condition was one of the highest on his list. It wasn't just the act of preserving evidence that led to this respectful relationship. Without a laboratory, modern equipment or up-to-date scientific documentation, there wasn't much to be gleaned from the body anyway. No, Dr. Siri showed the utmost respect to the cadavers that passed through his morgue because he knew their previous owners would be back.

Through no fault of his own, the good doctor hosted the spirit of a thousand year-old Hmong shaman who had the annoying habit of attracting all the wrong sorts. Every post mortem grievance-holder came knocking on Siri's dreams – leaving clues as to how their lives had been deprived them. One doesn't pile up bodies in a freezer if their spirits are likely to gang up on one for doing so. One takes very good care of them, and one certainly doesn't lose them.

"Can you believe it?" said Nurse Dtui walking into the cutting room with a urine sample in one hand and a greasy pork spring roll in the other. She was an imposing young girl whose figure was testament to many such snacks. "We've got a hydroelectric dam down the road pumping out 150 megawatts of electricity but they still manage to treat us to power cuts every other night. I woke up in a pool of sweat at two this morning. I mean, the fan's the only thing between me and suffocation in this weather. Did you say something?"

"Yesterday's arrival, Mrs. Lightswitch," Siri said, staring into the empty freezer. "She appears to have fled."

"No. Are you sure?"

"Unless she's shrunk to the size of an ant, I think we can fairly say she's not here, don't you?"

"Then they must have come for her?"

"Who?"

"The relatives. They probably wanted to get her on the pyre before the heat turned her."

"I was the last one out yesterday evening and she was still in here then. Did they break in and abscond with the body in the dead of night?"

"Did you remember to lock the front door?"

"Dementia hasn't set in just yet."

Dtui put her unfinished snack in a kidney bowl and went to stand beside Siri who was waving his arm back and forth in the empty freezer like a magician illustrating how empty his top hat is.

"No signs of a break in when you got here this morning?" she asked.

"Everything was perfectly normal."

"Who else has a key?"

"Only our trusted morgue assistant - and I believe Mr. Geung is still convalescing in Thangon – and Suk, the hospital administrator."

"Aha. Then it has to be him."

"What does?"

"Comrade Suk ran off with Mrs. Lightswitch."

"What would Comrade Suk want with a body?" Siri asked.

"Perhaps her husband pressured him to release it."

"Before the autopsy? The hospital would never have agreed."

"Why did she need an autopsy, anyway?"

"Because she was dead?"

"You know what I mean, smarty pants. We only handle suspicious cases from the hospital and government stuff. She wasn't either, was she?"

Siri had disappeared to his waist inside the freezer and was still waving his arm in front of him. His voice emerged like an echo from a mine. "Her husband's a doctor here."

"Really? We've got a Dr. Lightswitch at Mahosot?"

"He uses his first name, for obvious reasons: Dr. Bounmee."

"Not the gynecologist?"

"That's him. It appears he insisted on an autopsy."

"What did she die of?"

"The doctor's certificate says respiratory failure under suspicious circumstances. I didn't have a chance to have a good look at her before I left yesterday evening."

"You're sure the porters put her in the freezer and not the mop cupboard? They aren't the sharpest limes on the tree, you know."

"I know. I checked the body before I went home just to make sure they hadn't put her in face down. She was here all right."

Dtui watched the doctor's bottom sway from side to side.

"You're doing something ghostly in there, aren't you?" she said.

"If she'd been removed forcibly there'd be bad spirit in here." He slid out and stood beside the nurse. "But I don't feel anything. It would appear she was happy to go."

Dtui shuddered.

"No matter how many times I'm exposed to your sorcery, it still gives me the willies, Doc. What do you think we should do? Write her off as missing in action?"

"Dtui, my love, lest you forget, this is a socialist state. Everything is stamped and signed for in triplicate. If you lose something, you spend the rest of your life being made to pay for it. That includes Comrade Lightswitch."

"All right. Where do we start?"

"Step one, I go to find out whether anyone borrowed the director's key."

"What should I do?"

"You hang around here in case she comes back."

⚘

In the People's Democratic Republic of Laos, being a director had more to do with who your uncle was than whether you could do your job. Administrator Comrade Suk had been in charge of a battalion of infantry on the Vietnamese border when they called him south to run the hospital. As far as Siri could ascertain, his medical training amounted to a First Aid badge in the Youth Movement. But he delegated well and, to the relief of most, was rarely in his office, which was the case on this occasion. Suk's secretary led Siri into the sparse office where six heroes of the revolution hung in a line behind the modest desk, imprisoned in their wooden frames. They scowled at Siri. He glared back at them. These were the men who'd stolen his retirement and forced him to run the morgue. Almost fifty years membership of the Party and they still begrudged him a few years of peace. If he'd just had six tomatoes…

The secretary distracted him from his animosity and pointed to the wall cabinet where the spare departmental keys hung on numbered hooks behind the glass doors. They were all there, including number 17, the morgue key, and the key to the cabinet was locked in the desk drawer whose own key was in the pocket of Comrade Suk somewhere in the south. He'd been gone since Tuesday and nobody could have taken anything from the cabinet in his absence without breaking the glass, which showed no signs of damage.

Back at his building, Siri rechecked the door for evidence of a break in. Its lock was particularly free of scratches and jimmy marks. Few people went to the trouble of breaking into a morgue. Once the door was locked from the outside, it was impossible to open from the inside. The only windows in the squat concrete bunker were seven feet off the ground and louvered. All of the louvers were in place – an anomaly in glass deficient Laos. The Department of Justice had splashed out on an expensive Soviet air-conditioner to be used only during examinations, and the authorities didn't want any of that expensive conditioned air getting out. Hence the windows.

Siri and Nurse Dtui sat pondering. Impossible though it seemed, a dead body had been smuggled out of the morgue without anybody seeing or hearing anything. Without any leads as to the 'how', they set their sights on the 'why'.

"It seems to me," Siri said, "that there are two logical reasons why anyone would want to get a corpse out of the morgue in such a hurry. The first, as you rightly said, is when the family wants to get it cremated before the juices start to curdle in the heat. The second, and I'm perhaps being a little over dramatic here, is when they want to avoid an autopsy. To that end, I think I should go to have a word with Dr. Bounmee."

"You think he killed his wife?"

"I know a lot of husbands who would like to."

"But you said he insisted on the autopsy."

"He did. So, let's think deviously for a second. Suppose a husband, a doctor at that, kills his wife using some drug he has access to…"

"In the gynecology department?"

"I'm conjecturing here."

"Sorry."

"He kills his wife, sends her to the morgue in the evening when he knows we all have to hurry off to tend the cooperative vegetable garden, and insists on an autopsy. He knows full well we wouldn't examine her until the following morning. He then smuggles the body out of the morgue during the night and disposes of it together with whatever evidence it might be carrying."

"Not realizing we probably wouldn't have a clue what she died of even if she'd stayed.'

"Obviously not. But he'd be off the hook because we were responsible for the body and he'd shown concern as to her death. And... he works in the hospital where he has access to departmental keys. He could have made a copy. He might have been planning this for months. I wonder...?"

"The death certificate?" Dtui took the standard TT567 Medical Practitioner's Certification of Demise with its two smudged carbon copies from the in tray on her desk and looked at the signature. "Well, what do you know?"

"Her husband signed it."

"He certainly did. What has the world come to when a gynecologist can sign a death certificate? We'll have dentists and beauticians doing it next. Okay, Doc. I'm with you on the husband theory."

"You are?"

"Well, we haven't got anything else to go on. What do I do while you're off interrogating the gynecologist?"

"Can you ferret around at the hospital? Chat with those nosey nurse friends of yours and see if anyone has an idea what type of marriage the Lightswitches had. See if they fought a lot; whether he had a fancy piece on the side. That kind of thing."

"Ooh. Sanctioned tittle-tattle. I love it."

❦

This is probably as good a time as any to explain how a person might have acquired the name 'Lightswitch'. It all came about in 1943 when the Royal Lao Government announced that everyone in the country had to have a surname. Until then, the majority of the population had, like French poodles, been perfectly content with the one name. It irked some folk that they should be encumbered with such a bulky nomenclature just to be perceived as civilized by the western world. In rebellion, some people like the father-in-law of the deceased, created silly names for themselves. Electricity was a relatively new arrival in Laos at the time so rebellious Somphet named himself *Sawitfyfah*, after seeing an actual light switch in the capital. It was his belief that the government would baulk at such frivolity and force something more conservative upon him. But, no. A month after filling in the form, his new identity card arrived with Lightswitch written in large indelible letters, and from that day on, his wife and son and, eventually, the wife of his son would be wired with same name.

But it appeared that the current Mrs. Lightswitch had gone off.

❦

Siri arrived at Dr. Bounmee's residence early in the afternoon. The sun breathed its heat onto little brick house and wilted the morning glory that clutched desperately at its walls. He walked in through the unlocked gate and stepped cautiously through a minefield of sleeping dogs that lay in the front yard. The front door was closed – unusual for mid-day Vientiane. He called out.

"Sorry. Anyone home?"

There was no reply from the house but one of the dogs growled and farted in its sleep.

"Hello?" he tried again.

He was about to leave when the door opened a fraction and one eye framed in wrinkles looked out through the gap.

"Yes, what?" came a voice.

Siri walked up onto the first step and said, "Sorry. I'm Dr. Siri Paiboun from Mahosot. I'm looking for Dr. Bounmee."

The door opened wider to show more wrinkles and the rather sad face of an elderly woman. She was simply dressed in a T-shirt and an old weather-worn pasin skirt. Her hair was tied back with a rubber band. In her hand she held a duster of fine partridge feathers.

"He's gone, Doctor," she said. "He spends all his time at the hospital." Her voice was as tired as an old wash rag.

"Sorry, Auntie. They told me he'd worked last night and come home for breakfast."

"He never comes home in the daytime. I don't know where he goes."

"How long have you worked for him?"

"More years than I can count."

"So you know the doctor quite well."

"Know him? Me? I just clean the house, do all the dirty work," she said. "I've got a key. I'm supposed to be here. You can check if you don't believe me."

297

"No," Siri laughed. "I'm quite certain you're who you say you are. I was just wondering where the doctor might have gone if he didn't come here." She shrugged. "His bags and belongings are all where they should be?"

"What do you mean?"

"He hasn't gone on a journey somewhere?"

"He wouldn't tell me his plans, would he? I'm just the servant, here."

"He doesn't treat you well?"

She looked into Siri's eerie green eyes as if deciding whether to tell him a secret.

"I'm fed well enough," she said.

"How did you get along with Mrs. Lightswitch?"

The corners of her mouth turned up briefly – more of a crack than a smile. "Mrs. Lightswitch won't be suffering any more," she said.

"You think she suffered?"

"I have to go," she said, and slammed the door.

❦

That night, Siri went to sleep with a heavy heart. He'd never lost a body before. He'd spent the afternoon following up on leads and acting a lot more like a policeman than a coroner. But he had no qualms about playing Inspector Maigret. Why not? When you're an old fellow with an attitude, you can convince people you're almost anything without actually telling them so. But he'd come up with no leads as to where Dr. Bounmee might have fled. Dtui's research had been no less frustrating. Nobody could recall ever having seen the wife. She never attended hospital functions and he didn't mention her at work. It was as if she didn't exist. Dtui had also done a tour of the local temples but none of them had received an urgent request for a cremation.

Siri's dream that night was no more helpful. He was often visited by the spirits of those who had passed through the morgue. He'd been hoping Mrs. Lightswitch might stop by and tell him where she'd been removed to, but she didn't show up at all. Instead he had to sleep through a thoroughly confusing fable about an elephant. The animal went to sleep and Siri could see its dream within his own. It was a ferocious beast in the dream. Its trunk was a weapon that thrashed its enemy, and a tool that ripped trees from the ground. It boasted of its magnificent trunk to the other elephants and they bowed before him. But then the elephant awoke to find that in real life, his trunk and his tail had changed places. Wherever he went he was mocked and ridiculed.

Siri awoke as confused as he normally did. Half of the dreams he had meant nothing at all. The other half were deeply significant to cases he was working on. Unfortunately, he had no idea which were which. Even the significant ones were so cryptic, the case was often long behind him when he finally worked them out.

∮

Siri and Dtui sat at their respective desks without an original idea between them. He told her about his dream but all she could think of was that he should stop eating garlic before bed.

"Isn't it about now that you say, 'I think we're overlooking something obvious'?" Dtui said.

"I think we're overlooking something obvious," said Siri, obligingly. "But it's more likely we don't have all the pieces yet. What had Bounmee's maid been too afraid to tell me? Why has nobody ever met Mrs. Lightswitch? And how did Bounmee manage to be conveniently around to sign her death certificate?"

"And how could he be so calm as to work night duty so soon after his wife had died?"

"Good point. The good doctor certainly has a lot of questions to answer if only we could find him. Without a body, we can't even get the police to look for him. No, let's focus on the wife for a second. What is it we don't know about her?"

"Apart from where she is?"

"Yes, apart from that."

"We don't know where they found the body."

"That's true, we don't. We don't know where she was coming from or going to the day she died. That might help. I wonder whether the porters brought any artifacts in with the body. There might be something in her bag. Did they say anything to you?"

"Who?"

"The porters."

"When?"

"Nurse Dtui, you really will have to stop sniffing the ether during your lunch break. I'm asking whether the porters mentioned a bag or anything being found with the body."

"Well, how should I know?"

"You checked her in."

"I did not. You did."

"I certainly did not. Wait. Are you saying you weren't here when they brought in the body?"

"I didn't know anything about it till you told me she was gone this morning. I assumed you'd signed for her while I was over with the filing clerk. How did you get the certificate?"

"It was here on my desk when I came back from the toilet. I assumed you'd put it here."

"Nope."

"We most certainly didn't have an official delivery if nobody signed for the body. Those bureaucrats would sooner take the corpse home with them than leave it here without a signature."

"So somebody smuggled it in?"

"We'd have to assume so. This gets more and more peculiar."

❦

When Mr. Geung walked into the office he saw two extremely blank colleagues sitting at their desks.

"H…h…hello, Comrade Doctor Siri an…an…and Comrade n…n…Nurse Dtui,' he said with a big assorted-tooth smile on his face. He was a sturdy, greasy haired man in his forties who wore his Down Syndrome elegantly. He had been the morgue assistant since long before Siri or Dtui arrived there and they greeted his return with hugs and great relief. Once they'd established that his dengue fever was behind him and that he was fit and ready to resume his duties, they sat him down at his own little desk and began to share their mystery with him.

Once it was told, they asked him if he had a logical explanation for it all. He put his fist against his forehead and considered for a moment. Of course, having Down Syndrome he didn't have a logical explanation for anything, but he did have a story of his own to tell.

It was a story which sparked a thought in Dr. Siri's mind – a thought that led to one of those, 'How could I be so stupid?' moments. The 'How could I be so stupid?' moment led to a confrontation, which led to the discovery of a body and the arrest of a perpetrator - but not necessarily the body or the perpetrator that Dr. Siri and Nurse Dtui had anticipated.

The Story

Mr. Geung had cancelled his trip home. He figured that if he wasn't well enough to work, he wasn't well enough to convalesce. He hadn't quite grasped the concept. At sunrise the previous day, he'd been building up his strength by walking briskly around the hospital grounds. He'd arrived at the rear at the morgue to find all of the louvers from the cutting room embedded in the soft, freshly hoed dirt of the garden below it. As he was responsible for the upkeep of the morgue, he'd gone to the maintenance shed, dragged back a ladder and replaced the glass, pane by pane, giving each a good polishing beforehand. Luckily they were all accounted for and undamaged.

The Thought

Dr. Siri considered this fact. Somebody had apparently broken into the morgue by removing the louvers. They had pilfered the corpse from the freezer and, being unable to exit through the locked front door, had manhandled the dead weight of a body back out through the narrow window high in the wall. All this was done without breaking any of the louvers that lay on the ground outside: a momentous task. Impossible to imagine, unless...

The 'How Could I Have Been So Stupid?' Moment

Dr. Siri slapped himself on the forehead.

"Come on," he said.

"Where are we going?" Dtui asked, waddling after the little man as he hurried out of the morgue and across the crunchy brown grass.

"To the records department for a copy of Bounmee's contract," he said. "Then a brief stop at the state electricity commission."

The Confrontation

Siri, Dtui, and the captain from the temporary police headquarters on Sethathirat Road arrived at Dr. Bounmee's house a little before eleven. The yard dogs growled and howled behind the unlocked front gate, but not because they were protecting the house. Once Siri pushed open the gate they all fled through the gap.

"What on earth are they running from?" Dtui asked.

Siri looked around the yard, at the holes dug in the dry flower beds and the vines ripped from the walls.

"They're hungry," Siri said. "I'd guess nobody's been feeding them."

The visitors walked to the front door and were met by the unmistakable scent of death. The police captain with a handkerchief covering his mouth and nose, boldly followed the others in through the unlocked front door. The stench led them to the kitchen where they found the body hunched over the dining table with its face submerged in a bowl of half-eaten rice porridge. A large meat knife was buried deep between the shoulder blades. It was the last breakfast Dr. Bounmee would ever have. He still wore his white hospital shirt although the blood had soaked through it to leave only the collar starched and pristine white. From the state of the corpse, Siri estimated he'd been dead for some twenty-four hours.

Dtui looked at Siri, "So, he was already dead…"

"…When I came by yesterday. So it would seem," Siri confirmed. The sound of retching echoed down the hallway. The policeman had retreated to the front porch leaving the pair alone with the corpse.

"So, she could be anywhere by now."

"She could be," Siri agreed. "But I doubt she'll have gone far."

He went to the door that led off the kitchen area, the usual location for a maid's room in colonial homes such as these. He tapped lightly on the door and turned the handle.

"Are you sure it's safe to go in there?" Dtui asked.

"Oh, I doubt she has any more anger to vent. She's done her deed."

He pushed open the door to the small room and there before them was the old lady lying stiff on the single bed. Her arms were crossed on her chest and her tired eyes stared at the unmoving fan on the ceiling. Siri crossed to sit at the end of the bed and Dtui filled the doorway.

"It's over, Auntie," Siri said. "No more suffering."

The woman slowly tilted her head in the doctor's direction as if she'd only just noticed his presence.

"Hello, Doctor," she said. "I'm afraid my husband can't see you right now."

"I know, dear. I know."

ff

Dr. Siri, and Comrade Civilai, his only ally on the Lao Politburo were sitting on a log beside the Mekhong working their way through a couple of baguettes that could have been fresher. They were hard work for two fellows long in the tooth. Civilai's baguette was four inches shorter than his friend's because Siri had done all the talking so far.

"So," Civilai said at last, "Attempted suicide by freezer. I bet you haven't seen that too often in your career. She sounds like a real fruitcake to me."

"That's very sensitive of you."

"Well, excuse me for stating the obvious. I don't know too many normal women who spend the night in a freezer then go home and knife their husbands to death."

"She was disturbed, no doubt about that, and terribly depressed. Her husband had treated her like a hired help. He was ashamed of her, hardly let her out of the house. It finally sent her over the edge, but she had to have some of her wits about her to conceive such a devious plan. She wanted her husband to suffer, perhaps ruin his career if she could, but she wasn't courageous enough to be around to see it go down in flames.

"He kept death certificates with his papers. She took one and forged his signature – signed her own death warrant you might say. I checked his real signature on his hospital contract. She wasn't much of a forger."

"And she just waltzed into the morgue and climbed into the freezer?"

"She must have been outside waiting for her chance. Dtui left and I went for a pee and she just snuck in."

"And if everything had gone according to plan, she would have been dead by morning and they would have blamed her husband. It almost worked."

"It was very clever. She had a note on her that said 'In the case of my unexplained death, please let it be known that my husband is trying to kill me. I have proof.' She took a handful of sleeping pills, jacked up the temperature control in the freezer and waited for it all to be over."

"Couldn't she have thought of something more dramatic?"

"This was perfect: peaceful and non-violent. I imagine she didn't want to suffer any more than she already had. She would have had us all fooled if it hadn't been for the power cut. Fate begrudged her the dignity of death. The power company said the electricity was off for three hours. She would have woken up when the effect of the pills wore off, and realized her plan had failed. She had no choice but to climb out of the window."

"What made you realize the morgue had been broken out of rather than into?" Civilai handed Siri his flask of berry juice to help wash the bread down. Someone on the Thai side of the river was killing a pig.

"The louvers," Siri said. "None of them was broken. It's almost impossible to break in through a locked louver window without cracking one of the panes first. She must have stood on the gurney, dropped the louvers into the garden, and climbed down after them."

"Ah, the wisdom of a man who has perfected the art of break and entry. What do you think turned her from suicide victim to murderess?"

"Who can say? The frustration? All those years of built up hatred for a man who showed her no respect? I wouldn't be surprised if Bounmee hadn't even noticed she was missing. He just turned up from his late shift and ordered his breakfast as usual. I imagine by that time she felt she had nothing to lose."

"Why didn't you recognize her the first time you went to the house?"

"I'd never actually got a good look at her face. No need for a light bulb in the freezer. I just saw her feet sticking out and left her in there."

❦

With the stodgy lunch inside them, the two men found themselves shoeless and paddling in the cooling water of the slow moving Mekhong.

"You know, Little Brother," Civilai said. "I think this may have been the first case you've managed to solve without the aid of your spooky friends."

"Well, tell the truth, I did get a little help. But I didn't really understand it until it was all over. Dtui pointed it out to me."

"You should give that girl a raise."

"I'm surprised at you, Comrade. Didn't they teach you in Hanoi that money is not a motivating factor in a socialist state?"

"I must have missed that class. Meanwhile…?"

"She reminded me of that old Lao saying about married couples being the front and back legs of an elephant. Naturally, the woman is always supposed to be the hind quarters."

"Naturally."

"It seems Mrs. Lightswitch got tired of wagging her tail. There's a moral there, Old Brother."

"Enlighten me.'

"If you don't want to end up face down in a bowl of rice porridge with a knife sticking out of your back – you be nice to your wife."

Afterword

I'm sure most writers find that when they do research for a book, they come across a lot of stuff that's fascinating but that just doesn't fit in the story no matter how hard they squeeze. Every time I go to Laos I come back with a sackful of facts and anecdotes that I can't put in anywhere. that's why having this opportunity for a Dr. Siri short was so nice. It's like a repository for fun bits that didn't work in the books. "Mrs. Lightswitch" is a direct translation of the name Sawitfyfah *belonging to a hill tribe's man I met in Xiang Khouang. The history of surnames is true. I also met a Mrs. Waterpipe and a family called "Pudding." –C.C.*

OLD GUN

KEN BRUEN

Ken Bruen (born 1951) has been a finalist for the Edgar, Barry and Macavity Awards, and a winner of Shamus Award for Best Novel of 2003 for The Guards, *the first of his Jack Taylor novels. Many people claim to have Ken Bruen stories, but here's something almost nobody knows: Ken has a degree in art.*

†

OLD GUN
by Ken Bruen

Man, I'm old, tired too.

The fuck did that happen?

Like, I was going along, minding me old biz, and wallop, I look in the mirror, always a bad idea and there's this old guy peering back.

I reeled back, horrified, he had that white stubble and the rheumy eyes, looked like he'd been dead for 2 days… and didn't smell a whole lot better

Jaysus, a time, when I was with *The Cause*, running on the Falls Road, dodging the rubber bullets, I had me a full black beard, like Gerry Adams in his own prime, see Gerry now, the whiskers coming in grey n white

Salt n pepper, that's what they say when you're losing it, you're white mate, no other way of saying it.

Despite all the young hotheads, they reckoning I'm past it, they wanted this job done, they figured they'd wheel me out, one last gig

The guy who asked me, going

"With all due respect Mr. Farrell, you're the only one who could pull this off."

Bollix

The little pup, like I didn't know it was a no return event, the shooter was going down and why use one of the young flash Boyos? No, keep them on ice, use the sell by date codger

Yeah, legend, that's what they call me, I've been called worse, though not to me face.

On account of me temper, I don't deny it's got me into *situations*. That's a word I learned from the Brits, those bastards, they will literally kill you with politeness, in the real sense of the word, heard one of their Eton fucks say, as he put a bullet in a young Provo

"Nothing personal old bean, purely business."

The second bullet tearing off the young kid's forehead and the Brit going

"Rather messy."

I got some time with that officer later, made a point of it, did the ol kneecap routine to get him focused and after I danced a few cigarettes along his mouth, and the voltage along his spine, I said

"Yah cunt, this is real personal."

He knew

And after I gut shot him, I dragged his polite arse out on to the Ormeau read, put a sign on him:

"Sorry seems to be the hardest word."

I always liked me pop tunes

Gut sucker, takes maybe four hours to die and not nice, no, not nice at all. They tell me he whined for what seemed like days......and you know what, he lost all his manners, calling people names

Don't train em like they used to

First soldier I ever took a hurly to, he spat in me face before I cut his throat, calling me a *Fenian bastard*.

I might not have liked him but Christ, I did respect him

I would have been seventy two if I made me next birthday, born January 3rd, I used to listen to Kris Kristofferson, *Jesus was a Capricorn*. The boyos, they're real big on Country and Western, it's all the fecking loss and keening, that and the weather, gets you good and bronach, that's an Irish word, means soul sick and gives you serious motivation to sink the Jameson.

I've been Stateside for going on four years now, I dunno do I miss home, I miss the crack. But with all the new prosperity, America is kinda like the way the oul sod has become, Starbucks, McDonald's, Gap, all the kids talking like apprentice Yanks

Why?

Suppose cos they can.

You don't really need to know the reasons I had to leave, but had to, take me word on that. I' m too old for any more prison time. They wanted to send me to Boston but I always felt that place had notions. I'm in south Philly, literally on a whim. One, I love saying the name and I'm old enough to indulge a whim and, two, I heard a song by Springsteen, the time when I was still doing the rifle specialties and it stuck in me head. From a movie or something. Anyway, it had that air of longing and sorrow that is right in there in me soul.

Got me a small place on South Street and it's Spartan, bare as beggary. What do I need.

Bottle of Jameson, some soda bread and finally got me a dog. Mutt I got from the pound, He's old too, they were going to put him down and he gave me that canine look, all pleading eyes, like he was saying... *I'm fucked, whatchagonnado*. I call him Armalite, but on the street, someone asks me his name, I say *lite*. I like him more than I expected, he's got his ways, and late in the evening, when I put on the whining music, the sad suicide stuff, he whines right along, I pour two fingers of Jameson and a toddy in his bowl and we sip, listen along to Waylon, Johnny Cash, Merle, I'd swear that old dog knows the sentiment.

The Highwaymen, like the best of the movement, they're nigh all dead. I have a song from home by The Furey Brothers, *When you were sweet sixteen.*

That's my song for Molly, liver cancer took her from me ten years ago and the light went out in me, still flickers, as long as the Brits are in the Six, it has to but it's dimming.

Jeez, she'd a mouth on her, I don't take shite from anyone, never have, never will but Molly, she'd lash me with her tongue and I'd be quiet as a nun. Even carrying a piece, an Irish woman gets on your arse, you shut the fuck up. And defend you? Christ, they might give you God's own bollicking at home but let any fooker say a word agin ye, Irish women will fight yer corner to their last breath.

She was barely sixteen when I met her, a dance hall in Lurgan, I'd just killed me first squaddie and I was in that zone between euphoria and vomit. The show bands were at their height, all blue blazers, trombones, black dyed hair, Brylcreem and were massacring...*Only The Lonely*.....

I'd washed the blood off my hands but felt the smell all over me, I'd downed five pints of the black, it felt like it was about to come up, O'Brien, me Unit leader, took out a flask, said

"Tis poteen, get a shot of that in you, stops yer hands shaking."

It did.

O'Brien was real old style, had been interred, worked over by The Para's and was as hard as granite, he'd taken me under his wing and after the soldier had been kicked into the shallow grave, O'Brien intoned

"Dia leat (God be with you)"

I was very young, very raw and had expected him to spit on the body, I asked

"Didn't you hate him?"

He was silent for a long moment then sighed, said

"He's not much more than your age, probably from some backstreet in Coventry, he no more knew why he was here than you fully understand yet, I hate what he stands for, he was just a poor bastard who should be following the football, getting a few pints and a wank on a Saturday night"

I'd slugged the poteen and it burned, but in a good way and emboldened, asked

"So you don't hate the British army."

He turned from the mound of clay, said

"More than you'll ever fooking know son."

I'd give the same speech me own self over the years, long after we buried O'Brien, well, what was left of him, a plastic explosive blew up in his face. What he taught me was that anger is a waste of time, but hate, funneled and focused, is the most powerful weapon on earth and best left to simmer.

The show band went into a ladies choice next, the grimmest torture known to an Irishman. I was looking for the exit when I heard

"Would you dance with me?"

Was she codding?

Her face, walloped me heart like penance and was a crown of thorns in me soul. Like all Irishmen of me era, I had two left feet, couldn't move to save me life but she took me hand, by now, covered in sweat and led me through a waltz. It finished, Thank Christ and she asked

"Would you like a mineral?"

They didn't, of course, serve booze in the ballrooms, you could have club Orange Or… Club lemon.

I couldn't believe she wanted to spend time with me, to let me buy her a soft drink, I said

"I cant believe you'd let me buy you a drink?"

Her eyes, green, I swear by all that's Holy, they were light green with a fleck of grey, those eyes danced in her head and she smiled, a small twist in her front teeth that made her all the more appealing and she said

"Well, you're no oil painting but you have something."

Like I said… Irish women…

And that's how it began, I was never sure, over the next thirty years why exactly she'd chosen me but maybe, just maybe, God in his whatever, decides

"Give the bollix a break."

And I took it, with both grateful hands

When they said she had liver cancer and would linger on, in desperate pain, for months, I felt all the lights go out. I'd sit by her bed and the morphine only helped a bit, she'd look at me, those green eyes, now darkened by fear and agony, would plead with me, I asked

"Alanna, what can I do?"

She took my calloused hand, kissed the fingers, said

"Matt, mo croi (my heart), make it stop."

As she finally got some sleep, I took the pillow and made it stop, tears falling like Galway rain on the white bleached case, sobs raking my damned soul.

A time after, preparing to leave for America, sitting in a shebeen in West Belfast, a song on the radio, Marianne Faithful ….*Sister Morphine*….I downed two large Bushmills with Guinness chasers and felt a chip of stone slide into me heart. I never cried again, not so's you see. My unit commander gave me the new papers, said

"Philadelphia, odd choice."

I said……nothing

February in Philly is vicious but you know, I kind of like it, it's so freaking uncompromising, like a priests sermon at the beginning of Lent, Me and Lite, we wrap up real warm, take a walk by the Delaware River, the Irish Monument is there. It's too cold to sit but we stand in silent salute for a minute and I tell Lite about some Irish history, he pretends to be interested but like the new Irish youth, he's purely interested in his own self.

Yesterday, they sent a guy, I knew they would and it was just a matter of time. He came to my small apartment and his look said

"The fuck is this?"

The young, they don't do simplicity or if I mentioned Thomas *Merton's* cell, he'd think it was some rapper with his , what do they call them…*posse?* He was in his late twenties, wearing a very expensive leather jacket, vulgar in it's newness, I think, I hope I'm wrong but did it have epaulettes? He had gorgeous teeth, I know, he showed them, a lot. Put out his hand, said

"I'm Tiernan."

The hell kind of Irish name is that. What happened to Paddy and Mick? He was full of vim and piss, had a sweatshirt with Notre Dame on it. He gushed

"What a pleasure to meet you."

I let that piece of nonsense hover then asked

"Why?"

He was thrown but rallied, did the smile gig then

"You're a legend, I mean you…"

I cut him off, said

"Can I get you a drink?"

He sat carefully in the old leather armchair, his face saying

"This looks like it came from Goodwill."

It did

He said he could go a sparkling water.

Yeah

I went into the kitchen, poured a glass of tap water, put a spiddgen of washing up liquid in for the sparkle and poured me own self a Crested Ten. I handed him the glass, said

"I'm all out of lemons."

He took a tiny sip, made a grimace, said

"That hits the spot."

I sipped the Jameson, asked

"What's the job?"

He took the long route but the gist was, AF NI......Aid for Northern
Ireland, were cutting back on their activities due to the Peace Process
but a man named Beaton, one of their top executives, had been
indicted for tax fraud and in exchange for immunity, was giving the
real intent of the organization. Needless to say, this would cause havoc.
The kid said

"We need him to go away."

He took out a slip of paper, said

"This is his home, he's got some Federal Marshall babysitting him
and we need for Beaton to be ......am......quiet by this Friday, that's
the day he goes into court."

He reached into his jacket, laid a package on the battered coffee
table, said

"That's your persuader."

I considered the yarn and could see how it was. Me, an old
paramilitary, gets crazy, guns down the informer and gets rid of their
problem, and shows that the day of the rabid dogs like me, were drawing
to a close. Neeedless to say, I wouldn't be around to talk. The kid said

"Beaton has heard of you and is delighted to welcome one of the
old heroes into his home, he's expecting you for drinks on Thursday
evening."

He didn't ask me if I'd do it, the very fact he was there, was the
implied command. I asked

"And I'm to walk out of there.......how?"

He gave a practiced grin, said

"We have a car waiting for you, move you to Canada before they
know what's happened, a nice pension waiting for you in Montreal,
you'll like it there, some great Irish pubs."

I unwrapped the package, Nine Mill, loaded. The metal gleaming,
I asked

"And the Federal Marshall, he's going to let me walk?"

The kid smiled, ready for that, said

"He'll be .....neutralized."

The kid was to be my driver, said he'd wait outside and he'd pick
me up at 6.00 on Thursday, how would that be?

I gave him a smile of my own, not as bright but certainly as phony, asked

"And my old dog, will he like Montreal."

Armalite was snoozing in the corner and the kid gave him a
contemptuous glance, said

"We'll take care of the mutt."

That was the plan, the kid stood up, and I asked

"You know the names of the signatories of the 1916 proclamation?"

He was flustered, tried
"Am......sure, I, ...well, off hand, I cant name them all but ..."
I said
"Name two?"
He couldn't
I said
"See you Thurs."
The next few days, I put my affairs in order, didn't take long.

Five, Thurs evening, before the kid was due, I put on my combat
jacket, the one I'd had all the years, the only item, apart from Molly's
rosary beads and her cameo that I'd brought from home, I took off my
Claddagh wedding band, left it on the table, put *The Men Behind The
Wire* on very loud and called Lite over, patted his grizzled head and put
a round behind his left ear. I laid him on the couch, he looked like he
was sleeping.

I was waiting outside when the kid pulled up in a dark Buick, I
got in and he said
"The jacket, you look like Travis Bickle."
"Who?"
We got to the house, it looked expensive, every light on, the kid
was antsy, asked
"You know what to do?"
I nodded and shot him between the eyes.

I got out of the car, the engine still running and walked up to the
door, the nine down by my side, rang the bell, it had chimes, it sounded
like "Amazing Grace." A tall man opened the door, the Marshall, and
before he could react, I sucker punched him, then crashed the Nine on
the top of his skull. Walked in and turned left into what I figured was
the lounge and a corpulent man in a smoking jacket stood up, a snifter
of brandy in his hand , alarm on his face, demanded
"Who the hell are you."
I said
"The past."
Shot him twice. One in the back of the head, give it that
professional flourish, there was log fire going and it made me think of
the peat fires back home. Molly loved a real fire. I poured a brandy,
not what I'd normally choose but hey, I was on new territory, I sat in
the armchair before the fire, put the drink to my nostrils, it sure was
vintage. An Irish poet, I don't remember the name, had a title, "All the
old songs and nothing to lose"...came into my head.

I raised the Nine to my mouth, I knew how it would taste, bitter
and metallic, much like the new Ireland, I began to recite the names
of the signatories.

Afterword

The story was inspired by an old IRA activist who went on the scrap heap after the peace process. My favorite old timer movie is Charlie Varrick *with Walter Matthau. My grandfather told me that any day you can sit up and eat an egg, you're ahead of the game. —K.B.*

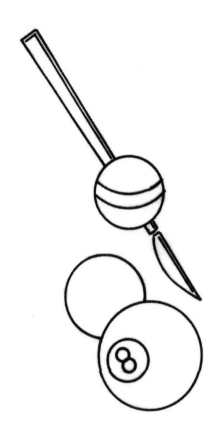

PART FIVE:

FELONS AND FRIENDS

ENCORE

MILTON T. BURTON

Milton Burton (born 1947) has taught, been a cattleman and served as a legislative aide for the Texas House of Representatives. His debut novel, The Rogues' Game, *was published by St. Martin's Minotaur in 2005, and his follow-up,* The Sweet and the Dead, *will appear later this year.*

ENCORE
by Milton T. Burton

When retired Texas Ranger Captain Bonaparte Foley called me at my aunt's house in Highland Park and asked me to fly to Houston with him, I didn't ask why; I asked when.

"As soon as we can get out to the airport," he replied. "It's just a little something I'm working on."

"Of course," I said, grinning. "You chased crooks for a living for sixty years, and you've been chasing them for fun ever since you retired. So what else could it be?"

He snorted in dismissal. Instead of answering my question he set the hook a little deeper. "You might get a story out of it when it's all over," he said.

Aside from going to the mailbox for interest checks, writing occasional true crime articles for national magazines is my only paying activity. I've been called a trust-fund hippie, though the trust fund part is all I'll admit to. A thirty-eight-year-old ex Marine with shortish hair and neat dress hardly qualifies as a hippie even by the broadest definition. But Foley knew I couldn't resist a story.

We met at the Southwest Airlines ticket counter at Love Field. At eighty-one the old man was still spry and tough, still carried a special Ranger commission, and still packed the same old .45 Colt automatic that had been his constant companion for more than sixty years. He still worked occasionally as a private investigator, but I didn't know if today's trip was part of a paying job or some personal tangent of his own.

We had a short wait before we boarded the Southwest flight to the coast. "It's the Carson case," he said as soon as our plane had lifted itself off the Love Field runway. "You remember me telling you about it, don't you?"

"I'll never forget," I said. "Who could?"

Indeed, who could forget the story of Jude Carson, a wealthy oil man who had disappeared into the bowels of the Big Thicket of East Texas in the gathering dusk of a cold fall evening back in November of 1930? And it was a compound tragedy; with him had been a twenty-five-year-old woman and her two little children—the daughter of one of Carson's old friends who was hitching a ride with him back home to Beaumont. Four people, along with the five-thousand-pound Pierce

Arrow sedan in which they were traveling, vanished off the face of the earth without a trace. Ever.

"It was murder," Foley said. "I knew it then, and I know it now. And at this moment I'm closer to the truth than I ever have been."

He reached into his inner coat pocket and pulled out a the battered old notebook he'd had ever since I'd known him. "It was one of these three men," he said.

I glanced at the page and gasped. "I recognize two of these names," I said.

"You should. They're all wealthy men up at Fillmore. Pillars of the community."

"But what possible motive—?"

"Oil leases," he said, cutting me off. "The Daisy Bradford Number 3 well had just blown in up in Rusk County ushering in the Great East Texas Oil Field. And Carson was known to have several hundred acres leased right south of Kilgore in what became the heart of the strike. But a week before he was killed, he sold all his interests in the field to a holding company that was owned jointly by these three men."

"But—" I began.

"I know what you're going to say," he replied, shaking his head. "The sale was bogus. The signature on the mineral deed was forged, and somebody bribed a guy named Arthur Holt who worked in the county clerk's office to backdate the paperwork. Not long afterward this Holt fellow turned up driving a fine new Buick roadster. On a fifty dollar a month salary, mind you. Then two months later he was killed. The murder was never solved. There were a lot of unsolved killings up there in those days. Hell, it was a boomtown deal with thousands of people pouring in from all over the country, and half of them thieves and hustlers of every kind you can imagine. The governor finally had to declare martial law to keep order."

"So Carson's leases must have been worth—"

"Several hundred million dollars, eventually. But back to Carson. He was last seen at a little country store right on the edge of Saratoga."

"I remember," I said.

"Well, what I didn't tell you is that the kid working there had been a guy named Luther Nolan—"

"Damn," I exclaimed. "And Nolan and his wife were found murdered in their beds last week."

"Right. Both with a couple of .22 magnum bullets in the head."

"Professional killers?" I asked.

He nodded. "Almost certainly. But at any rate I spent two days at Saratoga and finally ran down Nolan's best friend, an old man named Crosby. He told me that Nolan had known who the killer was."

"But how did he know?"

"The man had been with Carson when they stopped to gas up the car. And he came back the next day to tell Nolan he better keep his mouth shut."

"But why wait six decades to kill him?" I asked.

The old man sighed. "Who knows? According to Crosby, this guy had been by several more times over the years. He thought the bastard enjoyed baiting Nolan. Now maybe he's had enough of his game and decided to tie up his last loose end. But Crosby once saw him too."

"Really?"

He nodded. "He came by a big school construction project near Livingston where Nolan and Crosby were both working."

"Did he give you a description?"

He shook his head. "Jut that he was a tall man, and that fits all three of the jackasses on this list. But there was another guy there that same day who recognized him too, a commercial electrician. Old Crosby didn't remember this electrician's name, but he'd kept his business card. It took him three days of rooting around in drawers and what-not to find it, but he called me last night."

He flipped his notebook to another page and showed it to me.. It read, "Antonio Bagnianni."

"But how did this electrician fellow come to know the killer?" I asked.

"According to Bagnianni the same guy had killed his cousin not too many years before."

§

An hour later we drove away from the Avis Agency at Houston's Hobby Airport in a big Ford Crown Victoria, the model with the high-horsepower overhead-cam V-8 and fuel injection. The thing ran like silk and I pushed hard down the Gulf Freeway through the thin, midmorning traffic. In a little over an hour we passed the Galveston City limits, crossed the channel on the Interstate 45 causeway, and found ourselves in the town one famous evangelist once called the cesspool of Texas.

I don't think his estimation was accurate since my own vote for that honor would go to the state capitol, but there was once a time-and it's a time not too many years past-when Galveston was an exotic, sin-filled place. I would love to be able to go back to the early 1940s and spend a week in the Hotel Galvez during WW II. In those days, Houston, swelled with much of the war-born wealth of the nation, was the country's second busiest port, and Galveston was the playground of the South. Oil men, shipping magnates, industrialists, admirals, foreign sailors, spies, whores, card sharks, thieves and hustlers of every stripe—all flush with cash and eager for thrills—gambled and capered in the Maceo brothers' clubs, and danced to the music of such famous artists as Guy Lombardo and Tommy Dorsey. Burns and Allen were booked at the Hollywood Lounge every fall and Harry James was a regular at the Balinese Room. Each night sleek Packards and Cords and Lincolns whisked regally along the city's streets, stopping to disgorge their richly-dressed passengers at the casinos and nightclubs that lined Seawall Boulevard. Couples stopped to linger under moon-drenched palms, while lines of vessels from half the nations of the earth stretched to the horizon, riding the swells, each awaiting its entry to the Ship Channel.

All a part of the past. The slot machines and roulette wheels are long gone now, and Post Office Street is staid and respectable, its whorehouses either torn down or transformed into antique shops and boutiques. The old Balinese Room—once the most opulent nightclub/casino in the South—still sits on its pier out over the Gulf, deserted and forlorn, a weathered, time-eaten hulk at the end of its famous catwalk. Now the city does the best it can with museums and restored sailing ships and festivals like the annual December *Dickens on The Strand* blowout. Many of the antebellum homes are open to paying visitors in the spring and summer, the fishing is still good most years, and the hotels show a fair profit. The town draws its share of tourists, but like Natchez and Savannah and a hundred other places one could name, each with a rich past and a dim future, it can only try to capitalize on stories of its wicked history while time passes it by. And ever-realized but never spoken are two haunting facts: people who come to tour old homes and watch Dickens festivals don't have the kind of free-wheeling, free-spending exuberance that marked the city's visitors in decades gone by, and when they go, they don't leave behind them the kind of money once left by those who once came to frolic in the gambling dens and the whorehouses. I'd loved Galveston since childhood, but I'd never wanted to live there. The place always made me sad.

We took 61st Street through town, and as soon as we were on the Gulf side of the narrow island, I turned southward on Seawall Blvd. The weather was as miserable on the Coast as it had been back in Dallas. The drizzle had stopped, but the sun showed no signs of breaking through the heavy overcast, and the weatherman promised more rain and cold weather for the rest of the week. The morning's news said a tropical storm was brewing south of Cuba. The tide was out, but a good hard surf was up with the Gulf's gray waters rolling onto the beach in two-foot breakers.

We had no trouble finding Antonio Bagnianni's home. His wife told us he was surf fishing on the beach and gave us a pair of canvas folding chairs to take with us.

The object of our quest sat in an aluminum and nylon-web chaise with his back to us, a long spinning rod in a holder at his feet. A large cooler rested beside his chair, and as we drew closer I could see that he was reading the Houston newspaper. We walked around in front of the man and unfolded our chairs. Once we had them stable in the soft sand, we sat down and nodded hello. The man regarded us thoughtfully for a moment, then returned out nods. "Who the hell are you?" he asked.

"Bonaparte Foley," my friend replied. "And you're Antonio Bagnianni, aren't you?"

Bagnianni nodded. Even sitting he was an imposing man. In many ways he reminded me of an Italian version of Foley. He was taller and slimmer, with longer arms and legs and less muscle, but he had the same Roman nose and eagle-like brow above strong, forceful eyes, which in his case were dark brown rather than Foley's pale blue. His hair was thick and wavy and almost completely silver. He wore canvas-topped boat shoes, a denim coverall and a thick cotton sweater. A yellow slicker lay folded beside the cooler.

"Catching any?" Foley asked.

Bagnianni reached down and flipped open the cooler. A sand shark at least two feet long rested on ice beside a dozen or so bottles of beer.

"Not bad," Foleys said with a nod. "But I need to talk to you about something more important than fishing."

"So talk."

"Do you happen to remember a man named Luther Nolan?" Foley asked. "You worked with him on a construction job years ago up around Livingston."

Bagnianni nodded. "I thought that name sounded familiar when I read it in the paper. He was the guy who was killed up at Saratoga a few days ago, wasn't he?"

Foley nodded. "Have you ever heard of a fellow named Jude Carson?"

"No, I don't think so. Why?"

"He's the reason I came down here to see you. In 1930—in November of 1930 to be exact—he vanished. I was a young Ranger back then, and I investigated his disappearance. Carson was an oil man and he had some leases in the East Texas field which had just been discovered a month earlier. I'm convinced that somebody murdered him and stole his leases. They were eventually worth hundreds of millions of dollars. Whoever did away with Carson also had to have killed a young woman and her two little kids who just happened to be riding with him that day."

"Kids?" Bagnianni asked.

"Yeah, two little children, a girl and a boy, four and five years old. I'm also sure the same man had Luther Nolan and his wife murdered. Nolan was the last person to see Carson before he vanished. He was just a kid himself back then, and scared to death because somebody had gotten to him before I did. That same man came back over the years to remind Nolan to keep his mouth shut, and once when he came to see him it was on a job. A school down at Livingston. The same job, in fact, that you worked on with Nolan. And you recognized him. . ."

Bagnianni grimaced and nodded. "I knew the bastard, alright."

"Luther Nolan's friend told us that you threw down your tools and left the room when that man entered. He also told us that you later said this fellow had killed your cousin. You left because you wouldn't stay in the same room with him I need to know who he was. Do you object to talking to us?"

"Nolan's friend had it wrong. It wasn't my cousin who was murdered. It was my brother. My older brother."

"I'm sorry," Foley said. "I truly am. You have my sympathy and understanding. But it seems to me that's all the more reason to help us, my friend."

Bagnianni peered speculatively at Foley for a moment. "You're an old man," he said. "Hell, we're both old men. I've heard of Bonaparte Foley, though. In the old days I read about you in the papers. I remember that string of sex killings you stopped right here in Galveston back during the War. You used to be mean as hell."

"My disposition hasn't improved a whole lot with age," Foley replied.

"I won't give you the man's name. I'll tell you that right now. But I don't mind talking about my brother. I'd like for you to know how he died. Then you'll be aware of what kind of monster you're dealing with."

Foley nodded. "Fine. We've got plenty of time."

"My brother's name was Michael," Bagnianni began. "He fought in the Pacific, too, harder action than I ever saw. When we were kids growing up here in Galveston, Mike was always the wild one. He cut school, he tried to hang around the casinos, he swiped whiskey and drank it, and he always had plenty of girls. I guess it was his easy way with women that did him in. After the war he was a rodeo cowboy for a couple of years. A bronc rider. We'd both loved horses when we were kids and we learned to ride at an uncle's place back on the mainland. Mike could ride anything, a natural horseman. Mike was pretty successful in rodeo for a while, but in 1949 he took a bad fall and broke his arm in half a dozen places, and the doctors never did get it put back together right. The bones had been sticking out everywhere, and when it finally healed, it was shorter than his other arm and almost completely useless for anything but dealing poker.

"Mike took to gambling, something he'd always been good at. From then on he made his living at the card table and gravitated up to Fillmore to get in the big games the oilmen played there at the Maybach Hotel. He stayed away from towns like Houston and Dallas because he said a gambler had too much competition there, but he claimed Fillmore was just the right size for his tastes. And he had a few sidelines too. He dealt some in cattle—probably stolen cattle—from time to time, and sometimes he ran a couple of women. I don't approve of the things he did, you understand, but he was my brother and I loved him. And he sure never did anything to deserve what finally happened to him. Can you understand that, Captain Foley? Loving a brother, yet hating the way he acted and what he did for a living?"

"Sure," Foley said with a shrug. "I've got a black sheep or two in my own family. Everybody does"

"Yeah, I guess that's right. At any rate, back in those days the sheriff up in Fillmore was a man named Rip Garner. He was really something of a political boss, as well. He's held the office for better than twenty years, and he was tight with the local power structure, the oilmen who ran the town. And he hated my brother. Mike had seduced a couple of young women. Girls really, eighteen or nineteen years old. They were legal age, but nice kids from good local families. Garner told Mike that if he ever did it to another young girl, he'd kill him. Mike wasn't worried. He called Garner a draft-dodging, chicken shit sonofabitch. He also told him that if he was so hot on killing people, he would have joined up during the war and fought the Japs or the Germans. And he was right on that count. Garner didn't have much personal courage, but he didn't mind doing things by proxy, especially when he had a powerful ally.

"Along about the same time, another man came on the scene who had his own reasons to want Mike dead. He was an oil operator up there in Fillmore, a very rich man who was one of the pillars of the community, a real big-shot. He had a twenty-five-year-old woman on his payroll who'd come to work for him as a secretary. And she was a knockout. People say that in no time at all she became this man's mistress. Like a lot of middle-aged men, he preferred young women and, he could afford to indulge his tastes. He lavished money and gifts on her, bought her a Cadillac convertible, set her up in a fancy apartment. This little arrangement worked out fine for about a year, then she met up with my brother. And in no time at all Mike he had the girl *and* the title to the car this rich fellow had given her."

Bagnianni fell silent and sat motionless and silent for a time, staring out across the gray waters of the Gulf, then he resumed his story. "One day this rich guy caught Mike in one of the private clubs there in Fillmore. He pulled a gun and threatened to shoot my brother. And you know what Mike did? He laughed at the guy. Laughed at one of the richest and most powerful men in Texas, who also happened to be pointing a pistol at his head. Balls. Whatever else anybody can say about Mike, they can't deny that he had balls. He told the fellow that he wasn't about to shoot him in front of witnesses. Or anywhere else. But he didn't take the threat seriously enough, because the man's grudge against my brother gave him a sort of community of interests with Sheriff Garner. Both of them wanted Mike out of the way, and that's just what they did. They got rid of him."

"How?" Foley asked.

"He was set up. One night Mike and one of his girls drove up at one of his friend's houses. At least the man claimed to be Mike's friend. He owed Mike a few hundred bucks and he called that day and said he was ready to pay up. My brother said he'd stop by for the money about nine that night. When he and the girl got to the guy's apartment they were in a hurry, so my brother sent her in to pick up the cash while he waited in the car. When she got back outside no more than five minutes later the car was sitting there, idling away, empty as could be. And my brother hasn't been seen since."

"I suppose you know what happened, though," Foley said.

"Sure I know what happened. Garner had a deputy on the force working as a dispatcher who had once been a cop in Dallas. He was a crooked cop, everybody said, and I imagine he was because he sure as hell didn't draw the line at getting involved in murder. And he knew the right people to call over in Dallas for the kind of job the sheriff and his millionaire buddy had in mind. They snatched Mike and took him out to the Fillmore airport. This oilman had a big twin-engine Lockheed Lodestar that would hold six or eight passengers. They forced my brother onto the plane and took off, headed southward. One of the attendants at the airport actually saw it happen. After the story of the disappearance hit the papers, he went to the sheriff and told him what he knew. Garner laughed and told the guy he better forget all about it."

"Where did they take him, Mr. Bagnianni?" I asked.

"Out there," he said bitterly, pointing toward the Gulf. "They took him out there somewhere about fifty miles off the coast and threw him out of the plane. Alive and conscious, kicking and screaming."

"Damn," Foley muttered.

"I wanted vengeance for my brother. Me a Sicilian? What else would any man want? I tried. The Maceos were friends of mine. I went to Papa Rose and demanded justice. He said the man was too big, too important, and he told me to go home and forget about it. I had other contacts that I tried to use. The son of an old friend of my father, a man my family had helped come to this country, was one of Angelo Scorpino's capos down in New Orleans. I went to him and demanded that the favor done his father be repaid. The guy was willing, but he had to get Scorpino's approval. They had me come down to New Orleans to talk to Scorpino himself. He told me the same thing; the guy was just too big to hit.

"I almost did it on my own. If it hadn't been for my wife and kids I would have. And almost certainly I would have gone to the electric chair. For years my brother's murder ate at me. In my mind I killed him time and again. I shot him, I hung him, I burned him alive and I threw him from a thousand airplanes. It almost ruined my marriage and my health, but time did its work and I made peace with the fact that my brother was dead and nothing was ever going to be done about it."

Foley shook his head. "That doesn't have to be true." He reached inside his jacket and pulled out his battered notebook and flipped it open. "Look at these names, Angelo. The man who killed your brother was one of these three men, wasn't he?"

Bagnianni shook his head. "No. I'm not looking at any names. And I'm not giving you any more information, either. I've said all I intend to say." He stared once more out across the Gulf while Foley and I sat quietly, unwilling to disturb him. After what seemed like five minutes he turned back toward us and nodded once again. When he spoke at last, his voice was soft and a little weary. "I'm sorry, Captain Foley. I can't do it. I just can't do it."

"Why not?" Foley asked. "You say you almost killed him years ago. Why not help me now? Just tell me the man's name and I can have the whole bunch in jail by tomorrow night."

The man looked at Foley tiredly for a few seconds, then sighed. "I may as well tell you. I got a phone call a few weeks ago warning me to forget about what happened that day down in Livingston."

"Was the call from the man himself?" Foley asked.

Bagnianni shook his head.

"You know," Foley said, "they may not have killed you because they were busy tying up other loose ends and just haven't had the time to deal with you yet. Which is all the more reason you should give me the name."

"But I told them I wouldn't talk. . ." He looked a Foley sadly. "I gave them my word."

"That doesn't mean a damn thing to these guys. You need to give me his name and we'll have him locked up."

He shook his head once again.

"Then you should leave Galveston for a while. Do you have any place you could go for a few days?" Foley asked.

"Leave?" Bagnianni asked, puzzled.

Foley nodded. "Hell yes! If you won't talk, you need to get out of town as soon as you can. Remember what happened to the Nolans."

"Well, I've got an old friend who lives down in the Valley. He's always after us to come visit. I guess I could go down there."

"Go visit him," Foley said. "As soon as possible. Today. And be damn careful about who you tell where you're going. Still, the safest move is for you to help me."

Angelo Bagnianni shook his head a final time. "I may pack up and leave for a few days, but I'm just too old and tired to get involved. I slept well enough last night, and I want to be able to sleep again tonight. Don't you ever feel old and worn out? After a lifetime of fooling with men like these, haven't you had enough? Don't you ever just want to sit in the sun and not be bothered?"

Foley looked at Bagnianni, his eyes both kind and sad.

"No," he said gently.

❦

And that was all. Two days later Bagnianni was found shot to death in his to fishing chair on the beach—a .22 Magnum bullet in the head—and Foley's last link to Jude Carson's killer was broken. Within a decade all three of Foley's suspects were dead of old age, and my old Ranger friend himself was pushing ninety. After that day in Galveston we never spoke of the case again; Foley never mentioned it, and I didn't broach the subject, knowing that there are situations where it's better to just let things lie where they fall. Yet there are times when I'm watching the evening news, and I hear some wet-behind-the-ears police information officer end a *Crimestoppers* segment with, "Remember, crime doesn't pay." Then I want to grab the smug young fool by the throat and bang his head against the wall about three times and make him listen while I tell him the story of Carson and his three ill-fated passengers. For the sad truth is that with a little luck and a lot of brass, crime can be made to pay and pay handsomely. It has done so countless times before, and it will doubtlessly do so again. I've often heard Foley say that there's very little justice to be had this side of the Jordan. Devout Presbyterian that he is, he believes strongly that the River has another side where all the wrongs of this world will be righted and redress will be made to the poor and unfortunate. Myself, I'm not so sure.

Afterword

One personal characteristic of mine that has been commented on—for good or for ill—is that most of my friends are friends of longstanding—forty to fifty years in some cases. —M.B.

CRANKED

BILL CRIDER

Bill Crider (born 1941) is the author of the Sheriff Dan Rhodes series, which began with the Anthony Award-winning Too Late to Die. *(The 13th Rhodes novel,* A Mammoth Murder, *was published in spring 2006.) He also runs the very popular "Bill Crider's Pop Culture Magazine," and has a fabled collection of Gold Medal paperbacks. He's probably even better read than Charles Ardai.*

CRANKED
by Bill Crider

After the meth lab exploded, Karla decided she'd walk to the truck stop.

It wasn't her fault that some moron had fired a shotgun and blown the place up. Karla had been lucky, having jumped out a window before the blast, but she'd been cut by flying glass, and the hair on the back of her head was a little bit singed.

She still looked pretty damned good, though, better than any of the skanks at the truck stop, that was for sure. She knew she wouldn't have any trouble getting a ride out of town, and she might be able to get away before anybody found out she was still alive.

She didn't think anybody else who'd been in the meth lab was alive. The place had gone up in flames just seconds after the explosion.

Karla felt a little bad about that, but none of it would've happened in the first place if that drug task-force Nazi hadn't sent her in there with a wire. Whatever had happened, she figured the whole thing was on him.

Not that he'd see it that way, the self-righteous bastard.

Karla didn't like walking in the heat and humidity. The mosquitoes sang around her ears, and her whole face felt greasy. She could still smell the cat piss odor of the meth lab, and she supposed the stink was in her clothes and hair. She didn't feel a personal feminine freshness, either.

But she had to stay off the road, so it would take her a while to get to the highway. She'd still look better than those truck-stop ho's, anyway.

She heard sirens in the distance and walked back farther into the trees. First came a sheriff's car, and before long a couple of fire trucks came tearing along the county road, dragging rooster-tails of dust along behind them. Karla didn't think the fire trucks would do much good, not the way the house had been burning. As if she cared.

§

Lloyd hadn't taken his meds for two days, and he was feeling damned sharp, considering. He was fully dressed under the covers, except for his shoes, which were stuck under the side of the bed. He thought he was looking good, and he'd look even better when he put his teeth in.

Lloyd knew that in his case *better* was a relative term, but at least with his teeth in he'd look a little less like Gabby Hayes.

His daughter, Lou, came into the room like she did every day when she got off work. She looked a little disappointed, as usual, that Lloyd hadn't kicked off yet.

She was a skinny blonde, but the color was out of some bottle. She'd had brown hair as a kid, but it had gone gray early, not like Lloyd's, which still had a lot of black in it even though he was seventy-six. Lou had her mother's disposition. That wasn't a recommendation.

"How're you today, Daddy?" she said, the same as every day.

Usually Lloyd could hardly answer because his mind was so fuzzed with the drugs. They gave them to everybody in The Home because they liked to have the inmates nice and quiet all the time. In a lucid moment Lloyd had just pretended to take the shit and spit it out later. After two days he was almost back to normal.

But in Lloyd's case, *normal*, like *good*, was a relative term. Lloyd had never liked to play by the rules, which was how he'd wound up in The Home. He'd stayed drunk for a week and a half after the doctor had told him what was wrong, and Lou had gotten him committed. He'd been a handful at home, he knew that, so he didn't blame her much. By the time he was halfway sobered up, they'd got him full of the meds and he was trapped.

He knew he hadn't led a godly life, and maybe this was his punishment for all the things he'd done before he got sent to the pen that time. He'd put that behind him after his release, but things had a way of catching up with a man.

He'd been a healthy, strong guy for most of his life, and once in the pen he'd jerked an ax handle away from a building tender who'd knocked his teeth out with it. Lloyd had cold-cocked the building tender with the ax handle and spent two weeks in the cooler, but it had been worth it. His false teeth always reminded him of that building tender, the bastard.

"Daddy?" Lou said.

Lloyd came back from wherever he'd been and looked at his daughter with what he figured was the right amount of confusion and distrust.

"Sure could use a Co' Cola," he said.

Lou looked at him sternly, the bitch. She hadn't sprung for so much as a single Co' Cola since he'd been in The Home, nor even a candy bar. Made him spend his own money, of which there was damn little left.

"Some change in the drawer," he said.

Lou sighed. She walked over to the cheap nightstand by the bed and pulled open the drawer. Three quarters lay in bottom. She glanced down at them and then at Lloyd, who gave her a pathetic, pleading look.

"Oh, all right," she said.

She took the quarters from the drawer and left the room to go to the soft drink machine, which was in the big rec room, quite a distance from Lloyd's own room.

As soon as she cleared the door, Lloyd sat up, turned around, and put on the old black walking shoes he'd bought at Wal-Mart. He liked them because of the Velcro straps.

He stood up and looked over at the other bed where a dried-up fella named Jones lay on his back with his eyes and mouth wide open. He was just about mummified. In the month and a half he'd been in The Home, Lloyd had never heard Jones say a word.

"I'm bustin' outta this joint," Lloyd told Jones.

Jones didn't respond. Maybe he really was a mummy. Lloyd didn't waste any more time on him. As he'd hoped, Lou had left her purse on the room's only chair.

Lloyd took her billfold out and helped himself to the money inside, only twenty-one dollars. It would have to do, and he figured she owed it to him.

He also helped himself to her car keys. Then he put the purse back down and went out into the hallway. He looked both ways. Nobody in sight. There was an exit door at the end of the hall to his left, and he didn't think it was alarmed. What with the drugs, nobody ever tried to leave, so there was no need to go to the trouble and expense of wiring the doors.

Lloyd walked down the hall, his rubber soles squeaking on the linoleum floor. He hesitated for a second when he came to the door, then took hold of the bar and pushed. The door opened, and no alarm sounded, so Lloyd slipped out and let the door close silently behind him. He looked around the parking lot until he saw Lou's old Chevy Mailbu. A piece of crap, but it was all he had.

He took his teeth out of his pocket and stuck them in his mouth, moving them around until they felt right. When they did, he gave a porcelain grin. It felt good.

Whistling "San Antonio Rose," Lloyd headed for the Malibu, grinning again as he thought of the look on Lou's face when she got back to the room and found him gone.

The grin faded when he saw that the needle on the Chevy's gas gauge was sitting on the red E. Shit. He'd have to buy gas, and he didn't have but twenty-one dollars. He could remember when you could fill the tank for a hell of a lot less than five bucks, but not anymore. Well, he'd worry about that later. He wheeled out of the parking lot and headed for the truck stop.

❦

Royce Evans and Burl Isom were tooling along in Royce's rattletrap Dodge Ram pickup. They looked a lot like the two dumbasses in the Dodge ads on TV, but they didn't know it. They thought they looked like George Clooney and Brad Pitt in *Ocean's Twelve*, only taller.

It was the crystal that gave them that illusion, which is one reason they liked to amp up. They had plenty of other reasons, too, but that one was good enough.

Trouble was, staying amped cost money, and Royce and Burl didn't have any.

"Shit," Royce said as he drove the Dodge into and out of a chug hole, causing him and Burl to bounce their heads off the roof. Both of them laughed like monkeys.

"Where we gonna get us some money?" Burl said when the pickup had stopped rocking. It could have used new shocks, but fat chance that Royce would spend any money on something like that.

"Shit if I know," Royce said. "Can't get it from Karla. She's in jail."

Karla worked for a housecleaning service called the Kweens of Kleen. She'd let Royce into a couple of houses, and he'd pilfered a thing or two. Karla had taken the fall for him, which was how she'd wound up as in informant for the county's one-man drug task force.

"We ought do what Clooney would do, him and Brad Pitt," Royce said. "Knock over a casino or something."

"Closest one's Coushatta," Burl said. "We could be there in an hour, but them damn innians would tomahawk us if we tried it."

"Fuck the innians. We could take 'em. But we ain't got an hour to spare. Let's knock over the truck stop."

"How we gonna do that?"

"Check this out," Royce said.

He leaned over and opened the glove compartment. A Glock niner slid out and bounced off the floor of the truck.

"Holy shit," Burl said, picking it up. He looked it over and put it back in the glove compartment. "Where'd you get that thing at?"

"Stole it off a dead innian," Royce said, and he and Burl went off on another laughing jag.

After he managed to get control of himself, Burl said, "Goddamn, Royce, you kill me. You are one funny sonuvabitch."

He reached out and slugged Royce in the right arm, and Royce lost his grip on the steering wheel. The truck slewed from one side of the road to another, the headlight beams shining into the ditches and fields.

Royce fought the wheel, but he couldn't keep the truck out of the ditch. It went down the steep side, ripping through the tall weeds, tilting dangerously. Just before it hit the bottom, Royce clamped both hands on the wheel and wrenched hard to the left. For several seconds the truck cruised along the side of the ditch. Burl stuck his head out the window and howled like a ruptured wolf until Royce man-handled the truck back up on the road.

Royce looked over at Burl and said, "Wanna do it again?"

Burl laughed even harder than before. Finally he wiped the tears from his eyes and said again, "Goddamn, Royce, you kill me. You are one funny sonuvabitch."

ff

By the time she finally got to the Trucker's Heaven, Karla was frazzled, but that didn't keep her from being impressed, as she always was with the way the place looked. It was the liveliest place in the county, acres of concrete for the big trucks to park, lit up like Las Vegas. Twenty-four gas pumps for the four-wheelers in front, diesel in the back. Everything you could want in the big rambling building: restaurant where you could get a chicken-fried steak big as a pizza; a store that sold DVDs, CDs, candy, beer, jerky, you name it; showers; bedrooms where you could pick up a phone and order a massage of just about any body part; fast food burgers and rotisserie chicken; a sound system that pumped country music into the air twenty-four hours a day.

Karla thought the real heaven, in which she believed powerfully as only someone who never attends church can, must be a lot like that, but heaven probably didn't have quite as many truckers. That would be okay with Karla. Most of the ones she'd met in the past had been nice enough, but not all of them. You could never be sure. However, Karla had held onto her .22 pistol when the meth lab blew up, so she figured she'd be fine. She threaded her way through the cars and gas pumps and walked up to the big glass doors.

ff

Lloyd hated Trucker's Heaven. He hated the lights and noise, which reminded him of some cheap carnival midway. It made him long for the days when he'd pull up to one of the two pumps at the

Sinclair station and Harry and Larry, the Derryberry twins, would come striding out in their uniforms and gray caps with a green dinosaur on them and fill up his car; check the oil and water; air up the tires, and sweep out his old Ford with a whisk broom while Lloyd sat there in the front seat in comfort.

Now he'd have to get in line to buy gas that cost him as much as three or four good meals would have back in the day, and he'd have to pump it himself. If the tires needed air, he'd better have some quarters because the compressor wouldn't work without payment. And nobody was going to look under his hood, either.

It was okay, though. All he wanted to do was gas up and get out of there.

First, however, he'd have to pay. Nobody gassed up at Trucker's Heaven without sticking a credit card in the pump or paying inside first. Lloyd parked at the pump, got out, and went to pay. He figured he'd get twenty dollars' worth of gas and use the dollar that was left over for a candy bar. What he'd do for money after that, he didn't know. It might not even matter.

✠

Royce made a hard right turn off the feeder road onto the concrete lot at Trucker's Heaven with tires squealing. He sailed into a parking spot between a Hummer and an Escalade and threw on the brakes just in time to keep from running up over the curb and into the ice machine that sat on the walk.

Neither Royce nor Burl was wearing a seatbelt. Burl slammed into the dash, which he thought was funnier than anything else that had happened so far. Royce had been braced for the stop, so he didn't quite bang his head on the steering wheel.

"Hand me that pistol," he said.

Burl couldn't stop laughing, but he managed to open the glove compartment. The pistol slid out and fell to the floor.

"Shit," Royce said. "You can't do anything right."

He leaned over and picked up the Glock.

"Lemme use it," Burl said between giggles.

"You don't have enough sense," Royce said. "Let's go."

"What about masks? We can't let 'em see our faces."

"We'll pull up our t-shirts. Like this." Royce reached a hand into his outer shirt, a green, yellow, and red aloha job that he probably thought was invisible, and pulled his t-shirt up over his nose. "See?"

Burl got the giggles so bad that he slipped off the seat into the floor and doubled up under the dash.

"You're an asshole," Royce said. "Just for that, you can stay in the truck."

Burl nearly strangled himself as he tried to stop giggling and got back up on the seat. He pulled his t-shirt up over his nose, narrowed his eyes, looked from left to right, and said, "Let's go."

"Not while you look like that. We gotta be inconspicuous."

They unmasked, got out of the truck, and stepped up on the walk. Burl looked toward the door.

"Hey, Royce, that's Karla. I thought she was supposed to be in jail."

"Damn," Royce said. "And who's that old fart with her?"

Burl shrugged. "Never saw him before."

"Maybe he's her grandpa. Well, they just better not get in our way. Come on."

"Can I put my mask on?"

"Go ahead."

Burl pulled up his t-shirt and giggled all the way to the door.

❦

Lloyd thought the girl in front of him sure did have a nice shape, and she even said "thank you" when he opened the door for her. Showed she had a good upbringing.

He looked around before he went in and saw a couple of redneck idiots headed his way. One of them had his t-shirt pulled up over the lower half of his face, and the other one had something in the hand he was hiding behind his back. It sounded like one of them was giggling, but Lloyd couldn't be sure, what with the Cornell Hurd Band blasting over the speakers. Anyway, his hearing wasn't what it used to be.

Whoever they were, Lloyd wasn't going to hold the door for a couple of assholes like that. He started inside, but Royce sped up and jerked the door out of his hand.

"Get out of the way, you old fart," he said.

Lloyd didn't take that kind of shit from anybody. "Look here," he said.

"Shut the fuck up," Royce said, pulling his t-shirt up over his nose and sticking the gun in Lloyd's skinny belly. "And get the hell outta my way."

Lloyd doubled over, not because of the pistol barrel in the belly but because of what was already in there that the doctors said was going to kill him.

"Yeah," Burl said, shoving Lloyd on into the store and into a cardboard bin of bargain CDs. "Get the hell outta my way."

The bin collapsed, and Lloyd went to the floor amid a pile of plastic.

Karla looked around at the noise. "Royce? Is that you?"

"Hell, no."

Royce pointed the Glock at the man behind the high counter. "Gimme all your money."

Burl stood by, giggling.

"Burl?" Karla said. "What the hell do you two think you're doing?"

"Robbing the joint," Burl said between giggles. "How'd you know us with our masks on?"

A woman in the candy aisle overheard him and looked around. She started to scream when she saw Royce's pistol.

Royce turned and fired off a shot that went over the woman's head to shatter the glass door of one of the big refrigerators holding soft drinks, fruit juice, and water.

The man behind the counter grabbed the mic that he used to talk to the people pumping gas.

"We have a robbery in progress," he said. "Call 911. Call 911."

People all over the parking lot pulled out cell phones and started punching in the number.

"Shit-shit-shit," Royce said.

Karla thought he was wasting his breath, and so were those people making calls. All the cops in the county would still be out at the meth lab, sifting through the ashes. It would take them a while to get organized and get to the truck stop.

Three burly truckers intent on foiling the robbery started toward the front from the Hickory Holler restaurant in the back, one of them carrying a chair like it was a kid's toy.

Royce shot him. He fell against a popcorn machine, dropping the chair. The other two men ducked into the chips and peanuts aisle.

"Goddamn," Burl said.

"Royce," Karla said, "you're cranked out of your mind. Put down that gun."

Royce wasn't listening. He turned back to the cashier and put a bullet into a carton of Marlboros on the shelf behind him.

"Gimme the money. C'mon, c'mon."

The cashier said, "We put it all in the vault slots. All's I got is about fifteen bucks."

"C'mon, c'mon."

Lloyd finally got untangled from the CD bin and knocked the CDs off him. Trucker music. Red Sovine, Dave Dudley, C. W. McCall. Lloyd figured truckers were the only ones using CB radios anymore. He stood up and said, "Hey, asshole."

Burl looked at him over the rim of his t-shirt. "Which one of us you mean?"

"You'll do," Lloyd said and kicked him in the balls.

Burl's t-shirt slipped down to reveal his whole face, but that was the least of his concerns. He grabbed his crotch and fell to his knees, trying to get his breath, tears running down his face.

Royce grabbed the money the cashier put on the counter and turned to Burl.

"Get up, dumbass. We gotta get outta here."

"No, you don't," Lloyd said. "Lemme have that gun."

"Screw you," Royce said and pulled the trigger.

The bullet missed Lloyd and blew the cotton brains out of a teddy bear in a bin of stuffed animals

"Now look what you did," Lloyd said.

"You old bastard."

Royce was ready to pull the trigger again, but Karla said, "Don't you pull that trigger, Royce. I have a gun, and I'll shoot you in the knee if you do."

Lloyd had known the girl had a good upbringing. She was sticking up for her elders.

Royce looked at her and slammed the Glock into her wrist. She dropped the .22 and Burl picked it up as he struggled to his feet, his left hand still holding his crotch, tears running down his face.

"Shoot the old fart," Royce said, "and let's go."

He grabbed Karla's good arm and dragged her through the door.

Lloyd walked up to Burl, who was bent halfway over and trying to get his finger through the trigger guard of the .22. Lloyd took hold of the pistol and twisted it up and back. He heard Burl's finger snap. Burl fell to the floor, assumed the fetal position, and whimpered like a baby, his hands clutched together at his groin.

When Lloyd started past him, however, Burl stuck out a foot and tripped him. Lloyd staggered into the thick glass door and hit his forehead on it. He turned around and shot Burl in the ass cheek. Burl screamed like a panther.

"Jesus," the cashier said. "You're one mean old dude."

Lloyd gave him a blindingly white grin. "You ain't seen nothing yet, sonny."

f

Royce shoved Karla into the floorboard on the passenger side of the truck and started to back out of the parking space, but he couldn't see too well because of the Escalade on one side and the Hummer on the other.

Which is why he didn't notice the Camaro.

The driver of the Camaro didn't notice Royce, either, because he had his windows up, was talking on his cell phone, and listening to Gwen Stefani with his speakers cranked up loud enough to drown out the Cornell Hurd Band from Trucker's Heaven's speakers.

The rear of the truck hit the front of the Camaro, turning it halfway around. The driver, who had no idea what had happened, jammed his foot at the brake, missed, and hit the accelerator pedal. The Camaro shot forward and crashed into the grille of a Trans Am that its driver was filling with regular unleaded.

The Trans Am was shoved backward about ten feet, not a bad thing in itself. The bad thing was that the hose was still jammed in the filler hole and was torn from the pump. Regular unleaded sprayed all around.

An alarm sounded, Gwen Stefani said, "This is my shit," and the clerk inside Trucker's Heaven hit the automatic shut-off button, but it was already too late because the right front hubcap popped off the Camaro, spun a foot or two, and struck the concrete, sending up a couple of sparks.

And that was all it took to turn Trucker's Heaven into Trucker's Hell. Fire was all over the Camaro and the Trans Am. The guy who'd been at the pump had run out of the way, and the Camaro's driver jumped out and ran, too, as did everyone else who was at the pumps.

Karla tried to get out of the floor of the truck to see what was happening, but Royce hit her in the forehead with his fist and knocked her under the dash.

The pickup had stalled when it hit the Camaro. Royce ground on the starter but couldn't get it to catch.

"Fuck this," he said, when he looked back and saw the parking lot aflame.

He jumped out the door of the truck and ran around the Hummer, where Lloyd was waiting for him.

"Where's that lady you had with you," Lloyd said. He had to yell it to be heard over the screams, the country music, and Gwen Stefani.

The Trans Am blew up about then, so if Royce answered, Lloyd didn't hear him. Lloyd hadn't expected an answer, however. He had a feeling that Royce hadn't had a very good upbringing and didn't respect his elders.

Royce grabbed for the Glock he'd stuck in the waistband of his pants, intending to shoot Lloyd. He wasn't likely to miss, since they were standing only about two feet apart.

Lloyd had the .22, and he wouldn't mind depriving the world of one more piece of white trash. He'd have done it, too, if he'd known how many bullets he had left. He'd already wasted one on that asshole in the store, and he didn't want to waste another.

He was standing by the freezer that held bagged ice, so he reached out his left hand and flipped the door open, swinging it as hard as he could back into Royce, who had the pistol almost out of his waistband.

When the door hit his hand, Royce pulled the trigger. His scream could be heard even above Gwen Stefani, who was declaring yet again that she wasn't no hollaback girl.

Lloyd stepped over Royce, who was now lying on the none-too-clean sidewalk with blood on the front of his pants.

"Maybe you just shot the end of it off," he said.

Lloyd gave him a little kick for good measure and went to the truck. He looked in the driver's side door and saw Karla in the floor. Off to his right another car blew up with a *fwoomp* that shook the parking lot. Lloyd could feel the heat from the fire through his clothes.

"We better get outta here," Lloyd said. "What do you think?"

"Let's go," Karla said, wiggling out from under the dash.

Lloyd pulled himself up into the driver's seat. The engine turned over the first time he tried it, and he drove past the burning cars and pulled onto the service road. Looking in the rearview mirror, he saw his daughter's Chevy consumed by flames. He hoped she had good insurance.

"Whichaway you headed?" Lloyd said.

Karla fluffed her hair. She wished she'd had time to freshen up and use the toilet. Maybe she could do that a little farther on down the road.

"I was thinking of visiting my aunt up in Paragould, Arkansas. She might give me a job in her beauty parlor. Where you going?"

"Never been to Arkansas. What's it like there?"

Karla started to answer, but she closed her mouth when she looked up and saw the sheriff's cars, a couple of fire trucks, and a DPS car headed for them, flashers going, sirens yowling.

"Don't think they'll be interested in us," Lloyd said. "There's this big fire back there behind us, and they'll be going to that."

Karla looked back just as there was another explosion. A fireball rose in the sky, and she thought it was even brighter than when the meth lab went up. She wondered if Arkansas was far enough away, but she guessed it would do.

"Arkansas is all right," she said, turning to give Lloyd a good look. "You want to go? We could have us some fun."

"Damn, girl, I'm old enough to be your granddaddy. Considering the way I spent some of my time when I was younger, I might *be* your granddaddy."

"I don't think so. My mama's not from around here. She had me up in Paragould. You never been there, have you?"

"Nope."

"Okay. So how about it?"

Lloyd stopped at a red light. When it changed to green, he turned left, drove under the highway, and turned left again. When he was headed north on the highway, he said, "You sure you want me to go along?"

"Like I said, we could have us some fun if you did."

Lloyd thought about it. "I got to tell you two things before you decide for sure. For one thing, I ain't led a blameless life."

Karla nodded. "That makes two of us. What's the other thing?"

Lloyd didn't think he'd tell her about the stomach problem. Why worry her? He wondered how much fun a man his age could stand and how long somebody who was damn near dead would last with a woman like this one. By God, maybe he'd just find out.

"Well?" Karla said. "What's the other thing?"

Lloyd gave her a grin.

"These ain't my real teeth," he said.

Afterword

I wrote this story because of another one that I did for a blog project started by Dave White and Bryon Quertermous. That story was called "Raining Willie," and I liked the character of Karla so much that I kept wondering what happened to her after the crack house blew up. I figured the only way I'd ever find out was if I wrote something else about her, and "Cranked" was the result. Now I find that I'm still wondering about her, which means that sooner or later there's probably going to be another story. Since you mentioned it, I wanted to put in a favorite bit of wisdom from one of my grandmothers here. Unfortunately, they weren't much for pithy sayings, so I thought maybe I'd give you one from Pappy Maverick, who was nothing if not a bundle of pithy sayings. Here's one I think Karla would like: "Man is the only animal you can skin more than once." Maybe not words to live by, but they'll have to do. —B.C.

THE DEADSTERS

ROBERT WARD

Robert Ward (born 1945) is from Baltimore. He lives in Los Angeles and writes novels. His latest, Four Kinds of Rain, *is due out October 2006 from St. Martin's Minotaur, which is also reissuing his P.E.N. West Prize-winning novel* Red Baker *(1985) in paperback. He's currently working on a new novel,* Immunity.

f

THE DEADSTERS
by Robert Ward

After a relatively successful West Coast trip in which he'd robbed five retirement communities in Laguna, Long Beach, and The Inland Empire, Johnny Z. hit his old hometown, Baltimore, Maryland at five A.M. on a rainy Monday; by six A.M. he'd taken down an old croaker he knew, Dr. Mike Franko, on North Avenue for his free samples of Vicodin, five packs of Lunesta, and the big hit, three packages of Oxycontin. How he did it was artfully simple. Doctor Mike had a mail slot in the front door of his old row house, in which the postman dumped all the free samples from the various drug companies who craved the doc's biz. Using a little file he had in his pocket, Johnny did a quick pry and slash on the lock, opened the oak door and dumped all the samples into his backpack. Not a soul was alerted, and an hour later, Johnny was sailing on a Vike high that made him feel like Baltimore was the kindest place this side of Disneyworld. The dark, narrow trash-filled downtown streets, the crumbled red brick buildings all bespoke not of poverty, drug addiction, or the sublime indifference of the rich to the plight of the poor, but rather, character, earthiness, and dangerous pleasures. He was home, stoned, a happy man.

By seven o' clock industrious John had met up with an old woman named Luvleen Early, just off the bus from Fayetteville, West Virginia. Luvleen was looking for her lost brother, the guitar playing Chuckie, down in Fells Point. After buying the old country gal a couple of glasses of cheap red wine, and hearing her sad tale he offered to be her guide into the chaos of the Baltimore nightworld, and only minutes later he'd relieved her of three hundred dollars which he explained he needed to pay bribes to various "cats he knew" who could shed light on her missing bro. He agreed to meet the hunched and arthritic old woman at his favorite bar, The Horse You Came In On, at nine o' clock, with news that would reconcile her with her kin.

But by eight thirty that evening John had already forgotten her name.

He loved old people. They were the easiest prey in this unfair world. Of course there was a downside too. You had to stand around with them, listen while their enfeebled minds dawdled over a decision, watched as their liver spotted hands pulled out the bills. And their smell...ahhhh. That moldy hey I'm fixing to die real soon odor. Oh no man, that he hated most of all. Couldn't the old buzzards use a little Old Spice or something?

But still, they were such easy pickings. In California, using some fake cards he'd boosted in Kansas, Johnny was easily able to get work in the various retirement homes with their Disneyesque names -Sunnyvale Arms, and New Morning and his favorite, Happy Vale…and within a few days he'd relieved half the residents of most of their life savings. There was one little hitch. One of the geriatric set, a guy named Barney, had gotten hip to him so he had to croak him with a scarf. But hey, the dude wasn't long for this world anyway. The way Johnny figured it, the guy would be all stroked out in a few weeks so wasn't he doing the old gentleman a favor? He thought so. Though the Long Beach Heat might not agree.

So now he was stoned and flush and it was time for a slightly different amusement:

Johnny stood in front of an old and revered establishment called Mort's Billiard Parlor and smiled to himself. Here was a chance for him to make some more walking-around money, this time by using his God- given skill at pool. (Why the place was called a "billiard parlor" he never knew since there wasn't a true billiard table in the joint). Despite the fact that he was a career criminal young John had been raised in the Holy Church, and practically the first Bible lesson he had learned was that it was a sin to waste one's talents. His own talents, unfortunately, involved chicanery, breaking and entering, and conning old timers out of all their worldly goods…not exactly what the Good Book had in mind, to be sure. But at least this one talent, pool playing was legit. He could sink any ball, make nearly any shot, was a master of English, and mase. You wanted right spin, he had it down. You wanted to draw the ball, no problem. You needed to shoot around a blocking ball, he could handle that with ease.

He wouldn't call himself a pro. Not yet, but he had noble thoughts of going that way, getting out of the hustler life, moving toward the dignity of tournament play. Possibly in a few years he would even make it to ESPN, and become something of a national treasure. The colorful con man who righted the ship and now stood as a beacon of honest sportsmanship to other misguided souls.

❦

The place was dark, except for the shaded lights which beamed down on the rich green felt of the tables. There were twenty tables, ten on each side of the long narrow room. Like any good joint the front tables were occupied by the best players. About half the other tables

353

were being used by college kids, guys with tattoos all over their arms, and baseball caps worn lameass backwards on their heads. At the rear of the hall, obscured by shadows there were even a few girls playing. Johnny shuddered at the thought.

He walked over to the wall rack and chose himself a cue, then leaned up against the knotty pine wall, and watched the old man playing at the first table. Jesus more old people…What with modern medicine practically everyone was living way too fucking long. The guy was kind of pathetic looking, he thought, skinny, but not in a healthy way. More like concentration camp thin. His hair, what there was of it, was snow white, and his eyes were sort of bleary, the right one seriously bloodshot.

He dressed in the costume of early poolhall-hipster, circa 1958, with a black velvet vest, a midnight blue shirt buttoned to the throat, a skinny alligator belt, black flared pants with pleats, and Cuban heeled shoes, probably made from a tropical lizard of some unknown origin.

He looked like a throwback, Johnny thought, a guy who'd just stepped out of a time machine.

Yet, when he shot none of that mattered. He was good, very good. His stroke was smooth, his eye dead on. He could make the cue ball jump, twist and turn. He knew about angles and he knew bank shots.

Johnny watched him take on a younger man in a game of eight ball and destroy the dude. He ran the numbers and then hit the eight in…and the game was over before it had begun. The other guy managed to sink one ball. When the game ended the kid laughed, and shook his head.

"Geez, Mister Millwood, you've still got it."

The old man rubbed his ribs, then cackled his reply:

"Nah," he said. "I ain't got nothing anymore. My stick used to be magic, but not no more. Too shaky. "

"Aww come on," the kid said. "You're just being modest. You're the best I ever seen."

"Yeah," Millwood said. "But you ain't seen much."

The kid laughed as he handed Millwood twenty bucks. The old man took it with a shaking hand.

Johnny watched him slip the money into his trouser pocket. He had trouble making the maneuver and pulled out a wad of bills about as thick as a brick.

Jesus, Johnny thought, the old guy was loaded. Opportunity was calling. Johnny rubbed his stick, and devised a little plan, The guy was good, sure, but not "legend good".

He'd seen it wherever he traveled. The local hero, who beats all the stiffs in the room. But once the guy gets up against a really hot player…like Johnny Boy himself…he'd crack from the pressure. These old guys always did.

"He's really something, isn't he?" a voice said.

Johnny turned and was surprised to find an older woman standing next to him. She had red-hennaed hair, and Lolita heart-shaped sunglasses. Her face had once obviously been something to look at. Great bones, blue eyes that looked right through you. But whatever sex appeal she'd had, hey, that was long ago and far away…her skin was now creased and lined like an old map. Her mouth curled down and she had put too much lipstick on her thin cracked lips. Her fake red hair hung in Lulu Brooks bangs which must have wowed the boys thirty years ago, but now her hair looked like the tangled strings in an old mop.

Her red sweater and black Capri pants looked ridiculously inappropriate for someone her age.

"You and him an item?" Johnny said to her.

"That's right," she said. "I'm Millie and he's Marty . We're the Millwoods."

Johnny had to repress a laugh. Mille and Marty Millwood. Jesus, even their names sounded like they came out of a '50s sitcom.

"So you want to play a game young man?" Marty Millwood said, his old face cracking in a smile.

Johnny turned and looked at him. The old man was eager. He stared at Millie. Lame Lolita was ready too.

Millwood was pulling that wad of money out of his pocket again.

And suddenly Johnny knew just where this was going, how he would control it all.

"Hey, "Johnny said. "How about we play for fifty to start?"

"Fifty sounds fine young man," Marty Millwood said, rubbing his chest.

Johnny nodded but inside he felt a leap of joy. That rubbing the chest bit, that was the "tell". A lot of old cons rubbed their chest or their noses when they were setting up their mark. The old hawk was sure Johnny was a pigeon, just like the first kid…so that's just what he would be.

The game began:

Millwood broke and sank a ball, but then missed an easy shot on the six-ball. Johnny, shooting stripes, knocked in two in a row, but purposely missed on the five.

Millwood had two easy shots, but managed to miss one of them. He cursed to himself and rubbed his stomach again.

Another "tell" Johnny thought. He was setting him up. Making the game close…Johnny bit his lower lip and gave a deep breath, as though he was having an anxiety attack. He knocked in another ball, but then scratched on the four.

Millwood licked his lips and looked across the table at Millie.

This was it, Johnny knew. The kill.

Millwood made a difficult shot in the side pocket, hit two more in and then made a two rail bank shot on the eight ball and the game was over.

Johnny handed over the money, as he shook his head.

"Good game," he said. "But I bet I can beat you. Mister. I just got a little sidetracked. Been on the road all night."

Millwood gave his wife a little smile and said:

"Would you care for another game?"

"Sure," Johnny said. "And this time I'm going to show you!"

He grit his teeth like a frustrated nerd. The older man laughed and nodded his head:

"Rack 'em up, kid," he said. He'd dropped the friendly old guy attitude now. There was more than a measure of contempt in his voice.

Johnny racked the balls, and made a little hissing nose like "Gee I'm frustrated." When he looked over at Millie, she was smiling at him, like a lizard about to stick a fly with her eight-foot tongue.

Johnny lost the second game, and then the third. He played a little worse each game as though the frustration was building inside of him to such an extent that he couldn't control his shots anymore.

He jiggled his feet a little and sighed heavily when he missed.

They played for a fourth time and he nearly tore the felt trying to deaden the cue ball.

He lost again…

And stared down at his shoes, like he was too ashamed to meet Millwood's bloodshot eyes.

"Well," Millwood said. "Seems you're having a run of bad luck son."

"Yeah," Johnny said. "That's right. Bad luck. I'm just tired. You gonna be around tomorrow old man?"

"Why yes, I am," Millwood said.

"Well, I want a chance to win my money back," Johnny said.

"Be happy to give it to you son," Millwood said.

"I'll be here," Johnny said. "Four o clock?"

"Sure, my boy," said Millwood. "Sounds fine."

It was then that Millie spoke up.

"Oh Rog," she said. "We can't tomorrow. We have an appointment at the doctor's."

She looked at Johnny and made a face:

"I have some very difficult digestive problems."

"Too bad," Johnny said. "So when do you come back?"

"Well, that's a tough one," Millwood said. "Cause I have to fly out to California on business the next day and I won't be back for a week."

"Well great," Johnny said. "It's not much of a player who takes two hundred and fifty bucks from a guy and won't give him a chance to win it back."

Millwood scratched his head and looked at his wife.

"The young man is right, Millie," he said.

"But Rog, I have to go to the doctor, and you know I hate to go alone…"

Johnny sighed deeply. As Marty smiled.

"Listen," he said. "A week's not that long. Give me your phone number and I'll call you as soon as I return. Then we can meet over at my place and play as late as you like."

"Your place?" Johnny said.

"Yes, why not? I have a table that's quite a bit better than this one, and the drinks will all be complimentary. We live just across the way on Federal Hill."

"No limits?" Johnny said.

"Fine," Marty Millwood said, chalking up his cue. "Like true sportsmen."

"You're really gonna call me?"

"Of course," Millwood said. "We'll make a grand night of it, son."

"Fine," Johnny said. "Have a good trip."

"I intend to," Millwood said. "And I'll make sure I practice while I'm out on the coast. I suggest you do the same."

Johnny smiled. The old man wasn't all that good but he was confident, that was for sure. He turned to go, but Millie called to him.

"Smile Johnny!"

What was this? Johnny turned around and a flash went off in his face.

"Gotcha," she said. "I'm doing a book of pool hall players," she said. "Gonna self-publish it on the Internet!"

"Whatever," Johnny said.

And walked out the door.

ƒ

During the next week, Johnny found himself worrying about Marty Millwood. What if he never called back? Was it possible he'd been hustled by him? The thought bothered him. Here he'd lost 250 bucks to the old dude, and maybe the guy wasn't going to call him at all. Maybe the son of a bitch didn't even live over on Federal Hill. He called information but found out only that Millwood's address and phone number were unlisted. The son of a bitch…Christ, it wasn't as if he hadn't been hustled before…that was part of "the life"…every once in a while you ran into a grifter smarter than yourself and you just had to live with it.

But to be hustled by an old guy…a guy who kind of reminded him of his father, Woody, the card shark, dope runner from Norfolk Virginia, the son of a bitch who had turned Johnny out into the "life" then hustled him out of his own money and disappeared ten years ago. That was all part of it.

Old people with their blue veiny faces, and their old nose hairs, and their weird smelling touch-o'-death skin. Old people with their intestinal problems, and their pathetic dye jobs and their fucking out of it clothes. Old people like old bread, old mould, old broken down bones, their organs rotting inside.

How he hated the sons of bitches.

Yes, yes, of course he knew it was nature's way, but that didn't mean he had to dig it. No, Johnny thought, just like he was beyond the law he'd be beyond nature too…Of course the irony was that to beat nature you had to die…but that was ok by him. He didn't want to be some old fart in a wheelchair, with tubes sticking out of his nose, ears and ass, while some condescending nurse gave him shit for not eating his fucking stewed prunes.

"You gotta be regular, Mr. Johnny, haha."

No, fuck that.

He'd rather take thirty pills of the big Vike and say sayonara motherfuckers. That was the way he'd go…the last big high, the Big Wave, and then oblivion. He'd end his life just as he'd lived it, by his own ramshackle rules, no whining, no begging, and fuck all the squares.

But meanwhile, what if he'd been fucked by that slick son of a bitch oldster, Marty Millwood?

It bugged him, drove him nuts…the old man and the old broad, conning him. If word got out in the hustling community? Oh man, he'd be a laughing stock.

§

By the fourth day he was so wound up that he started riding around Federal Hill in his stolen Porsche checking at the Hollins Market and all the local bars to see if the old man was hanging out. Cause if he had hustled him maybe there was no California trip…And if he saw either

Millwood on the street there was some serious arm breaking that was going down.

But he never saw even a glimpse of either Marty or Millie, and by the fifth day he had decided that if he'd been ripped off he'd know soon enough, and meanwhile, if the old man was going to come back he'd better get some practice in.

I mean it wasn't like it was going to be easy to beat him. The old guy was good…and there was no use going into the match unprepared.

So he hustled down to Mort's and played the local guys, beating all comers at eight ball, then wiping up two of the regulars in straight.

By the seventh day he felt cocky again. If the old guy had beat him and split town, then so be it, but if the guy called he was ready to kick his ancient ass.

Hey, ho, he was Johnny Boy, Johnny fucking G and he was ready baby.

Wasn't it true? Baby, you know it was.

ff

Johnny spent the sixth night ripping off his best friend Terry Zane for three hundred dollars for a bottle of fake Methedrine pills (caffeine pills he'd boosted from the Save-On) and now he was sleeping in. Well, he was trying to anyway. He hadn't really caught many Z's that night, wondering if he was going to get a call from the goddamned creeping Millwoods. He was ready, had actually gone out and ripped off a new stick from the Big Five, a beauty, a Scorpion cue worth three hundred and fifty five bucks.

He didn't have to wait long. At nine in the morning the phone rang. It was Millie Millwood herself, her voice a croaking kootchie koo, like she was trying to seduce Rudy fucking Vallee.

"Ho honeybun," she said. "How you doing?"

"Fine," Johnny said, trying to sound cool.

"Marty wants to know if you want to play a little pool with him tonight."

"I could get into that," Johnny said.

"Cool," Millie said, her voice squeaking like an injured penguin. "You come by our place around eight. We're at 620 Hollins. Oh, we've invited a few other people. I hope you won't mind."

"As long as they don't disturb us," Johnny said.

"No way. They're all old friends. They understand the game comes first. Bye."

Johnny hung up and shook his friends. He just bet they were old friends. As in fucking a-moldering-in-the-grave-old. Jesus, what a scene. How had he ever gotten into this whole little deal?

He shook his head, and fell back on his bed. When he shut his eyes he saw Marty Millwood hovering over him, his bloodshot eyes reflected in his triple thick lenses.

Johnny shook it off, and got up out of bed. He felt dead-tired, but he didn't want to sleep now.

Man, he didn't need any more Marty and Millie dreams. After he took the creeps tonight he wasn't going to ever see either of them again.

❦

Johnny couldn't believe it. In some of his dreams the Millwoods lived not in a house but in an old hotel...a hotel with no name.

Now, as he stood in front of the place he realized that this dream, submerged in his Viked out memory, had been prophetic. There was only one old hotel left in Federal Hill, The Calvert Hill Hotel. It stood along side of Federal Hill itself, kind of lopsided, leaning toward the harbor below. An old hotel, Johnny thought, ready for the wrecking ball, just like Marty and Millie themselves.

"A piece of cake," Johnny thought, gripping his Scorpion as he headed inside. He liked the sound of his own words, steady, cocky. Hey he was the guy, the man, the fucking hombre, no? Oh, yeah he was.

No doubt.

Still, as he passed through the dirty double doors to the lobby he felt a chill run down his spine.

❦

"Hello, John," Marty said, as he opened the door. "You look particularly well tonight."

"Thanks," Johnny said. "You're looking good yourself, Mart."

Actually, Johnny thought, Marty did look pretty well, considering he was ripe for a coffin. The old man had some color in his cheeks, and his eyes looked clear and focused.

The fact that he wore an absurd bo-ho striped ascot, circa 1925 Paris, of course, made him seem more than faintly ridiculous. And what was with the red velvet smoking jacket, like some character out of one of those S.S. Van Dyne novels Johnny's dead mother, Val, used to read, while covering her face in Noxzema and smoking camels in the Baltimore backyard heat?

From behind Marty came Millie, dressed in some vintage Victorian black lace number replete with red rose corsage. Christ, Johnny

360

thought, they were doing the Adams family. Where the fuck was Lurch or Cousin It?

The apartment itself was like something from the gilded age. The chairs all looked ancient, cane backed babies, and the walls seemed to be papered in some kind of crushed velvet. The décor was halfway between Edith Wharton and a bordello.

And the friends…there seemed to be a good sized crowd of them… were all ancient, really ancient Johnny thought as his hosts introduced them to the group.

"John, this is Diana Hare," Marty said. "She's been one of the great patrons of the city. Single handedly paid for the new wing of the Walter's Art Gallery."

"Pleased to meet you," Johnny said.

"As I am you," Mrs. Hare said, sticking out her hand in an awkward way. "I've heard so much about you."

That was when Johnny realized that she was blind. He reached toward her hand, and pressed it tightly. It felt soft, squishy to him, as though the bones inside were already turning into oatmeal.

"And over here," Milly said. "We'd like you to meet Don Dietz."

Johnny turned around to meet the next guest, but was shocked to find an amazingly over weight man with an oxygen mask strapped over his nose and mouth. He gave Johnny a thumbs-up, as Marty listed Mr. Dietz's many contributions to the city's architecture.

"Donald has built over forty of our city's finest buildings," Marty said. "Buildings which are on the historical register."

"Way to go, Don," Johnny said, backing away from the grotesque figure as fast as he could.

The rest of the guests were equally worn out, and each of them was some kind of high achiever.

There was Scott McKenna, a poet who had won the Pulitzer Prize, but who had lost both his legs to diabetes, and there was Sally Callahan, a once beautiful blonde singer who had had both breasts cut off due to recurrent malignancies and there was Billy Weaver, the psychologist, who was paralyzed on the right side of his face due to Lyme's Disease he'd picked up while vacationing on the Eastern Shore. And more, a woman named Daisy with a crushed hand, a man named Perry with what looked like a hole in the middle of his head, from some brain disease Johnny had never heard of…and a fairly youngish girl-only 72-named Susan who had a tumor sticking out of the side of her neck.

After the fourth or fifth terrifying introduction, Johnny felt light headed, and had a panicky desire to escape.

He gladly accepted a drink, straight vodka, from Millie, downed in one swift gulp, and held out his empty glass for a refill.

"Hey Marty," he said. "Are we ready to play?"

"Of course, John," Marty said.

"What will be the stakes?" Johnny said.

"That's up to you?" Marty said. "As my guest you should decide."

"All right, then," Johnny said. "How about two hundred a game? For starters."

"Fine," Marty said. "Two hundred it is. Follow me."

ǁ

The game room was all oak and brass, and the table was amazing, with a deep green felt that seemed like more like a summer lawn on a great estate.

Johnny could barely believe his luck. It was as though the table had been invented expressly for him.

All his fears of losing to the old crock vanished and he played the games of his life.

He won the first contest running six balls in a row, and by the second he knew he couldn't lose. Marty Millwood on the other hand played in a decrepit fashion. His confidence seemed to have disappeared, and he missed shot after shot.

Within five games of eight ball Johnny had won back all he had lost...and pressed on with his bets.

"Let's up it to five hundred," he said, after he'd gone five hundred and fifty up.

"That's steep John," Marty said.

"I can handle it, Johnny said, accepting another drink.

He downed his fourth straight Chopin and felt it kick in with the Vicodin he'd just swallowed. A fine mixture, he though. It was as though his insides were running like his Porsche.. all the gears meshing, the engine just cruising along. There was a road in front of him, twists and turns but he couldn't run off of it if he tried. He was in the groove. Oh yes, and wasn't he the man?

"I bet you can handle just about anything, John," Marty said.

"Yeah," Johnny said. "As a matter of fact, I can."

"I bet you can handle women," Marty said.

"Oh yeah, I can handle women," Johnny said. "See the thing is about women, they only got power over you if you want them, which I don't."

"Not ever?" Marty said.

"Nah," Johnny said. "I want sex sure, but a woman, nah...I need sex I pay some chick and walk away free."

"I see," Marty said. "And what of family? Don't you ever want a family, John?"

"No way," Johnny said. "I did that number as a kid. That was all I needed to see. Don't give me any kids, baby…oh no."

"What of old age, John?" Marty said. "Don't you worry about getting old alone? And believe me Johnny, you will get old someday."

Johnny laughed, chalking up his cue.

"No," he said. "I got that covered too. No offense, Mart, but before I'd get like those guests of yours in there I'd rather check out."

Marty looked at him in a serious way.

"You say that now, John. I said it myself when I was your age. But when the black angel comes stalking you son, you'll beg and plead with the Lord for one more minute of life, no matter how debilitated you are.'

"No I won't Martman," Johnny said. "I've seen enough of this life to know it ain't worth begging for."

"Really?" Marty said.

"Really," Johnny said. "Now can we lose the inquisition and just play pool?"

"By all means John," Marty said. "I meant no offense."

"None taken," John said. "Now wrack 'em up, will you?"

They played five more games and though Marty had a good run in the first one Johnny was red hot. There was no beating him. He made banks, impossible combinations, and he had total control of the cue ball. Every "lie" he got was better than the last, and most of his shots then were easy ones.

By the end of five games he had won over a thousand bucks of Marty's money.

"Want to go a few more at a grand apiece?" Johnny said, knocking back another cold Chopin.

He felt a wild abandon inside himself, like…like he was a God. Oh yes, the God of Pool, for sure, but in this crowd of soon-to-be-Deadsters the God of so much more. That was another thing about hanging with old people. You were the man…there was no one among them who could hurt him. Out there in the real world among his contemporaries he might be considered a punk or a loser…and if he gave anybody any shit about it, well, he wasn't the biggest or toughest guy in the world. But among the Deadsters….he was king. He could let them live or let them die. He could walk in the other room right now and just cut through them all, breaking their old bones, smashing their wrinkled heads like melons and what the fuck could any of them do about it? Nada.

What could Martman do about it, Johnny thought, as the old man walked to a picture of himself and Millie at the track about a million years ago when they were young.

He watched with a sneering sense of superiority as Marty moved the old photo and revealed a wall safe.

He saw him turn the dial a couple of twists and open the safe.

He moved up behind Marty, and looked over his shoulder, inside.

Jesus Christ, he had never seen anything like it. Money...piles of money...why the thousand bucks that he'd just won was nothing compared to the stacks of dough in the safe.

Johnny felt a crazy itch under his arms, and a wild jump in his stomach.

All that money wasted on this old fart who couldn't really enjoy it. What the hell would he buy with it, gold plated crutches?

Marty took a stack of bills, a small stack, and turned toward his guest.

"Here you are son," Marty said. "One thousand dollars."

"Fuck that," Johnny said. He grabbed Marty by the lapels and pushed the old man up against the wall.

"I want all the money. Every cent in the safe."

"John," Marty said. "This isn't the way son."

"It's my way," Johnny said. "Here's the deal. I'm taking the money and if you call the cops I'm going to come back and kill both you and Millster. You get it, Martman?"

Johnny had used his toughest voice. Low, growling. It was a performance really. Used to scare the living shit out of the old crock. It had always worked well in the old age homes out on the coast. Old people couldn't think too well, anyway. Their fucking neurons were all twisted up inside. And, of course, they were scared of...well, of practically everything. The horrors of war, a recurrence of terrorism, the upsurge in crime, hurricanes, tornados, earthquakes, global warming, cancer, heart attacks, dogs, cats, snakes, spiders and worms, you name it the elderly (what a word) were freaked by it. So grabbing a guy and jamming him up against the walls... well, that was the living embodiment of all their fears. They were helpless and they knew they were. A guy like Marty Millwood, he had no shot against a psycho like Johnny Z.

So how come he wasn't shaking in fear, wetting himself, crapping in his pants?

Instead he simply looked down at Johnny with clear blue eyes and then did something that sent a chill through Johnny's tattered soul.

Marty smiled.

He smiled in a cruel and unforgiving way, like it was him who had control here. Johnny tightened his grip on his lapel, and slammed the old man up against the wall again.

"You find something funny?" he said.

"Not exactly," Marty said. "Not funny-funny, if you know what I mean. More like ironic funny, son.'

"Yeah, well fuck your irony," Johnny said. "You turn around and grab all that money and you pull it out of there. Then you take off your fucking smoking jacket and wrap the cash inside it. Then you lead me outta here. We say goodbye at the door, and you go back and finish your night with the lame, the halt and the blind. You got it?"

"Yes, most emphatically," Millwood said.

"So do it. And remember one slip up and I'll come back and kill you and Millie. And don't think you can get a cop to hunt me down before I get you, Marty. Cause even if that happened I got plenty of friends who will come back and finish the job for me."

"All right my boy," Marty said. "I'm in no position to argue with you."

Johnny let him go and Millwood took off his smoking jacket, then turned back to the safe.

Johnny stood behind him…watching the old man fill the jacket with packet after packet of money.

Oh this was beautiful Johnny thought. He could split town and spend the summer in Miami. Be a high roller at the casinos. Maybe run this dough up into an even higher plateau.

Oh yeah, this was his finest shining moment. The big score.

Then Millwood turned and sprayed something in his face. It burned his eyes, and scorched his nose.

Mace!

The son of a bitch.

He staggered forward but Millwood, amazingly wasn't there.

"You motherfucker," he said, groping blindly forward.

Then he felt a terrible blow to his groin, and he fell to the floor on his knees.

"You bastard!" he screamed, holding his painful testicles.

"Good night John," Millwood said. Johnny looked up through the fog of pain and saw not Marty but Millie and her guests streaming into the room. He started to get up but she picked up a cue ball and smashed him in the temples once, twice.

"And one more for good luck," Millwood said.

"But not too hard," said one of the guests in the background. "We don't want to injure the property."

"Right, of course, "Millwood said. "Not too hard. But not too soft either. The rule is always the same, has been since Aristotle. Moderation in all things."

He then crashed the pool ball into Johnny's head.

Johnny saw some flashing lights, and heard the crowd ohh and ahhh. Then his little world went dark.

❦

Millwood and Millie brought in the gurney which was waiting in the large back room of their old apartment. The gently picked Johnny up, and laid him out. Then they , with their happy guests following closely at their heels, rolled him down the long old hallway, and, after Millie had unlocked it, into the Freezer Room, which the retired surgeon Marty Millwood had set up five years ago.

As he'd tried to explain to Johnny, Millwood's friends had been the crème de crème of Baltimore society. They had contributed the most to the city, given it their all…and it seemed to him a terrible thing that they now had to go and die while people like Johnny Z raped and pillaged and ruled the roost.

The problem was very simple. Old age, disease, dementia, death. In the end no one could beat the reaper. But you could certainly slow him down.

Which is why they'd started trolling the city at night. They searched in the pool rooms, in the houses of prostitution, in the lowest of low bars.

What the needed were candidates. People of low repute with healthy organs.

But there could be no mistake. The ones they chose had to have forfeited all of their potential. They had to be the worst of the worst. Like a guy who raped children for example, their first candidate five years ago.

Or a boy who had killed his parents while they slept because he wanted to take their money for drugs. Their candidate of last year.

Or a guy who made his living on beating up old people. A certain guy who hung out in a certain pool hall whenever he came back into town.

A certain guy who was a known killer but whom no one could ever pin anything on.

A certain guy named Johnny Z. The kind of guy you could take his picture and e-mail it to certain senior security groups like Sigma on the West Coast and they could tell you if he was the man that had robbed and beaten old people in Laguna, in Long Beach and the inland Empire. Not that they would ever testify. They were all too old and afraid to do that.

❦

Nowadays the parties at Marty and Millie's are a lot zippier than they used to be. Diana Hare, who used to be the life of the party back in the '70s before she went blind is doing fine with her new eyes. Johnny's corneas work amazing well for her. She dances around and has fallen in love with Don Dietz who has been helped immeasurably by Johnny's lung-tissue graft. Daisy of the crushed hand is doing better too since they sewed Johnny's fingers on her left hand.

Of course not everybody is a perfect match. Perry Pillas has the hole in his forehead. You could hardly expect Johnny's brain to help him or anyone else.

But those, as Marty and Millie like to say, are only temporary set backs.

The two of them have taken up drug dealing now…heroin, meth, coke…That's a great way to meet young scumbags.

They've got high hopes that in a year, maybe two, they'll find enough youthful healthy creeps to give their special group of accomplished friends new and even longer lives.

As for Johnny, he's still hanging around. Part of him is anyway. His shoulders, rib cage, and intestines. They're hanging on a meat hook back in the refrigerated room, in the darkest part of Millie and Mart's apartment. They keep a constant spray over his skin, to keep it hydrated, and a nice saline drip going into his right arm to keep what's left of him fresh. His face is pretty wrecked what with no eyes, no jaw, and half a nose. But the way his head is cocked, and what with the strange angle of his lips, why it's almost like Johnny Z is cracking his old, hustling smile.

Afterword

My mother Big Shirl, is in a retirement community in Baltimore. She told me a story about an attendant who stole some of her money. When my mom called her on it she denied it and my mother was powerless to do anything about it. We talked to the guys who run the place and they shrugged, "Without proof, what can we do?". My mother's word wasn't proof because as an older person, well, maybe her mind is faulty. That gave me the idea. What if the thief was a lot more aggressive? What if he threatened to kill anyone who called the cops? That was a cool setup. But what was the payoff? Well, how about an older person's association who dealt with bad guys that the cops wouldn't touch. And what if they used the bad guy's body to patch up their fellow senior citizens. That was the "tail" the story needed. A surprise on top of another surprise. To me that's what a good story does. Sucks you in looking one way and then bam, sneaks in a left jab, and knocks you out.

I've always hung out with older people, and always learned from them. I learned as a very young man that if you follow the guys on the street you hang with it's a case of the loud and blind leading the shy and blind. My role model for life was my own grandmother, who I've written about in my last book, Grace. *She lived in redneck Waverly in Baltimore, and she had interracial meetings at her house in the 50s. Black folks from Morgan College and from all the local churches came to Gracie's home and planned non-violent demonstrations. While they were walking in from their cars, rednecks on 38th Street came out on their porch and threatened their lives. These same brave people called my grandmother while my seaman grandfather was away, (they wouldn't have dared call when he was home because he would have broken their necks) and threatened to burn down her house. I know because I took some of the calls. I asked her about it once: "Gracie aren't you scared?" Her answer was, "Them? Those ignorant idiots. They're trash and we don't truck to trash." End of story. I've met a lot of great people, and a lot of brave people, but none more brave than Grace. She walked the walk, and never wrote one word about any of it. Nor asked for any fame or glory. Everyone who knew her, though, friend or foe, knew she was a force to be reckoned with. She was the greatest inspiration in my life. I feel that she has enabled me to go on writing when things looked hopeless. I miss her more each passing year. –R.W.*

JUST
FRIENDS

JOHN HARVEY

John Harvey (born 1938) is the author of ten richly-praised Charlie Resnick novels, the first of which, Lonely Hearts, *was named by the Times as one of the "100 Best Crime Novels of the Century." Amongst his other work, he has written three books featuring retired police detective Frank Elder, the first of which,* Flesh & Blood, *won the British Crime Writers' Association Silver Dagger and, in America, the Barry Award for Best British Crime Novel of 2004. The second novel,* Ash & Bone, *was short listed in 2006 for in the Mystery/Thriller category of the Los Angeles Times Book Prizes.*

JUST FRIENDS
by John Harvey

Thinking about this, I remember about Diane Adams: the way a lock of her hair would fall down across her face and she would brush it back with a quick tilt of her head and a flick of her hand; the sliver of green, like a shard of glass, high in her left eye; the look of surprise, pleasure and surprise, when she spoke to me that first time—"And you must be, Jimmy, right?": the way she lied.

It was November, late in the month and the night air bright with cold that numbed your fingers even as it brought a flush of color to your cheeks. London, the winter of fifty-six, and we were little more than kids then, Patrick, Val and myself, though if anyone had called us that we'd have likely punched him out, Patrick or myself at least, Val in the background, careful, watching.

Friday night it would have been, a toss-up between the Flamingo and Studio 51, and on this occasion Patrick had decreed the Flamingo: this on account of a girl he'd started seeing, on account of Diane. The Flamingo a little more cool, a little more style; more likely to impress. Hip, I suppose, the word we would have used.

All three of us had first got interested in jazz at school, the trad thing first, British guys doing a earnest imitation of New Orleans; then, for a spell, it was the Alex Welsh band we followed around, a hard-driving crew with echoes of Chicago, brittle and fast, Tuesday nights the Lyttelton place in Oxford Street, Sundays a club out at Wood Green. It was Val who got us listening to the more modern stuff, Parker 78s on Savoy, Paul Desmond, the Gerry Mulligan Quartet.

From somewhere, Patrick got himself a trumpet and began practicing scales, and I kicked off playing brushes on an old suitcase while saving for the down payment on a set of drums. Val, we eventually discovered, already had a saxophone – an old Selmer with a dented bell and a third of the keys held on by rubber bands: it had once belonged to his old man. Not only did he have a horn, but he knew how to play. Nothing fancy, not yet, not enough to go steaming through the changes of *Cherokee* or *I Got Rhythm* the way he would later, in his pomp, but tunes you could recognize, modulations you could follow.

The first time we heard him, really heard him, the cellar room below a greasy spoon by the Archway, somewhere the owner let us hang out for the price of a few coffees, the occasional pie and chips, we

372

wanted to punch him hard. For holding out on us the way he had. For being so damned good.

Next day, Patrick took the trumpet back to the place he'd bought it, Boosey and Hawkes, and sold it back to them, got the best price he could. "Sod that for a game of soldiers," he said, "too much like hard bloody work. What we need's a bass player, someone half-decent on piano, get Val fronting his own band." And he pushed a bundle of fivers into my hand. "Here," he said, "go and get those sodding drums."

"What about you?" Val asked, though he probably knew the answer even then. "What you gonna be doin'?"

"Me?" Patrick said. "I'm going to be the manager. What else?"

And, for a time, that was how it was.

Private parties, weddings, bar mitzvahs, support slots at little clubs out in Ealing or Totteridge that couldn't afford anything better. From somewhere Patrick found a pianist who could do a passable Bud Powell, and, together with Val, that kept us afloat. For a while, a year or so at least. By then even Patrick could see Val was too good for the rest of us and we were just holding him back; he spelled it out to me when I was packing my kit away after an all-nighter in Dorking, a brace of tenners eased down into the top pocket of my second hand Cecil Gee jacket.

"What's this?" I said.

"Severance pay," said Patrick, and laughed.

Not the first time he paid me off, nor the last.

But I'm getting ahead of myself.

That November evening, we'd been hanging round the Bar Italia on Frith Street pretty much as usual, the best coffee in Soho then and now; Patrick was off to one side, deep in conversation with a dark-skinned guy in a Crombie overcoat, the kind who has to shave twice a day and wore a scar down his cheek like a badge. A conversation I was never meant to hear.

"Jimmy," Patrick said suddenly, over his shoulder. "A favor. Diane, I'm supposed to meet her. Leicester Square tube." He looked at his watch. "Any time now. Go down there for me, okay? Bring her to the club; we'll see you there."

All I'd seen of Diane up to that point had been a photograph, a snapshot barely focused, dark hair worn long, high cheek bones, a slender face. Her eyes—what color were her eyes?

"The tube," I said. "Which exit?"

Patrick grinned. "You'll get it figured."

She came up the steps leading on to Cranbourne Street and I recognized her immediately; tall, taller than I'd imagined, and in that moment—Jesus!—so much more beautiful.

"Diane?" Hands in my pockets, trying and failing to look cool, blushing already. "Patrick got stuck in some kind of meeting. Business, you know? He asked me to meet you."

She nodded, looking me over appraisingly. "And you must be Jimmy, right?" Aside from that slight flaw, her eyes were brown, a soft chocolaty brown, I could see that now.

Is it possible to smile ironically? That's what she was doing. "All right, Jimmy," she said. "Where are we going?"

When we got to the Flamingo, Patrick and Val had still not arrived. The Tony Kinsey Quintet were on the stand, two saxes and rhythm. I pushed my way through to the bar for a couple of drinks and we stood on the edge of the crowd, close but not touching. Diane was wearing a silky kind of dress that clung to her hips, two shades of blue. The band cut the tempo for *Sweet and Lovely*, Don Rendell soloing on tenor.

Diane rested her fingers on my arm. "Did Patrick tell you to dance with me, too?"

I shook my head.

"Well, let's pretend that he did."

Six months I suppose they went out together, Diane and Patrick, that first time around, and for much of that six months, I rarely saw them one without the other. Towards the end, Patrick took her off for a few days to Paris, a big deal in those days, and managed to secure a gig for Val while he was there, guesting at the *Chat Qui Peche* with René Thomas and Pierre Michelot.

After they came back I didn't see either of them for quite a while: Patrick was in one of his mysterious phases, doing deals, ducking and weaving, and Diane—well, I didn't know about Diane. And then, one evening in Soho, hurrying, late for an appointment, I did see her, sitting alone by the window of this trattoria, the Amalfi it would have been, on Old Compton Street, a plate of pasta in front of her, barely touched. I stopped close to the glass, raised my hand and mouthed "Hi!" before scuttling on, but if she saw me I couldn't be sure. One thing I couldn't miss though, the swelling, shaded purple, around her left eye.

A week after this Patrick rang me and we arranged to meet for a drink at the Bald Faced Stag; when I asked about Diane he looked through me and then carried on as if he'd never heard her name. At this time I was living in two crummy rooms in East Finchley—more a bed-sitter with a tiny kitchen attached, the bathroom down the hall—and Patrick gave me a lift home, dropped me at the door. I asked him if he wanted to come in but wasn't surprised when he declined.

Two nights later I was sitting reading some crime novel or other, wearing two sweaters to save putting on the second bar of the electric fire, when there was a short ring on the downstairs bell. For some reason, I thought it might be Patrick, but instead it was Diane. Her hair was pulled back off her face in a way I hadn't seen before, and, a faint finger of yellow aside, all trace of the bruise around her eye had disappeared.

"Well, Jimmy," she said, "aren't you going to invite me in?"

She was wearing a cream sweater, a coffee-colored skirt with a slight flare, high heels which she kicked off the moment she sat on the end of the bed. My drums were out at the other side of the room, not the full kit, just the bass drum, ride cymbal, hi-hat and snare; clothes I'd been intending to iron were folded over the back of a chair.

"I didn't know," I said, "you knew where I lived."

"I didn't. Patrick told me."

"You're still seeing him then?"

The question hung in the air.

"I don't suppose you've got anything to drink?" Diane said.

There was a half bottle of Bell's out in the kitchen and I poured what was left into two tumblers and we touched glasses and said, "Cheers." Diane sipped hers, made a face, then drank down most of the rest in a single swallow.

"Patrick ..." I began.

"I don't want to talk about Patrick," she said.

Her hand touched the buckle of my belt. "Sit here," she said.

The mattress shifted with the awkwardness of my weight.

"I didn't know," she said afterwards, "it could be so good."

You see what I mean about the way she lied.

❦

Patrick and Diane got married in the French church off Leicester Square and their reception was held in the dance hall conveniently close by; it was one of the last occasions I played drums with any degree of seriousness, one of the last times I played at all. My application to join the Metropolitan Police had already been accepted and within weeks I would be starting off in uniform, a different kind of beat altogether. Val, of course, had put the band together and an all-star affair it was—Art Ellefson, Bill LeSage, Harry Klein. Val himself was near his mercurial best, just ahead of the flirtations with heroin and free form jazz that would sideline him in the years ahead.

At the night's end we stood outside, the three of us, ties unfastened, staring up at the sky. Diane was somewhere inside, getting changed.

"Christ!" Patrick said. "Who'd've fuckin' thought it?"

He took a silver flask from inside his coat and passed it round. We shook hands solemnly and then hugged each other close. When Diane

375

came out, she and Patrick went off in a waiting car to spend the night at a hotel on Park Lane.

"Start off," Patrick had said with a wink, "like you mean to continue."

We drifted apart: met briefly, glimpsed one another across smoky rooms, exchanged phone numbers that were rarely if ever called. Nine years later I was a detective sergeant working out of West End Central and Patrick had not long since opened his third night club in a glitter of flash bulbs and champagne; Joan Collins was there with her sister, Jackie. There were ways of skirting round the edges of the law and, so far, Patrick had found most of them: favors doled out and favors returned; backhanders in brown envelopes; girls who didn't care what you did as long as you didn't kiss them on the mouth. Diane, I heard, had walked out on Patrick; reconciled, Patrick had walked out on her. Now they were back together again, but for how long?

When I came off duty, she was parked across the street, smoking a cigarette, window wound down.

"Give you a lift?"

I'd moved up market but not by much, an upper floor flat in an already ageing mansion block between Chalk Farm and Belsize Park. A photograph of the great drummer, Max Roach, was on the wall; Sillitoe's *Saturday Night and Sunday Morning* next to the Eric Amblers and a few Graham Greenes on the shelf; an Alex Welsh album on the record player, ready to remind me of better times.

"So, how are things?" Diane asked, doing her best to look as if she cared.

"Could be worse." I said. In the kitchen, I set the kettle to boil and she stood too close while I spooned Nescafé into a pair of china mugs. There was something beneath the scent of her perfume that I remembered too well.

"What does he want?" I asked.

"Who?"

"Patrick, who else?"

She paused from stirring sugar into her coffee. "Is that what it has to be?"

"Probably."

"What if I just wanted to see you for myself?"

The green in her eye was bright under the unshaded kitchen light. "I wouldn't let myself believe it," I said.

She stepped into my arms and my arms moved around her as if they had a mind of their own. She kissed me and I kissed her back. I'd like to say I pushed her away after that and we sat and drank our coffee like two adults, talked about old times and what she was going to do with her life after the divorce. She was divorcing him, she said:

she didn't know why she hadn't done it before.

"He'll let you go?"

"He'll let me go."

For a moment, she couldn't hold my gaze. "There's just one thing," she said, "one thing that he wants. This new club of his, someone's trying to have his license cancelled."

"Someone?"

"Serving drinks after hours, an allegation, nothing more."

"He can't make it go away?"

Diane shook her head. "He's tried."

I looked at her. "And that's all?"

"One of the officers, he's accused Patrick of offering him a bribe. It was all a misunderstanding, of course."

"Of course."

"Patrick wonders if you'd talk to him, the officer concerned."

"Straighten things out."

"Yes."

"Make him see the error of his ways."

"Look, Jimmy," she said, touching the back of her hand to my cheek, "you know I hate doing this, don't you?"

No, I thought. No, I don't.

"Everything has a price," I said. "Even friendship. Friendship, especially. And tell Patrick, next time he wants something, to come and ask me himself."

"He's afraid you'd turn him down."

"He's right."

When she lifted her face to mine I turned my head aside. "Don't let your coffee get cold," I said.

Five minutes later she was gone. I sorted out Patrick's little problem for him and found a way of letting him know if he stepped out of line again, I'd personally do my best to close him down. Whether either of us believed it, I was never sure. With or without my help, he went from rich to richer; Diane slipped off my radar and when she re-emerged, she was somewhere in Europe, nursing Val after his most recent spell in hospital, encouraging him to get back into playing. Later they got married, or at least that's what I heard. Some lives took unexpected turns. Not mine.

ff

I stayed on in the Met for three years after my thirty and then retired; tried working for a couple of security firms, but somehow it never felt right. With my pension and the little I'd squirreled away,

I found I could manage pretty well without having to look for anything too regular. There was an investigation agency I did a little work for once in a while, nothing too serious, nothing heavy, and that was enough.

Patrick I bumped into occasionally if I went up west, greyer, more distinguished, handsomer than ever; in Soho once, close to the little Italian place where I'd spotted Diane with her bruised eye, he slid a hand into my pocket and when I felt where it had been there were two fifties, crisp and new.

"What's this for?" I asked.

"You look as though you need it," he said.

I threw the money back in his face and punched him in the mouth. Two of his minders had me spread-eagled on the pavement before he'd wiped the mean line of blood from his chin.

At Val's funeral we barely spoke; acknowledged each other but little more. Diane looked gaunt and beautiful in black, a face like alabaster, tears I liked to think were real. A band played *Just Friends*, with a break of thirty-two bars in the middle where Val's solo would have been. There was a wake at one of Patrick's clubs afterwards, a free bar, and most of mourners went on there, but I just went home and sat in my chair and thought about the three of us, Val, Patrick and myself, what forty years had brought us to, what we'd wanted then, what we'd done.

I scarcely thought about Diane at all.

ℰ

Jack Kiley, that's the investigator I was working for, kept throwing bits and pieces my way, nothing strenuous like I say, the occasional tail job, little more. I went into his office one day, a couple of rooms above a bookstore in Belsize Park, and there she sat, Diane, in the easy chair alongside his desk.

"I believe you two know each other," Jack said.

Once I'd got over the raw surprise of seeing her, what took some adjusting to was how much she'd changed. I suppose I'd never imagined her growing old. But she had. Under her grey wool suit her body was noticeably thicker; her face was fuller, puffed and cross-hatched around the eyes, lined around the mouth. No Botox; no nip and tuck.

"Hello, Jimmy," she said.

"Diane's got a little problem," Jack said. "She thinks you can make it go away." He pushed back from his desk. "I'll leave you two to talk about it."

The problem was a shipment of cocaine that should have made its way seamlessly from the Netherlands to Dublin via the UK. A street value of a quarter of a million pounds. Customs and Excise, working on a tip-off, had seized the drug on arrival, a clean bust marred only by the fact the coke had been doctored down to a mockery of its original strength; a double shot espresso from Caffè Nero would deliver as much of a charge to the system.

"How in God's name," I asked, "did you get involved in this?"

Diane lit a cigarette and wafted the smoke away from her face. "After Val died I went back to Amsterdam, it's where we'd been living before he died. There was this guy—he'd been Val's supplier ..."

"I thought Val had gone straight," I said.

"There was this guy," Diane said again, "we—well, we got sort of close. It was a bad time for me. I needed ..." She glanced across and shook her head. "A girl's got to live, Jimmy. All Val had left behind was debts. This guy, he offered me a roof over my head. But there was a price."

"I'll bet." Even I was surprised how bitter that sounded.

"People he did business with, he wanted me to speak for him, take meetings. I used to fly to Belfast, then, after a while, it was Dublin."

"You were a courier." I said. "A mule."

"No. I never carried the stuff myself. Once the deal was set up, I'd arrange shipments, make sure things ran smoothly."

"Patrick would be proud of you," I said.

"Leave Patrick out of this," she said. "This has nothing to do with him."

I levered myself up out of the seat; it wasn't as easy as it used to be. "Nor me." I got as far as the door.

"They think I double-crossed them," Diane said. "They think it was me tipped off Customs; they think I cut the coke and kept back the rest so I could sell it myself."

"And did you?"

She didn't blink. "These people, Jimmy, they'll kill me. To make an example. I have to convince them it wasn't me; let them have back what they think's their due."

"A little difficult if you didn't take it in the first place."

"Will you help me, Jimmy, yes or no?"

"Your pal in Amsterdam, what's wrong with him?"

"He says it's my mess and I have to get myself out of it."

"Nice guy."

She leaned towards me, trying for a look that once would have held me transfixed. "Jimmy, I'm asking. For old time's sake."

"Which old time is that, Diane?"

She smiled. "The first time you met me, Jimmy, you remember

that? Leicester Square?"

Like yesterday, I thought.

"You ever think about that? You ever think what I would have been like if we'd been together? Really together?"

I shook my head.

"We don't always make the right choices," she said.

"Get somebody else to help you," I said.

"I don't want somebody else."

"Diane, look at me for fuck's sake. What can I do? I'm an old man."

"You're not old. What are you? Sixty-odd? These days sixty's not old. Seventy-five. Eighty. That's old."

"Tell that to my body, Diane. I'm carrying at least a stone more than I ought to; the tendon at the back of my left ankle gives me gyp if ever I run for a bus and my right hip hurts like hell whenever I climb a flight of stairs. Find someone else, anyone."

"There's nobody else I can trust."

❦

I talked to Jack Kiley about it later; we were sitting in the Starbucks across the street, sunshine doing its wan best to shine through the clouds.

"What do you know about these types?" Jack asked. "This new bunch of cocaine cowboys from over the old Irish Sea?"

"Sod all," I said.

"Well, let me give you a bit of background. Ireland has the third highest cocaine use in Europe and there's fifteen or twenty gangs and upwards beating the bollocks off one another to supply it. Some of them, the more established, have got links with the IRA, or did have, but it's the newer boys that take the pippin. Use the stuff themselves, jack up an Uzi or two and go shooting; a dozen murders in Dublin so far this year and most of the leaves still on the fucking trees."

"That's Dublin," I said.

Jack cracked a smile. "And you think this old flame of yours'll be safe here in Belsize Park or back home in Amsterdam?"

I shrugged. I didn't know what to bloody think.

He leaned closer. "Just a few months back, a drug smuggler from Cork got into a thing with one of the Dublin gangs—a disagreement about some shipment bought and paid for. He thought he'd lay low till it blew over. Took a false name and passport and holed up in an apartment in the Algarve. They found his body in the freezer. Minus the head. Rumor is whoever carried out the contract on him had it shipped back as proof."

Something was burning deep in my gut and I didn't think a couple

380

of antacid tablets was going to set it right.

"You want my advice, Jimmy?" he said, and gave it anyway. "Steer clear. Either that or get in touch with some of your old pals in the Met. Let them handle it."

Do that, I thought, and there's no way of keeping Diane out of it; somehow I didn't fancy seeing her next when she was locked away on remand.

"I don't suppose you fancy giving a hand?" I said.

Jack was still laughing as he crossed the street back towards his office.

§

At least I didn't have to travel far, just a couple of stops on the Northern Line. Diane had told me where to find them and given me their names. There was some kind of ceilidh band playing in the main bar, the sound of the bodhran tracing my footsteps up the stairs. And, yes, my hip did ache.

The McMahon brothers were sitting at either end of a leather sofa that had seen better days, and Chris Boyle was standing with his back to a barred window facing down on to the street. Hip-hop was playing from a portable stereo at one side of the room, almost drowning out the traditional music from below. No one could accuse these boys of not keeping up with the times.

There was an almost full bottle of Bushmills and some glasses on the desk, but I didn't think anyone was about to ask me if I wanted a drink.

One of the McMahon brothers giggled when I stepped into the room and I could see the chemical glow in his eyes.

"What the fuck you doin' here, old man?" the other one said. "You should be tucked up in the old folks' home with your fuckin' Ovaltine."

"Two minutes," Chris Boyle said. "Say what you have to fuckin' say then get out."

"Supposin' we let you," one of the brothers said and giggled some more. Neither of them looked a whole lot more than nineteen, twenty tops. Boyle was closer to thirty, nearing pensionable age where that crew was concerned. According to Jack, there was a rumor he wore a colostomy bag on account of getting shot in the kidneys coming out from the rugby at Lansdown Road.

"First," I said, "Diane knew nothing about either the doctoring of the shipment, nor the fact it was intercepted. You have to believe that."

Boyle stared back at me, hard-faced.

One of the McMahons laughed.

"Second, though she was in no way responsible, as a gesture of good faith, she's willing to hand over a quantity of cocaine, guaranteed at least eighty per cent pure, the amount equal to the original shipment. After that it's all quits, an even playing field, business as before."

Boyle glanced across at the sofa then nodded agreement.

"We pick the point and time of delivery," I said. "Two days time. I'll need a number on which I can reach you."

Boyle wrote his mobile number on a scrap of paper and passed it across. "Now get the fuck out," he said.

Down below, someone was playing a penny whistle, high-pitched and shrill. I could feel my pulse racing haphazardly and when I managed to get myself across the street, I had to take a grip on a railing and hold fast until my legs had stopped shaking.

✦

When Jack learned I was going through with it, he offered to lend me a gun, a Smith & Wesson .38, but I declined. There was more chance of shooting myself in the foot than anything else.

I met Diane in the parking area behind Jack's office, barely light enough to make out the color of her eyes. The cocaine was bubble-wrapped inside a blue canvas bag.

"You always were good to me, Jimmy," she said, and reaching up, she kissed me on the mouth. "Will I see you afterwards?"

"No," I said. "No, you won't."

The shadows swallowed her as she walked towards the taxi waiting out on the street. I dropped the bag down beside the rear seat of the car, waited several minutes, then slipped the engine into gear.

The place I'd chosen was on Hampstead Heath, a makeshift soccer pitch shielded by lines of trees, a ramshackle wooden building off to one side, open to the weather; sometimes pickup teams used it to get changed, or kids huddled there to feel one another up, smoke spliffs or sniff glue.

When Patrick, Val and I had been kids ourselves there was a murdered body found close by and the place took on a kind of awe for us, murder in those days being something more rare.

I'd left my car by a mansion block on Heath Road and walked in along a partly overgrown track. The moon was playing fast and loose with the clouds and the stars seemed almost as distant as they were. An earlier shower of rain had made the surface a little slippy and mud clung to the soles of my shoes. There was movement, low in the undergrowth to my right hand side, and, for a moment, my heart stopped as an owl broke, with a fell swoop, through the trees above my head.

A dog barked and then was still.

I stepped off the path and into the clearing, the weight of the bag real in my left hand. I was perhaps a third of the way across the pitch before I saw them, three or four shapes massed near the hut at the far side and separating as I drew closer, fanning out. Four of them, faces unclear, but Boyle, I thought, at the centre, the McMahons to one side of him, another I didn't recognize hanging back. Behind them, behind the hut, the trees were broad and tall and close together, beeches I seemed to remember Val telling me once when I'd claimed them as oaks. "Beeches, for God's sake," he'd said, laughing in that soft way of his. "You, Jimmy, you don't know your arse from your elbow, it's a fact."

I stopped fifteen feet away and Boyle took a step forward. "You came alone," he said.

"That was the deal."

"He's stupider than I fuckin' thought," said one or other of the McMahons and laughed a girlish little laugh.

"The stuff's all there?" Boyle said, nodding towards the bag.

I walked a few more paces towards him, set the bag on the ground, and stepped back.

Boyle angled his head towards the McMahons and one of them went to the bag and pulled it open, slipping a knife from his pocket as he did so; he slit open the package, and, standing straight again, tasted the drug from the blade.

"Well?" Boyle said.

McMahon finished running his tongue around his teeth. "It's good," he said.

"Then we're set." I said to Boyle.

"Set?"

"We're done here."

"Oh, yes, we're done."

The man to Boyle's left, the one I didn't know, moved forward almost to his shoulder, letting his long coat fall open as he did so, and what light there was glinted dully off the barrels of the shotgun as he brought it to bear. It was almost level when a shot from the trees behind struck him high in the shoulder and spun him round so that the second shot tore through his neck and he fell to the ground as good as dead.

One of the McMahons cursed and started to run, while the other dropped to one knee and fumbled for the revolver inside his zip-up jacket.

With all the gunfire and the shouting I couldn't hear the words from Boyle's mouth, but I could lip read well enough. "You're dead," he said, and drew a pistol not much bigger than a child's hand from his side pocket and raised it towards my head. It was either bravery or stupidity or maybe fear that made me charge at him, unarmed, hands outstretched as if in some way to ward off the bullet; it was the mudded turf that made my feet slide away under me and sent me sprawling headlong, the two shots Boyle got off sailing over my head before one of the men I'd last seen minding Patrick in Soho stepped up neatly behind Boyle, put the muzzle of a 9mm Beretta hard behind his ear and squeezed the trigger.

Both the McMahon's had gone down without me noticing; one was already dead and the other had blood gurgling out of his airway and was not long for this world.

Patrick was standing back on the path, scraping flecks of mud from the edges of his soft leather shoes with a piece of stick.

"Look at the state of you," he said. "You look a fucking state. If I were you I should burn that lot when you get home, start again."

I wiped the worst of the mess from the front of my coat and that was when I realized my hands were still shaking. "Thanks, Pat," I said.

"What are friends for?" he said.

Behind us his men were tidying up the scene a little, not too much. The later editions of the papers would be full of stories of how the Irish drug wars had come to London, the Celtic Tigers fighting it out on foreign soil.

"You need a lift?" Patrick asked, as we made our way back towards the road.

"No, thanks. I'm fine."

"Thank Christ for that. Last thing I need, mud all over the inside of the fucking car."

*

When I got back to the flat I put one of Val's last recordings on the stereo, a session he'd made in Stockholm a few months before he died. Once or twice his fingers didn't match his imagination, and his breathing seemed to be giving him trouble, but his mind was clear. Beeches, I'll always remember that now, that part of the Heath. Beeches, not oaks.

Afterword

I've been mulling over for some little time a novel which centers round three childhood friends who come to adulthood in London in the late 1950s, a police officer, a mixed-race jazz musician, and a chancer and club owner who frequently steps the other side of the law. Writing this short story gave me an opportunity to give those characters a preliminary walk around the block. —J.H.

Coming Fall 2006 from **Busted Flush Press**

STONE CITY
by Mitchell Smith

Trade paperback reprint of Mitchell Smith's 1990 crime novel.

"*Stone City* blew my doors off. While reading this lost masterpiece, I tried to conjure up other instances where I was so thoroughly placed within a foreign world so perfectly, awfully, brilliantly evoked and could think of only two – *Catch-22* and *One Flew Over the Cuckoo's Nest*. Violent, passionate, brutal, frightening – yet oddly seductive and redemptive, *Stone City*, for me, is the be-all, end-all novel about life in a modern American penitentiary. Praise be to Busted Flush Press for rescuing this perfect, bloody gem."

– C. J. Box, author of In *Plain Sight* and *Blue Heaven*

"*Stone City* is the cold light of day. Writing as sharp and raw as a shiv. Mitchell Smith nails the surreal reality of prison life and just keep going deeper. This one is scary – you'll keep looking over your shoulder and steering clear of wire clothes hangers. There's no higher praise than that."

– Anthony Neil Smith, author of *Psychosomatic* and
   The Drummer

"Mitchell Smith's *Stone City* is a literary tour de force, as well as a novel that delivers an emotional wallop nearly unparalleled in my experience. Dark, disturbing, multi-layered, and nothing short of brilliant, this book belongs at or near the top of any list of the best crime novels of all time."

– John Lescroart, *New York Times* best-selling author of
   The Hunt Club

"After reading *Stone City*, I want to burn every frame of *Oz* and start all over again."

– Tom Fontana, Emmy Award-winning writer/producer,
   Homicide: Life on the Street and *Oz*

"*Stone City* might be the best novel of its kind ever written. This republication of Mitchell Smith's stunning work, long out of print, is a cause for celebration."

– George Pelecanos, Edgar Award-nominated author of *Drama City*

Available Fall 2006 from your favorite bookseller.